DANCE OF THE RETURNED

DANCE OF THE RETURNED

DEVON A. MIHESUAH

THE UNIVERSITY OF
ARIZONA PRESS

TUCSON

The University of Arizona Press
www.uapress.arizona.edu

We respectfully acknowledge the University of Arizona is on the land and territories of Indigenous peoples. Today, Arizona is home to twenty-two federally recognized tribes, with Tucson being home to the O'odham and the Yaqui. Committed to diversity and inclusion, the University strives to build sustainable relationships with sovereign Native Nations and Indigenous communities through education offerings, partnerships, and community service.

ISBN-13: 978-0-8165-4640-4 (paperback)
ISBN-13: 978-0-8165-4641-1 (ebook)

Cover design by Leigh McDonald
Designed and typeset by Leigh McDonald in Adobe Jenson Pro 10.25/15 and Telmoss WF (display)

Publication of this book is made possible in part by the KU Hall Center for the Humanities Vice Chancellor for Research Book Publication Award, and by the proceeds of a permanent endowment created with the assistance of a Challenge Grant from the National Endowment for the Humanities, a federal agency.

Library of Congress Cataloging-in-Publication Data
Names: Mihesuah, Devon A., 1957– author.
Title: Dance of the returned / Devon A. Mihesuah.
Other titles: Sun tracks ; v. 90.
Description: Tucson : University of Arizona Press, 2022. | Series: Sun tracks: an American Indian literary series; volume 90
Identifiers: LCCN 2022000982 (print) | LCCN 2022000983 (ebook) | ISBN 9780816546404 (paperback) | ISBN 9780816546411 (ebook)
Subjects: LCSH: Missing persons—Oklahoma—Fiction. | Choctaw Indians—Oklahoma—Fiction. | Time travel—Fiction. | LCGFT: Detective and mystery fiction.
Classification: LCC PS3563.I371535 D36 2022 (print) | LCC PS3563.I371535 (ebook) | DDC 813/.6—dc23/eng/20220415
LC record available at https://lccn.loc.gov/2022000982
LC ebook record available at https://lccn.loc.gov/2022000983

Printed in the United States of America
♾ This paper meets the requirements of ANSI/NISO Z39.48-1992 (Permanence of Paper).

To the dreamers

We had prophets, back before any other races came other than Native Americans living. We had prophets that prophesized long time ago, that these things were going to happen.

—CARMEN DENSON (MISSISSIPPI CHOCTAW),
JANUARY 12, 2000, IN *CHOCTAW PROPHECY:
A LEGACY FOR THE FUTURE* BY TOM MOULD

DANCE OF THE RETURNED

HATAK HOLHKUNNA
THE DREAMER

*As dreams are the fancies of those that sleep, so fancies are but
the dreams of those awake.*

—SIR T. P. BLOUNT

Fuji lay still, his head on soft pillows. His breathing was almost impercep-
tible. Unusual for a large man.

In his first memory, he stood in darkness. Warm breezes stirred his
hair and caressed his skin. In the second, he looked up to see a shimmer
of daylight. A feminine voice urged him to climb toward the circle of blue.
He struggled upward, lungs aching. Sharp rocks and brambles scraped
and lacerated his legs until he emerged into a brilliant world. A dormant
part of his brain registered that he was looking at grass, flowers, and trees
for the first time.

Fuji rolled onto his back and sighed. Other memories came quickly,
just as they did every night. He and the others stood in the upper world,
scared and shaking. Animals beckoned them to follow to search for food
and water. Fuji dreamed of wide, clear skies, full moons, and thundering
hooves. Still asleep, he shivered under his green blanket. Then he felt
the burning summer sun. The grass beneath his feet shriveled. The dirt
cracked. He began to sweat, and threw off his blanket.

He felt exhausted from wandering dark underground tunnels and from crossing wide plains of buffalo grass. He flinched from the pain of frostbite, of childbirth, of sprains, of broken bones, and the despair of losing loved ones. He was born countless times and died of infections, injuries, diseases, and old age. He was born repeatedly, and the memories of innumerable ancestors flashed through his mind, all complex and too indistinct to recall.

Through the flash of time that was the history of his people, Fuji experienced his tribe's struggle for survival, identity, and peace. As usual, when he awoke the next morning, his pillow was wet with tears.

PART I

When he was 14 years old and in the spring time, he went
into the woods to have his dream (the guiding spirit of destiny).
He fell asleep and slept for three days and nights and in his
dreams he was among wild roses, the bees were humming,
the birds singing, water splashing, geese cackling and white
feathers were falling like snow.

—JOSEPHINE USRAY LATTIMER, "THE LEGEND OF
EZEKIEL ROBUCK"

I

Mosholi
The Vanishing

Monique adjusted the metal nose strip on her mask for the tenth time in as many minutes. The elastic bands around her head had stretched out, and the mask kept slipping down her nose. She knew she should give up and put on a cloth one, but she preferred the dust mask that Steve sold at his auto-parts store. It did not hug her face and pulse up her nostrils when she inhaled, like cloth. But still she sweated, her temples pounded, and she couldn't get a lungful of air. She wiped her forehead and panted.

Monique knew that Steve was smiling because the corners of his eyes crinkled. He did not sweat, nor did he look winded.

Of course he feels fine, she thought.

Steve wore his favorite Hannibal-Lecter-as-a-hockey-goaltender mask. Monique hated that image and argued that Steve was not the one forced to look at his face. She preferred the mask made of bright-yellow-sunflower material. Steve did not like that one. He also rejected the one with a black background and green glow-in-the-dark constellations.

Steve looked at his wife and flinched, alarmed by her furrowed brow and flushed skin. "There is an end to it, Moni."

She coughed. "Doesn't feel like it." She hacked so many times she thought she had busted a gut. "I'm hot. And really tired. I need a nap."

"It's nine thirty in the morning."

"I've been tossing since three."

He said nothing and picked up her Hydro Flask. He unscrewed the top and lifted it to her. "Lemonade and electrolytes. You have to stay hydrated. And the vegetable soup will be ready by eleven." He had gathered broccoli and spinach from the cold frame that morning, as well as a few early potatoes from the mounds by the fence. From where Monique lay in bed at six that morning, she'd heard her husband's knife hitting the chopping block. She'd listened to him open the freezer and imagined him rummaging for the tomato sauce she had processed the previous October. A cabinet opened and she'd visualized him taking out black pepper, onion, and garlic powder. The door slammed. A few moments of silence meant he was in the garage looking in the icebox for a jar of turkey-carcass broth.

She knew he hoped to make her happy with a thick and spicy soup. Right now, however, she had no appetite. Her head ached. "No. In a minute." She closed her eyes and concentrated on breathing. Thunder boomed. "Thank God," she said. "Please rain." Rain and thunder relaxed her. Light rain outside enhanced smells of tree bark and foliage that evoked more sensory pleasure than a Dairy Queen Double Oreo Blizzard. Sometimes.

"Dang it," Steve said. "I wanted to mow before the storm."

Monique wiped her sweaty forehead with her T-shirt and then took a deep breath. But not too deep because the mask retained pizza odor. "Grass in the front isn't tall enough. You just want to get on your machine."

"I like to mow."

She sighed loudly for effect, then lifted the trowel and scraped approximately a quarter pound of pigeon shit off the third perch from the top of the coop, second from the west wall. Dry and dusty crap fell into empty feed bags at her feet. The bags made it easy to drag the heavy scrapings out the door. Some of the dry droppings fell through the floor grate to the ground, where the earthworms would eat the poop and leave the castings for Steve to rake up and toss into the compost bin for Monique's garden.

She eyed the shelves where the birds perched. Only six more to go in the hens' side of the coop. Then she and Steve would move to the cocks' area. The sliding screen door remained open to allow the once-segregated hens and cocks to co-parent their squabs.

Monique exhaled again dramatically.

"We're almost finished," Steve said as he worked quickly. He knew Monique hated to help him scrape. Robbie was finishing homework, otherwise he'd do it.

She did not reply.

Monique thought it a great idea when Steve said he wanted to race pigeons like he had when he was a teenager. Raising birds was supposed to be a relaxing distraction after his long days at work. Moreover, he wouldn't hound her about quitting her job. This was Steve's hobby, not hers. Yet, somehow, he had roped her into not only cleaning his racing-pigeon coop but also helping him vaccinate birds and band babies—then, prior to the first race of the season, catching each bird and documenting their sex, color, birth year, and band number. Hen, blue bar, 2019, #0867. Cock, grizzle, 2020, #0754. And so forth. During the months prior to spring and summer racing seasons, Steve loaded up the birds in the crates and drove them various distances for training tosses. Closer to the first race, he'd drive fifty to a hundred miles before work to release them at dawn. Most birds came home, but hawks and high wires took many of them. The losses were greater during races. And that was what she hated most about the sport. She appreciated the athleticism of the birds, but the attrition rate was far too high. Their human handlers just sat on their butts and waited for the fatigued birds to step on the finish line—that is, the antenna pad.

"Mom!" Robbie called as he approached the coop. "You left your phone in the kitchen. You got a ca—" he broke off in a squeak. Their son was going through puberty. His uneven voice sounded as if he was attempting to emulate the Bears Papa, Mama, and Baby all in one sentence.

Monique looked at him through the screen. "From?"

"Your captain." He held up her phone.

Monique took off her glasses, mask, and gloves as she exited the coop. She felt relief as the breeze hit her uncovered face. She exchanged her gear for her phone. "Almost done," she mouthed. Robbie put on the gloves and opened the coop door. Monique patted his arm in sympathy.

"Monique here," she said into the phone.

"It's Hardaway." Captain Phil Hardaway, the jovial giant. "We got a missing person."

"Who?"

"East James."

"You mean James East?"

"No. I mean East James. You know a James East?"

"Uh, no. I just thought his first name might be . . . never mind. Who reported?"

"Robb Novler. He's a new officer here. He and James are on the Cedar County volunteer fire department together, and James didn't show for his EMT final Thursday night. He had to be there. Then he missed the mandatory truck cleanup this morning. That's unusual, apparently."

"Not in our jurisdiction."

"He lives in Norman." Her wheelhouse.

"Right. Okay. This is Sunday afternoon. Maybe gone since Thursday morning or afternoon, that's what—seventy hours or more?"

"Yeah."

"Long time."

"Novler wasn't worried too much about the EMT exam, but he sure was today."

"Right. James married?"

"Yeah."

"Why didn't his wife call in?"

"Novler called her today to see if he was at home. She said no. Novler also said she was evasive and sounded odd."

"Evasive and odd how?"

"She didn't seem concerned."

Monique pulled a Kleenex from her pocket and wiped her nose. "Maybe they had a fight, he left, and she doesn't want people to know. Or he got drunk and is recovering from a headache on a friend's couch. He could be with another woman."

"Maybe."

"Kids?"

"Two. Seven and five. Boy and girl."

"How old's James?"

"Twenty-seven."

"Maybe he wasn't prepared for his EMT final and backed out. I failed my first EMT final because I bandaged a femoral bleed on a guy who was wheezing. I should've dealt with his breathing first. It's easy to mess up."

"So why miss the truck wash?"

"Maybe embarrassed."

"Just talk to the wife. Name's Lulu."

"Why not get a patrolman to deal with this?" Hardaway was silent a few seconds.

"She's Indian."

"Which one?"

"Choctaw. Same as her husband. And you."

"And that's why you called me."

"Well, yeah. Could be hinky and you do that best."

"We could call tribal police," Monique offered.

"If he shows up dead on tribal land, then yeah."

She sighed. "What else?"

"I wouldn't give her a heads-up. Just go."

"Right." Monique rubbed a temple and wondered if a cool shower would deter her growing headache. She knew that pigeon-shit dust covered her hair. "Send me her info. I have to shower."

A few seconds later, Monique had the number and address of Lulu James. "Gotta roll, guys," she shouted because Steve was still scraping.

"Now what?" Steve yelled back.

Monique put her phone in her pocket. "A man is missing."

"He dead?"

"I don't know. He's not where he's supposed to be."

"Name?"

Monique was tired of shouting. "Never heard of him."

"Where you gotta go?"

"Steve. Stop."

Robbie paused his troweling.

"Moni . . ." Steve trailed off. She saw through the screen that he put his hands on his hips and directed his gaze to the treetops. Monique knew his drama pose. She waited for it.

"You need to do something else. It's Sunday. This job . . ." His long braid swayed when he shook his head.

"Is mine. We discussed this." She did not want to lose her temper. "I like it."

"Wasn't long ago that you almost didn't make it."

"But I did."

"Covered in blood. So was everyone else. I was there."

"I have to go." She started for the house. "I need to hurry." Thunder boomed again, but farther away.

"Bye, Mom," squeaked Robbie. "Love you."

"I love you too, Robbie."

They went through this routine every time Monique got a call. Steve knew the demands of her career, yet he felt compelled to discourage her from working. He made no sense—if he got his way, that would mean no paycheck. Their constant bickering over her job had become tiresome and predictable.

She hurried to the house as she called her partner, Chris Pierson. He had moved from New York after his divorce four years ago and found that he liked the slower pace of Oklahoma. He had even said *y'all* a few times. The two worked well together. A year before, they'd found themselves in the midst of a murder investigation at the local museum, and one of the perps had slashed Chris's right pectoralis. He'd required surgery and three months in a sling, followed by two months of rehab. Now he could brag about his jagged scar. He finally felt better enough to ask Monique's friend Rachel McCarthy, a forensics investigator, out for dinner. That move was gratifying for Monique, because Chris now paid closer attention to his wardrobe.

"Chris," she greeted.

"Monique," Chris answered.

"Got a call."

"For what?"

"Missing man."

Chris said nothing, but she heard children laughing and adults talking. "Chris, where are you?"

"Well, uh . . ."

"Hey, Monique," said Rachel in the background.

"We're in Bricktown. Just went through Crystal Bridge."

The Crystal Bridge Conservatory, part of Oklahoma City's Myriad Botanical Gardens, was a spectacular, glassed-in botanical garden housing thousands of plants and a waterfall. It stood on the edge of Bricktown, a neighborhood known for its shopping, sports venues, museums, and housing the city's large zoo.

"I love this place," Rachel said, louder this time.

"Yeah, it's always nice. Chris. Gotta come with me. Sorry, buddies."

Chris did not respond for a few seconds, but Monique heard disappointment. "All right," he said. "I'll meet you at your place in an hour."

"Bricktown will be there next weekend."

He clicked off.

"Said I was sorry," she muttered.

She left the pigeon-poop-soled shoes on the porch, scratched her dog, Rover, behind the ears, and took the butterfly clips out of her hair. She bent at the waist, shook her head, and despaired at the amount of grayish particles that fell to the porch floor. "Damn," she said. Heading inside, she flipped her long hair back over her shoulders and found a plastic-bristled brush from the kitchen bathroom drawer. She cursed and yelped as she quickly ran it through a chunk of hair that had caught static. She wanted to wash her hair, but the thick mane took a long time to dry. "Good enough," she said. She undressed as she moved down the hall to the shower. She twisted her semi-clean hair into a high bun, brushed her teeth, and then stood under a cool shower. "I'd rather stay in here," she said to herself before turning the water off and dressing in her usual uniform of a white cuffed blouse and black slacks. She felt certain that East James was hiding in a hotel with a girlfriend, but because she did not know what the day might bring, she wore her flak vest underneath her shirt.

Her small silver hoops were already in her earlobes and her cheeks still flushed from the heat of the coop, but she added a few swipes of blush any-way, along with some eye shadow and mascara. With her Beretta Pico in her ankle holster and the .40 Glock secured under her jacket, she walked in her socks toward the garage, past the delicious-smelling stew. She stopped, opened the lid, and dipped into the mix with the wooden stirring spoon, then took a bite of a perfectly cooked pea, bits of potato, mushroom, and a few pieces of barley, all seasoned with pepper, garlic, and chile powder. She put the lid back on, sighed regretfully, and continued to the garage.

She donned her comfortable New Balance walkers, took a Diet Rite from the garage fridge, popped the top and guzzled half of it, then tore open a crunchy peanut butter Clif Bar and took a large bite. As Monique stood chewing, she felt pleased that her hair had no flyaways from the bun and she hoped her deodorant would work hardest when she needed it most.

2

AIYOKOMA
CONFUSION

Monique sat in her unmarked Ford Police Interceptor sedan watching Chris park his Chevy Caprice under a stately pecan tree. Chris unfurled his long legs and ducked his head as he exited his vehicle. He tucked in his shirt as he walked up the driveway. His had allowed his red hair to grow out a few inches after his first date with Rachel and he had not shaved in a few days. The look suited him. Now he appeared to be over thirty.

"That was quick," she said.

He plopped into the passenger seat and pulled a tie from his jacket pocket. He looped it around his neck. "We took two cars."

"Sorry to take you away from the fair flowers."

"Me too." He did not look at her.

Monique felt a twinge of guilt. "Rachel understands. It's her business too."

"Yeah, I know. What's up?"

Monique clicked her seat belt and started the engine. She slowly pulled into the street as she relayed Hardaway's message. "Missing guy named East James. He didn't show to his EMT final at the Cedar County volunteer fire department Thursday night and he missed the department's

mandatory meeting today. Hardaway found out about it from a new officer named Robb Novler. He's also a volunteer."

"Novler? Haven't met him."

"Me neither. Anyway, we're going to see James's wife. Lulu."

"Lulu? You don't hear that name every day."

"Nope."

"You mean the wife didn't call it in too?"

"Not so far. Mrs. Lulu James definitely has not reported her husband's
absence. Novler called her to ask about him. So, unless Lulu is witless,
she must be aware that people have noticed that her husband is AWOL."

"Maybe she's glad he's gone."

"If that's the case, why?"

"Yeah. Does she know we're coming?"

"Nope."

"So we don't know how she'll react."

"Correct." She reached over and tapped his chest. "You're wearing. Good.
This is probably no big deal. Still, you never know."

"I'll never not wear."

"Some women find scars sexy."

"Maybe." He massaged his right shoulder. "I'd rather break my arm
than go through that again."

Traffic was light on the Sunday afternoon. Churchgoers had completed their after-church shopping, and the Oklahoma City Thunder vs.
Utah Jazz basketball game was about to start. Perhaps residents sat in
front of their televisions, and maybe some attended the final day of the
University of Oklahoma and Oklahoma State baseball series.

The James family lived on the southern outskirts of Norman, about
six miles from Monique's home. She slowed as she reached the long rows
of storage sheds, and turned on Raptor Lane. An empty Dairy Queen
sat on the corner. Next to the boarded-up building was a decrepit used
clothing store, the white paint peeling and windows laced with cracks.
The front door stood open and a few racks of clothing blew in the breeze

alongside an old tricycle, a push mower, and miscellaneous junkyard items. A wooden fence separated the businesses from the residences. The detectives scrutinized the old houses. Sofas and folding chairs adorned the porches. Some properties had paved driveways, but most were dirt. Wood or metal tornado-shelter doors were visible in most of the yards.

"Old homes," Chris observed. "That's a cool rock house. Look at the chimney." He pointed to a small home with an elaborate brick chimney. A strutting turkey was fashioned from small stones set between the column's bricks and mortar.

"Yeah," Monique agreed. "Some buildings in Oklahoma, especially around the Wichita Mountains, have cannonball rock walls. You know, round rocks. Looks like they cleared the lot and used the stones. You'll see wire gabions filled with round rocks in the country. Makes sturdy pillars."

The owners of the second yard on the street had posted a Children Playing sign. Another appeared two more houses down.

Monique stopped in front of a wood-sided house with a wraparound covered porch. A four-foot-high metal cutout bison adorned the front flower bed. A light-blue Ford Taurus sat, nose out, under the carport. A white Chevy Sonic with a bumper covered in stickers had been left in the unmowed grass by a barbecue grill and three plastic chairs. She studied the house.

"This is it," she said, without looking at the address on her notepad.

"How you figure that? The buffalo?"

"It's a bison. Buffalo are in Africa. And no. Look at the decal on the bumper of the Sonic. Far-right one."

"Where? You mean that little flag?"

"Look closer."

"It's upside down."

"Indeed it is. Signal of distress. The American Indian Movement has used it as a symbol. Doesn't mean these people are part of AIM, though. Lots of Indians fly it like that. There's also a peeling medicine wheel next to the feathers decal on the back driver's-side window. And Steven Paul Judd stickers on the rear window."

"And a *shampe* sticker on the bottom right," Chris added.

"Well, well. Good for you. Although I think that's just Bigfoot on a bike."

"I thought they're the same thing."

"Maybe." *Shampes* are big, hairy creatures that many Choctaws believed followed them on the removal trail. Some argue that they are the inspiration for *The Legend of Boggy Creek*. Other tribes have similar beings, like Sasquatch.

"You got a lot of weird things to keep up with. Little People, deer men, owl shifters."

"You remember." She glanced at the notepad before sliding it into her jacket pocket. "Yep. This is it."

Monique walked to the front door first. Chris stayed behind her, his fingers on his sidearm.

She pushed the bell, but she did not hear a ring. She tried again. Silence. She glanced back at Chris. She tried the glass storm door and found the handle broken. Propping it open with her left foot, she knocked on the wooden door and then stepped back.

The door opened. Monique looked up, expecting Lulu. Instead, a child of about seven peeked out.

"Hi," he said.

"Hello," said Monique. "Is your mother here?"

The boy with enormous brown eyes and black hair nodded. "She's on the potty."

"I see. Well, can you please tell her to come to the door as soon as she can?"

"Okay." He left the door open as he ran to inform his mother of the visitors.

Monique exhaled, puffing her cheeks. Chris shrugged. They heard the television inside the house. Blue jays in the neighbors' blackjack oaks shrieked and a child several houses down laughed. Chris peered over Monique's shoulder to the door.

"Hello," came a chirpy voice.

Monique turned. Standing in the doorway was a dark-skinned, bespectacled woman of about twenty-five. She stood roughly five feet five—five feet six or seven if you counted the thick bun on top of her head—and at about 140 curvy pounds. Her smile and eye crinkles were honest and her T-shirt and cutoffs were tight. No space for a gun. "You need to see me?"

"Yes. I'm Detective Monique Blue Hawk." She pulled back the left side of her jacket to reveal her badge on her belt. Lulu gave it a quick glance. "This is my partner, Detective Chris Pierson." He stepped forward, his badge raised. Lulu eyed his ID for a split second, not long enough to read it, and then focused again on Monique. "Is your husband, East, here?" Monique asked.

"No he isn't," she said as if he had stepped out to the grocery store.

"Has he been here today?"

"Not today."

"What about yesterday?"

"No," she smiled. "Not yesterday either."

"When was the last time you saw your husband, ma'am?" Chris asked.

"Oh, let's see. Uh, I don't really remember what day." She did not appear concerned.

"You can't recall?" Monique asked.

"Hmmm. Maybe Saturday."

"You mean yesterday?"

"No, I mean last Saturday." She pursed her lips. "Yes, that's right. Not since that afternoon. Around three."

"Mrs. James," Monique said, "your husband has been reported missing." Lulu did not flinch.

"May we come in?"

"Of course." Lulu stepped back and went to the plush brown sofa against the far wall. She turned, sat, and crossed her legs. A girl of about five years old holding a stuffed animal ran to her and climbed into her lap. Monique and Chris surveyed the small living room.

A sewing table stood in front of the television, material cascading from either side like blue waterfalls. Bolts of colorful material leaned against the wall. A puffy-sleeved blue cotton dress embellished with purple, turquoise, and red ribbons, and a white apron with lavender stitching hung from a portable rack. A long purple skirt with yellow, red, and green ribbons sewn around the lower half dangled behind it.

Monique was transfixed. "Beautiful," she mouthed.

"Who else is here, ma'am?" Chris asked.

"Just me; *amvllatek-vt*, Eloise; and *amvlla-vt*, Silwee."

"*Nanta?*" the boy yelled.

"Nothing. Hush," Lulu admonished. Monique noticed that she had diamond tattoos around both wrists. The same markings of the diamondback rattlesnake that Monique wore around her left ankle. She got the tattoo in high school after seeing them on her father and her uncle Leroy. No one in her family objected to her being tatted at age sixteen—as she recalled, her uncle had suggested it. "Go for it," her father had said.

"Mind if I look around?" Chris asked.

"Go right ahead. Watch out for snakes."

Chris stopped. "You have snakes?"

She laughed. "I'm just playing."

Chris arched a brow. He walked down the short hall. He inspected the first room. Piles of toys and stuffed animals surrounded two twin-size beds. The room across the hall was a bit larger. Sewing projects covered the unused bed. He strode to the attached bathroom and pushed open the door. Just a tub with shower, a toilet and sink. He went to the last door at the end of the hall. He turned the squeaky knob.

At the same time that he pushed open the door, Lulu called to him from the front room. "No, really. Watch out for snakes."

Too late. Shrill barking and two dark shapes burst from the room. One hit Chris in the knees and knocked him into the wall. Monique's hand went to her Glock and then she realized that the shapes were a longhaired dachshund and a mixed-breed Toto. The two barreled down the hall, careened into the coffee table, and swerved onto the vinyl floor. They hit a throw rug and slid. The children laughed and cheered.

"What the hell?" Chris muttered.

"The wiener dog is Sidewinder," Lulu yelled. The dachshund twirled in circles until she fell and lay on her side. "The mutt is Cottonmouth." The mixed breed that might have been a cairn terrier and a beagle jumped onto the sofa, farted, and then sat panting.

"Like I said. Watch out for snakes."

"Holy shit," Monique said.

"They just had a bath."

Silwee laughed. "Shit!" he repeated. "Dash hound!"

"I'm sorry," Monique said. "I didn't mean to—"

"No worries," Lulu said.

"Shit!" Silwee repeated.

Chris quickly scanned the master bedroom and bath and hurried back to the front room. He ascertained that no one else had entered and then quickly searched the kitchen, small mudroom, and two closets.

"Like I said. Just us," Lulu reiterated. "And the snakes."

"Don't tell me," Chris said. "*Kill Bill.*"

Lulu laughed. "The cat's Elle Driver." She pointed to a carpeted cat tower next to the bookshelf. A one-eyed, orange-faced tabby stared out at Monique. "Our Deadly Viper Assassination Squad."

Silwee shrieked. "Shit!"

"Mrs. James—" Monique started.

"Call me Lulu. *Binili*—sit down." She motioned to the two-person sofa and chair under the front window. "Blue Hawk. That's Pawnee. I know some Pawnees. The council house was damaged by fracking."

"Correct," Monique agreed. "You're Chahta."

"That's also right. Where you from?"

"I was born in Red Oak."

"Red Oak. Small town."

"My parents were visiting my grandma. Her allotment is there. I arrived in this world early. My grandmother knew how to deliver me."

Lulu nodded, and Chris sat in the chair. Eloise jumped from the sofa, ran to him, touched his knee, and then ran back to her mother. She giggled.

Monique started talking again before she sat. The sofa springs were broken and she hoped she didn't have to stand quickly. "Mrs. James—"

"Lulu," Lulu repeated.

"Okay. Lulu. As we said, we're looking for your husband, East."

"Daddy!" Silwee interjected, laughing.

"Let's start again," Monique said.

"He's not here," Lulu said.

"Where is he?" Chris asked.

"I don't know," Lulu shrugged.

Chris leaned forward, elbows on his knees. "A friend let the police know after he didn't show up for a mandatory meeting at the fire station today. And he missed his EMT final Thursday night."

Lulu nodded.

Monique stared at the woman. Lulu did not appear worried about her husband and she showed no evidence of crying. Nor did her children seem upset.

Monique asked, "Has he called you?"

"Just once."

"When?"

"When he arrived at the dance grounds."

Cottonmouth ran to Chris and leaped into his lap. She wiggled until Chris stroked her back.

"And where was that? Where did he go?"

"*Hilhvt im ia tuk,*" she answered, watching Monique.

"A dance?"

"Yes."

"Can you be more specific?"

"There was a dance and he went to it."

Silwee went to a small table in the corner. He plucked a framed picture from the collection and brought it to Monique. "Daddy!" he said.

A man of about twenty-five stood next to a truck in a gray tank top and baggie nylon shorts. Monique could not discern his height, but he was beefy, like a high school football lineman. His dark, tousled hair appeared wet. His smile was huge. A pleasant face. He also had diamond band tattoos around his forearms and calves. A dozen large catfish lay displayed on the truck tailgate.

"East?"

"Yes. He loves to fish. He noodles."

"Noodles?" Chris asked.

"Catches fish with his hands," Lulu explained. "Noodlers stick their hands in crevices where the catfish are. Big ones clamp down on your hand so you can pull them out. Or you can just take hold of the fish's gills."

"With your hands?" Chris asked. "Is that hard?"

"When you first start out, it might be."

Noodling was more than that, Monique knew. Catching a large cat had its dangers. A big, strong fish might knock a human off balance and try to keep him under, or they might ram into a torso, or cut with their barbs. And catfish were not the only denizens of Oklahoma fresh waters. The thought of encountering a thirty-five-pound snapping turtle—or a rare hundred-pound alligator snapper with an attitude and vise-grip jaw—gave Monique a chill.

"Okay," Monique said. "Let's back up. You saw your husband before he went to the dance. Where was the dance?"

"Ummmm. East of Ada."

"What kind of dance? Was it at a bar?"

Lulu laughed. "No! He stopping drinking two years ago."

"*Sa hochaffo!*" Lulu's daughter interrupted. "Hungry!"

"Do y'all want a drink?" Lulu asked the detectives.

"Yes." Monique answered. "That would be great."

Lulu got up and went to the kitchen. Monique heard ice clink. "Silwee," Lulu yelled from the kitchen. "*Miti! Tushpa!*"

Silwee stood and ran to the kitchen. He came out a few seconds later carrying a large University of Oklahoma baseball cup. He stuck his tongue out in a concerted effort not to slosh. He handed it to Monique.

"*Yakoke*," she said.

The boy grinned and returned to his sister. Lulu brought another cup to Chris. She held up her right index finger and then turned around. Her children followed. The two came running back with gingersnaps. Silwee giggled as he handed one to Monique. Eloise stopped two feet from Chris and tossed one to him. Cottonmouth intercepted and swallowed it. Eloise laughed. The children ran back to the kitchen and emerged with juice bags and a box of Wheat Thins. Eloise gave a handful to Chris. The kids then sat on the floor, snickering and crunching.

Lulu sauntered back into the room and sat. She crossed her legs.

"You said that East went to a dance?" Monique asked.

Lulu clarified. "Ceremony." She pronounced it *cer-mony*.

"A ceremonial dance?"

"Detectives," Lulu said with a smile, "East went to a dance. A ceremony, really. He's not here and I haven't seen him. Don't worry. He's fine."

"What dance?"

"Renewal."

Monique racked her brain, but could not recall a Renewal Dance. She was familiar with the Duck, Turtle, and Raccoon Dances, and of course the popular Snake Dance. Everyone was. Choctaws donned their post-colonial tribal clothing to take part, but Monique wondered how many possessed knowledge of culture extending beyond the dancing. Those dances were not religious ceremonies and neither were powwows. The latter were pan-Indian social events and, for some, a source of income. She knew of some Choctaw powwowers who wore impressive Plains attire and who sat at Plains drums and sang songs unrelated to Choctaw culture. The daughter of a Muscogee friend had danced for years in her cloth ribbon dress, but one day showed up in full Kiowa buck-skin regalia, complete with feathers, beadwork, and her hair in braids. Monique was so shocked at the cultural transformation that she nearly fell off the bleachers. Clearly, the girl felt she was not flashy enough in her own tribal dress.

Monique knew it couldn't be the Sun Dance. That was not a Choctaw ceremony and, besides, it was too early in the season. Those dances lasted four days. Her husband did not Sun Dance, although some of his fellow Pawnees pledged to Sun Dance with Lakota friends in South Dakota. She had gone with Steve four summers to Mission to support them. The long preparation, the promises to not to engage in bad behavior, not to think bad thoughts, and not to imbibe or take drugs was arduous for many people. On top of that, dancing without food or water for four days with a skewer through one's skin proved impossible for some. Dragging bison skulls was particularly challenging. Monique was no saint. She knew that even if she were member of a Plains tribe, she was not worthy to partici-pate in such a rite. Still, she gave small flesh offerings from her shoulders. The old man who took her skin was skilled with the sharp blade and the scars were faint.

The way Monique understood it, the Sun Dance was a renewal dance of a sorts. The purpose was for committed dancers to sacrifice for the good of the community. One could dance for someone, such as an ill or distressed family member or friend. One of Steve's friends danced for his alcoholic father. Another danced for murdered and missing Native women. Yet another acquaintance participated because he deemed him-self cool with scars on his chest. He picked at the scabs to make them more prominent. Not everyone danced for the right reasons.

Monique snapped out of her reverie. "East was planning on attending his EMT final?"

"I guess so. His books are still on the kitchen floor under the table. That's where he studies. He also has to watch online videos. We saw a scary one about radiation burns last week."

Monique recalled that unit. Her class watched an old black-and-white film about the aftermath of the Hiroshima bombing. No one who saw that could forget images of melted skin and shadows of incinerated humans etched onto buildings and sidewalks. "Why did he leave Saturday?"

"He said he was going to help get ready."

"I see. Why isn't he home yet?"

"Probably tired. Resting."

"Where?"

"Any number of places. We got lots of friends. And he likes to sleep outside. He'll be back."

Monique felt like she was spinning her wheels in mud. "Do you know of anyone else who danced?"

"Sure. Silan Bohanan. Mike LeFlore."

Bohanan was a familiar Choctaw name, and every tribal citizen worth their salt knew of Silan Lewis, the Choctaw Nationalist who, along with other disgruntled Choctaws, killed Progressive Choctaws in 1892. Lewis had been a sheriff of Gaines County, but the newly elected Progressive chief, Wilson N. Jones, removed him. The chief was one of the wealthiest men in Indian Territory—much wealthier than most white men. Twenty other Nationalists, known as the Last League of the Choctaws, participated in the killing spree, but Lewis was the one sentenced to die. The partisan judge released him on his word that he would return for his execution in Wilburton. And he did. One of Lewis's political enemies was supposed to execute him, but instead of shooting Lewis through the heart, as per the law, Lyman Pusley instead shot him in the right side of the chest, through a lung. Lewis lingered until a sheriff suffocated him with a handkerchief.

Many Choctaws called that murder because Lewis was supposed to die by bullet, not by hankie.

Monique understood Silan Lewis. The Bohanans had named their son well.

"Have they danced before?" she asked.

Lulu shrugged. She kept her smile, and Monique took that to mean that yes, they had.

Chris chewed as he put Cottonmouth on the floor and stood. The dog looked up adoringly. "Mrs. James," he said, "we need to look around your property." Actually, they needed a warrant, but Monique was willing to wager that Lulu did not know that.

"You think I buried him under the woodpile?"

"Did you and your husband have any difficulties? Did you recently have a fight?"

Silwee and Eloise stopped laughing.

"We never fight," Lulu said calmly as she stood. Monique wondered if she took Xanax. "I'll show you around."

The adults, children, and dogs walked into the front yard. Chris put his hands on his hips as he surveyed the front of the property. There was no place to hide. He walked to the north side of the house and saw a line of tall rosebushes.

Lulu opened the gate to the backyard and the dogs and children ran in. In the back of the property was a detached garage and the heavy metal door of a storm shelter.

"Do you have a key to the shelter?" Monique asked.

"Not locked."

Chris pulled back the heavy, squeaky door. It dropped to the ground, revealing a dark underground space. He pulled a penlight from his jacket and shone the small light inside.

"There's a flashlight on the second step," Lulu said. Silwee did not hesitate. He grabbed the light and ran down into the dark.

"Whoa there," Chris said.

Silwee giggled as he turned to shine the bright light into Chris's face before continuing down the steps.

"Lulu," Monique said as she watched Silwee, "please." She motioned for Lulu to proceed in front of her. Lulu nodded and quickly descended toward her son.

Monique used her iPhone flashlight as she placed her long feet sideways on the narrow steps. She reached the floor then took the large light from Silwee and shone it around the room. The beam revealed a space larger than most tornado shelters. A twin bed stood next to one wall, four rolled sleeping bags on top, along with three trash bags stuffed with what looked like blankets or clothes. Along another wall was a stack of five cases of bottled water, canned fruits and vegetables, a tool kit, a filing cabinet with bicycle helmets on top, a shelf with three radios and four battery-operated lanterns, and another shelf piled with jigsaw puzzles. There was no child-size plastic toilet. Instead, they'd opted for four plastic containers with heavy lids. A shovel and three-foot crowbar leaned in the corner. Monique knew that could be used to pry open the door in case it became blocked by debris. She also knew if the house landed on the entrance, the family would have a long wait.

More importantly for their immediate purposes, there was no place for a man to hide. "Lotsa stuff," Chris said.

"You haven't lived here long enough to see an Okie tornado," Monique said. "An F5 twirling over two hundred sixty miles per hour and a mile wide will destroy everything. It'll put balled-up trucks in the treetops. See the movie *Twister*. That'll give you an idea."

"Comin' up on the anniversary of the 2013 Moore tornado," Lulu said. "Less than ten miles north of here. Killed a buncha people and wrecked the town. That one took off our roof. The entire woodpile disappeared. And a cow landed in the flower bed across the street."

Monique nudged Chris. "That's why your apartment complex has a shelter," she said.

"I guess I should finish my bug-out kit."

"Good idea. Come on."

They left the shelter and entered the garage. The interior resembled a hardware store. Hundreds of tools hung from pegboards. Propane tanks were stacked in one corner, next to a welder's torch. Jars filled with nuts, bolts, screws, and washers lined the wooden shelves. Loops of orange extension cords hung from the rafters. Many tools were still in their plastic wraps.

"East likes flea markets," Lulu explained.

There was nothing but a modest woodpile on the south side of the house. There was no basement.

The children led the group back inside via the wooden porch and screen door. They kicked small plastic balls to the dogs, whose yipping reverberated through the house.

"All right," Monique began. "Lulu, you need to stay in town in case we want to ask you more questions."

"Not going anyplace. Silwee's birthday party is next week."

"Planning something big?"

"His whole class is coming over." She smiled in anticipation. "Already sent out invitations."

Monique nodded. "Here's my card with my number. Call me when you hear from your husband." She almost said "if," but the children were listening.

"Okey dokey."

Monique turned reluctantly and walked to the car. Chris followed and they both got in.

She started the car.

"Very accommodating," Chris said. "And she's not worried." Monique drove back down Raptor Lane and stopped at the sign.

"So where is he?" Chris asked. "At a friend's? A girlfriend's? A relative's? Maybe he went noodling."

Monique stared straight ahead. Clouds obscured the setting sun. It would be dark in another thirty minutes.

"No. She's hiding something," Monique said.

"Like what?"

Monique watched a pair of crows conversing on a mailbox.

"Monique?" Chris prompted.

She took her lip balm from her pocket and thoughtfully coated her lips. "She is. She really is. We need to speak with Bohanan and LeFlore."

"All righty."

Monique snickered at his use of a Southern phrase spoken in a New York accent.

Chris called in their names. He jotted down the information as dispatch recited their addresses. "You heard. Bohanan lives in Coalgate and LeFlore is in McAlester. They're out of our jurisdiction."

"The guy who's missing is *in* our jurisdiction."

"We should inform tribal police. They'll have a heads-up in case James ends up dead on tribal land."

Monique did not respond.

Chris drummed his fingers on his knee. "Monique."

"No. I don't want to complicate things. I need to call Hardaway and brief him." She thought a moment. "On the other hand, James probably went snagging."

"Is that like noodling?"

"Ha! Sort of. And you can get hurt." She sighed. "I'll call him when I get home. It's too late to call on Bohanan and LeFlore. Long day, and I'm as tired as a mother."

"You are a mother."

"True that. But I'm really tired. There's a reason no one says 'tired as a father.'"

"Uh, actually, I think the phrase is 'tired as a mother fuc—'"

"All right."

"Just saying."

"We'll start early. Be at my place at six thirty. We'll drop in on Bohanan first." She pressed the accelerator and the dust flew.

3

Iksho Hatak
Men Gone

"Pooped," Monique said as she slurped her Budweiser. Her second, half-consumed bowl of spaghetti with extra tomato-and-pepper sauce sat on her side table. She felt way past full.

"You had a long day," Steve agreed. He had piled his long wet hair into a topknot. Monique liked how his thick hair looked when he unfurled it in the mornings. "Up at six, ran an hour. Then you helped me in the coop for one whole hour." He leaned back in his leather recliner, his stained towel-as-a-napkin on his chest. "I made dinner."

"This wasn't necessary, Steve. You made a Crock-Pot of soup this morning. You don't have to be a martyr."

Steve kept his eyes on the television. Monique glanced past him to see that Robbie's light shone under his closed bedroom door.

"Don't start," she warned.

"I'm not starting anything."

"You made more food because you're pouting. And you also knew I had to go."

"This is Sunday."

Steve never yelled. He merely made quiet comments in a passive-aggressive manner.

Monique's head throbbed.

"Something bad happens every day, Steve."

"You think this is a crime? Sounds like a runaway husband to me."

"Maybe."

Steve speared some noodles, then twirled his fork. His fork scratched the plate. Monique's father ate his spaghetti like that. Her father told her that he could not understand why anyone would cut spaghetti into pieces when they could twirl it. She mentioned that to Steve on their first date at Bellini's in Oklahoma City. She ordered eggplant parmesan and he ordered basic spaghetti with meatballs. She stared as he chopped his noodles with his fork. When he asked her what was wrong, she shook her head and took a bite of eggplant. He pressed, and she admitted that cutting noodles was a pet peeve and then proceeded to tell about her dad's eating habits. Instead of being annoyed, Steve laughed, stopped cutting, and began twirling.

"Anything else about food?" he had asked.

"Well, um, cereal with milk in a bowl is weird to me. I eat it by the handful."

"Okay. I don't usually eat cereal."

"I tried to eat an oyster once and spit it out."

"That makes sense. Tastes like snot to me. What else?"

"Salad dressing on sushi. Pimiento cheese in California rolls. Why put cheese on fish?"

"Some people like it on fried fish. You know, sandwiches."

"Yeah, but by the time it's deep-fried, it doesn't even taste like fish. Except catfish. And I would certainly never put cheese on that."

"Of course. Most french fries don't taste like potatoes either."

"My aunt liked beer mixed with Clamato."

"Well, it is a thing now."

"Gross."

They continued, talking about likes and dislikes. Movies and books. Over time, they understood each other so well they often forgot to interact. Except to complain.

"Damn cilantro is in everything now," Monique said the last time they went out to dinner.

"I love it," Steve countered.

"Yes, I know. You always say that when I say I don't like it."

"Just eat it."

"It tastes like soap. And I'm not the only one who feels that way."

"It's in your head."

"Do you like the taste of shampoo?"

"It doesn't taste like shampoo."

"Right. Fresh and bright." Monique tapped her plate with her fork. "Why would anyone put cilantro on fried okra? Where's that waiter?"

And on they went. The replacement side dish of okra had no cilantro and that made Monique happy. She doused it in ketchup. Most evenings out featured some kind of minor trauma over unexpected ingredients. Monique got mad, they argued, and then eventually all was better. Over time, anticipating the arguments became more tiring than the arguments themselves.

"Tomorrow is Monday," Monique said.

Steve set his bowl of pasta on his side table. He had paused Kevin O'Leary of *Shark Tank*, whose face was screwed up as he tasted a product christened Lima Bean and Peanut Cheese Dip. Steve often paused shows so he could advance through the commercials. He waited for her to speak.

"Chris and I are headed to Coalgate and McAlester to talk to two men in the morning."

"You think they got your missing man?"

Monique had no obligation to tell her husband anything about her work. Still, she always revealed enough to keep him off her back.

"They might know where he is."

"Who is he?"

"Choctaw guy. I already told you that. He was at a dance. Ceremonial maybe. That's what his wife said."

"What dance?"

"Renewal."

"What's that?"

"I don't know."

Steve took a sip of ice water.

"Maybe he needed to get away for a few days."

"It's been longer than that. And his wife is unconcerned."

"Well, there you go. Maybe he's having an affair and she knows it. Maybe she doesn't want to talk about it."

"I didn't get that impression. And their little kids didn't act like they missed him."

"Mom probably told them he was on a trip and would be back soon."

"True. I'll find out more tomorrow."

"How's your back?"

"Tweaked."

"Wanna back rub?" This was Steve's way of saying he was sorry for causing ruffled feathers.

"More than anything."

Crepe myrtles and pecan trees shaded the Bohanans' L-shaped brick house. The attached carport protected a green 1990 Volvo 240 with a crashed-in passenger door. A red-and-gray crew-cab Dodge diesel faced the street. Coolers, life vests, and fishing poles in a ready-to-roll bass boat stood hitched behind it. Two gray-faced German shorthaired pointers ambled to Monique's car as she parked in the dirt driveway. One had a chewed-up tennis ball in her mouth. The other barked once and stood still, waiting to see what might happen.

The detectives got out. "Doggies," Monique held out her hand for them to smell as she walked to the door. The old dogs followed.

The inner wooden door stood open, and a thin, black-haired woman of about thirty appeared at the glass storm door. She opened it as they approached. She wore red cat-eyed glasses, a high ponytail, jeans, a gray T-shirt stenciled with the words *Oka Lawa Camp*, and a yellow visor with the bill outlined with white, green, and red beads.

Monique knew the place. Outside McAlester. Protesters of the Diamond Pipeline organized the camp in 2017. Monique noticed that the woman wore the same diamond tats on her biceps as East and Lulu James.

"Mrs. Bohanan?" Monique asked.

"Yes, ma'am," she said.

"I'm Detective Monique Blue Hawk and this is Detective Chris Pierson." The two displayed their IDs.

Mrs. Bohanan glanced at the badges, but not long enough to read them. Monique took note of her indifference. "We're looking for Silan Bohanan," Monique said.

"That's my husband. I'm Jodi."

"Fine. Good to meet you. Where is he?"

"He went to the Shop-N-Hop for ice. He'll be back in a few. You want to come in?"

"We'd be delighted."

The detectives climbed the two cement steps and entered. Jodi held the door so the arthritic bird dogs could follow. The morning sun shone through the large front windows and hit the potted plants that took up the space along the sill. A ninety-inch smart television occupied the north wall. Movie DVDs filled the wall-to-wall shelves underneath. Even with the sofas situated at the opposite side of the room, the effect was similar to sitting in the front row of a movie theater.

"Now that's a screen," Chris said.

"Yeah," said Jodi. "Needed three people to carry it in here. I hope we don't have another quake. Damn frackin', right? The screen's not secured to the wall yet. Y'all want a drink? Sweet tea?"

"Maybe in a minute," Monique said. She took in the room. The house was old but well maintained. The threadbare carpet was clean and the walls smelled of new paint. A gas wall heater barely fit between the television and the hall doorway. A box of long matches and a clamshell filled with coins sat on top of the heater. The floor creaked when Jodi walked.

"Plenty of food here too." Jodi motioned to the kitchen table overflowing with loaves of bread, potato salad, bags of chips, covered casserole dishes, and a roast chicken. Monique thought that was an odd breakfast spread.

"No thanks," Chris said.

"I'm good," Monique agreed.

Another woman of the same age, donning cutoff jeans, a camo T-shirt, and flip-flops, came down the hall carrying a plastic tumbler filled with soda. She wore red lipstick on full lips and her thick hair in a perfect fishtail braid over her shoulder. She also had the diamond tattoo on her upper arm.

"This is Saralese LeFlore," Jodi said.

"Hello," she said.

Monique extended her hand. "Are you related to Mike LeFlore? From McAlester?"

"Yup. My husband."

Monique raised her brows and Chris coughed.

Just as Monique thought *jackpot*, a truck with a glasspack muffler and headers pulled up outside. Monique knew the sound. Some of Steve's best auto-parts customers wanted obnoxiously loud exhaust systems.

"Guys are here," Jodi said.

Monique looked through the window to see a beige Chevy Silverado park on the grass next to the boat. Two men exited the truck. The driver went to the bed, pulled out two large bags of ice, and dropped them into the red ice chests in the boat. The passenger was the first in the house. He carried two full grocery bags in one hand and a half-eaten hamburger in the other. He swallowed, then pushed the remainder of the burger into his mouth.

"This is Silan," Jodi said. She took the bags and went into the kitchen.

Silan waved, chewed, and held up a finger. His deeply tanned skin peeled from sunburn. He appeared thin and tired, like an ultramarathoner who'd just finished a rim-to-rim-to-rim Grand Canyon torture run—except he wore Teva sandals instead of sneakers. Band-Aids covered the tips of the fingers on his left hand, and the sclera of his right eye seemed inflamed.

He took the tumbler that Jodi had brought in, drank all of it, and then smiled, revealing one missing canine tooth and another silver one. Silan stuck out his hand first to Monique. "It's not pink eye," he said. She took his hand. He held her gaze a few seconds.

"Nice to meet you."

He held his hand out to Chris and stifled a yawn. "Excuse me," he said before sitting on the sofa.

Next in the door came Mike LeFlore, a bit shorter and with longer hair. He, too, was thin, and his skin and lips flaked from sunburn. Instead of Tevas, he wore Merrell trail running shoes, the right one loosely laced. He walked with a pronounced limp. Like Silan, he held half a burger in one hand, and a Subway bag filled with two foot-longs in the other.

Jodi introduced him to the detectives. He put down the bag and shook their hands, but winced at the slight squeezes. Both men wore jeans and T-shirts. And diamond tattoos. Silan's wrapped around his forearms. Mike's adorned his biceps.

"Headed to Atoka Reservoir?" Monique asked. That was the only logical spot.

"Yes, ma'am," answered Mike. His voice was deep and confident. He took another bite of his burger.

"Nice bass boat," she said.

"Oh yeah," Silan said. "That's my baby." He took the Subway bag from Mike and pulled out a sandwich.

"I thought I was your baby," Jodi said, adjusting her beaded visor.

The LeFlores and Bohanans laughed. They did not seem nervous. No one had asked why Monique and Chris were there.

"Stuff in the kitchen too," Jodi reminded him. She did not look the least bit alarmed at her husband stuffing himself.

"I saw that." He unwrapped the thick sandwich and took a bite.

Monique watched the men eat. She wondered what the heck was going on. They were ravenous.

"We're here to ask you some questions," Monique said. "Actually, Mr. LeFlore, we were headed to McAlester to see you next. This is convenient."

"I'll say it is," answered Mike.

Monique's eyebrows furrowed. "Pardon?"

"I mean, yeah. Saves you a drive, for sure."

"Right. Let's do it this way. Chris, you and Mr. LeFlore—"

"Mike," Mike LeFlore interjected.

"Okay. Chris, you and Mike go out back and talk. Mr. Bohanan, can we please sit down?"

"Of course," Silan said. "But call me Silan. Hey, honey," he said to Jodi, "how about you and Saralese make sure the ice chests are closed and see about the grill?"

Jodi winked. "Yessiree." She went to the kitchen to get a chair for Monique, and then she and Saralese went outside with the dogs.

"Detective Chris," Silan said, "there're chairs on the back porch." Chris gave a thumbs-up and followed Mike through the kitchen and into the mudroom. Monique heard the back door open and shut.

After Silan settled on the couch and Monique on the kitchen chair, Monique pulled out her pen and small notepad.

"We're looking for a missing man. East James. We understand that you both saw him a few days ago."

"That is correct," Silan said. He took another bite.

"Did you know that he is missing?"

"No," Silan said. He put down the sandwich and pulled a Snickers from his pocket.

"He's been gone a few days and people are concerned."

Silan did not respond. He bit off a third of the candy bar. Melted caramel strands stuck to his chin.

"His wife hasn't seen him," Monique added.

"Hmmm," he mumbled indifferently, before pushing the remainder of the bar into his mouth.

"Where did you last see him?" Monique asked.

"At a dance."

"What kind of dance?"

"Ceremony." Silan nodded.

"Which one?" Monique prompted.

"Renewal."

"Renewal?" She repeated as if she had never heard this before. "You mean like spring? Time to plant?"

Silan took Life Savers peppermint candies from his pocket and held out a piece to Monique. She shook her head. Silan took his time opening a piece. "Sort of," he said.

"Walk me through it," she said. "When you arrived and so on."

"Well, I drove my truck over the night before the dance," Silan said. "Got there Sunday about four. Mike drove up about twenty minutes after me."

"Was East there?" she asked.

"Yes," Silan answered. He unscrewed a bottle of orange juice and chugged the entire contents. "Saw his truck parked by the shed. He got there the day before."

"How do you know that?" Monique asked.

"His tent was set up and his stuff was laying around it. That. And he told us." He laughed.

Monique sighed. "Okay. What kind of truck?"

"A blue ninety-four F-150 Super Cab," Silan said. "He loves that truck."

"Goes off road a lot?" Monique asked.

"Yeah, man," Silan answered. "He was always going on dirt. Hunts deer, turkeys, pigs. But he's not a BTJ."

"What's that?" Monique asked.

"Big Truck Jerk." He laughed. Monique thought that was an ironic statement considering Silan's annoying truck.

"East doesn't drive distances in that thing. He mostly uses that little Sonic and Lulu drives the Taurus."

"I see. Where was this dance?"

"East of Ada," said Silan.

"Where is east of Ada?"

"Off Highway 75. On Rock Creek. Off Muddy Boggy."

Monique clicked her pen, then stopped. Muddy Boggy Creek, actually a river, was at least 170 miles long. But her uncle Leroy Bear Red Ears lived off Highway 75, east of Ada. On Rock Creek.

"Whose property?" she asked.

"Bear Red Ears," Silan answered. He watched Monique's reaction. Monique froze. She wondered if she appeared as shocked as she felt.

"What?" she asked. Blood pounded in her ears. She bit the inside of her left cheek and winced. "You're telling me that this dance was at Leroy's?"

"Yes, ma'am."

Silan found more food in his pockets. He pulled out a stick of jerky and a granola bar. One of the shorthairs in the yard barked.

"He's my uncle," she said quietly.

"Yeah? Well, we had the dance at his place," Silan said. "East's truck was by Leroy's shed when we got there."

Monique sat still, her heartbeat now slamming her ribs. She feared her blood pressure was rising.

"And you saw East?" she asked.

"Yup, after we went in the house."

"Then what?"

"Had beans, man! Leroy cooks a mean pot of beans."

Monique had tasted Leroy's spicy beans many times throughout the years. The last time, she and Chris ate three bowls each after Leroy performed the cleansing ceremony for them. After they almost died in the hollow.

"Yeah," Silan continued. "Uses a lot of tomatoes."

"Tomato water," she clarified.

"Yeah. Tomato water, chiles, onions, and what's that brown powder?"

"Cumin," she answered.

"That too. And lots of black pepper and garlic. He puts chunks of chiles in his corn bread and some sweet corn too. Then cheese on top of the beans. Man, I ate way too much."

That was how Monique made beans. She learned from Leroy.

They were silent a few seconds. The morning was warm. If these people were going fishing, they should have left long before now. The men knew East was missing. And they knew that she was Leroy's niece.

"You knew we were coming," she said.

"Not me," Silan said. He retained a slight smile, and Monique knew he was lying.

"Let me make myself perfectly clear. A man is missing. You saw him. Where is he? Is he still at Leroy's?"

Silan shrugged. "Dunno."

"Haven't you talked to him?"

"Can't."

"What do you mean?"

"He doesn't always use his cell phone."

Jodi knocked at the door and stuck her head inside. "Did you ask if she wants tea?" she asked.

The woman already had offered her tea.

"Oh. You want any tea?" Silan asked. "Sun tea. It's good." He stood and went into the kitchen.

"No," Monique said.

She heard him drop ice into the cups. "Well, East has gotta be someplace," he said from the next room. "Probably on his way home."

Monique sighed heavily on purpose. She was annoyed and frustrated and wanted him to know it, but she also did not want to lose her temper.

"What happened after you ate dinner?"

"Sat around the fire and talked," Silan said as he returned to the sofa.

"Did you drink?"

"Had a case of Fresca and cooler of tea."

"I mean alcohol."

His smile disappeared. "No. We went to sleep early. Dance started at sunrise."

"How long did this ceremony last?"

"Two and a half days. We stopped a few times to sit in the shade. Then went until dusk. Stopped around midmorning the third day. We finished early."

"How do you complete a ceremonial dance early?" As far as Monique knew, ceremonies were not whimsical. They followed prescribed prayers, chants, songs—all passed down through the generations. If anything, they went overtime.

Silan shrugged. "Leroy finished it."

"Then you left?"

"No. Stayed until the next morning. Thursday. Ate. Then drove home."

"Did East go home?"

"Dunno," Silan said. "Mike left first. I pulled out after him."

Monique's thoughts swirled. If Silan and Mike were the last people to see East on Thursday morning, that meant East James had indeed been missing for four days.

"You and Mike look like you danced for a month. What did you do to your fingers?"

Silan wiggled his bandaged digits. "I got ahold of a hot coat hanger. You know. S'mores. We craved chocolate and onions."

"Onions on s'mores?"

He laughed. "Yeah. After the dance, we craved sweet stuff and onions. I couldn't wait for my marshmallow to cool, so I grabbed for it and got the wire instead."

"You'd have to be pretty hungry to eat that," Monique said. "I've seen Sun Dancers after four hot, dusty days and they don't look as exhausted as you two."

As she had observed, Sun Dancers did not eat or drink for four days. They danced in inclement weather. Monique had seen dehydration, sunburn, tangled hair, and deep piercings that resulted in excessively torn flesh. She even watched one man's skirt fall down, yet he kept leaning backward until the skewers pulled free. She wondered if Mike and Silan had scars.

She said, "If you ate like this all the time, you'd be three hundred pounds. What have you been doing?"

One of the dogs barked again.

After a few seconds, Silan said, "Oh yeah. Man, we've started running."

"And just how far are you running every day?"

Her phone vibrated. She ignored it.

"Too far." Silan laughed.

A car pulled into the driveway. Monique watched through the window as a tall man with thick black hair dressed in jeans and an untucked dress shirt exited a red Hyundai. Jodi and Saralese greeted him. The three looked to the house as Jodi spoke. The man retrieved a box out of the back seat and passed it to Jodi.

"Who is that?" Monique asked.

"Andre Grayson," Silan said.

Monique knew the name from the last few issues of the tribal newspaper, *Biskinik*. "He's running for chief, right?"

"Yep."

"Mike and I are running for council," Silan said. "Vote for us."

"I'm not in your districts."

"Oh, right," Silan said.

Monique considered the two rugged dancers and their chances.

"Looks like he dropped off some campaign signs," she said. "I want to talk to him."

Before she could stand, Andre quickly got back in his car and drove off. Clearly, he had nothing to say to the detectives.

"Huh," Monique said, huffing. *And a bit obvious,* she thought. "Who else was at the dance?"

"Ummmm, let's see. There was Mazey Spring, Peta Hayes, Deb Hollow Tree, and Rob Scanlon."

Monique scanned the names she wrote down. She recognized Mazey Spring as a one-time council member. He would be about seventy-five now. "Were they all councilmen?"

"All of them," Silan said.

"Did your wives go too?"

"Not this time."

"You mean you've done this before?"

"Mm-hmm. Coupla times."

"At Leroy's?" She blinked. *Why did she not know about this dance?*

"Yeah." Silan smiled.

Monique's phone vibrated a few seconds, then stopped.

Jodi stuck her head in the doorway. "Coconut LaCroix in the fridge," she said.

"No thanks," Monique said.

Silan sat quietly. Relaxed. As if he had nothing else to do. Fishing clearly was not his priority.

Monique's phone vibrated again. Her screen said it was Hardaway. She stood. "Excuse me." She walked outside to her cruiser, which sat far enough away from where the wives rearranged the boat gear for privacy. She called Hardaway.

"Monique," Hardaway said. "Where're you?"

"Coalgate."

"Officer Novler did a bit of checking and it appears that more than one person has gone missing at a dance."

"Who else?"

"A guy named Ron Barnes. He was on the Tribal Council but had resigned. Back in 2005. Same kind of deal. Went to a dance and never came home." Monique kicked at a stone on the driveway.

"Where did he live?"

"Antlers."

"Do you know where the dance was held?" She held her breath.

"Off Muddy Boggy Creek."

She puffed her cheeks, then sighed. *Leroy*, she thought.

"Monique?"

"I'm here. We'll check it out."

She watched Jodi and Saralese retrieve boxes from Silan's truck and carry them to the boat. After depositing the boxes, they walked to the back of the house.

"Call in later." Hardaway disconnected.

Monique walked over and peeked into the boat. Bungee cords secured a small grill to the back of a chair. Bags of charcoal, tortilla chips, and bread stuck up out of the boxes. Another held granola bars, peanut butter, trail mix, Little Debbie Oatmeal Creme Pies, and Band-Aids. Cases of Gatorade and V8 peeked out from under the seats. Three ice chests were filled with steaks, sliced cheeses, deli meats, yogurts, fruits, and condiments. A container with a white top sat in the drink holder in the back. She picked it up and saw that it was a jar of adult gummy vitamins.

Monique went back inside. Chris sat with notebook in hand, listening to Silan talk about large-mouthed bass.

"Yeah, we want to start a bass team," Silan said. "There's a tournament at Lake Eufaula end of April." He swigged some tea.

"Either of you know Ron Barnes?" Monique interrupted.

Silan stopped lifting his glass to his mouth long enough for Monique to know his answer. "Not me," he said. Then he took a long drink.

"Me neither," Mike said. He crossed his right leg over his left and tugged at the loose laces.

"Did you know he disappeared from a dance in 2005?"

Silan shook his head. "I didn't dance then and wouldn't have paid attention."

"I was only seventeen," Mike added. "I didn't watch news."

Monique calculated how old she was at the time. She had no excuse. She had been twenty-eight.

"What happened to your foot?" she asked Mike. "Saw you limping."

"Dirt got hot in the afternoon. You know. I also stepped on a rock. Burned my sole and got a stone bruise."

Monique thought that unlikely. "It's not that hot right now."

Mike shrugged.

"You're injured and you're out running?"

"Well, I took the morning off," Mike answered.

Monique raised an eyebrow and stared at him. Chris stayed silent. She blew air out through her nose, then said, "All right. We're finished here. For now." Everyone stood. "I know that you're fishing down the road, but don't go anyplace else," she told them.

"Thank you for your time," Chris said to Silan and Mike.

"Here's my card," she said, handing one to each man. "Call me if anything else comes to mind." She regarded both of them. "We'll be in touch."

She patted the head of one of the dogs, who jogged to her as she walked down the cement steps. Chris quick-stepped to keep up with her.

Chris started to speak. "Not now," she said.

Monique unlocked the cruiser. She got in and started the engine.

Chris clicked his seat belt, then slapped his knee. "Man. That was weird."

Monique put the car in gear and backed out of the driveway.

"Those guys've been through a wringer," Chris said.

"Yeah. But what wringer?"

Two kids playing soccer in a yard a few houses away waved as they drove past. Chris waved back.

"Tell me what Mike said."

Chris relayed his question-and-answer session with Mike LeFlore. The answers were basically the same as what Silan had told Monique.

"They did more than just dance," Monique said. "And they did it for longer than two and a half days."

"Who's Barnes?"

"Look him up," she told him.

Chris typed on his phone and scrolled. "Not much. Ron Barnes is twelve and plays baseball."

"Chris. Seriously? Look under news."

"Right." He punched keys and scrolled more. "Okay. Here he is. Ron Barnes. Choctaw. He was a council member. The story says he went to a ceremonial dance near Muddy Boggy Creek on April 14, 2005, and did not show up to work the following week. Widowed. One kid. This is a reposted story—from three years ago. One of those 'On This Day' pieces."

"What else? Who reported it? Quotes from anyone?"

"The article isn't very long. Just finishes by saying that the investigation is ongoing." He scrolled some more. "Here's another one, but it says the same things."

"We need to see what Novler found. Call him."

Chris called dispatch to discover that Novler was working a car-and-truck collision. He sneezed.

"Dang," Monique said. "Gesundheit."

"Thanks."

"Someone's thinking about you."

"What?"

"A sudden sneeze means someone is thinking of you."

"Didn't know that."

"If a cheek burns, it means someone is talking smack. It feels as if someone slapped you."

"I thought that's when my ear itches."

"Just if the left ear itches."

"What about the right one?"

"Someone said something nice about you. Or it means you need to clean your ears."

"You're a wealth of information, Monique."

"Thank you."

"How far is it to Leroy's?" Chris asked.

"Less than thirty minutes."

Her heavy foot pressed the accelerator.

4

HATAK HOPOKSIA
WISE MAN

Chickens followed Leroy Bear Red Ears along the garden fence as he pulled up dead raspberry canes. He left a few stalks to provide support for the healthy canes that he hoped would bear fruit in a month. He cut thick, dry okra stalks at the base before moving on to inspect the sunflower heads. If the birds had picked all the seeds, he cut those too, and tossed them over the fence for the burn pile. Old pepper and tomato plants and cucumber vines went over next. Birds no longer needed the brush for protection from the cold winds. He studied the dried milkweed stalks along the south fence and determined that there were no butterfly chrysalises attached before launching them over the fence like javelins.

Crows and jays cawed and screeched in the nearby cottonwood and pecan trees. They, along with opportunistic sparrows, watched in anticipation of finding unearthed insects and seeds. They planned to descend on the garden as soon as Leroy left.

Garden work was his hobby, his obsession, his love. Late spring in Oklahoma is the time to clean the beds and to plant. After months of cold winds, Leroy would be busy until November. A tall chain-link deer fence surrounded the five raised beds, cucumber and winter squash arches, roasting-ear patch, and future rows of beans, amaranth, tomatoes, and okra. Pots and growing bags filled with rich earth from the creek bottom nourished potatoes, peppers, and bright flowers that would soon crowd the front porch.

In summer, each morning before sunrise and before the heat made outdoor work unpleasant, Leroy walked the dirt roads through neighboring corn and soybean fields. These were not plants for human consumption; rather, they fed cattle and machinery. He grumbled at the wasted water and depleted soils, then spent a few hours tending to his plants and animals.

A black-and-brown shape landed in the midst of the chickens. The birds squawked and flapped, feathers flying as they scattered. Lorraine, Leroy's tortoiseshell cat, posed like Bastet, pleased at the chaos she caused. She watched nonchalantly as the agitated flock regrouped by the garden gate. The diminutive Polish cock, Smudge, stood at attention in front of the hens, staring at Lorraine. He emitted a war cry, and then the flock rushed toward Lorraine, heads outstretched and bodies swaying side to side like small, feathered dinosaurs. Lorraine turned and dashed for the back fence, jumped over, then turned to look through the chain link at the angry birds. The cat knew she couldn't kill them, but she took great satisfaction in pissing them off.

Leroy laughed. "They'll get you someday." Lorraine ignored him.

He dug up a few potatoes that managed to survive the winter. He did not use a rototiller in his old garden, instead allowing the earthworms, fungi, and other small organisms to continue their life cycles. He still used a shovel to break up a few lumps and hard patches. He tossed white June-bug grubs to the chickens.

Lamb's-quarters were already up. In a few days, the plant would be big enough for him to snip leaves to add to his dandelion-and-pigweed salad. Pokeweed emerged along the south fence, the same place as it had the past ten years.

The chickens scratched in the dirt, heads down, in hopes of finding more grubs. Leroy squinted up at the sun and smiled. Monique and Chris would be here soon.

5

ONSSI
EAGLES

"Are you ever gonna get up and help me move the fridgerator?" Gena Vaughn asked her brother Fuji.

"In a minute," he answered, without turning to look at her. Fuji watched the pair of golden eagles circling the field behind their property. A soft breeze swept across the plain, nudging the buffalo grass and carrying early-spring butterflies and floating seeds on its current before dissipating.

Fuji spent many of his afternoons on a metal fold-up chair behind the screen door, observing the birds that nested in a tall cottonwood tree. He never exercised and ate too much of the federal government's fatty commodities. Fuji was a large man of twenty-one, whose spare tire bulged out under his faded navy-blue T-shirt.

His mother, Christine, saw a *National Geographic* magazine when she was a child. She became enamored with the spread on the Fiji islands that included a photograph of a handsome island man holding a large fish in his muscular arms. She hoped her son would grow up to be as darkly sinewy as the Fiji man was, although she liked the sound of Fuji better than Fiji, so that's what she named him.

By the time Fuji turned fifteen, it became clear he would look different from Christine's ideal. He had the same height and straight white teeth as the Fiji man, but he did not look like the islander. Fuji's round face, with eyebrows that arched in the center and drooped at the far edges, gave him a soft and gentle look to match his demeanor. The opposite of Gena. His persona matched that of his thoughtful and gentle father, Ingram, also known as Inge, who died from heart disease and diabetes at age thirty-five. Christine could not deter Inge from his favorite meals of bacon and eggs, ham, and macaroni and cheese. He didn't like her salads and vegetables, so he made his own meals.

Gena was angry with Fuji's stretch marks. Of all the commodities they could choose, Fuji liked the least healthful: hard, yellow-orange cheese and white bread slathered with butter or mayonnaise. He chased his sandwiches down with a can of peaches packed in sugared syrup.

"Fuji!" Gena repeated. The chair squeaked as Fuji shifted his weight.

Gena was not a gentle personality. Her now-dead Muscogee father named her after Gena Rowlands, who played a mob guy's girlfriend in the movie *Gloria*. Gena stood five feet nine, five inches shorter than Fuji, walked softly like her mother Christine, and spoke loudly like her two little brothers.

She slapped Fuji's back to get his attention. "Brother! *Halito*! Time to clean under the fridge. That smell is from the stew you made last week. It spilled over and no one cleaned it up. And for sure there's a dead mouse in the trap."

Fuji moved slow and quiet and did not appear annoyed by his sister's lecture. He just stood and pulled up the shorts that had slipped halfway down his ass.

"Finally," she said. "Get on that side and we'll slide this thing back and forth."

The strong Fuji pulled the white over-under refrigerator from the wall by himself. "That good enough?"

He sat down to watch the sky again. With a grimace, Gena scraped and swept up the hardened mess. Their mother worked two miles away in the tribal registrar's office in Durant and by the day's end felt too tired for housework. Gena usually cleaned and made sure her ten-year-old twin brothers, Gary and Walt, helped. Fuji pitched in, but only after Christine bribed him with something sweet.

After completing her task, Gena pulled up a chair by her brother and watched the eagles. "Sure would be nice if our neighbors moved and took their junk with them," she said. Bags of trash and old furniture covered their neighbors' place. The Vaughns' clean property had no garbage in sight.

"One yard full of garbage makes the entire area look bad. Doesn't it embarrass you?"

Fuji shrugged. He did not pay attention to his neighbors, and for the next two hours, he gazed through the screen while cracking open sun-flower shells.

That evening, Gena, Fuji, Gary, Walt, and their mother sat around the kitchen table. They dined on greasy fried chicken and french fries that Christine brought home from Popeyes. Gena ate the coleslaw in hopes of avoiding artery-clogging grease, although the mayonnaise likely rendered it as fattening as the chicken.

Walt pulled chicken and fries from the bag and plopped them on the table. "What did y'all do today?" Christine asked them. The pink-cheeked twins had been at their grandparents' all afternoon. Christine grinned because she knew that her mother enlisted the ten-year-olds to prepare her garden for planting.

"Plowed and plowed and plowed," said Walt, the family complainer. "I'm soooo tired." The fastidious boy wore his hair slicked back into a neat, thick ponytail.

"No, you didn't, you liar," said Gary. "Grandpa has that tiller thing and he plowed it. We just moved rocks." Also hair conscious, Gary preferred his hair short, the top moussed and combed straight up.

"Same thing, chicken face. We had to stand out there all day and move rocks."

"Couldn't be that many rocks, son," said Christine. "They've had that garden in the same place since before you were born and most of the rocks are gone."

"Well. We had to put seeds in and my back hurts."

"Go to bed then, you baby," said Gary.

"Enough, you two." Gena said. "You need to help Fuji in our garden here."

"Oh man," Walt whined.

Gena sighed. "It's not that big. You can manage an eight-by-four-foot raised bed." Walt shrugged and dragged his chicken through ketchup.

"I cleaned the kitchen," Gena said.

"I noticed," Christine said. "Looks good."

"Fixed my loom so I can start beading."

"Need to check out your bead supply, Gen. Auntie Vic still wants you to make her a belt. You gotta do it this year."

"I know."

The breeze blew through the screen doors and windows. Late spring brought warm afternoons and brisk evenings. Walt pressed his fingertips onto the hard french fry pieces in the bottom of the sack and licked them.

"What's going on at work?" asked Gena.

"Same old stuff. We got a couple dozen applications today from people wanting to enroll."

"We're a popular tribe," Gena said.

"I don't know if that's the reason or if people think they'll get money every month. Applications are back up. Only three that I looked at today have proof that they're Dawes Rolls descendants. I get depressed when I see that some of these people wait until they're forty to try to enroll. Like they never knew they were Choctaws. Or maybe they did know and don't care."

"Cherokees deal with that too, except more so," said Gena. "Anything about the candidates?"

"People are just now filing."

"I hope we get Andre and B. O."

"Who?" Gary asked.

"Andre Grayson and B. O. Banning." The two unlikely candidates were running for chief and assistant chief. Prior to their candidacy, both forty-somethings seemed more destined for careers as clients in a drug and alcohol rehabilitation house than potential CEOs of a financially successful tribal Nation.

"You may have seen them at the hog fry in Durant last summer," Christine said.

"Why's his name B. O.?" Gary asked.

"He smelled bad," said Gena. "You know—body odor." The twins laughed. "Even though B. O. started bathing, the name stuck. A lot of people think *Body Odor* is funny and won't call him by his real name, Brian Oar."

"Neither Andre nor B. O. were too smart when they were younger," Christine explained. "Then a couple of years ago, they stopped drinking. They started the Learn Your Traditions initiative. They got bumper stickers—*Self-Sufficiency* and *Tribal Pride* and *One for All and All for One*." Christine pointed to one that hung on the corkboard by the light switch. "Those guys could win. A lot of people don't like them, though." She poured more root beer into her plastic tumbler.

"Yeah," agreed Gena. "They're too honest and want to address our poverty."

"So what's the problem?" asked Walt.

"We're not rich, that's what," laughed Gary.

"No, that's not the problem," said Christine, wiping crumbs from the table. "For some people, being in charge is more important than the good of the group." She picked up her glass and talked as she went to the freezer for more ice. "The only way we can survive as a tribe is to recognize our differences and work through them. B. O. and Andre pledged to do that and they'll do their best. But they can't do it alone." She turned to eldest child. "Fuji?" Christine had to prod her son to talk.

"Leroy's having a Renewal Dance next week," Fuji said.

"What?" Christine was surprised.

Fuji did not respond.

"Fuji." She sat down and leaned into him. "Look at me." He sat back and obeyed his mother.

"You don't need to go to that dance."

"I'm going to."

The twins stared, mouths full of chicken.

"Son, Ron Barnes didn't come back from one of those dances." Fuji stayed occupied with his chicken.

"Fuji."

Walt swallowed. "Who's Ron Barnes?"

"A guy who didn't like anyone else," said Gena.

"That's not true," said Fuji quietly. "Ron was unhappy with our tribe. Too many white people."

"White people?" Walt asked.

"Those who act like them," Fuji said. The confused twins fidgeted.

"Ron would be about sixty-five or seventy years old now," Christine added. "He followed Leroy Bear Red Ears since he was a teenager then got active in the American Indian Movement in the early 1970s. He said he didn't like it much because some of the leaders only wanted attention. AIM's rhetoric about tribal rights was exciting at first, but he also agreed with his tribe's elders that violence would not be the way to achieve goals. He came home and wasn't surprised when conditions for Indians in South Dakota didn't change for the better after the take-over. Many were murdered. Anyway, Ron liked what the AIM guys said about Indian rights and treaty breaking in front of the cameras, but he was worried about their behavior behind the scenes. He said they were sexist."

"What's sexist?" Walt asked.

Christine cleared her throat. "Men treating women bad." She almost said *Screwed every Native and white female who presented herself and left behind God knows how many offspring,* but thought better of it. She recalled a comment a Lakota friend made about Russell Means's memoir, *Where White Men Fear to Tread.* "Should have subtitled it *And Where White Women Aren't,*" she said after seeing the book cover. "He doesn't even mention Anna Mae Pictou Aquash." And why would he? The male AIM leadership had ordered the murder of the Mi'kmaq activist and mother of two.

Walt and Gary stopped eating. Their family and extended family were replete with strong females who took pride in their tribe's history and culture. Their mother, sister, aunties, and cousins took charge of not only household duties—they also changed car tires, hunted deer and turkey every fall, and had served on the council. The twins did not understand the concept of men taking advantage of women.

Christine wadded up the dirty napkin she'd used to wipe the table. "Anyway, Leroy's brother Strong Bull and Strong Bull's wife, Ninah, were at the dance. So were Andre and B. O. They always said they knew nothing about Ron's disappearance. Right, Fuji?"

He took a swallow of root beer. Gena slapped his arm.

Fuji nodded. "I guess."

"Ron and his son, Kurt, kept to themselves most of the time," Christine continued. "Ron was friendly and Kurt's friends liked to fish the pond behind his house. He dammed a creek and made that pond himself." Walt and Gary grinned at each other conspiratorially.

"Don't get any ideas," Christie warned. "Anyway, after the dance, some kids knocked at Kurt's door to borrow poles. They couldn't find Ron or Kurt so they told their parents. Kurt was at his auntie's house in Antlers, but nobody found Ron. Then tribal police questioned Leroy. All he would say was that Ron came to the dance, went through the ceremony, and afterward his truck was gone."

"Where was it?" Walt asked, eyes wide.

"It had come back to his house. But Ron wasn't there."

"What happened to him?" Walt prompted.

"Some thought he was murdered, but police couldn't find any evidence. No odd tracks around the dance grounds, and no strangers in the area. Ron didn't have enemies and didn't have anything worth stealing. One of the officers knew Leroy and swore he had nothing to do with Ron's disappearance. He thought it was a matter they'd never solve. So he got the case closed."

"Wow," said Gary. "Where's Kurt now?"

"I'd guess that Kurt's about forty years old, and he lives in the house. Y'all know him. He's the one who reroofed our house two summers ago. He married that pretty girl who runs the nursery with the big greenhouse and fishpond. I buy hanging baskets from her."

"Oh yeah," said Walt. "The plant place where cats sleep in the pots."

"Yes. Fuji, who all's dancing?" Christine asked.

"Not sure."

"I don't like the idea."

Fuji shrugged. "You already said that. But I'm dancing anyway. It's safe, Mom. It's just a dance at Leroy's. I'll be home after a few days."

Christine stared at her son. Walt, Gary, and Gena watched her chew the inside of her cheek. "All right," she said in resignation. "What do you need?"

Everyone exhaled.

"Just my ties and skirt." Fuji took several long swallows of his drink. "Was gonna ask you to hem the red material we got last year."

"What's the Renewal Dance?" Walt asked.

"It's a dance to bring back the old ways," Fuji answered.

"The buffalo aren't coming back, Fuji," Christine said. "And white people aren't going away. So why do you keep waiting for that to happen?"

"I never said they would."

Gary laughed. "But that's what *renewal* means, right? Then you can go running across the prairie on a horse and fall off. And you don't even know how to shoot a gun."

"Hey, did Choctaws eat buffalo?" asked Walt. "Even if you killed one, you wouldn't know what to do with it."

Everyone but Fuji smiled at the imagery.

"The Old Ones back in Mississippi mainly saw deer and bears," Christine said. "*Yvnnvsh* stayed farther west, but our ancestors did see some."

Christine knew that many tribes never saw buffalo at all. Nevertheless, through the decades, the animals became symbols of the collective tribal past. Their destruction represented the colonization of all Natives. Many believed their reappearance would help foster their decolonization.

"Fuji," Gena reached for his hand. "Maybe you could just . . ."

"We've lost our way," Fuji interjected.

"I'm not lost," laughed Walt. "You lost Gary?"

"Not me."

Gena sighed. "Okay, you two," she scolded.

Fuji wiped his mouth with his napkin. "You two don't know anything."

Christine felt pride that her eldest son spoke Chahta anumpa and was well versed in tribal history. She also fretted that Fuji appeared to be turning into a red version of the religious fanatics who believe that Jesus hides in comet tails or that sleeping with poisonous snakes brings enlightenment. Fuji wholeheartedly believed that whites would destroy themselves with their greed and pollution. Then, he reasoned, Indians would have the country to themselves. While she knew that human self-destruction could happen, the idea that buffalo would again run in vast herds and that the land could become as it was before contact seemed not only ridiculous, but also scary.

"You and Rene can live in a tipi and wear buckskin," Walt kidded him.

"Yeah, and she can make you buffalo cheeseburgers for dinner," laughed Gary.

"Breakfast and lunch too." Walt thought himself hilarious.

Fuji did not smile. He was not angry at their teasing him about Rene because he had been in love with her since grade school.

The quiet and pretty Rene Gibson also followed Leroy Bear Red Ears. She and her two brothers were raised listening to tribal stories. Their parents, Rosa and Arlan, insisted on their speaking Chahta anumpa at home.

"If you do bring back the old ways, then new ways gotta go, don't they?" asked Gary. "Whatcha gonna do without your stuff? Can you handle losing TV and your car?"

"No mac 'n' cheese," added Walt. "No ice cream. No—"

"Won't bother me any," his big brother interjected.

That was what troubled his mother.

6

NUKOA
FRETFULNESS

Gena lay in bed watching the stars that twinkled between the billow-ing lavender curtains. She pondered her brother. She loved Fuji and felt uneasy about his participation in a dance that she did not know much about. Was it the same as the Ghost Dance? Did dancers expect that whites would go away, the dead of their tribe would arise, the buffalo herds would return, and all would be as it was prior to contact?

What if Fuji participated? Would he suffer cognitive dissonance after-ward like the people who waited in vain for the Second Coming of Christ on New Year's Eve in 2000 and the Mayan apocalypse in 2012?

Gena sipped from a glass of watered-down root beer that sat on her bedside table. Smells of birds, new grasses, and fruit-tree blossoms wafted into her room. She breathed deeply, then sneezed. A whip-poor-will ser-enaded the night creatures.

Fuji was smart. Their mother hoped he would enroll in the commu-nity college, but she soon realized that his thoughts mainly focused on religion. He also avoided white people. He didn't dislike them; he just never seemed interested in mainstream society. Gena figured that Fuji could not face reality.

She rarely saw her brother upset. Fuji was adept at taking the path of least resistance to avoid arguments. He never yelled and he never poked fun at anyone. She concluded that no, Fuji would not fall apart when the dance failed. He would sit and think and deal with whatever came his way. Quietly.

But what if the dance didn't fail? Well . . . it would.

Gena found herself enmeshed in a whirlwind of choices. She had thought numerous times about leaving Durant. She had enrolled in Bacone College in Muskogee two summers ago and liked it. At the awkward age of nineteen, Gena possessed a confusing and volatile mix of knowledge that is the curse of many Indians: a year of college among Natives from a variety of tribes, which made her aware of career and social possibilities. She tried hard to break free from her tribe, which she often found stifling. But for reasons she could not explain, she felt pulled back. Ironically, she often sat on the sofa watching *Dancing with the Stars* and absurd soap operas, wishing she could go somewhere.

Now, Gena lay on her soft bed in her T-shirt and gray sweatpants and stared out the window. A coyote howled in the distance and, seconds later, neighboring dogs yipped in attempts at answering. She thought of asking Fuji if she could join him in the Renewal Dance, but she was afraid of the consequences.

7

Amoshi
Uncle

Monique drove north on Highway 75, taking large bites from a turkey sub. There was not much to see besides red cedars lining portions of the road, newly sown farmland, and red-tailed hawks atop telephone poles scouting for snakes, rabbits, and mice. She studied the road ahead, wondering what Leroy might have to do with a man's disappearance. She vaguely heard Chris speaking.

"And you never know how a man might act out when he's mad," he said as he stuffed barbecue chips into his mouth. "Maybe he just decided to leave and zone out by a lake for a few days."

She snapped back to attention. "What?"

"East James. Maybe he got mad at his wife and left for a while."

"Maybe. But she wasn't upset."

"Black widows usually aren't."

"I don't get a murdering vibe from her."

"You never know."

"True."

They ate the rest of their lunch in silence.

As they approached Leroy's place, a dozen turkey vultures circled over the cornfield beyond. The corn was only knee high, so the birds could see whatever was rotting below.

"Probably a dead deer in there," Monique said.

Chris watched the black birds coasting on the thermals, fascinated at how none of them flapped their wings. Their graceful sailing relaxed him. "Hopefully that's all it is."

"Look at those redbuds," Monique said, gesturing to the pink-blossomed trees that lined Leroy's driveway. "And check out the dogwoods over there." She pointed to the four trees by the pond. Tall cottonwoods grew on the opposite side.

"Spring's busting out," Chris said.

"The dogwood blossoms are cool," she said. "They're in the shape of a cross. Four petals. Christ's cross was made of that tree's wood. At the end of each petal is a little dent—like they're perforated with nails. The middle of the flower looks like the crown of thorns. Sort of."

"No kidding."

"That's the story."

"Huh," he remarked.

"Didn't you go to Sunday school?"

"Yeah, but I don't remember much about it."

"I didn't. I read about them from a brochure at the arboretum. Anyway, dogwoods aren't as common as they used to be."

They approached Leroy's property and saw three trucks and a Subaru hatchback parked on the west side of his house.

She turned into Leroy's drive. "Who're these people?" Chris asked.

"I don't know. And I don't see James's truck," Monique said. "Maybe it's around back."

They saw Leroy in his garden, his floppy-brimmed orange angler hat a beacon. He took no chances: Many of Leroy's clothes were orange because his property backed to public, forested land. Bullets had hit his house, truck, and shed many times in the past decade. This was turkey season and he wanted to make certain that hunters saw him. There were plenty of careless hunters out there, and some yahoos shot at anything that moved.

Lorraine streaked toward them across the open space between the garden and house. "Whoa!" Chris yelled. "Watch out."

Monique stopped in front of the carport. The cat leaped onto the hood of the car. She crept to the window and stared at Chris.

"That freaking cat is nuts," he said.

"She likes you."

"How does she know I'm in here?"

"Cats work in mysterious ways. I told you someone was thinking about you. It's been a year, but she remembers."

The detectives got out and stretched. Leroy walked toward them, a shovel in one hand and a bucket in the other. Lorraine jumped from the hood onto Chris's left foot.

Chris reached down to scratch behind her head. "Hey, cat. Long time no see."

Lorraine's purr was unnaturally loud. Monique's grandmother—Leroy's mother—had had a black cat like that. She'd always said, "Noche Negro's engine is running."

Leroy's old, heavy wheelbarrow sat under the shade of a redbud. Monique saw straw encrusted with chicken poop, bits of onions, sweet potato peels, eggshells, beet greens, carrots, apple cores, and other detritus. She knew the edible parts went to the chickens and crows. He would shovel the leftovers into his twirlable compost bins after the birds picked what they wanted from the colorful jumble.

"*Halito ibitek,*" Leroy said. He set the shovel and bucket down next to the toolshed. Her fit uncle walked quickly with no limping or slouching. No sunburn, and he appeared well fed.

Leroy had clearly not endured whatever Silan and Mike had experienced. Or, he had managed better. He walked toward her with his arms out.

"*Amoshi,*" she answered.

"Not going to hug too tight," he said. "I'm dirty." Lorraine meowed loudly. "Oh stop," Leroy admonished. "And how're you, Chris?" He extended his hand.

"Not bad."

"Chest healed?"

"All healed. Except for the scar."

"It's a reminder," Leroy said. "Not a bad thing. So, what brings you here?" Leroy asked as if he were truly curious. Monique knew better. This was a sly old dog.

"Well . . . there's a missing man," Monique said. "East James. And we were told by his wife that he danced here last week."

"I see."

"You see?" she echoed. Leroy shrugged. "Is he here?"

"Nope."

"Was he?"

Lorraine reached up Chris's leg and dug her front claws into his pants. "Owww," he said. "Dang, you weirdo."

Lorraine backed off, lifted her paw, and licked it. She turned her head away, insulted at the rejection.

"Let's go inside," Leroy said.

"Who's here?" she asked.

"Old friends."

They followed him through the garage door and into the den. Curtains billowed in open windows. Something roasted in the oven. Monique thought it smelled like venison.

"I felt like cooking," he said.

She and Chris removed their sunglasses. Four men stood. "Monique, you know everyone here." Actually, she only knew Mazey Spring and started to say so, but Leroy added, "You met them when you were a child." That was news to Monique.

"Oh," she said. "Well, hello again, I guess. And this is my partner, Chris Pierson."

The men were dressed in jeans and flannel or work shirts. Mazey Spring and Deb Hollow Tree wore boots, Peta Hayes wore running shoes, and Rob Scanlon went barefoot. Mazey favored a cowboy hat while the others had on gimme hats in different colors. All had short black-and-gray hair except for Deb, who wore a ponytail.

Each man held out his hand. Monique and Chris shook them in turn. Mazey smiled and revealed no upper teeth.

"Glad ta meet y'all," said short, wide Peta. Fifty years before, Peta played as a linebacker for the University of Oklahoma. He remained powerful, thanks to the weights in his garage and a daily regimen of flipping an old four-hundred-pound Goodyear tire in his backyard.

Lorraine trailed Chris. When he sat in the large rocker, she jumped into his lap, lay down, and curled.

"So now you're nice," Chris said.

"I told you she has a crush on you," Monique said as she sat on the sofa. Everyone knew to leave the recliner for Leroy.

"We'll be outside," Peta said as the four men filed out the front door.

"Don't go anyplace," Monique called after them. "We want to talk to you in a minute." Mazey turned and gave her two thumbs up.

Leroy busied himself in the kitchen. Monique and Chris knew it would do no good to tell him they weren't thirsty or hungry. They heard ice cubes clink. Leroy emerged with two plastic glasses filled with amber liquid and ice. He handed them to the detectives.

Monique took a sip. "Hmmmm. Cedar?"

"Yup. With a bit of agave."

He went back to kitchen and returned with a bag. He held it out to Monique, who pulled out two cookies that looked like Fig Newtons.

"They're really brown," she observed.

Chris took a few.

"Got them out of a bin in a health-food store."

He sat in his recliner, worked the control on the side, and lay back as the footrest lifted his legs. Steve did the same at home. "So, what's up?" He bit into a cookie.

"I told you. East James."

"Okay."

"His wife, Lulu, said he came to dance here. Silan Bohanan and Mike LeFlore were here too."

"That is true."

Monique set her tea on the floor and pulled out her notepad. She pointed toward the door. "We were told that Mazey Spring, Deb Hollow Tree, Peta Hayes, and Rob Scanlon were also here."

Leroy sat with his fingers laced across his belly. "Yes. They were here."

"Leroy," she prompted. "East is missing."

"Missing," Leroy repeated.

Monique had her legs crossed so tightly she worried about thrombosis. She uncrossed them, then tapped her left toe on the ground.

"What went on here? Silan and Mike looked like they'd just returned from the Marathon des Sables."

Leroy laughed. "I watched a documentary about that. Hot. One grain of sand in your sock will ruin your foot." He kept smiling. "You can get a heck of a blister."

"Yes, you can. What happened?"

"We had a dance."

"And East James was here."

"I just told you that."

"He danced."

"Yes."

"Then what?"

"He left."

"He's not at home. We went to his home. He's not there. And he missed two important meetings."

Monique watched Leroy look out his front window at the cardinals cracking sunflower seeds at the feeder. Hulls rained onto the sidewalk. Monique shifted her gaze to Chris, who petted Lorraine. The cat was not asleep. She stared at Monique.

Monique glanced back at Leroy. He lay back in his chair and appeared at ease. "Renewal Dance. I've never heard of it. Why haven't I heard of it?"

"Not everyone has."

"What's it about?"

"Renewal."

"Can you be a bit vaguer?"

"Sure."

"Leroy, I . . ." she trailed off and sighed. Lorraine continued to watch her. "When did East get here?"

"Saturday afternoon."

That matched what Silan and Mike had told her. "Then what?"

"We had dinner. Then went to sleep."

"And the next day?"

"We talked a lot. He helped in the garden. Fixed the shed door. He's a carpenter by hobby, you know."

"You did that all day?"

"Pretty much. We also burned the grass. Smell it?"

"Sort of. And?"

"The wood on the east side of the coop was warped. We replaced it."

"So he came early to help around the place."

"Pretty much. Then the others got here around three. We talked, ate dinner, went to sleep."

Monique glanced at Chris. He knew better than to interrupt.

"Up early to dance on Monday," Leroy continued. "Did that all day. Then to sleep early. It was hot. Got up early Tuesday to dance. Not as hot. Danced awhile. Rested. Danced. Slept." Leroy slowly ate another cookie. "We were finished Wednesday around noon."

That also correlated with what the others had told her.

"It sounds like someone got too excited about all this," he continued. "Last I saw East, he was fine."

"His truck is not at his house."

"It's not here either."

"Did you see him drive away?"

"No."

"His wife is not excited. She acts like it's no big deal."

"It's not."

Monique and Leroy regarded each other. She knew she couldn't beat him in a stare-down. She glanced at Lorraine. She couldn't out-glare the feline either. The cat had eyes like marbles. Monique blinked.

Chris cleared his throat. "Do you have any idea where he is?" he asked.

Leroy shifted his gaze to the ceiling. "Not really."

"This is serious," Monique said. "He's not at home, hasn't been to his EMT final, missed his regular firefighter meeting, and is not here. This is the last place where you, Mike, and Silan saw him."

Leroy shrugged again.

Monique stood and went to the door. She saw through the glass that the four men sat at the picnic table next to a crepe myrtle.

"Peta, would you please come inside?" She planned to speak to these men individually so none of their testimony could influence the others'.

To her chagrin, all four men came back in. They smiled and sat around the den table.

Monique glanced down to catch Lorraine still watching her.

"Umm. I wanted to talk to Peta."

The men smiled at her. Monique opened her mouth, then hesitated. This was not normal interrogation procedure, but she also knew these men were not going to budge. "All righty," she acquiesced. "I need to ask you some questions. It's my understanding that East James was here last Saturday and y'all saw him when you arrived."

"That's right," Peta said.

"True," Mazey agreed. His voice sounded as if his vocal cords were old, stretched rubber bands.

"We were here," Deb added. He smacked his gum. That drove her husband nuts. She'd stopped buying gum because Steve could not abide her chewing with her mouth open.

"Yep," Rob the tallest and thinnest of the group said. His deep-set eyes gave him a look of intensity, reminding her of the Cherokee actor Wes Studi.

"When did you arrive?"

"Sunday around, oh, fourish," Peta said. Everyone else nodded.

"When did you last see him?" She didn't ask anyone in particular, but Deb answered.

"Well, let's see. We ate beans after the dance. Then I left."

"Same," Peta added.

"We left after they did," Mazey pointed to Rob, who nodded in agreement.

"What about the other dancers?"

"We all left about the same time."

"None of you saw East leave?" The men shook their heads.

"So the last person to see East was Leroy."

She squinted at her uncle. Leroy appeared deep in thought, then said, "Probably."

"Do any of you have an idea of where he might be now?"

The men contemplated the question. Mazey pursed his lips. Deb closed his eyes. Rob rubbed his chin. Peta crossed his arms and searched for an answer on the ceiling.

Peta spoke first. "Around here someplace."

"Got to be," Deb said.

"I agree," Mazey said. His voice made her shiver. She thought his vocal cords would rupture.

"No doubt," Rob added.

"Already told you," Leroy said before Monique could ask him again. "He's nearby."

Monique ground her teeth in exasperation. "He's already considered missing. More people will become involved in this."

"Makes sense to me," Leroy said. "Let's see what happens."

Monique sighed and finished her tea. She stood and walked to the kitchen for more. As her cup filled with ice from the refrigerator dispenser, a few pieces fell to the floor. She picked them up and tossed them in the sink. She glanced to the mudroom and saw that the recycle bins overflowed with boxes of crackers, cereal, cookies, and empty cans of orange Diet Rites. An upside-down roasting pan dried in the sink. A foil-covered cookie sheet sat on the stovetop. She peeked underneath and saw large hunks of corn bread flecked with pinto beans. Two pies cooled on the countertop.

She heard Chris say from the other room, "Took a while to raise my arm over my head. The pectoral was really tight after the reattachment."

Leroy's usual fare covered the rest of counter: two jars of peanut butter, a half-full bowl of Cutie clementines, bowls of apples and pears, a bunch of bananas, tall glass jars filled with granola and flakes, bags of dried hominy and dried corn, and a bowl of eggs. She opened the refrigerator. The shelves brimmed with casseroles, fruits, bunches of greens, plus almond, soy, and cow milks. Glass containers of pasta with red sauce, various cheeses, and condiments of every color.

The dishwasher was open, full of clean plates, glasses, pans, and silverware. It appeared to Monique that one feast was recently over and another was about to start.

She returned to the den. The four visiting men had moved back outside.

"Find what you're looking for?" Leroy asked.

"What am I looking for?"

"You're the detective."

"Silan and Mike were starving."

"They need to pay closer attention to their diets."

Monique set her glass down and crossed her arms. "Leroy, for crying out loud—help me out here."

"East is not here. If you didn't see him at his home, then he isn't there either. Has his wife filed a missing person's report?"

"No. She's very casual about him being gone."

"If a spouse goes missing, isn't the one who's left the assumed assailant?"

No one said anything. Leroy could take Monique aback. The elder, dark man with long hair, tattoos, and vast tribal knowledge could bust out legalese, pop-culture trivia, and witticisms with anyone. Lorraine continued to stare at her.

Chris said. "If he doesn't come home pretty damn quick, we'll treat it as possible foul play."

"It's only been four days," Leroy said.

"Many things can happen in a few seconds," Monique said.

Leroy nodded. "Maybe. But it's not as if he has known mental issues, is senile, or is a small, vulnerable person who could be abducted. He's a fairly big guy. I also know he carries a bat and a tire iron behind his front seat."

"He could have been exhausted and fell," Chris offered. "Maybe he's laying out there someplace."

"Then you'd find his truck." Leroy lowered his footrest. He stood and walked to the mudroom.

"Might have been stolen," Chris countered. "Or he could have driven off the road and into a deep ditch."

"Doubtful. Monique, let's go outside."

"Chris needs to hear what you have to say."

"No, he doesn't."

Chris sipped his tea. He didn't appear concerned. Lorraine shifted and lay on her back, purring. "Don't worry about me."

Monique and Leroy went out the mudroom door and into the backyard. She heard Rob ask, "So ya find any good fishin' spots lately?"

Birds at the feeders flew into the trees, but the chickens came running.

"Sparrows," Leroy said. "Those little shits eat everything. They're invasive, you know."

"I know."

"They kill other birds and break eggs. Got into my bluebird houses and killed one of them. And they get into those." He motioned to the raised purple-martin houses. He had three twelve-room bird apartments atop telescope poles. "Native birds are disappearing and invasive species take over."

Monique had heard all this before.

She considered her uncle. A man of secrets. To her assessment, he didn't look much older than he did when she was a teenager. Now he was seventy-five. He always had been thin, yet he exuded energy—like a skinny marathoner who didn't appear to have the strength to lift a bag of dog food, but could run for a hundred miles. Where did his vitality come from? Her mother—his sister—had not fared as well. Her vigor evaporated, sucked dry by a drunk driver when she was forty-four, shortly after the murder of Monique's brother, Brin. Maybe Leroy absorbed what they left behind.

"Did East seem sick? Troubled?"

"No." The chickens pecked around their feet.

"Did he mention an argument with his wife?"

"Not a word."

"So what am I supposed to do now?"

"He'll come home."

"I have to report this."

"I've heard that repeatedly in the last fifteen minutes."

A hawk screeched as it soared over the house. Seconds later, another hawk approached from the south and screamed.

"Gotta watch my hens this time of year. Lots of coyotes and coons around too."

Monique admired the raptors, thankful for the moment of beauty. "You should dance," Leroy said, abruptly changing the subject.

"What? The Renewal Dance?"

He put on a glove, then squatted to pull up some poison ivy encroaching under the carport.

"Sure."

"What for?" She regretted saying that. Leroy stood and then faced the purple martins that sat atop their houses. Their distinctive chirps sounded to Monique like encouragement.

"Not everyone gets a chance," he said.

She thought again about dances she had seen and dances of which she had been a part. Social dancing, mainly. Not religious, just a way to connect with others.

Leroy said, "It's not a social dance."

She blinked. Leroy seemed to know what she was thinking. So had her much older uncle, the deceased Strong Bull, also known as Jerry, and his feisty ninety-year-old widow Ninah.

"We have to keep on," she recalled overhearing Ninah say to Monique's father twenty-three years prior at a family potluck at a cousin's house. They were talking on the front porch. Monique stood around the corner, inspecting a birdbath shaped like a cat's open, upturned mouth.

"What now?" her father replied.

"We'll tell you tomorrow," Nina said in a hushed tone.

"How long this time?" he asked.

Monique did not hear her quiet answer. She had no idea what they were discussing. She waited too long to ask her father—he died two weeks later.

Then she recalled the strangers who attended Strong Bull's wake. None of the Choctaws she saw that day appeared even part white, so unlike the blond-haired, pale-skinned people who attended the Nation's Labor Day festivals. These people were friendly, but with closed faces. They were true Choctaw Nationalists, unconcerned with amassing wealth and immune to the white world of political pandering. People who knew more about spirituality than she ever would.

"What does me dancing have to do with East James?" she asked Leroy, shaking off her memory. "How will that help find him?"

Leroy shrugged again. "Can't say that it will help with that. But it might help you."

Maybe she did need help. But dancing for enlightenment seemed too much like a self-help project from an online personal development blogger.

"I don't meditate and I hate yoga."

"Not talking about that."

"Psychological exercises bore me. Mentally and physically."

"One of your problems is that you avoid exertion."

She started to remind him of her daily workout regime, which exhausted her.

He quickly said, "I don't mean running and lifting weights."

She had no response to that. He didn't mean she never challenged herself physically.

"Self-acceptance is sometimes hard," he added.

Perhaps she did need some clarity. A few years prior, Ninah sent Monique the Tribal Council's audacious declaration that decreed the Choctaw Nation a "Christian Nation," much to the dismay of tribal traditionalists. This should not have been too surprising. Missionaries had infiltrated the tribe before removal in the 1830s, and their influence devastated the link between Choctaws and their knowledge of and adherence to traditions. Many had bought into what the proselytizers were selling, and that included marrying white men and women, becoming acquisitive and patriarchal in attitude. That influence had continued unabated for almost two centuries.

How does this make you feel? Ninah had written on a yellow note stuck to the declaration. That was a good question. She had thought about that a lot lately. No vote. No debate. Just a declaration by the Tribal Council determined to sever ties with all non-Christian beliefs. Of course, these were not the first colonized Indians to assert their beliefs on everyone else.

Nationalist and Progressive Choctaws had fought—many times with fatal results—after the Civil War. Arguments and struggles over wealth, cultural beliefs, land, and personal power were nothing new in any politics. And so she was familiar with factions, personal choices, and their consequences. One of her ancestors signed the removal treaty of 1830, also known as Treaty of Dancing Rabbit Creek. Her father told her that story when she was in grade school and she still wondered about it. Why would he sign such a document? Did he not know the pain and suffering it would cause? She hoped not. Even now, she spent her life wondering about his motivations and feeling ashamed for something a family member had done almost 190 years prior. A consolation was that his son had been a Nationalist, one of those Choctaws who fought against the unrelenting white intruders, railroads, Christianity, and tribal leaders concerned with lining their pockets. Not surprisingly, Progressive political rivals waylaid him on the road one evening in 1884. They bashed in his head and shot him point-blank. A Progressive judge and jury declared the assailants innocent.

The reality that Choctaws engaged in such intratribal bickering left her disheartened. Monique shut her eyes and recalled her confusion at reading the declaration, which was so outrageous that all she could do was to hand it to her Pawnee husband and laugh. Steve, however, did not laugh.

"So are y'all Indians or not?" he had asked.

"You can be a Christian and still be an Indian, Steve."

"I know that. But why make a formal declaration that falls right in line with the colonizers? Don't you people have any sense of history and the genocide and cultural destruction that Christiani—" He stopped and started to turn away, but then faced her again. "And your tribe is worth, what, several billion dollars, yet some of your citizens live in poverty?"

It was not a new conversation. "Yes. I do know," she had answered.

Back in Leroy's yard, she countered her uncle's suggestion: "Wait a sec. What do you mean 'one of your problems'?"

Leroy pulled more ivy shoots. He appraised her face and smiled.

"What?" she challenged.

"You should see your expression. You get mad over nothing."

"Oh really?"

"You could use some anger management."

Monique found herself grinding her teeth again. Steve often said the same thing. "That's not true."

"You're getting mad now." He stood and pulled his glove off inside out. He faced her. "Ever since Brin died."

Monique huffed. "What about him? Everyone is angry about it. He was murdered."

"That is true."

"Of course I'm mad." She couldn't think of anything else to say.

"You've always been a sparkler. Always done your own thing, worked hard. Sort of a type A personality. Your brother's death made you resentful. Suspicious."

"I am not."

Leroy shrugged.

Monique's cheeks reddened. She felt hot. One thing Leroy got right was her type A personality—but she did not like listening to something that she did not want to hear.

"What is this dance supposed to do? You just did one. You're doing another?"

"Yes. Fuji and some friends requested it."

"Fuji Vaughn?"

"The very same."

Monique met Fuji for the first time nine years ago at Ninah's home in Citra. She recalled that the tall adolescent seemed shy, intense, introspective, and profoundly sensitive. Like Leroy, he seemed to know more than he let on; he acted like a fifty-year-old in an eleven-year-old's body. At other gatherings, he remained quiet, politely fielding questions before managing to slip away unseen. The last time she saw him was a few months ago at a wake. Although only twenty-one, he sang with Leroy, Ninah, and the other elders. He did not falter. If Fuji planned to dance, that meant one of two things: either the dance really would be easy because Fuji was not in good shape physically, or perhaps it would be so profoundly religious that she would not understand what was going on.

"Who else will be there?"

"Some folks. They have questions too. It's a small group."

"Mike and Silan are exhausted. What did you do to them?"

"I didn't do anything to them."

"Yeah, but—"

"You run. You lift weights. You're fit. I promise you it's not the Sahara race. We'll talk tomorrow and I'll explain. Dance is on Friday and you need to be here Thursday afternoon."

"Can't do it. Got to work."

"You certainly are intent on convincing yourself not to do this. You can take a few days."

"Have to find East James."

"Chris is a competent detective. Besides, East will come home."

"I dunno. Even if East shows up, the dance is too soon. And I might be too old. Too set in my ways."

"When was your last vacation?"

"Uh . . ."

"Yeah. Too long." Leroy watched a hummingbird flit around the feeder. "First hummer of the year."

"How is this a vacation?"

Leroy smiled. "You get away from work for a while."

"Hmmmm. I had LASIK surgery a few years ago and can't handle bright lights. I can't look at the sun."

"Why would you do that?"

"Aren't I supposed to?"

"You can if you want to. But I don't recommend it."

"Well, I don't want the sun on my face all day. I can't stand it. When I run, I use a neck scarf that I can pull up over my nose. At my age, it's hard enough to keep wrinkles away—and windburn sets me back."

"Wear your scarf. I don't care."

"Oh."

"Sunglasses?"

"The first day."

"Hat?"

"Same."

"Why not after the first day?"

"You just can't."

That did not make sense.

"Does this Renewal Dance make dancers feel . . . rejuvenated?"

"It's not called the Downer Dance."

She thought a moment. "Maybe you're right. I need a jolt. I'm getting more cynical. I worry about this world. Robbie. The kids he'll have some-day. Birds, insects, koalas, fish, water. Everything is changing and I'm not doing anything about it." She avoided mentioning her short-fuse problem.

"No one person can do everything, Monique."

"I know. But if I could do something, I would."

Leroy smiled without comment, then walked out from under the car-port, Monique behind him. They watched Chris walk to the pond and stop next to a dogwood tree. Lorraine shadowed him like a dutiful dis-ciple. When he stopped, the cat walked in circles around him, rubbing against his legs. Chris bowed his head to inspect a four-petaled flower in his hand.

Leroy followed her gaze. "Many things are possible," he said.

"Chris!" she yelled. "Let's go." He walked toward her, still looking at the flower.

Monique turned to Leroy. "I'll talk to you tomorrow."

Chris patted Lorraine, shook Leroy's hand, then got into the cruiser. Monique started the engine then slowly pulled out of Leroy's driveway. Lorraine trailed the car as if it were a mouse.

"Don't hit her!" Chris warned.

"I'm not going to hit her," Monique replied. "Goddamn. She's like a dog that chases tires." She continued to back up and then put the cruiser into drive and headed down the street. She spotted Lorraine in the rearview mirror. "Now she's sitting in the road like that damn cat in *Pet Sematary*."

Chris opened his window and stuck his head out. "She's okay," he yelled over the rushing air.

She accelerated.

Chris sat back and sighed. "Now what?"

"I don't know."

"Slow down," he said. She eased off the pedal.

"We'll be home by five," she said. "We'll talk to Lulu again in the morning." Chris drummed his fingers on the handle of his door and mumbled.

"What?"

"I wish I understood you people."

"Us people?"

Chris continued to look out his window.

"I know what you mean," she acquiesced. "I wish I understood us too."

8

ANUKTUKLO
DOUBT

Monique and Steve watched Dr. Jeff, Rocky Mountain Vet, spay and neuter dozens of dogs and cats on a Planned Pethood trip to Cozumel.

"He does that so fast," Steve marveled.

"His wife, Petra, does it faster," Monique said as she struggled to get
the skin off her baked salmon.

"If I had his skills and the money to do that, I'd go all over the country.
Too many unwanted animals. Cats, especially."

"I'd go to Africa," Monique said.

"To spay and neuter what? Everything's endangered over there."

"I didn't say I'd fix anything. I got other skills. I'd be a poacher killer."

"That's cold."

"No, it's not. How do you justify killing an elephant for tusks?"

They continued arguing throughout an episode of *Dr. Pimple Popper*.
Monique maintained that all poachers needed eradication, while Steve
countered that poachers did what they did because they had no other
means of revenue. "They would stop if there were other ways to make a
living," he said. "They could make more money showing off their wildlife

to wealthy tourists than they could taking a rhino horn. Africa needs to get its economics in order."

No one won the argument, so they settled on sex in the Jacuzzi before falling asleep.

The crickets ringtone from her iPhone hit Monique's ear. She jerked awake.

"What's that?" Steve asked, still asleep. Foogly, who slept in her usual spot behind his bent knees, meowed and stretched.

Monique grabbed her phone and threw off her covers. She glanced back to make certain that Steve was still in the bed and then hurried out of the bedroom, quietly closing the door behind her. She strode down the hall to the kitchen.

"Go ahead. Who is this?"

"Lulu!" came the perky voice.

"Lulu? What's wrong?"

"Nothing. East is here."

"He's home?" Monique focused on the clock on the microwave. The green numbers read 2:24.

"He sure is. Wanna talk to him?"

"Yes. Put him on."

Monique slid down the wall until her butt hit the floor. The wood connected hard with her coccyx. She gritted her teeth and listened to the shuffling on Lulu's end of the line. She heard loud voices and children laughing.

"Hullo?" came a hoarse, masculine voice.

"Who is this?"

"East James."

"How do I know it's you?"

Heavy breathing. "I guess you don't. But it is."

"Where have you been?"

"I just took my time coming home." He sounded exhausted.

"Are you okay?"

"Yeah."

"Daddy! Daddy!" Silwee yelled.

Monique heard a jumble of mumblings in the background. Silwee kept yelling, "*Kil-ia! Kil-ia!*" *That's odd*, Monique thought. *Go where?*

"Why were you gone so long?"

"I was nervous about that EMT test. I wasn't ready for it."

"Daddeeee!!!" Eloise squealed.

"You left for four days because of a test?"

"Well, yeah. I have test anxiety."

"I'll say. Where were you?"

"Just in the country. Stayed with friends. You know."

"Not really." Silwee and Eloise laughed. Monique sighed. "All right. Do you plan to take any more trips at test time?"

"Oh no. I'll be ready for my makeup."

"*Miti!*" Silwee whined.

"Come on" where?

Monique stared at the numbers on the stove clock. She winced and hoped she would go back to sleep after the call. "It's good to know you're home. You sure you're okay?"

He paused a beat. "Yes."

"All right. We'll follow up in a few days. Good night," Monique said before clicking off. She held the phone to her chest for a few seconds, then slowly stood and walked back down the hall to her bed.

She eased under the covers. Steve threw an arm over her chest and snored. She stared at the ceiling. East claimed to be anxious about the EMT exam and decided to disappear. That sounded lame.

She was too tired to ruminate more about it, although before drifting off to sleep she whispered, "Nervous, my ass."

9

AHNI
WISHING

Friday afternoon, Monique backed her cruiser into Leroy's driveway and parked next to the garage. She rolled down her window and sat in the quiet. A swallowtail butterfly glided past the windshield and landed on the rue in the whiskey barrel. Purple martins chased insects in the clear air. It had sprinkled earlier and she smelled the newly burned pampas grass that Leroy preferred as a windbreak alongside his carport. Green blades emerged from the back stubble.

A furry shape landed with a whump on the hood. Monique jumped. "Shit! Lorraine! How do you always know I'm here?" Lorraine meowed in response. Monique rolled up the window, opened the car door, and Lorraine jumped to the ground, then up into Monique's lap.

"You know what we're doing, right?" Lorraine purred and looked up at her. Monique stroked her back. "Not talking, huh?" Lorraine rumbled. Monique scratched the furry head for a few minutes, enjoying the calm.

"Maybe we should get moving."

Lorraine emitted a quiet half meow. Monique took a deep breath and put her left foot on the ground. Lorraine jumped down and sat, waiting.

Monique took her weekend bag from the back seat and the ice chest from the trunk, then locked the cruiser. She stuffed her keys inside a bag pocket.

Monique wore Adidas running shorts with mesh lining. Leroy told her she could wear underwear, but she felt more secure wearing shorts under her ankle-length skirt.

Lorraine followed as Monique made her way to Leroy's open back door. She heard men laughing. Leroy saw her through the screen and lowered his recliner. "Set your things on the porch," he told her.

He slid back the door and gave her a hug as she stepped inside. He slapped his palms together. "Tell you what. Monique, get a drink if you want. Plenty of juice in the fridge. Then take your stuff to the arbor and set up your spot. The others will be here soon. Last chance to be by yourself for a while." He winked at her and grinned.

Deb, Mazey, Rob, and Peta sat around the table, sipping from cans of Diet Rite or tumblers filled with clinking ice. They waved and she nodded.

Monique chewed the inside of her cheek. "You better not be bullshitting me about all this, Leroy."

The men laughed.

Monique carried her belongings to the shade, the orange juice and ice in her Hydro Flask sloshing as she walked. Lorraine trailed behind her. "You're such a predator," Monique said.

She stopped under the twenty-by-fifty-foot arbor. Leroy rebuilt it ten years ago with strong redwood poles topped with crossbeams and lattice. He planted wisteria vines that wound throughout the trellis, unintentionally providing cover for black rat snakes. Monique spread her tarp and dropped her rolled-up sleeping bag. The tortoiseshell cat waited for the human to sit.

Monique surveyed the open area. It looked the size of the Sun Dance arenas, minus the cottonwood tree pole in the center and cedar boughs over the arbor. The mowed grass smelled good. Like summer. She stood with her hands on her hips, trying to spot any worn areas. Was this where Mike, Silan, and East danced? If so, they did not wear down the grass. She also could not ascertain what accounted for their exhaustion and sore feet. Mike said he burned his sole here. Maybe they danced elsewhere.

Monique sat and stretched her legs out in front of her, the rolled-up sleeping bag a backrest. Lorraine made herself comfortable on Monique's thighs and purred.

This was a good vantage point. Purple martins soared and chirped. A peeper frog sang from somewhere amid the woodpile. Canadian geese honked as they landed in the pond. Hens scratched in the dirt and Monique once again wished she had chickens.

She shifted her gaze upward. Glowing clouds inched across the blue sky between the vines that had not yet produced perfumed blossoms. She heard the gentle dings of Leroy's porch chimes in the distance. Despite the peace and calm of the moment, blood pounded in her temples, which reminded her that she might not leave Leroy's without a headache.

Breathe, she told herself. *Here you are. Calm, Calm, Calm.* Lorraine turned her head and stared up at her. "Stop judging me," she said.

Monique had to decide within a day that she would dance. She knew that was not enough time to think through this challenge. Still, here she sat. Her right quad still ached from a ten-mile run two days prior. A dumb thing to do, but she had always allayed her nervousness with intense exercise. Despite her soreness, she figured that the dancing Leroy planned would not be terribly arduous. Stepping backward and forward? Side to side? She probably would not have to lift her legs high, and she could always stretch.

Steve had reacted to the news that she would be gone a few days better than she'd predicted. He knew that Leroy's power was similar to that of a nuclear reactor. Steve respected Leroy yet remained wary of him.

"Yeah, I agree with Leroy," Steve said. "It'll be good for you."

Monique felt pleased, but then paused, suspicious. "Why?"

"You need to do more stuff like that."

She asked, "Like what?" but she knew exactly what he had meant. Steve, a Pawnee, came from a family that regularly attended Native American Church meetings. That was not traditionally Pawnee, because peyote ceremony originated in Mexico. But between his relatives who spoke the language, NAC meetings, some family members who participated in Sun Dances in South Dakota, and the times Steve took Robbie to visit his parents (who had little use for thin-bloods), Monique often felt like the lesser Indian of the family. Monique got along with Steve's parents and brothers, but despite the medicine people in her immediate family, the passionate and confident Pawnees intimidated her. Steve always invited her to come along, but she either had to work or said she did.

Her husband also argued relentlessly that she should spend less time at her job and more time with her fellow Choctaws. Well, here she was, about to spend time with them. She felt uneasy. Steve knew that she would. And that was exactly why he pushed her to participate.

Monique considered the crows on Leroy's garden fence posts. One dropped into the garden and returned to the post with an old corncob. The bird set it on the post in front of the second bird and cocked its head. The recipient bird pecked at the treasure. The first crow hopped up and down twice, happy to share. Monique laughed. The black bird cawed at her.

"Corvids are cool," she said aloud. Lorraine dug her claws into her thigh. "Ouch, damn it. Don't do that."

Lorraine purred.

Just then, an older-model gold Prius rushed into the driveway, followed by a cloud of dust.

Monique and Lorraine watched Fuji and Rene climb out, then Fuji's mother Christine. The three spoke for a minute, group-hugged, and then Christine got back in and drove off. Fuji and Rene walked to Leroy's front door. Lorraine yawned. Monique was not yet in the mood to start a round of "Kumbaya" with Fuji the Mystic, so she stayed where she was.

Next came a pine-green, four-door Dodge Dakota truck equipped with a lift kit, upper and lower fog lights, and all-terrain tires that parked next to Leroy's 1975 Subaru, whose silver paint had almost worn away. Monique scrutinized the ridiculous truck. She believed she could learn a lot about a person by their choice of vehicle. Some people did not have much choice, of course, and bought what they could afford. On the other hand, she was aware of drivers who spent all their money on a car or truck to project an image, instead of choosing practicality. Steve owned an auto-parts store and he had seen plenty of jacked-up trucks with big off-road tires that rarely encountered dirt or bumps larger than a curb. In her experience, the more jacked up the suspension, the more attention the driver craved. Some owners raised their trucks absurdly high, dangerous for the driver because of the altered center of gravity—they could tip over. If the brakes were not upgraded to match the large tires, the vehicles couldn't stop adequately. Jacked trucks also were potentially lethal for drivers in small cars. And how do you take someone out in such a silly ride? Offer your date a ladder?

Monique recognized the man who climbed out wearing khaki shorts and a lavender T-shirt adorned with a retro Doors image. Art Blue, the thirty-six-year-old son of Hazel and Will Blue, a nice couple she'd met at Strong Bull's funeral, was not an attention seeker. She had heard from Leroy that the formerly poor family had invested in an oil well and their apparently barren allotment revealed its underground treasures. Clearly, the truck reflected Art's new affluence. The vehicle he purchased after his windfall might have served as his expression of exuberance.

She sipped from her Hydro Flask as she watched Art.

"Be sure you're hydrated," Leroy had told her. "Start drinking more and add some electrolytes to the water. Eat fats and protein. Beans, cheese, put some turkey or chicken in it. No sugar. The night before, you can have pasta or sweet potatoes, but don't eat a huge pile of spaghetti. Have a little and put cheese on it. No beer. It'll dehydrate you."

She took his advice and ate a bean, cheese, and potato burrito for dinner and another one for breakfast. She'd seen in a documentary that the Rarámuri ultradistance runners of Mexico drank corn beer. That did not sound tasty, and she was not planning to run a hundred miles. Still, she would be hungry. Monique had the metabolism of a shrew and the attention span of a squirrel. Hunger and boredom scared her. She needed a steady supply of food and mental stimuli.

She once again wondered if she would make it through whatever Leroy had planned.

Art spotted her and jogged over, the long part of his mullet flowing as he moved. "And there she is!" he yelled. "We're saved!"

Oh brother, she thought. Her first impression of Art when they met a few years prior was that he was a bit of a nerd, and he just confirmed it.

She moved Lorraine off her legs and stood to meet him. "I didn't know you'd be here," he said.

"Yeah, well, Leroy convinced me." He gave her a hug.

"Ha ha. Good. Let me get my things. I take it we're bedding down here?"

"Yup. Leroy's Airbnb. I'll help." They walked back to Art's truck.

"Who else is coming?" he asked.

"Fuji and Rene are in the house. You know them? I know Fuji and only met her once."

"I met them a few times," he answered. "She's quiet."

A dusty white Ford truck pulled into the drive and parked next to Art's Dodge. The door opened. The driver sat in the front, looking down at his phone.

Art said, "Hey, you remember John Impson, right?"

At the sound of his name, the owner of the truck got out. He waved. "Of course."

Monique held out her hand and they shook. John had also been at Strong Bull's funeral and the dinner afterward at Ninah's house. Tall, rugged, square-jawed John. He had been a marine and he still looked it with a flat buzz cut; he was muscular, but over the years had accumulated a layer of what Monique referred to as "snack fat." She had some too, courtesy of popcorn, beer, and periodic injuries. All older athletes had it, she figured, but they would lose it quickly if they devoted time to fitness and diet as they once had. Competitor that she was, she squeezed his hand hard. If he could dance all day, so could she.

"How's the criminal-apprehension business?" he asked.

"Never a shortage."

"Yeah, I bet." He nodded toward the road. "And here comes Miss PPO," he said, then pulled his duffle bag from the truck bed and dropped it on the ground. A cool breeze emerged from the warmth of the afternoon. It whipped through the trees and wrapped around their legs. Monique closed her eyes in appreciation.

They watched thirty-two-year-old Grace Oldson, a.k.a. Miss Permanently Pissed Off, drive her red Ford into the yard and stop under a cottonwood tree. Grace got out, followed by her girlfriend, Elaine Sellen, who'd been sitting next to her on the bench seat.

Grace stood five feet seven and was broad in the rear. Her father said she had "breeder's hips" and she hated him for saying it. Of course, because he was a white man, she hated everything about him. Grace wore black-rimmed glasses for farsightedness and was partial to nail polish. This month, she wore black and purple on alternating nails.

Her tall partner was a year older. Elaine wore her usual button-down shirt that hid the large tattoo of the nickel Indian on her chest that she regretted. She had poor posture because she did not want to call attention to her large breasts, but most people thought that she stooped out of deference to her partner.

Both women wore their hair long, with Grace favoring short, thick bangs. Elaine said "hi" with a smile. Grace gave a sullen *halito* in their general direction as they walked past to the arbor.

"Bitch," Art said quietly.

"She's good at it," John replied.

Monique did not know either of the women and had no opinion. She recalled what the former Cherokee chief Wilma Mankiller said about arguing in public. Something along the lines of "Don't ever argue in public with a fool, because people walking by won't know which one of you is foolish."

John pulled a Nike zip-up long-sleeved shirt over his head. He did not worry about his hair catching in the zipper.

"Larry's coming too," said Art.

Around the bend came a hailstone-dented Chevy S-10 with a home-made blue paint job. The paint dried thick in some places and thin in others. Some of the blue spray had hit the windows and the bumpers because the painter had not covered them with newspaper. The sad truck had no front or rear bumper. It stopped next to John's truck.

"And here he is," Grace affirmed.

"Hey, dudes," the skinny man said through his open window. Larry Chinisa, thirty-six, got out of his truck, took three steps, tripped over nothing that the group could see, and almost fell.

"Jeez," said Grace.

"Wow, man, almost wiped out," Larry grinned as he pushed his black dreadlocks over his shoulder.

"What's up, Larry?" asked Art.

"Nothing much. Been working on the truck and the fence. Cows keep getting out." Art knew Larry worked harder at his family's ranch than did his older brother, who thought that standing around and watching counted as work.

"Yeah, I bet you have," Art said in a poor attempt at humor. "You lazy ass."

Larry looked hurt.

John shot him a disapproving look. Art's brutal honesty combined with his piercing, deep-set black eyes gave people pause. John often was angry with Art for giving him unwanted advice, which Art referred to as "helpful suggestions," but for the most part John found it easy to deal with him because he could criticize Art right back and he would not be offended. Art liked to argue because he was good at it.

"Get the ice chest outta the truck," Grace barked to Elaine as she walked back toward her truck. The two women had their own issues.

"And she's off," John said.

"Maybe she'll wear herself out," Art said.

"Fat chance, buddy," John countered.

Leroy opened the screen door with a flourish and stepped outside, followed by the four elders, Mazey, Deb, Peta, and Rob. They were friendly and said hello, nothing else.

"Tomorrow we start when the sun comes up," Leroy said to the dancers. "You can eat dinner, but no food or drink after nine o'clock and nothing in the morning. Drink a quart of water before you go to sleep. I know you'll have to get up to pee, but drink up anyway. No earrings, jewelry, elastic hair ties, or makeup. After dinner, we'll talk more about it. Eat even if you're not hungry."

"Four days isn't a big deal," Larry said. "Sometimes I'm not hungry and don't eat hardly anything for that long." Art assessed Larry's bony physique and believed him.

"Larry," Leroy began. Then he said each name in turn to get their attention. "Monique. Art. John. Elaine. Grace. Fuji. Rene." Then he repeated himself. "Eat even if you're not hungry."

"Well, okay," Larry said. "I brought some pork rinds and dip."

"Great," Art muttered. "That'll keep our energy up."

"And I brought bologna and cheese," Larry added. "Oh man, dang. Forgot the bread."

The four elders brought their dinner contributions to the picnic table. Mazey brought ham sandwiches. Peta opened a Cool Whip container. "This is turkey dip," he said. "Mixed with mustard, pepper, and celery." He placed a box of saltines next to it. Rob brought a tuna casserole and Deb opened a container filled with Cajun-seasoned catfish.

Art and John pulled an ice chest from John's truck onto the tailgate, each grabbing a handle. Between the two of them, they'd brought cold sliced luncheon meat, wheat bread, macaroni salad, and several six-packs of Pepsi. Rene and Fuji donated Rice Krispies Treats, canned peaches, a chocolate cake, and a bucket of fried chicken.

Monique retrieved her dish. She didn't have time to do anything that morning except to drop some chicken breasts in the Crock-Pot. The meat cooked for seven hours, then she put the hot pot in the ice chest.

Grace, a skilled cook, loved potlucks because she was sure to get positive attention. "I have an ice chest full of traditional foods," she announced.

"Cool," Larry said.

"Corn and . . . corn?" Art asked. Grace glared at him, nostrils flared.

"I brought us *banaha*. For those of you ignorant of our foodways, Art," she glared at him, "that is cornmeal and turkey in cornhusks, boiled in water and hickory oil. And no, these are *not* tamales." She held up a plastic container. "Here is Minnesota *manoomin* with cranberries." She reached in and took out another one. "This is sautéed lamb's-quarters topped with pecans."

Monique thought she wanted applause.

Art snickered. "Bravo," he said. "*Top Chef* fare, for sure."

Grace stood up straight, opened the containers, and piled her plate high with her righteous sustenance.

The others loaded their wobbly paper plates with a polite sampling from everyone's contribution.

"This is too bland," Art muttered to Larry. "That *banaha* looks like tamales, but no salt, no garlic, no Tabasco."

"It's supposed to be like this," Larry whispered back.

"You know I can hear you," Grace said. "Precontact food does not include garlic. Or beef, or pork, or chicken, or wheat, or—"

"We get it," John interrupted.

Grace huffed and dropped another helping of *banaha* onto her mound of rice.

The diners ate in silence until John got up for more. Everyone followed suit and filled their plates a second time with mainly colonizers' fare, then mingled quietly with the four elders. The men revealed that they would drum, and cheerily offered opinions on mundane issues.

"Whaddya think of the new red postal delivery jeeps?" Mazey asked Peta. He was careful to keep the chicken from falling between the gap in his teeth.

"Now I can see her coming," answered Peta. "My *ofi* hears that bad muffler. She barks when that jeep's a mile away."

"I'd like her to drop off my mail earlier in the day," said Deb.

"I got a box at the post office," said Rob, "so I don't care." They all laughed as if it were a hilarious joke.

"Old folks," John whispered to Art.

"Be careful what you say," Art warned. "Last I checked, you were forty-three and counting."

Great. I'm the oldest dancer here, Monique thought.

Everyone felt stuffed a short time later. They stashed leftovers in Leroy's refrigerator, deposited trash bags into the bed of Deb's truck, and then sat waiting for Leroy to emerge from the house. He did when the moon came up. It was not quite full, but it would be in two nights.

Leroy unfolded his lawn lounge chair next to the drummers, then sat back and put his feet up. "Are you ready?" Leroy asked the group.

"Yeah, man, I'm ready." Larry laughed as if he were preparing to ride the world's biggest roller coaster.

"Tell us why you want to dance," Leroy asked.

"Uh. Well, let's see. To bring back the buffalo!" Larry thought that a wise response.

Leroy held Larry's eyes for a second, then nodded. "Art?"

"The tribe needs to work together more. I'm dancing to make the tribe strong and unafraid. We need to get back to traditions more. Everyone is starting to scatter. People leave and when they come back, they just visit. They don't want to get involved. The council needs to stay with what's important. You know, culture and environment. Protect our land and not just make money from ruining it."

Leroy stared at Art with no expression.

Art tucked wayward hairs behind his ears and continued. "Not every-one knows about our traditions and many people don't even want to learn. It's a real problem. Sort of like . . . like planets revolving around the sun. Each has to stay in the tribal solar system, but they're all different dis-tances away from the center. You know, the sun is the strong, tribal core and the planets are our members who stay various distances away from that core of knowledge. Does that make sense?"

"If it makes sense to you, it does," Leroy answered. Art felt deflated.

"We need to find our center," Elaine said softly. "Our identities. Oth-erwise, we're brown people who act white."

"We have to decolonize," Grace interjected. "We have to get rid of the whites and make things as they were in the beginning. We need to raise the blood quantum requirement for tribal membership to one-quarter. One-half would be even better."

John laughed.

"What?" Grace demanded in her typical bombastic fashion. The vocal activist always made herself known to anyone within earshot, and that included the last decade of Tribal Councils. She had become notorious for starting arguments about gender and racial equality. She relentlessly lob-bied for severing ties with whites and returning to traditions, even though she could not specify what she meant by that. "Furthermore, everyone needs to know our traditions and ceremonial songs."

"That's not realistic, Grace," John countered. "Only Leroy and other medicine people need to know every single song. There's no way we can know them all unless we want to follow him. Besides, most members don't live around here."

"And if you were a real Choctaw, you'd want to take the time to learn," Grace said.

"That's what a real Choctaw does?" John asked her.

"All Natives should know their culture. Their songs, ceremonies, and history. And they sure don't sign up to be a marine."

"What do you know about the military, Grace? All you do is sit around and gripe about everyone, including your girlfriend. You think you're traditional. What's that hairdo and nail polish? You drive a car and wear glasses, and don't tell me you don't watch TV."

"You're a sellout, just like a lot of our people," Grace argued. "Decolonization is the only way the tribe is going to get complete sovereignty and get back our lost traditions. That includes a return to equal gender roles."

"Are you saying 'decolonization' will help you be less verbally abusive?"

"I am not abusive!"

Elaine listened and silently prayed that Grace and John would burn themselves out. So did everyone else. No such luck.

"Grace," said John, "what makes you think that any tribe can decolonize? Every tribe in this country has scars, but nobody tries to get completely back to traditions. If invaders hadn't come over, tribes still would have developed and changed, intermarried more, and created things to make life easier."

"You don't know that. Whites have made this country what it is: polluted, violent, competitive, and racist. Our Tribal Council needs to understand that. Whites abuse Turtle Island as fast as they can, and they treat Indians as if we're stupid kids sitting on uranium so they can pay us pennies to take it. Then they leave their tailings piles and make us sick."

"Other tribes let the colonizers do that to them, Grace."

"They don't know any better!" she yelled.

"And we never used the term 'Turtle Island,'" John said. "If you're planning on recovering traditions, at least use your own tribe's concepts and not swipe from another."

She paused, considering how to respond. She opted to ignore it. "We're becoming white people! White education is killing us. And if the tribe had voted for me as council member, then I would be able to do something about it."

"Cool your jets," John said. "You're pretty much like white people, Grace. You're just brown. Or should I say, sort of brown?"

"I can't help who my father is."

"Well, if we completely decolonize, then at least half of you has to disappear."

She powered on. "Our women have been sterilized, our lands taken, and our images used on butter and tobacco."

"You used to smoke it."

She paused to swallow. "And white people have no business on our land. We need to get all of them out."

"Does that include your dad?" John asked.

Grace whipped her head around to glare at John faster than a sentry gun ready to fire. "My mother needed to marry a white man because the colonial regime made her feel insecure, and she felt the only way she could be equal to the oppressor was to have one love her. Frantz Fanon says—"

"Fanon! And where did you get the idea to read his work?" John laughed and that made her furious.

"There's nothing wrong with me reading!"

The rest of the group moved their heads right to left like fans at a volleyball game, wondering whose nose would bleed after a bull's-eye spike. Elaine tried not to become involved when Grace became angry, which seemed to be most of the time. She'd witnessed this same argument a year prior at another gathering and could not help but say something.

"Grace, I agree with you," Elaine had said at that winter council meeting. "But do you have to be so harsh? I mean, we can't change completely, and whites aren't going to leave. And we need the white people here because they help finance the bingo hall and the travel plazas and smoke shops and your dad's fishing business. And that last one's not even tribal."

Grace had had no logical comeback. Nevertheless, she'd blurted out, "They'll leave if we make them!" Then Grace grabbed Elaine by the arm, pulled her out the door, and screamed at her the entire way home about how she was stupid and didn't know anything about Indians.

Now, Monique glanced at Leroy. She was not the only one who felt impatient.

"You're talking in a circle," John said. "Foucault says that to know something is to have power over it. And here you are saying education is the enemy. You owe what you are to it. If you weren't educated, you'd be sitting around doing nothing except waiting for the next shipment of commodities to come in."

"I don't eat commodities and you know it."

John lowered his voice in a futile attempt to slow her down. "Grace, we don't have to believe everything we learn, we just need to be aware of the world and then try and understand it. We don't have to change our beliefs and start thinking that we came over the Bering Land Bridge. But we need to know that's what others think."

"The way to regain our traditions is through religion," Grace said, her eyes burning a hole through John.

"You're a great example of that."

"Not the white man's religion, stupid. Ours."

"So you want to go back to head-flattening and using bone pickers? You've got a chip on your shoulder the size of Mount Rushmore and think you're right about everything. Even when you know you're wrong, you can't admit it."

Undeterred, she continued. "Some of our members are one-four-thousand-ninety-sixth degree Choctaw blood, and that is unacceptable. Descendancy without cultural connection is a bullshit way to allow people into our Nation. The council needs to pay attention to the traditionalists." She sat back against Elaine's legs and nodded to Leroy, satisfied that somewhere in her diatribe she had produced the right answer.

Then she glared back at John and dared him to challenge her. He did not.

Leroy hardly glanced at her while he nodded. The "decolonization" reasoning had grown tiresome. These youngsters did not know what that actually meant.

The demure Rene spoke in her low, husky voice. "We're surrounded," she said to a point over Leroy's shoulder. She lifted her head, revealing a long scar running the length of her jaw. A drunk bingo player had hit her aunt's car five years ago. The crash killed her aunt and the glass shattered, slicing Rene's face. Rene had cut her hair to chin length in mourning, but now her heavy tresses had grown back to where they fell prior to her lopping them off. She had what Monique referred to as "impossible hair," waist length and as thick at the ends as on her head. Same hair as Monique's grandmother.

Rene continued. "We are so into what the outside world has to offer that we forget our roots. I try, but I keep getting pulled away from what I should be doing." She looked at Fuji.

Fuji stood. "The world is what it is. We have to somehow deal with it." He paused to examine the grass and dirt clumps at his feet. "One way is to dance so we can change it. Only a few have this chance."

Monique felt a tingle in her neck. Leroy had also told her that not everyone had the opportunity to dance. Fuji just said something similar, but somehow, what he said did not have the same meaning.

Leroy considered him and Rene before nodding. "John?"

"To make the people strong in dealing with the world," John said. "To find ways for us to work together to solve problems instead of arguing all the time. I've just about given up believing that all members of the tribe can or even want to come together as a whole. We have money because a lot of members work hard. But some drink too much, they snipe at each other and won't even say hello to each other in the grocery store. There are plenty of bitchers and moaners ready to undermine what others gain." He paused. Monique saw his jaw muscles clench. "Sometimes it seems that our tribe's only goal is to make more money. And we do. We're worth billions. But we got hundreds still suffering. You should have heard what was said at the council the other night. Like B. O. says, 'Those who don't get elected get pissed.'"

He paused and took the toothpick from his mouth, considering the mangled sprig of wood. "The way we're approaching sovereignty isn't right. We need to think about how we politically organized ourselves before outsiders imposed their form of government on us."

Leroy nodded and looked to Monique.

"I, uh—" she stammered. She felt her face heat up. Public speaking was not her strong suit. "I need to understand what it means to be a member of this tribe. I need to come to peace with what my ancestor did." Leroy did not change expression.

"What did he do?" Grace asked.

Monique cleared her throat. "Signed the removal treaty."

"Why did he do that?"

"I wish I knew. Money. I don't know. There are no photographs of him or his wife. He was a headman from Okla Hannali. He signed his name with an *X*."

"Maybe he felt he had to," Art said.

"I've always hoped so. His son had the opposite ideas. Progressives killed him forty years later for resisting the intruders into Moshulatubbee District. That's all I have."

Grace cleared her throat. "Shitty thing to live with."

"Enough," Leroy interjected. "What is it you want to know, Monique?"

"Why. Why would he do it? Thousands died after that treaty."

"Are you saying that you feel guilty?"

"Yes."

"Historical trauma," Grace interjected. "You don't have to experience an event to be traumatized by it. You feel the effects of the past. Right now."

Monique knew that past traumas often dictated peoples' actions, but she had not experienced the trauma of the long-ago removal. She only imagined the horrors that her ancestors and other Choctaws endured—or died from—in the effort to reach a new land. Was empathy for their plight the same as the real struggles experienced during the arduous removal? No. She considered that witnessing present-day self-destructive behaviors and despairing at the self-loathing, poverty, and helplessness of her fellow tribespeople also shaped her perceptions of the past. Environmental destruction, racism, treaty abrogation, violence, and stereotyping were all legacies of colonialism. It was all around her. Even Steve's family consistently expressed anger and suspicion because of their punishing past. And they could indeed express it. One brother was a mixed martial arts fighter and the other a roofer so burly and intimidating that Monique thought he could use his hands instead of a hammer. That one took his frustrations out on the nails.

Bingo, Monique thought. *Historical trauma*. That was the name for it. A traumatized soul. *That* was her problem.

"What your ancestor did stops you," Rene said.

Monique considered that. *What stops you?* What was she *not* doing because of how she felt? Rene's perceptive remark caused Monique to flinch.

"I get it now. I inherited the legacy of the pain from those who came before me. Those who suffered from what my ancestor did. Now I have to deal with it and move on. But it's hard."

Leroy exhaled. "Stop it."

"Stop what?"

"You didn't inherit anything, Monique. Stop acting like you did."

The others looked at each other, unsure about the new direction of this conversation. The four drummers smirked.

"You're not special," Leroy said, his face deadpan. "There are a lot of descendants of treaty signers walking around."

Monique gasped as if Leroy had slapped her. "You're saying I shouldn't feel guilty?"

"Correct. You're not the victim type, Monique. Tell us what's really bothering you."

She felt her face heat. "What do you mean?"

Leroy stared into the trees beyond their camp, as if he had all the time in the world. Monique huffed and folded her arms across her abdomen. It was clear that Leroy was going to wait on her.

"Okay. My brother, Brin, was killed," she told the others. "White guys stabbed him to death. They didn't serve time."

"That's what really drives you," Rene said quietly.

"Yeah. Obviously."

"You became a cop."

Monique nodded. "Yes."

"You're angry," Rene went on.

Monique glanced at Leroy, who still gazed into the darkness. "Very," she whispered.

"Actions of an ancestor stops you from acting, and the killing of your brother motivates you," Rene theorized. "You're caught between the two emotions."

"Besides," John interjected, changing the subject, "Andre and B. O. keep telling me I have to dance."

Monique sighed in relief. She had avoided another goring. Nevertheless, she felt that the animal had only moved into the shadows.

"Hey, man," said Larry. "Me too. Andre called one night and we talked for a long time. That's why I called Leroy to get started."

"Same here," said Grace. "He and B. O. came by one night. Elaine fixed dinner. Even though they weren't invited." She shot an angry glance at Elaine.

Leroy and the four other elder men stood. "Sleep and I'll wake you when it's time." Lorraine ran to him and jumped into his arms. "I hear your wishes. We'll see what happens."

"What the hell does that mean?" Art muttered. Monique wondered the same thing.

Four of the five elder men walked toward the house. Peta came toward the group and pulled something out of his breast pocket. "I'd use this in the morning," he said in his happy voice as he tossed it to John. "Pass it around." He smiled big and turned to go.

"What is it?" asked Grace.

"Yeah," added Art. "What he give us? Painkillers?"

"A bag of weed?" Larry sounded hopeful.

"No, you dumb shits," John said as he held up the object. "Coppertone. SPF 100."

That night, while lying in their sleeping bags, Art and John watched the bright stars. "This whole thing is off somehow," said Art. "Leroy isn't telling us something."

"Yeah, I caught that," answered John. "Most of the time when we meet, he talks a lot. Not tonight. I want to know more about this dance. It's not like the Sun Dance, right?"

"I hope not," Art said. "I can't handle being pierced."

"You'd already know if piercings were involved," Monique said. She still felt the sting of Leroy's rebuke but wasn't sure what to do about it. "Leroy isn't going to surprise anyone with a scalpel."

"Scalpel?" Art asked.

"Used to use eagle talons. When I went to Mission years ago, dancers brought their own scalpels because of HIV."

"I think this is one of those things that you got to experience," Art speculated. "Maybe he can't describe it."

"No," John disagreed. "He could. He's not going to. Something's going to happen."

"Big marine like you. Afraid?" Grace asked. She and Elaine lay ten feet away.

"You don't mess around with religion, Grace," John answered. "You'd be a fool not to be afraid of it. But, of course, you're not afraid. Good night."

Monique held her breath waiting for the reply.

"Asshole," she heard Grace mutter.

Leroy Bear Red Ears and his friends watched the campers through the den window. They lay still as fallen logs. The men heard their quiet voices.

"We were just here," Deb said.

"Yup," agreed Rob.

Leroy sighed. "Are we doing the right thing?" he asked. He stroked Lorraine as he considered for the hundredth time what they planned to do.

Mazey put his hand on his old friend's shoulder and squeezed.

"I wish Strong Bull could be here to help us," Leroy said quietly.

"We all agreed," said Rob. "We have to."

"That's right," Deb said. "It's the right decision. Don't worry."

Leroy nodded. Lorraine purred in agreement. "We need to sleep, old friends."

The drummers went to their blow-up mattresses scattered in the den and dining room.

Leroy stared at the campers for few seconds, then said a prayer before shuffling down the hall to his bedroom. They all slept soundly though the night.

10

NAN ISHT AIOKPACHI
THE GIFT

Leroy awoke the eight sleepers with a gentle song ten minutes before Smudge crowed at 6:45 a.m. There was only a hint of light in the eastern sky.

Although the cool, cloudless morning promised a lovely day, Leroy had checked out National Weather Service—the dancers were huddled in their bags now, but he knew that the rising sun combined with no breeze would increase the afternoon heat.

Leroy wore a red skirt and his leather vest with a black beaded bear outlined in bright red. The sleeveless garment revealed lean arms and weathered skin. The black beads shone as if wet and the bear seemed to breathe. His diamond tattoos circled his arms like a snake.

"Zip your bags and fold them over so bugs won't crawl inside. Then dress," Leroy said. "Come to the grounds. No one will bother your things."

Bleary eyed, the dancers changed clothes. No one paid attention to anyone else. They were unsure of what to wear, so they went with Sun Dance clothing—the men chose skirts and vests or no tops and the women wore skirts and loose tops.

Art wore a brown-and-green-striped skirt that reached above his ankles. "You look like a carpet," John told him. John's was sea green. Elaine put on her blue blouse and green cotton skirt and Grace wore a red skirt and baggy tan shirt she knotted at her waist. The women felt both half-naked and liberated without their bras.

Monique chose a gray T-shirt and an ankle-length purple skirt with pockets that made her feel secure. She loathed pants and skirts without pockets. Unlike Elaine and Grace, Monique wore a jog bra to prevent gravity from tearing her breast skin more than it already had. The neck scarf could be pulled up over her nose and protect the skin around her mouth—she feared lines around her lips. Just as important, she was not going to part with her mesh running shorts underneath her skirt. She wore her sunglasses and planned to keep them on until Leroy took them off her.

"This is not the Sun Dance," Leroy told them. "Sun Dancers dance for peace and healing. Some dance for loved ones and for health of the community. We do too, but we also dance for other things." He eyed their skirts. "What you have on is fine."

He turned to walk across the grass. "No sweat first?" Monique asked.

He stopped. "No. Why?"

"Well, I just thought that—"

"Everyone get in a circle."

"Are we all good to go?" John asked the group.

"I'm cold," Grace said, wrapping her arms around herself.

"Not for long," Monique said as she slathered on sunscreen and lip balm and then tossed the tubes onto her pile of gear.

"Let's hit it," John said. The dancers adjusted their clothing and spread out around the dance arena.

Art walked behind Larry. "What's that on your skirt?" he asked.

"Cool, huh?" Larry had found some red paisley and a strip of black-and-white houndstooth material on a bolt at Dollar Tree. His mother sewed the pieces together with the large strip of paisley on top. A Spider-Man patch covered a small rip in the back. Larry wrapped the skirt around himself and secured it with a medium-sized safety pin.

Art shook his head and rolled his eyes.

Grace marched in with her head up, believing that she would change the course of her tribe with her dancing. Monique walked behind her, but at the other end of the psychological spectrum, simultaneously fearful and cynical.

The four elder men sat around the large drum under the arbor's shade. They began a light beat, an easy cadence. Once the dancers arrived inside the arena, they formed a circle and imitated Leroy's gentle marching movements.

Supporters could not attend the Renewal Dance. Christine and Gena wanted to attend at least part of the time, but Leroy firmly told them no.

"No matter, Mom," Fuji had told the disappointed Christine. "I know you're with me here, always." He put his hand over his chest.

She hugged him tightly. "I love you," she said softly.

"I know," he answered. Then he did something she had never seen him do in all his twenty-one years: he winked. Worried, yet strangely calm, Christine got up at sunrise the next morning and sat in Fuji's metal fold-up chair to watch the eagles.

The dance began.

This isn't so hard, Larry thought as he sidestepped to his right. This seemed to be similar to the round dance at a powwow. *I can do this for hours.*

How is this weenie dance supposed to help anything? Art mused.

I'm thirsty, Grace almost said aloud but did not, considering that they had just started.

John was not deceived. *Easy now, but killer later.*

Monique liked the rhythm. So far, nothing they had done was difficult. She waited for the exercise-induced endorphins to kick in. She saw that none of the others seemed tired. Knowing Leroy, however, he had something more challenging in store for them.

She turned her head and was surprised to see a beaded squirrel on Leroy's vest. *I swear I saw a bear earlier*, she thought.

The drummers' tempo increased. Leroy changed the dance from the basic side step to two steps forward and two steps back. His arms moved upward with the forward steps. His arms and chin dropped on the backward steps. After ten minutes, Monique's shoulders began to ache from the repetitive movement. She wondered how long she could do this.

The beat slowed. Leroy kept his arms at his sides. Monique knew this break would be short lived. She took a breath, then the cadence increased suddenly. Leroy started a side-to-side and forward-to-back routine that Monique had to watch carefully. She felt a jolt of panic at the thought that she might not keep up. The drummers did not slow for thirty minutes. No one sang. The sweaty dancers glistened in the full glare of the sun. They kept on.

Monique's shoulders and arms ached. She saw that the others appeared to be in a trance. Mouths open. Gasping.

Except John, who felt energized. He ran most mornings and, so far, this dance reminded him of the long, slow runs he did every Sunday. He had a feeling, however, that things were about to take a turn. The increased tempo reminded him of the escalating physical challenges of marine training. *If I could do it then, I can sure as hell do it now*, he thought.

John had always sought out ways to test himself. He learned in high school that thousands of Indians had served in the military and that one in four were veterans. He took that as a challenge. Not because he was patriotic—rather, he wanted to push himself physically. He first considered the Navy SEALs. He regularly entered local 5Ks, raced in several mud runs, ran up Mount Scott a few times a year, and could bench 250. He ran five times a week on shady dirt trails and sprinted on the local high school track. He could swim, but did not have access to a pool year round. Was he fit enough to try? Probably not. Successful SEALs also possessed an enviable determination that pushed them through extreme physical and mental tortures. If John was being honest with himself, he wanted to be a SEAL just to prove that he could make it through their rigors.

John knew he had the potential to kill and feel comfortable doing it. That scared him more than the prospect of floundering in a SEAL training pool with his arms and legs tied. Becoming a marine also carried the possibility that he would have to kill. He knew that, as a marine, he might be assigned to perilous tasks in countries with crazy leaders and fanatical followers. Still, he assumed that there were safer career options being a marine than being a SEAL. He already had two years of aviation maintenance training in Tulsa and figured he could travel and work on helicopters after more training. Although John was strong and did not mind physical work, he almost quit because he did not fit the soldier mold.

"You're gonna be one of the few Indian recruits, son," his dad, a marine veteran, told him. "Get ready for shit, because it'll come straight at you."

Indeed, being Indian made him a novelty and he got into several fights with other recruits who called him Chief or Geronimo. Despite being in the minority, he was still one of many soldiers and he hated being a face in the crowd.

"You're not a team player," his dad said before he left for boot camp. "The military is all about discipline. Nothing is going to be on your terms. You gotta do what they say."

His father was correct. John remained too much of an individual to handle taking orders. He was neither a soldier ant nor a worker bee. John knew the most torturous aspect of training would be taking orders without talking—or fighting—back. He kept telling himself that once he finished, he would be a marine and nobody could take that away from him. However, until then, he would muster every bit of self-discipline to get through. Sure enough, after he completed training, he was just as proud as the commercial on television said he would be. He had *Semper Fi* tattooed on his right forearm, *Marines* on a bicep, and the tribe's seal over his left deltoid—the latter emblem with a bow, three arrows, and a calumet. Unlike the accepted Great Seal that depicted the bow only partially strung, John's tattooed, nocked bow symbolized that he was ready for war.

John then spent two years in Afghanistan and two in Pakistan as a helicopter mechanic. Four years of heat, dust, and constant worry about the Taliban was enough. When his time was up, he came home. Even in his comfortable Oklahoma bed, he dealt with nightmares and sleepless nights. Depression wracked his life, and for months, he struggled through his waking hours. Exhausted and confused, he decided to become a fishing guide. He felt more alive outside in his environment. However, he made little money and lived in a trailer with an adjoining outhouse.

Wanting something more, he completed his college degree, got his teaching certificate, and taught mechanics at the high school. He married Shirley Waters, a woman from the Blackfeet Nation who died from ovarian cancer two years after their wedding. Her death devastated and infuriated him. He had not dated another woman since.

John stayed connected to his tribe by blood and those unseen forces that draw Native people to each other. He enrolled in conversational Chahta anumpa classes for adults at the high school, attended council meetings, and volunteered to teach weight lifting at the community centers. He never grew his hair waist length as he did in high school, but wore it short like other male vets in the tribe. John often wondered what kind of Indian he was. Perhaps on this day, he would find out.

After four hours, the drummers stopped abruptly. The dancers continued to feel the rhythm that matched their racing heartbeats, and almost stumbled.

"Oh man," Art muttered.

"Holy shit, shit, shit," Elaine panted.

Leroy led the dancers from the arena to the arbor. He did not allow the weary group to lie down because they would have difficulty starting again if they got comfortable. He told them to lean on the wood rails for ten minutes and he would call them out with a whistle. Monique noticed that Leroy ordered the group back into the arena after the arbor shadow moved a few inches.

They filed out like exhausted soldiers on a ruck march. Leroy prayed in both words and song. The tired dancers listened closely in hopes that he would reveal a secret for finding energy to finish, but they could not understand his quick Chahta anumpa.

The drummers never slowed. Monique wondered about her motivation through bouts of nausea. She also feared her body would suddenly stop, like an Energizer Bunny whose dollar-store batteries ran out of juice. One second, it's pounding away on a drum, then the next it's a dead rabbit.

When she was younger, she could run for miles and hike all day, but as she grew older, even small injuries sidelined her. She no longer believed that she was immortal.

She gasped, licked her dry lips for the hundredth time. She saw that Leroy's beads had morphed once again. Now they were in the shape of a raccoon. She shook her head and then closed her eyes, afraid of falling in a heap of fatigue. Suddenly, three hazy, black-and-gray women appeared ten feet in front of her. They wore long skirts and long-sleeved blouses. All three wore their hair long and tied back. One held a hoe. The other two bent at the waist, maybe planting seeds. All three raised their heads at the same time and one screamed, although there was no sound.

She felt a hard slap on her arm. She blinked and the women were gone. John hit her again.

"Wake up," he said.

She stopped and almost fell. "Ouch. Wha—?"

"Done for the day, I hope," John croaked.

Leroy led the weary dancers out of the arena and back to camp. "Rest," he said, and everyone collapsed onto their bags.

Monique awoke around ten that night, chilled from sunburn. She took off her sunglasses, which had managed to stay in place, and roused the other dancers long enough to coax them into their bags. Their legs would cramp by morning if they continued to lie in the cool damp air.

She drifted off to sleep again, then awoke and scanned the mist surrounding her. She discerned riders on horseback. They were blurry, but she knew there were two. The rider on the left took a knife from the scabbard on his left thigh, while the other pulled a pistol from his holster. Her hands gripped hard objects. She felt confident and at peace. Monique smiled and took a step forward.

"*Onnahinli achukma!*" Leroy said loudly.

She gasped and opened her eyes. What was she dreaming? Who were those men? She never dreamed of cowboys. This vision was out of focus and gray, but she recalled it with clarity. Moreover, she felt with certainty that she was supposed to be there at that moment. To see those men. But why?

"Yeah, good morning to you too," she heard John mumble.

"Oh wow," moaned Larry.

"For once, I agree with you," Art said.

"Man, I'm thirsty." Larry added.

"No kidding," agreed Art.

"My back's killing me," John said.

"Is this a blister?" Art lay on his bag and held his foot up to John.

"Get your foot out of my face."

"Is it a blister or not?"

"I can't see one. Where's the sunblock?"

"It was on the picnic table," said Larry. "It's gone."

"Shit," said John. "My neck's really burned."

Monique sat up, still dazed from her dream. She had pilfered the Coppertone the night before. "I have it." She tossed it to John. The tube hit him in the temple.

"Shit. Thanks."

"Payback."

"My feet hurt," Larry said. "I think I got splinters."

"You don't have splinters. I have them all," Art said. "Or maybe glass. Damn, my little toes are on fire."

"Does anyone have ibuprofen?" John asked. "God, I hurt all over."

Elaine bent to rub the three-inch white scar on her throbbing knee, the result of surgery after a bike tumble and torn ligaments years before. Monique grimaced as she leaned forward against the table, supported by her outstretched arms, stretching her calves. Grace sat and gently rotated her ankle. She had sprained it last year while stepping off her sidewalk. The women said nothing as they managed their pain.

"Do we see a common theme here, ladies?" Grace asked as she stood and folded her bag.

Rene and Elaine had already folded theirs and stood waiting for everyone else. They all knew the answer to Grace's question, but no one vocalized it.

The aching dancers followed Leroy back to the arena. The drummers began with the same song they'd left off with the night before.

Thirst and hunger contributed to a miserable day. The warm morning blossomed into a hot afternoon. Leroy slowed the drummers when it appeared the dancers might falter, then sped them up after a few minutes. He walked around the circle several times and tapped each dancer to give them encouragement. Monique wondered why he didn't use an eagle or hawk feather. *I'm good at stereotyping*, she thought.

Used to long workouts, John and Monique were the strongest. Still, they began to crumple. Art put effort into swallowing, as did Monique. John felt the stirring of cramps in his calves.

Monique coughed. She prided herself on her fitness and physical strength. But she also knew that small injuries could impede a physical goal. She tried to swallow and could not find enough saliva. She thought about throwing in the proverbial towel. *If I feel like this, I wonder how the others feel.* A glance at Leroy caused her to gasp. His beads were now in the shape of a strutting tom turkey. He danced to her, as if on roller skates, and plucked the sunglasses off her.

Then she felt a sudden realization as sharp as a cattle prod to her ass. This was not a physical feat to master. This was something else. And her situation was about to take a turn.

With that idea, a cool breeze hit the dancers with the force of a bucket of cold water. Storm clouds appeared overhead.

"Where did those come from?" Larry muttered.

The clouds grew dark and moved faster than the day-to-night montages from a Disney nature film. The wind felt cold and damp. A powerful force sucked air out of the dancers' lungs. Monique noticed that the others were still moving, their eyes open. She yelled at Art, who was closest to her, and attempted to move to his side, but an invisible force kept her in place. She leaned forward until she was almost horizontal to the ground. The barrier that felt to Monique like wind fingers kept her from falling face-first into the dirt. The unseen hand gently raised her upright and forced her to stand.

The wind swirled faster, blocking the sun. Orange-and-yellow light filtered through the dust, creating an abstract art dance scene. Curiously, no dust blew into Monique's eyes. She watched Leroy dance, the old man's chin raised and arms outstretched. She saw with complete clarity the black beads on his vest transform into the shape of woman dressed in white. Monique panted, but did not falter.

Leroy began to pale, but Elaine and Rene on either side of him did not. Then Monique realized his bright-red skirt had turned gray and the white vest beads had dulled. No doubt, Leroy was fading. So were the drummers under the arbor. Although Monique could tell by the drummers' arm movements that they hit the hide forcefully, she could barely hear their sound.

"Leroy!" Monique yelled at the fading man. "Where are you going? LEROY!"

The wind rushed through the dancers' senses so fast and hard that they put hands to their ears and fell to their knees. Then they heard Leroy's voice through the chaos.

"For you!" he yelled. "For you!" Leroy yelled again before disappearing faster than a popped balloon.

His voice was the last thing the dancers heard before they closed their sunburned eyes and welcomed the cool, soothing darkness.

PART II

It may be that we are condemned to spend our whole lives in this strange, inaccessible place. I am still so confused that I can hardly think clearly of the facts of the present or of the chances of the future.

SIR ARTHUR CONAN DOYLE, *THE LOST WORLD*

II

OKCHA
AWAKENING

Monique perceived movement in the shadows twenty feet in front of her. She surveyed the area around her and realized that everything—the tree trunks, brambles, leaves—were indistinct and black and white. She squinted and made out the two blurry horses and riders approaching her, but she stood behind a large tree out of their line of sight. In the silent gloaming, she watched as the hazy riders turned their heads as if listening, but there was no sound. One man backhanded the other on the arm and pointed to where the inaudible sounds emanated. She followed his finger but saw only gray mist. Monique's breathing quickened as one of the men leaned to the left, intending to dismount. Her hands tightened around the same hard, cold objects she had held before.

Fuji spoke. "Did you hear Leroy?"

Monique twitched. She lay facedown, her head turned to the side, resting on something soft and smelling of moist greenery. Loud buzzing sounded in her left ear. She opened her eyes to see red clover. Bumblebees swarmed among the pink flowers.

"What?" Monique turned over to see an unusually blue sky. The sun was almost directly overhead. She licked her dry lips.

"I asked if you heard what Leroy said to us." Fuji stood with his hands on his hips. "He said 'For you.' And look. We're here."

Something nudged Monique's left leg and she turned her head to see Art's foot. He stared at the clouds.

"It's okay," she told him. "Deep breaths."

Monique sat up. She expected to be in the same spot as the night before, but instead of seeing just a few trees and willows, she spied a thick stand of cottonwoods crowded around the little field of grass. The trees blocked the view of distant landmarks. Clover carpeted the ground. Wasps flitted above yellow sorrel.

"Uh-oh," muttered John.

"No shit. We've been drugged and taken someplace," she said quietly.

"Maybe."

"Damn, Leroy. What did you do?" she asked the unseen man.

"He can't be too far away," John reasoned.

"He better not be," Grace said, straightening her top.

The air felt clean and light. Birds chirped loudly. Rene took a deep breath. "Filling," she said.

"What?" Larry asked.

"The air. It's . . . filling. The only times I breathe air like this is when I'm the Rockies."

Elaine pushed her thick hair behind her ears and looked down. Her top had come untied, revealing her breasts. She quickly adjusted the material. Her face reddened but no one paid her any attention. "Where's Leroy?" she asked. "I saw him disappear when the winds started."

Grace surveyed their small meadow. "Maybe he got lost. Where are we? Did the arbor blow away?"

"Grass is tall, man," Larry said.

Monique stood and straightened her skirt. "We better see what's going on here. First, is everyone all right?"

"I think so," Art answered.

"Yeah," said John.

Grace jumped sideways and screamed. "Oh my God! A snake!"

Elaine peered into the grass, reached down, and picked up the foot-long garter snake. It curled around her arm. "Just a bug eater, Grace. There's probably lots of them here. They crawl around in grass and clover." She walked to the edge of the trees and let go of its neck. The snake unwound from her arm and slithered gracefully into the foliage.

"Dear God, my head hurts," Grace said. "I need Tylenol. There's a bottle in my car." She looked around. "Where's my car? Where's Leroy?" She spun in a circle. "Mazey? Peta? What the hell? Deb? Rob? That cat? Where are we?"

Elaine put her arm around her. "Deep breaths."

Grace began to cry. "I'm thirsty."

"We all are. Let's take a walk," Monique said, hoping action might distract Grace.

The dancers followed Monique out of the cottonwood grove, through more clover, and across a field of lupines that grew interspersed with Indian paintbrush, their purple-blue and scarlet colors bright under the morning sun. They entered a thick stand of box elders that shaded a narrow stream. Robins hopped through the underbrush, searching for insects, while a crow cawed from a branch above them. More soft, buzzing clover grew at the edge of the forest.

John put his hands on the top of his head, as if out of breath, and assessed the situation. "We should walk around those hills and find a house or gas station so we can call Leroy."

"We're in the place we were last night," Fuji said.

"That's not possible," Monique said.

"Nothing's here," Art said.

"Look around you," Fuji said. "Everything is here."

Tiny drumsticks pounded Monique's left temple, the precursor to a headache. *Did I pass out? Am I in a coma?* She wondered. A glance at her feet revealed maroon nail polish beneath a layer of dust. Wind whistled through the cottonwoods.

Movement to the east caught her eye. A herd of does stood a hundred feet away, watching the dancers with huge, unblinking eyes.

"This isn't funny," Monique said. "Fuji, if you know something, you better speak up."

"Like what?"

"Like, how did we get here?" She answered calmly, but felt the opposite. She was tired, thirsty, and in no mood for a barefoot Outward Bound experience.

"You drove," Fuji answered in his placid voice.

"We got here in our cars?!" Grace screamed. "Like hell we did. Where is everyone? Where is Leroy's house?" She gasped, took a deep breath, and then blurted, "What did they do to my brain?"

"Oh, for crying out loud, Grace," Art said. "Cool it." Grace grabbed Elaine and sobbed into her neck.

John glanced at the deer. They observed the humans and did not move. He wondered why they were not alarmed enough to bolt. When he hunted, he was lucky to see their white butts running for cover. A buck in velvet blew and turned to the trees. The herd followed him and wandered off between the trunks.

Monique turned to the group. "We've been drugged and moved," she said. "Some sort of experiment to see what we'll do."

"Why, for fuck's sake, would Leroy be a part of that?" Grace asked.

"Leroy does things for a reason," Fuji said.

Monique touched her chapped lips. She was wary of Fuji. Ideological young people could be unpredictable and sometimes stupid in their zealousness. On the other hand, Leroy was big on teaching lessons. "Maybe this is a team-building exercise," she said.

"What?" Grace asked loudly. "Why? What is that supposed to do?"

"Tribal unity. I don't know. Regardless of what Leroy has planned, we have to stay calm."

"We need to get organized," interjected John.

"But first we need water," Monique said. "I feel strange."

Fuji walked through the clover and flowers and stopped. He waved them over. He knelt by the stream and then cupped water in his hands.

"No!" John yelled. "Don't."

Fuji brought his hands to his mouth and drank. John exhaled. "Just great. No telling what's in that."

Rene knelt next to Fuji and they drank and splashed until their clothes were wet. Larry joined them. "Hey, man. It's clean. Cold too."

"The spring is right there." Fuji pointed up the hill to a grassy knoll. Water bubbled and flowed toward them in the narrow stream.

"Ah hell," John said. He strode to the stream and lay on his belly, then scooped the cool water into his mouth.

Art, Grace, and Elaine followed him. Monique watched a minute, then relented.

"Okay," Monique said between gulps. "We should break into groups and walk in several directions. Pick a landmark and walk fifteen minutes one way, then come back here."

Everyone except Fuji and Rene stood still, hesitant to move. "Go on now," she encouraged. "Yell if you need help."

Elaine and Grace headed north. Fuji and Rene slowly walked south, so slow it was clear that they did not intend to go more than twenty feet.

"I'm heading west," Monique said.

"I'll go with you," John said. "Larry, you and Art go east."

"Let's not lose our direction," Monique told John. "Head for those tall trees on the rise." She pointed to box elders about eight hundred yards away.

They started walking. "Good thing there's ground cover," John said. "We'll wreck our feet once we hit rocks or a forest with downed branches."

"Yeah," she agreed. "Barefooting is not sustainable. But I don't intend to go much farther than to those trees."

The two examined the ground and the trees until they arrived at the grove. They surveyed the landscape. "No fences or evidence of any development here," Monique said. "It's all pristine."

"Let's go a bit farther," John said.

"This is bullshit," Monique said. "We should not be doing this."

"Yeah, I know. Just go with it."

The pair made their way through the trees, mindful of the fallen branches and thick undergrowth. "Ow! Oh shit!" John blurted. He pointed at his foot.

"Let me see," Monique said. She saw that he had stepped on a branch. One with enormous thorns. "Uh-oh. Honey locust. Can you pull your foot free? Be careful." She squatted to look. He had impaled his heel.

John grimaced. "You do it."

She took hold of his ankle and gently pulled his foot upward. "Damn!" he yelped.

She inspected the long, red-tipped thorn. "That's a good quarter inch." She focused on the offensive barb. "The tip appears intact. Wow. That is sharp."

"Shit," John said again.

"Those trees are murderous."

She pointed to a tall tree endowed with hundreds of hostile thorns along its trunk that stood twenty feet away.

"We need to pay closer attention to what's around us," Monique said. "If that had broken off in your foot . . ."

"Yeah, I know."

"How does it feel?"

"Burning."

"Okay. Let's back out of here and walk around."

They exited the shade and kept their eyes on the horizon as they circled the trees. They focused on trees to the north.

"There's no one here," Monique said. She felt her heart beat faster.

"Let's go to the top of that rise over there," John said.

"How's your foot?"

"Feels like I got jabbed with an acid-filled syringe." Monique nodded. Nothing she could do about it.

They negotiated branches and rocks to reach the crest of a small hill. Luckily, the rocks were sandstone and not sharp malpais that could shred boot leather. Soft spring plants cushioned their feet. From their vantage point, Monique and John could see that all around them were more trees and patches of meadows. The only noise came from rustling leaves.

Neither spoke. She slapped him on the back. "Come on. We have to get more water and find food." She turned and began the trek back to their starting point.

"No houses, no buildings, no roads," Elaine reported once the dancers regrouped. Grace sat on the clover, wiping her eyes.

"Ditto," said Larry. "No water tower and no corn or soybean fields. No cattle."

Monique looked up in hopes of spotting anything besides hawks, turkey vultures, and clouds. "No planes. No vapor trails. No noise except wind and birds." The clouds had no answers.

Grace sniffed.

"Even if we were dropped off in a North Dakota field, we'd see something," Art said. "An old fence, cut trees, tin cans, litter. *Something*."

"We're in the place we were this morning," Fuji said again. "See the rock wall over there? That's the back wall of Leroy's shed."

"No way," Larry said.

Monique stared. Indeed, the back wall of Leroy's shed was a natural wall of granite. She had been in that shed several times. Leroy thought the rocks would serve as a good back support and would keep the structure from blowing away.

"Can't be," Monique said. "I saw it the day before yesterday."

"It's why we danced, remember?" Fuji answered. "It's what we wanted."

"What?" yelled Grace. "What do you mean 'what we wanted'? Are you nuts?"

"This can't be the same place," John said. "We passed out and were moved."

"That's the only explanation," Monique agreed. "We're probably in western Oklahoma someplace. There's vast open space." As she spoke, she knew that was not true. This area was too lush and green. "Well, maybe someplace in Kansas. Arkansas has forests too."

"No," Fuji said.

"Fuji, I know you have high hopes for some kind of revelation. But, Fuji. Honey. This is not what you think it is."

"What do you think it is?"

"Clearly, Leroy has taken us someplace." Monique studied the trees. But this really did look like Leroy's property, sans buildings and gardens.

"He didn't take us," Fuji continued. "He sent us."

She ignored him. "We were drugged," she repeated.

"Yeah," Larry agreed. "Simple as that."

"You know that's not true," Fuji said. "Remember the granite wall."

"Well, there you go," Monique said. "There are lots of granite outcroppings around here. And Leroy doesn't have a spring." She shifted from one foot to the other. A pair of hawks circled the meadow, screaming. She did a double take. At least one hawk always circled Leroy's property. "Besides, what you think happened isn't possible."

"Why not?"

"What the hell do you mean 'why not?'" She coughed.

"We're where we're supposed to be."

"Fuji, don't be a brat." Monique scrutinized the sky. She coughed again. "I need more water. Whatever you and Leroy are up to, it's not funny."

"No, it's not."

"So, you two *are* up to something."

"No."

Fuji kept his gaze on her, but said nothing.

"Stop it."

"Stop what?"

"You're pissing me off. Are you going to stand there and tell me you aren't in on this with Leroy?"

"No," he said so quietly that no one heard him.

She crossed her arms the way she did when she wanted to make a point with her son, Robbie. "I think you better tell us what's going on here. What are we supposed to be doing? Sitting around and talking about our feelings? We don't have any food, no shoes, no medicine. I'm hungry and thirsty and I have a headache."

"No sunscreen," Larry added.

"Hush," Monique told him.

Grace sat up. "What's that?" The group turned to see a furry animal, larger than a squirrel, next to a cottonwood, standing still, eyeing them.

"That looks like a ferret," Art said. "A big one."

"That's not a ferret," John said. "It's a mink."

"A mink?" Grace repeated. "No way. There aren't any minks around here."

Fuji smiled. "A lot more now than there will be."

Monique admired the animal that was clearly a mink. Shiny fur, weasel head. Beautiful and mean. An animal that opportunistic trappers would kill in a heartbeat.

"I have an idea," Monique said. "Hey, Art."

"Yeah."

"Let's check out that direction." She pointed south.

"Fuji and Rene already went that way."

"Yes, I know." She eyed the couple who stood quietly in the clover. "No offense," she said without expression.

Fuji smiled and Rene nodded her head. They resembled benevolent monks.

"We're going to head out for a while. About thirty minutes out, then we'll come back."

"Yes!" Grace agreed. "Great idea."

"See that open space between the trees, about half a mile?" she asked the group. "That's where we're going first. Then from there we'll pick the next landmark."

"Looks pretty dense," John said. "Watch for thorns."

There was nothing to say to that, so Monique and Art started walking.

12

NUKSHOPA
FEAR

Monique and Art lay on their bellies by the stream. Both dunked their heads after drinking, then sat up and put their feet in the cool water. They had limped back to the group ten minutes prior and neither said a word.

"And so?" Grace asked, rushing toward them after they emerged through a stand of cedars. The tops of the taller trees shaded the small field. The two travelers looked like unfortunates from the Donner Party. "Tell us," she demanded.

Art laid back in the grass, his eyes closed. "Nothing."

"What? How far did you go?"

"Maybe a mile south," Monique said as she inspected a cut on her left heel. The nail on her small toe had partially ripped. "Our feet are trashed. We shouldn't have gone that far. I have a cut and a shit ton of splinters and stickers. I'm always barefoot except when I run or work. My feet are tough, but not that tough."

Art winced as he rubbed his right heel. "Mine are not calloused at all. I pulled out at least a half dozen vine thorns."

"You didn't see anyone?" Grace persisted.

"Anyone?" Art asked. "We didn't see a road, a cow, or trash. No deer stands, cattle tracks, and no evidence of old roads. We got to the top of a rise. All around us are thick trees and no open areas for farming or roads. There's a few open places east and southwest, but I'm pretty sure they're meadows. No crops. No cattle."

"That's what Monique and I saw when we went west," John said.

"Oh man," said Larry.

"Does anyone feel funny?" Monique asked the group.

Everyone except Fuji and Rene raised a hand.

"What I mean is, does anyone feel as if they've been drugged? Is your vision blurry? Are you dizzy? Uncoordinated? Any part of you numb?"

Everyone shook their heads.

"No," John answered. "What are you thinking?"

"I still think we were medicated."

"I've taken most drugs," said Art, "and I don't feel like I've taken anything."

"Well that's the confident statement I need to hear," Grace said.

"Yeah. What do you mean 'most drugs'?" Monique asked.

"We're not drugged," Fuji said again.

"Are we back in time?" asked Elaine.

"Well," Art started, "In that movie *Back to the Future*—"

"Stop," Monique interrupted. "Don't start that."

"Maybe not back in time," said Art. "Maybe it's still the same time and everything's changed."

"People have to be here someplace," Elaine said.

"We can't be back in time," Grace said. "It's impossible." Her hands trembled.

"How do you explain where we are now?" asked John. "Something sure as hell happened."

Larry shook his head, the dreadlocks swaying. "Man, the NBA finals are on next week."

"SO WHAT?!" screamed Grace.

"Remember what we told Leroy," said Fuji. "We all said we wanted to return to traditions and for the whites to go away."

"I didn't say that," corrected John.

"Neither did I," Monique added. "He pretty much beat me down to get me here."

"But you also got what you asked for," Fuji added.

"How so?" asked Monique.

"He means," interjected Rene, "that you will."

John turned his head quickly. "What?"

"Nothing." Rene suddenly took an interest in her feet and fell silent.

"Shouldn't fool around with religion. Especially this dance." John said. "I knew it." He kicked at a dirt clump with a bare foot. "Ouch. Shit. Damn."

"That thorn poke hurt?" Monique asked.

"Actually, yes. It does."

A thought niggled at her, but she couldn't catch it. She knew it would return. "So everyone's okay except for nerves, right?" Monique asked. "Who knows wilderness first aid?"

"Why do we need first aid?" asked Larry.

"It goes like this, Gilligan," she explained. "If someone gets hurt, we need to know what to do instead of figuring it out *after* something happens."

"But we don't have anything for emergencies," Larry replied.

"It doesn't matter," said Fuji. "We can do with what nature gives us."

"Spoken like a truly decolonized NDN," Monique said.

Grace laughed, but she was not amused. "What do you mean 'what nature gives us'? I want vaccines and medicines, and if I get something in my eye, I don't want anyone licking my eyeball to get it out. I want something to kill the pain if I break my leg. What if we need surgery? I still have my appendix!" Her voice increased in velocity. "What if I get a yeast infection?" She felt terrified at that thought and the tears welled again. "I don't have any shampoo! And how am I gonna trim my nails? My glasses! I have to squint!" She sat and cried into her skirt.

"I thought you wanted to get rid of everything whites brought to the New World, Grace," John said.

"I don't use much shampoo," said Larry, stroking a long, twisted mess of hair.

"You need to shave your head and start over Larry," said Art. "You probably have things living in there."

"What if we get lice?" Grace said, scratching her head. "And what is this on my leg?" She pointed to her right calf.

"Where?" John asked.

"Right there! This red circle."

"Looks like leprosy."

The group leaned in to see. "What?!!" Grace yelped.

"Yeah," John continued. "A sore that's a bit swollen. Does it tingle?"

"Sort of." Grace sniffed.

"Numb?"

"I . . . well . . ."

"John," chided Monique. "It's not leprosy. Cool it."

"Okay. You're right. I'm wrong. It's necrotizing fasciitis."

Grace stared at him, then swung her leg out. John jumped back to avoid a strike to his shin.

"Jerk-off," she muttered.

"Grace," said Elaine gently, "you have a bruise on your leg. That's all. I need to get more water. Come with me to the creek."

"And what about infections?" yelled Grace, her eyes wide. "We don't have penicillin. If I'm stung by a bee, I might go into shock. I don't want to die from a beesting. Elaine?"

"A wasp stung you last summer and nothing happened besides a small red bump and some pain. No anaphylactic shock."

"We need Kleenex and underwear," she continued. "I'm not doing a farmer's snort! What if a tooth filling falls out? What about you, Elaine? You've got celiac disease!"

Alarmed, Art asked, "What in the heck's celiac disease?"

"No big deal," Elaine explained. "I can't digest gluten."

"What's gluten?" asked Larry.

"You know, it's in bread, pasta, crackers, stuff like that."

"Should be easy for you. No wheat here," John said.

"What do you mean?" asked Art.

He shrugged. "Do you see any QuikTrips?"

"I'm not worried," Elaine said.

"Yeah, and what if we cut our feet?" asked Larry. "Art and Monique did already, and John stepped on a thorn. We need some shoes, right?"

John nodded.

"No Foot Locker that I can see," said Art.

Larry thought hard. "We could get some hide and sew on a sole."

"WITH WHAT?!" screamed Grace. Spooked, a small flock of birds rocketed from out of the big bluestem.

Larry jumped at her shrill yelp. "Good point," he said quietly. "Can't we grow some penicillin on cheese? Isn't it the moldy stuff?"

"Is that for a virus or bacteria?" Art asked. "And where do we get the cheese? How do we make it? Are there cows here?"

Larry picked at a torn fingernail. "Who knows how to milk a cow?"

"Cool it, Larry," Monique said.

Then Larry pointed to two circling hawks. "How much meat's on them?"

"You're out of line," Art said.

"SHUT UP!" yelled Grace.

"Well, she's right," said Art.

"God will provide," Fuji said.

"That's nice," Art said. "Warm and fuzzy."

"God gave us brains to solve our problems."

"Yeah, and look at all the brains we have here."

This foolish exchange reminded Monique of an eighth-grade sleepover. Still, some of what they said was on the money. They needed shoes, and a lack of medical supplies could be a problem if Leroy planned to abandon them for more than a few days. She knew CPR and had been an EMT decades ago, but that meant little in the face of a serious injury or disease.

"We can sit here and think of a million problems," Monique said. "That's a waste of energy. We have to stay calm and be very careful and don't take chances. We know basic first aid, but none of us knows how to set bones and there is nothing to stitch with. If it rains, there's no place to keep dry. And we have no pain medication." Monique knew aspirin was made from willows, but damned if she knew how to extract it. "If someone gets hurt, they stay put with another person. The rest of us hike to a road."

"What if there aren't any?" Grace asked.

"There are roads, Grace," Monique argued. "Leroy and the drummers put us in a deserted spot. We're supposed to find our way out. It can't be that arduous. We're not in the mountains, and the weather is warm."

She glanced at Fuji. His face appeared weirdly serene. She wondered if he was mocking her.

"Until that time, we need to get our shit together," John said.

"I'm starving," Monique said. She had picked a handful of dandelion leaves and inspected them for insects. Seeing none, she rolled them up and pushed them into her mouth. "Needs dressing," she said. The others followed suit.

"Yeah. And there's no toilet paper," Larry said, watching Grace and Elaine walk arm in arm to the water. "I can't just tear off pieces of my skirt. What are we gonna use?"

"Grass is good as long as there aren't chiggers on it," said John. "And there's the creek you can wash in."

"Now I understand the toilet paper rush when COVID-19 hit," Art said.

"Mullein works," Monique said. "It grows in my yard. Big soft leaves. Older lamb's ears leaves are big too. Maple leaves. And there's plenty of cottonwood leaves. Just use them before they dry out."

"What about when we have our periods?" Grace stopped and turned around. "I'm not using rabbit fur, so don't say it."

"Well, there's always tree bark," Monique suggested. She thought she might start laughing. "You have to pound it to make it soft, then . . ."

"And I'm not staying in a hut for a week!" She started to cry again.

"A hut?" Elaine asked.

"A menstrual hut where women had to stay during their periods!"

"No one in our tribe had to do that. You're thinking of a place in Africa maybe. You're losing it."

"Okay, enough," John said. "Listen up. We need to stay clean. Bathe every morning and night. Use this grass as a tooth cleaner. It's kind of like toothpicks. There's no shampoo, so you need to get your head in the water and rub your scalp with your finger pads every day. You gotta stay clean."

Grace pointed to the creek. "Should we be drinking the water? I was so thirsty before, I had to. It looks uncontaminated, but it might be dirty."

"If it's coming from that spring, there's nothing to pollute it except us and we should pee a good distance away from it," John said. "The water's clean but it may upset our stomachs until we get used to it. There're only a few bugs."

Grace gasped. "BUGS?"

"Little ones," said Elaine as she put an arm around Grace and led her to the clear water. "No ibuprofen, Grace. You'll make your headache worse, so stop crying."

"There is nothing to pollute the water yet," Fuji said.

"We're not in a different time," Monique chided. "Stop saying that. The water has to be bad somehow. Maybe not right here because it's coming out of the ground. Other streams could be bad. Even if no one is around here dumping their car oil or company waste upstream, deer and elk pee in the water. And turtles are major poopers."

"Can't we boil it?" Grace's voice was shrill.

"In what?" Art asked.

Grace put her hands over her face and wept.

13

YANNASH
BISON

After a late evening of talking, crying, and attempts at making a comfortable campsite, the confused dancers fell asleep on piles of clover. Thick branches of pecan trees obscured the night sky.

"Warm weather for at least six more months," John said as the sun rose. He lay on his back, enjoying the soft clover. "How long we gonna be here, Fuji?"

Fuji shrugged. "Don't know."

"Sure as hell not six months." Monique huffed as she rebraided her hair. "I'm thinking more like six hours."

"Yeah, well. Better make some plans in case it's longer than that," John said.

"No way would Leroy allow us to be here longer than a few days. It's too dangerous." She stood and went to the stream to drink and wash her face.

"We're in *Hash bihi*," Fuji said. "Mulberry month. And there should be lamb's-quarters. We're in the middle of spring."

"What's a mulberry?" asked Larry.

"Fruit on a tree," Art said.

"You ran around them when you were a kid," Monique said over her shoulder. "Or at least you did in your third-grade song."

Larry scratched his head. "I thought that was a bush."

"Mine are trees."

Fuji continued. "And there's lots of dandelions—"

"Dandelions!" Monique sputtered droplets as she spoke. "Ha! And lamb's-quarters!"

"What?" Art asked. "You like them?"

"Dandelions and lamb's-quarters are not from this hemisphere." She squeezed cool water from her braid. "They're from Europe and Asia."

"And so?"

"We're here, that's what."

"We know we're here," Art said. "What's your point?"

"Fuji says we're in a different time. We're not."

"Dandelions arrived here with the colonists in the 1600s," Fuji said. "At least. They spread fast."

Monique exhaled in exasperation.

"Well, no way we can survive winter," John mused. "If we're really stuck here, then we may need to think about moving."

"Like to Mexico?" asked Larry. Long grass stuck to his dreads.

"Maybe."

"That's absurd." Monique said. "We're not going to be here through spring, not through summer, much less winter. This is an exercise, and we'll be done with it in a few hours."

"Maybe you're right," John acquiesced. "But what if Leroy has other plans and we're here a lot longer?"

Images of Silan Bohanan and Mike LeFlore popped into her head. Sunburned, ravenous, and footsore. Plus, East James sounded terrible on the phone.

"Shit," she said aloud. Maybe they were in for more than a few days.

"What?" John asked.

"Nothing. I don't know. But maybe you're right and we should think a few days ahead."

"Yes, we should!" yelped Grace.

Monique held up her hands. "Hold on. Just a few days."

"Yeah," John said as he scrutinized Grace. "There's lots of water and green stuff here. We'll be fine. Uh, what used to grow around Leroy's property?"

Grace sat with her head resting on her on her knees. She stifled a sob.

"Berries?" Elaine offered. "Fruit trees?"

"I eat mulberries, dandelions, goosefoot, amaranth leaves," Monique said. She did not mention pokeweed, because she never learned how to cook the leaves. You could be poisoned if they weren't properly boiled. "Anyone else?"

The others shook their heads. Fuji knew the old Choctaw thirteen-month calendar and how it related to the seasons, but the only fruits and vegetables he and the others ate came from grocery stores.

"Pecans will be ready in fall. There's chicory starting to grow right over there." Monique pointed to green stalks and buds that would soon open into light-blue flowers. "The weather has to get hot before we can use the roots."

"You mean coffee?" Elaine asked.

"No. Coffee is made from beans. Later in summer, you can roast chicory root, grind it, and make it like coffee. Some people like it better than coffee. I don't. It upsets my stomach."

"Wow, that's real interesting," said Grace. She massaged her temples with fingertips. "But we don't have anything to make it with."

The group thought about their lack of utensils.

"I saw on a cooking show that you can sauté some kinds of chicory," said Elaine. "It looks kinda like lettuce. You need a pan, though."

"Thanks, Mrs. Anthony Bourdain," said Grace, wiping her eyes.

"Lots of birds here," said Larry.

"Hard to catch," said John. "Even if you do catch a dozen, those little birds don't have much on them. Hardly worth the energy unless we can find turkeys. Duck meat's high in fat, so we should think about how to hunt them."

"Dandelions are everywhere," Monique observed.

"There's always mushrooms, man," said Larry.

"You know the difference between edible and poisonous ones?" John asked.

"You mean some shrooms are poisonous? Wow."

"For God's sake, Larry," Monique said in frustration. "Mock oyster, pink oyster, beefsteak, amanita. Not every mushroom is a morel."

"Larry," Art could not resist asking, "how did you make it to thirty-six?" Larry did not answer. He was mulling over the poisonous-mushroom factoid.

"At the most, we might have to fast a day," Monique said. "None of us are ethnobotanists. I can forage some stuff, but I'm not an expert on plants."

Thunder boomed in the distance. "Great," said Art. "Rain."

"Maybe not," Monique replied. "Those big cumulonimbus clouds in the west may stay there. See how blue and clear it is everyplace else?" The tops of the clouds shone white, then faded to gray and blue-black below. Thunder rumbled. "At least, I hope."

From the corner of her eye, she saw Fuji put his mouth to Rene's ear and heard him say, "Heloba laid some eggs."

Larry also heard him. "Huh?" he asked.

"Heloba." Rene explained. "The Thunderbird. Her eggs roll around in the clouds and cause thunder."

A horizontal bolt lit the clouds like a laser. The group jumped.

"That's Melatha. He moved so fast to stop the eggs from splattering to Earth that he caused that lightning."

"Just freaking great," Monique said.

"We'll be fine," Fuji said. He and Rene sat down, smiling. Then Fuji stretched his arms overhead. "I love rain and thunder."

Monique recalled that she had thought the same thing a week ago.

"Yeah, well," said Art, "I do too. When I'm indoors."

Thunder boomed again. Then the ground vibrated—a deep bass rumble like an earthquake, except the ground did not move side to side. It grew louder. Everyone stood.

"That is *not* Heloba," Monique said.

The group looked in the direction of what sounded like a freight train bearing down on them. They peeked through the scrub oak to see a wide field of green with spots of flower color. A black ribbon spread across the field, covering the green, treeless strip. And it came fast.

"It can't be," John said.

"We wanted buffalo," said Art. "There they are."

"Is this buffalo country?" Grace asked.

"What was your first clue?" Monique asked. "And they're bison."

"You know what I mean," Art said.

"Buffalo live in Africa," Monique said.

"Buffalo," Art said, mesmerized. "Jesus. There must be hundreds of them."

"Bison," John repeated.

"Screw you, John," answered Art.

The herd stormed past the group. Thousands of hooves churned dirt and grass the width of a tennis court.

"Unbelievable," said Art.

"Yeah," John said. "And white bison hunters loved to shoot the hell out of them. Sometimes from trains. Left them to rot in the sun. They killed so many that by the turn of the century there were only a few hundred left."

Monique watched, transfixed. "Okay, so we're in South Dakota. On a bison ranch."

"We're on private property," John said. "It appears that Leroy knows someone and they let him do this little exercise."

"That's a pretty long drive with us asleep," Larry mused. Monique had to agree. At least ten hours, maybe more.

"That would be dangerous," John said as he watched the herd disappear into the distance. "How would he get drugs?"

"What's the challenge of shooting into a herd from a train?" Grace interrupted.

"Your dad's white," answered Art. "You tell us."

Grace slapped him hard across his right cheek. Art caught her wrist before she hit him again.

"No arguing," John said evenly. "We need everyone in order to get through this, and you better stop with your bullshit, Grace, or I'll tie you to a tree with that skirt you got on. You cool it too, Art." Art let go of Grace's arm. She turned and stomped off.

They turned their attention back to the plain, still speaking quietly. "Look, look there," John pointed. "One's down. May have a broken leg."

"Hey!" Art shouted to the group. "Come on. We got a buffalo."

Fuji stayed in front, running fast. The churned dirt meshed with soft springtime grasses and flowers felt soft under the dancers' bare feet. They reached the downed animal and saw that her front leg was broken above the hoof. She tried to rise. Slobber and snot flew as she lashed her head around.

"Now what?" asked Larry, breathing hard.

"So who's gonna strangle it?" Larry's skirt had come undone and his privates were in full view. Everyone ignored him.

"We have to tell the owner," Elaine panted. "We can't kill it. We'll get in trouble."

"Can't put that leg in a cast," John said. "That's why injured racehorses are put down."

"Yeah, but will we be arrested?" Elaine started to argue.

"Can't let that animal suffer."

"I agree," Art said.

"Good. So we need some spears," John said. "Art, you and Elaine see if there's some sharp branches in that oak grove over there. Everyone else find rocks that look like spearheads."

The group fanned out while the wounded bison flailed.

Monique stayed back. "John, we could get in trouble. These animals are expensive."

"You wanna go find the rancher? Did you see a fence? Any road out here?"

"Ranchers have to check their herds."

"Hurry up!" John yelled to the others. "Jeez, what's so hard about finding rocks? Look, Monique, if nothing else, we're putting it out of its misery. It could be hours or days before the owner finds her."

"Vultures tell ranchers when there's an issue."

"Then I guess we'll find out. But in the meantime, I'm not going to let this one suffer. And we can eat it."

Monique considered that a moment. "If we eat it, we'll have to pay for it."

John eyed the injured animal. "We'll worry about that later."

"All right." She then turned to find a sharp stone.

Ten minutes later, the dancers returned with a pile of rocks of various sizes. After the group dumped the rocks at John's feet, he and Art worked fast to force the sharpest onto the ends of several straight branches.

"Here." Art handed a heavy five-foot branch with a broken end to John. "This one's pretty good. It's heavy."

"You want me to kill her?"

"Well, yeah. You do stuff like that, don't you? I mean, you're a marine." Art was partially teasing, but mainly serious. He normally killed animals with rifles or arrows shot from compound bows. Clean, quick, and from a distance. Somehow, a close-up killing seemed more brutal.

John hesitated.

"It needs to be done," Fuji said. "She knows it." The animal stopped thrashing. She turned her brown eyes to John.

John took a deep breath, pulled his arm back and prepared to strike, and then with a thrust and a powerful turn of his hips like Barry Bonds hitting a homer, he stabbed into the animal's neck.

The sharp tip led the way past tough hide, fat, and muscle. The jagged end of the branch severed the carotid artery and the bison struggled for less than a minute before her tongue hung out and she stopped breathing.

Fuji and Rene fell to their knees to sing, thanking the bison for dying for them. Monique reached down and stroked the animal's head. Grace sobbed.

"What's wrong with you now?" Art asked her.

"You killed it!"

Everyone looked at her. John spoke. "Grace, she was going to die."

"But . . . but . . . I've never seen an animal killed before." Then her pitch increased. "I get meat from Save A Lot!"

"We couldn't put her leg in a cast, Grace," said Elaine.

"We could have tried!" she yelled.

Monique kept looking at the animal's eyes. Did the bison's spirit now see endless prairie and all the bison that had come before her? Her eyes burned.

"What do we do now?" Larry asked again.

"Haven't you ever killed a deer?" John asked.

"No, man. Not even a chicken."

"Need to get her guts out first," John poked the dead cow's belly with his big toe.

"Hang on," Monique said. "You mean you really want to eat it?"

"You see anyone who's going to stop us? Listen."

The dancers stopped moving. After twenty seconds, John said, "Nothing. No one."

"We're way out in a field, John," Monique countered.

"We can pay the rancher for the meat later."

"That's a terrible idea." She hesitated. "Well, maybe we could."

"Let's do it. Hand me that rock with the sharp edge."

Elaine handed him a piece of gray chert.

John started sawing on the animal's underside at the sternum, but the dull rock could not cut cleanly. He sawed fast and managed to open only part of the underside. He put his hand in the cut and started pulling on muscles to get to the stomach, but there were too many innards to remove through the small incision.

"Art, get in here and help me."

"Do what?"

"What do you think I'm doing, dumb shit? Pull the skin apart. This hide is tough." Art, Fuji, Rene, and Elaine and jumped in gamely while Grace and Larry watched in disgust.

"There's got to be a sharp piece of something around here," Monique said as she searched the ground.

"Gross," Art said.

"We've done this before," John said. "You go hunting with me all the time. Bull elk are bigger than this. What's your problem?"

"We had guns, sharp knives, and it wasn't this bloody and slow. That's my problem."

"You got any better ideas?"

Viscera plopped onto Art's leg, splattering blood onto his face and chest. "Shit. Guess not."

The dancers ripped and pulled until finally the opening was big enough for the remainder of the guts to slip out onto the ground. The udder was half-full of milk.

"It had a baby!" yelled Grace. "It has milk!"

"Grace, listen." John breathed hard and his hands dripped blood and various bison fluids. "If she did have a calf, it's nowhere around. It ran off with the herd." Then he turned back to work.

"He's right, Grace," said Elaine. "Don't worry about it."

"Yeah, man. Another mother will adopt it," Larry said. "I guess."

"Grace," said Fuji, "the baby's all right. I promise." He held her eyes with his until she relaxed. "Don't worry. This is how it's supposed to be."

"Uh, okay." Then she sat and hugged herself.

John sat back, gasping and covered with blood. The others stood looking in fascination at the gutted bison.

"Wow. All right. You did it," said Larry.

"No, we didn't." said John, standing. "That was the easy part."

"What's that?" Larry was pointing to one of the organs.

"Gallbladder," answered John.

Larry squatted down and pressed on it with an index finger. It burst and squirted green bile onto him. He licked his lips and screwed up his face as if he had tasted a lemon.

"There's your dinner," said Art.

Larry wiped his eyes and leaned down for a closer look at the dead ungulate. "Where's the steak part?" he asked.

They struggled to get the hide off for two hours. They cut the membrane under the skin to separate it from fat and muscle.

"You know," John said an hour into their ordeal, "in the old days, they'd tie the edges of the hide to ropes and the other end to horses, and then the horses would pull off the hide. And someone had a knife to help get the skin free."

"That was then and this is now," Art said.

"I think this is then too," John replied.

They all felt exhausted, and blood and gummy gut fluids saturated their clothes. Dirt caked their faces. Everyone's humor worsened.

"No. This is still now." Monique wiped her eyes with the back of a filthy hand. She sighed wearily and rested her sticky hands on the carcass.

"There's no sign of other humans," Art said. "We really may be alone."

"Baloney. Leroy wouldn't do that." Monique still felt certain that she was right. "Which begs the question: Fuji, why did Leroy do this to us?"

Fuji stopped cutting. His straight teeth appeared whiter surrounded by a dirty face. "Well, we asked him to. That's why we danced and prayed. What did you think was going to happen?"

"I thought it was symbolic," Art answered, breathing hard. "You know, pray for the old days and ways to return. Then we feel better about ourselves because we're asking for what we're supposed to."

"Are you serious?" Fuji asked.

"Yes, I'm serious. I mean, how many Ghost Dances worked?"

"True that," John said. "Big Foot didn't exactly get what he wanted. Ended up in a mass grave with the other Minneconjous. All those other tribal prophets told their people what they wanted to hear. Hope comes from faith. Like Christianity. Miracles don't have to actually happen. The anticipation of miracles give them meaning."

Art pushed his hair behind his ears, leaving gunk on them. "We hoped something would happen, but not this." He tossed his rock down and inspected the end of his index finger. "Now look at us. Here we are. We can barely skin an animal. We sure as shit won't survive very long. Why would we really want the old times back? What kind of wish is that?"

"I wish we had horses," Larry said.

"Yeah, well, we don't have horses," said Monique. "So keep cutting."

"Man, this whole thing is unreal," Larry said. "Did I hit my head?"

"That would explain a lot," Grace answered.

John snickered.

"Hey, what do you mean by that?"

"I NEED A KNIFE!" yelled Art. "I've had it with this rock!"

"We all need a knife, Art. Cork it," said a damp Elaine, returning from washing in the stream. "We have to make do." Art noticed that her posture was straighter and her wet skirt stuck to her legs. He felt too tired to argue.

"It's a wish that our tribe and other tribes have had for hundreds of years, Art." Fuji resumed cutting.

"I did not wish for the old days," Monique said.

"Neither did I," Art agreed.

Fuji ignored them. "The tribal prophets Wovoka, Kenekuk, and Tenskwatawa had the word of the Creator that if they did what they were supposed to, then the old times would come back. Well, the old times didn't come back to them, but it did for us."

"Nothing came back to us, Fuji," Monique said. "This is a simulation of a historic situation, nothing more." She kept looking to the sky, hoping to see a vapor trail.

John, on the other hand, had a feeling the old days had not returned; rather, they were now *in* the old days.

"It's a gift," Fuji continued.

"And you're not supposed to look it in the mouth," said Larry.

"You mean a gift *horse*," said John.

"I know. I wish I had one. And if I did, I sure wouldn't look in its mouth."

"This is a gift?" Art asked as he gestured to the clear, clean world around them. Fuji seemed puzzled at Art's question. "Well, yes. Of course."

Art and John glanced at each other and sighed.

"You know what they say," John said through chapped lips. "Perspective is everything."

The sky darkened and the top edge of the moon peeked over the eastern horizon. After another half hour John said, "We need to hurry in case it gets too dark."

"Hey, that moon is huge," Larry said.

"Same size at it always was," John said. "It looks bigger because it's full, the sky's clear, and it's big compared to the trees."

"No way."

"Put your thumb up and size the moon against your nail. I guarantee it'll be the same size across the sky. And Larry?"

"Yeah?"

"You do know that's sunlight reflecting off the moon, right?"

"Hey, yeah. I knew that."

"Just checking."

The dancers butchered into the night. The light from the nearly full moon allowed them to see enough to pull off the hide. The group struggled to turn the huge animal over to peel the thick skin from the other side. Just as John remembered why Leroy said they would need the moonlight, and Monique thought about how the light made the blood look black, the howls started.

"Wolves," Fuji said calmly.

"Oh no!" wailed Grace. She perched on a rock watching and crying while the others labored. She wanted the company of the creek but fear kept her close to the others.

"Wait a sec," said Elaine, sitting back on her heals. "There aren't any wolves in Oklahoma."

"There are now," John said.

"Can't be wolves," Monique said. "They're coyotes."

"Nope," John disagreed. "Those are wolves."

One howled again. Monique had to agree. That was not a coyote. "That means we might be closer to Wyoming."

"No," John said.

"Northern Rockies, then."

"Do you see any mountains?"

Monique let out a weary sigh.

"They won't hurt us," said Fuji. "They'll stay away."

"Provided they're healthy and have plenty to eat," added John. "Wolves don't attack humans unless they're starving or have rabies. Same with coyotes, and there are plenty around here." He paused, considering the carcass. "Need a fire to cook this before it spoils. It'll take a long time to cook it all. We need several fires."

"We need a lot of things," said Grace.

They finished dressing the bison before sunup. Tired and filthy men and women carried slabs of jaggedly cut meat up the hill and piled it onto flat rocks. The animal's ruptured intestines rested on the grass and smelled bad. The hide lay next to the coiled intestines, but without curing and stretching, the skin would soon dry and shrivel.

"Now we have to get this cooked," said John. "This meat will rot fast and flies will be here with the sun—those little fuckers will be all over the place. And we better make shoes out of that hide."

"We need No-Pest Strips," said Grace. No one responded.

"What do we say to the ranchers?" Monique asked. "How much will this cost?"

"They won't come," Fuji answered.

"Look at us," Monique said as she scrutinized her clothes and bloody arms and feet. "They'll think we killed this animal on purpose."

"Monique. There are no ranchers."

"Can we eat it raw?" Larry asked. "I'm hungry." Monique thought of Silan and Mike again.

"Could," answered John. "Wild game's the best meat there is. But you might get a gut full of parasites unless you cook it. No hormones, but plenty of cooties. Be my guest."

"Plains tribes ate raw liver and other parts," Elaine offered.

"And they had been doing that their entire lives. I don't know enough about parasites to say that's a good idea."

Larry wrinkled his nose. "Uh, I'll wait for fire, man."

Fuji scanned the plain. "Wolves are here."

"Let me see." Monique hurried to look down the slope. Sure enough, a stealthy pack of gray wolves slowly approached the carcass. The largest male circled the remains, then smelled the blood ring. It stepped closer and grabbed one side of the rib cage. The others moved to the opposite side of the carcass and cautiously bit the legs, the head. "Oh my God," she said. "They're huge." The sight of the powerful, long-legged animals transfixed her. "Incredible."

"They'll be gone before the sky turns blue," Fuji said. He stood next to her.

A lone howl from across the hills cut through the night, followed by an answer from one wolf near the carcass. After a few seconds, his relatives pointed their noses to the sky and sang.

John frowned at the mangled bison. He looked to Monique as if he had just stepped off the set of *The Texas Chainsaw Massacre*. "They can have it." Bones stuck up and a dark ring of blood-soaked dirt encircled the remains. "Looks like it stepped on a land mine and blew up. My dad would freak out if he saw that. He has a thing about cutting up game the perfect way. Man, we got to get knives."

Fuji turned back to their meat. "Come on."

"How did the Stone Age guys do it?" asked Larry.

"Patience," said John as he squatted in front of his fire circle. He busily struck rocks together in an effort to generate sparks.

"They spent a lot of time etching and flaking the sides off to make serrated edges so the rocks could cut easily," he explained. "And before that, they needed to figure out which rocks to use, which ones they could strike together to make fire. This kind won't work." He tossed aside a piece of purplish bornite. "And neither will this one," he said about a lovely chunk of silvery argentite.

John approached his frustration level as he struck another pair against each other with no result. He sighed. Meanwhile, Grace bustled around the field. She stayed occupied by collecting as many different rocks as she could find, but concentrated on the prettiest. "Maybe we could start a rock collection for show-and-tell," John muttered.

"Why not try two sticks?" Elaine asked.

"Too hard unless you know what you're doing," Monique answered. "Even using a hand drill and changing with someone else so you don't get tired hardly ever works. You'd get blisters before a spark. If only someone had glasses or a pocketknife, or even a silver earring."

"I watched Bear Grylls start a fire with a bag of urine," Larry said. No one replied to that.

"Could wait for lightning to start a fire," said Elaine. John raised his eyebrow. "I'm kidding."

"Leroy made sure we only had our clothes," said Grace, walking over with another armful of stones. "I never take off my earrings and I had to give them up. Can't we get metal someplace?"

"Heck no," John answered. "You have to know how to take metal material out of rocks and then mix it with other stuff. Melt it and work it." He shook his head. "So simple at home. Now look at us."

"Check on the wolves," Monique said to Larry. He walked to the edge of their rise and looked down.

"Just two are there," Larry answered.

"A lot of people wish they could live in the 'good old days,'" said John. "But I don't know how good they really were. No vaccines, water filters, dentists, real painkillers, vitamins, war-veteran counseling centers. Tribes still got lots of problems like poverty and bad health, but they can at least help themselves if they try. Even poor people in our tribe have access to services." He used the edge of his skirt to work a piece of dirt out of the corner of his eye.

"Problems sure as hell multiply when you're out in the woods trying to start a fire in a skirt," Art said.

"Scottish men did it," Elaine said.

"Okay. This rock has got to do the trick," John said. "It looks flinty." He struck it repeatedly on another and finally a few sparks jumped outward.

"You got sparks," said Elaine. "How do we keep them?"

"Dang, I should've got tinder first."

"What's that?" asked Grace.

"Dry stuff like grass and bark. A dead tree with a dry middle. Rub it between your hands to make it fluffy. Then we let the sparks fall on it and hope it catches." Grace and Elaine rushed off and returned shortly with armloads of dead grass and small twigs.

They made a semi-windproof bank of dirt. After striking the rocks for almost ten minutes, John watched a small flame rise from the dead grass.

"Yes!" he urged the tiny fire with a few small puffs of breath. "Come on, come on."

Larry watched from where he fanned the meat to keep flies off. When the fire grew, he yelled, "Fire! Fire!"

"All right. Let's get more wood," John ordered. They all were hungry, so no one sat still. "And see if there's any dried buffalo manure!" John yelled to Grace. "That burns good."

"Lots of manure out there where the herd ran," Monique said. "But it's not dry yet."

John nodded. "Okay, yeah. You're right. Fire's gonna be a big problem. If it rains, we're up the creek. And even if it doesn't rain, we can't keep this fire going forever."

"What do you want to do?" Art asked, folding his arms in front of him.

"We need a shelter for fuel so it stays dry. And for us so we stay dry. That's going to be some chore. Man, we could be in trouble."

"This will just be for another day," Monique said.

"You think," John muttered.

"John, Leroy would not put us in a dangerous situation for longer than a few days."

"It's already been two. We have no way of knowing what Leroy is up to. Fuji drank the Kool-Aid and is in dreamland or someplace."

They saw Grace step on something and then sit down hard. She struggled to pull her foot to her face to inspect it. John sighed as he watched her.

"Gotta deal with her, man," Art said.

"I agree," said Monique. "We need to get secure as fast as possible. Grace is going to snap." They watched as Larry stretched out his arms and faced the sky, mouth open. "And Larry's too calm."

"I noticed," John said.

"Do you want me to suggest to the others that we should decide on leadership?" Monique asked.

"That's a good idea. I think Rene knows something too." He watched Rene and Fuji laying strips of meat on rocks. "Those two are too touchy-feely to lead. Elaine's strong and a good voice. Larry's too much of a goofball."

"Well, you stand up to everyone pretty good. Especially me," Art smiled. "I'm the biggest pain in the ass here and I'll support you."

"Me too," said Monique.

"You're the law," John told her.

"I don't have my gun. I only have my hands and harsh language."

"If you wanna be leader, I'm fine with that," John said.

"I'll be the enforcer," Monique offered.

He snorted. "Ha. All right. I'll be the political leader and Fuji will be the religious leader. That's a balance. Okay?" John pushed kindling into the growing fire. "I had a feeling that the dance would be arduous, but I didn't think this would happen." He inhaled deeply. "Marines didn't teach me to survive with nothing. We always had a knife and shoes and a pack full of basic survival things. I'd say this is ten times worse. I mean, we have nothing to work with."

"Maybe we could use some bison bones," Monique wondered aloud.

"Sure. We can use the scapulas as bowls. And we can hit each other with the femurs."

"Let's get some wood," Monique said as she started down the hill.

John, Larry, and Fuji cooked the meat throughout the day while Grace and Elaine fanned flies away. Shiny black crows watched the activity from the tall spruce trees. A sentinel sat on a branch above the dancers, occasionally cawing his observations.

"Man, this meat cooks slow," said Elaine.

"Well, without a knife or meat thermometer, we can't tell when the middle of thick pieces are done," said Rene. "These smaller pieces roast pretty quickly, though."

"We can eat the charred edges of the bigger hunks, then cook them more when it starts to taste raw," said Fuji.

The dancers were ravenous after two days of fasting followed by two more of foraged greens. They sat around the fire and ate quickly.

Elaine saw Grace clench her teeth and before she could curse, Elaine said, "Think of it as a campout. You can have nicely cooked meat at home."

"And what if we *are* home?" Grace asked.

"Then you smile and say the cook did a great job, like you do at our house."

"We need to talk about group organization." Art said suddenly, talking loudly so everyone could hear. "We should pick someone who's strong as the leader. That person will get us lined out, and I suggest John. Fuji will lead us in any religious matters that might come up."

"Yeah, okay," Larry said.

"Good idea," Rene agreed.

"John won't tell us what to do. He'll suggest and we'll discuss things, but if anyone misbehaves then he or she will have to deal with the group. No one acts independently."

No one responded. "Okay?" John asked.

"Okay here," said Elaine.

"Us too." Rene spoke for Fuji, who had a mouthful of crispy meat.

"So you agree?" John tried to get everyone to answer so there would be no mistake.

"I do," Larry raised his hand enthusiastically.

"We know you do, Larry," said Elaine.

"Salt would be great," said Grace. "And a Diet Coke."

"Tabasco," said Larry.

"How do we get salt?" asked Grace.

"We could go to the ocean and get water and then let it evaporate," said Larry.

"Yeah, let's take a hike over to the Pacific, dumbass," Grace said as she pulled off a strip of fat with her teeth and tossed it aside. "Ugh. Gamy."

"Don't waste that," said John. "We gotta eat all of it,"

"Could've used the brain and sweetbreads," said Elaine.

"Sweetbreads?" asked Larry.

"The organs," Art informed him.

"Yuck," said Grace.

"If we're here a few more days, we'll be begging for a mouthful of it," said John. "This meat is going to go bad. We can't go through this again with the tools we have. There must be fruit trees or onions around here."

"Anyone know how to make rabbit sticks?" Monique asked. She believed that Leroy would appear in the next day and they wouldn't need bunny meat, but she wanted to appear helpful. "They're small and heavy. If you make them right, they're more accurate than rocks."

Everyone shook their heads no except John. "I can sort of make a snare," he answered. "Wire works best."

"We could make pemmican with the leftovers," said Grace hopefully. "It'll last longer."

"Do you know what real pemmican is?" asked John. "It's fat, meat, and berries. No sugar and no fruit juice like health-food pemmican. The real stuff's made for calories. Energy. Not for taste, and you'd gag on it. Flies'll lay their eggs all over any meat we try to dry. They're swarming over it now."

The group considered the uncooked portions. It was black with insects. Larry jumped up and waved his arms to shoo them away.

"We could keep smoke going," offered Elaine.

"Possible, but we'd have to man the fire all the time. If this goes out and we have to make another, we gotta make sure to use dry tinder," he explained. "Otherwise, it may not start. If we get damp wood, put the pieces by the edge of the fire and they'll dry."

The group shuffled their feet. John still wasn't sure they would do it correctly, so he offered more explanation. "This isn't like a woodstove. A big wind can put it out and a small rain can ruin the whole thing."

"Maybe we should sleep in shifts and some of us stay up to keep it alive," Monique suggested. "And to guard us."

"Guard us from what?" asked Grace.

"Nothing, probably," John said. "But we got wolves and we might have bears. Unless we hoist that meat up real high, they'll come around. They don't care if we're here or not."

Each person jumped up and the entire group worked to secure the cooked meat high in the branches of a tree across the creek. Larry managed to shimmy up the trunk of a cottonwood.

"Boy, oh boy," Art said to John from where he sat on a branch of an oak, forcing a large hunk of meat between two branches. "I forgot about bears. Man, we've hunted together for what, fifteen years, in Colorado, Wyoming, Montana? And every time we've secured the food in a tree. How could we forget something like this?"

"We don't run into bears in Oklahoma, Art. You wouldn't have thought of them. Here's another piece." John threw another chunk of meat to his hunting partner. "Let's keep some of it down here. We'll be hungry again in a few hours."

"But like Monique says, we may not be in Oklahoma."

"If we're up north, then yeah, there might be bears."

"Just like Grizzly Adams," Larry interjected. "Cool."

"You think 'cool' now," John said. "Wait till a bear bites you in the ass and we'll see what you say then."

The group ate again. John ate burgers and steaks on a fairly regular basis, but this was more meat than he had consumed in a month. Monique only ate fish, chicken, or venison two or three times a week, while Grace and Elaine were semi-vegetarians. Art had stopped eating red meat three years before in an attempt to lose weight. Monique wondered how the quantity of meat she had consumed would affect her digestive system. *Better get up and move*, she thought.

After the dancers ate, they wandered around the area, although not far from each other. They feared that the rest of the group might disappear.

Monique turned her face to the sun in defiance of the UV rays. She took in the red columbines covering the hillside amid the yellow dandelions. Pink rose mallows lined the creek banks and sticky purple thistles grew among the buffalo grass and yarrow. Birdsong filled the air at full volume.

By evening, the dancers were exhausted but too tired to sleep.

Elaine attempted to squeeze a splinter from Grace's foot. "You need to put your foot in the creek and soak it. Then the thorn'll come out easier. Tough to get it out with no tweezers."

Grace whimpered. "My God. What if my foot gets infected? Then gangrene? Oh no! They'll tie me down and amputate my leg with rocks and I won't have any pain medicine or crutches!"

"You'll be okay. Come on, let's get to the water."

John stretched his legs by the fire and listened to Grace's dramatics, more concerned about the flame going out.

Larry stayed busy wandering. "Dead porcupine over here!" he yelled from behind an outcropping of rock.

"How dead?" John yelled back.

"Skeleton dead."

"No good."

Grace and Elaine sat on the bank of the stream. Grace's foot soaked in the gently moving water. "What are we going to do?" Grace asked while wringing her hands in her dirty skirt. "And what are we going to wear when these clothes fall apart?"

"We won't be here that long."

"What if we are?"

Elaine shrugged. "Find food. And build shelter. A tipi or lean-to, or something."

Grace tried to tie her hair back with a long piece of grass but it broke when she pulled it taut. She threw the grass down. "Damn it."

"I'm kidding about tipis," Elaine said. "The way that buffalo got shredded, it'll take ten years to get enough hide. Deer and elk won't be much easier to dress, even if we get close enough to kill them. I doubt if anyone besides a few of us are fit enough to run after game. And we don't have an axe to cut tipi poles, anyway." Grace pushed a rock over with her toes and little mugwumps scattered. She pulled her foot back in alarm.

"They won't hurt you." Elaine tapped her toe in the sparkly water.

"We need different food," Grace insisted.

"There's fish," Elaine said.

"Yeah." Grace's brows knitted together with worry. She picked up a flat stone to skip it across the narrow creek. From the way her hand drew back, Elaine could tell it would hit the water and sink. Grace flung the rock at an angle. "Shit."

"You're good at catching fish."

"If I have the right equipment. Look, Elaine, it's important that you stay strong so I won't fall apart." She chose another stone.

"You depend on me for everything, Grace."

"What do you mean by that?"

"I'm not your mother and I'm not your crutch."

Grace threw the stone to the ground. It bounced and hit her shin. "Damn it!" She lifted her skirt to see a red scrape. "I know you're not my mother. But you're my . . . my . . ."

"Good friend."

Grace let go of her skirt and dropped her jaw.

Elaine stood. "I'll get some hair from the buffalo's tail and maybe that'll hold yours back. If it's too short, I'll braid some grass."

"You're more than that."

"What if I am? I still can't do everything for you. I won't always be where you want me."

"We have to stick together." Grace's voice rose.

"Grace. We *all* have to stick together. Remember that we talked about how it does no good to complain all the time? Be proactive. Jump in and help. Don't ask. Just do it."

"I do," she argued.

"No. You don't."

Grace huffed. "I do."

Elaine didn't look at her.

"I'll try," Grace said.

"The best way to feel better is to do something about what bothers you. If you can't solve the problem, find something positive to do. Gather wood, look for dandelions, wash your hair. Ask the others if they need anything."

"Yeah, I know."

Elaine held out her hand. Grace grabbed it as she started to stand. "You're right. As usual."

Elaine forced a smile and sighed. "You're welcome."

Fuji and Rene wandered down the hill, happy and content. Monique watched them go. It had been four days since they'd left their normal lives, and everyone besides Fuji and Rene was stressed and pissed. Fuji seemed invigorated. Where was Leroy? What if this little exercise was meant to last for weeks? *No way.*

Monique wondered what might happen if they were stuck here. How batshit crazy would the group be after weeks of minimal food and excessive exercise? Monique had a short fuse—she knew that if she didn't get answers soon her switch would flip and she'd see red. Angry-bull red. She hoped that wouldn't happen.

As she watched Fuji and Rene, she wondered what their role was in this escapade. They didn't appear worried, so maybe she should follow their lead. She intuitively knew they were in on this activity with Leroy. That meant they knew the plan. Like that this field trip would be over soon. On the other hand, it bothered her that they acted as if they belonged here. With that in mind, it seemed appropriate that the couple walked hand in hand through a field of buttercups, surrounded by butterflies before disappearing into a stand of cedars.

14

KANALI
MOVING

Monique found another thick patch of soft clover. She stepped into the greenery and felt a slight depression. She preferred to sleep on her side—this small hollow would accommodate her hip. There were no sticks or brambles and, even better, no poison ivy or oak. She'd have to go without a pillow. Insects buzzed around and, once again, she wondered about chiggers. No one in the group had mentioned the insects' dreaded bites. She had long ago given up sitting in grass in her normal life, even on a picnic blanket.

Intermittent cool breezes swept through the still night, but none cold enough to cause her to shiver. Still, she wished for socks. She wondered what Robbie and Steve were doing. Probably eating pizza or spaghetti. They would expect her home tomorrow. Four days of dancing plus one day before and one day after the dance. If she didn't return, Steve would drive to Leroy's and demand answers. *All I have to do is deal with this another night.* That thought made her smile. She could do it. Easy-peasy.

Monique listened to the far-off howls of wolves to the west and the shriller coyote sounds in the north. She brought her knees in closer. The secure fetal position. What were the dancers supposed to be doing out here? What did eating bison have to do with "renewal"? Leroy should have given them instructions. Unless he showed up in the next few minutes, Monique knew she would not get any answers that night. She listened to the feral sounds and the gentle breeze, then forced her mind to shut down.

"Rice-A-Roni," Larry muttered softly.

"Fuck a duck," someone else said. "God, enough of the sticks in my back, my ass, my ear," the voice continued. It was Art.

She opened her eyes. The sun had not yet cleared the trees. A quick perusal of the camp told her the others were awake but still prone and thinking.

"What's for breakfast?" Larry asked.

"Same thing you had for dinner," John answered.

"It's in the trees." Art added. "I need something different."

"Same here," Grace said.

The only ones who did not complain of either stomach upset or constipation were Rene and Fuji. Rene never whined and Fuji could consume almost anything.

"Then pick dandelions and lamb's-quarters," John suggested. "Or find onions. Catch a goose. What do want us to say?"

"Don't get your panties in a wad," Art said.

"I'm not wearing any."

"What can I use to brush my hair?" Grace asked.

"Your fingers," Monique said.

"I have a million tangles," she said, panting. "I need a comb."

Monique did not reply. Instead, she sat up and wove her fingers through her own tangled mess. The knots at the nape of her neck could make her panic. Once, in elementary school, she fell asleep with gum in her mouth. The wad fell out during the night and as she rolled over, the gum and hair combined to form a mesh akin to a sparrow's nest. Her mom removed it with scissors and left behind a bald spot on the back of her head. At that remembrance, Monique stopped and took a deep breath. Impatient, she tore apart a tangle and cringed at hearing her hair rip.

"Goddamn it."

John tried to dig dirt from under his nails with a stick but the ends splintered. He picked up another and tried again and it broke. He dropped the lightweight stem and it landed on his foot. "Screw you," he said to the offending stick.

"We can't just sit here and wait for something to happen," Monique said. "This is ridiculous."

"What are we supposed to be doing?" Grace whined.

"Yeah, really," Larry said. "I thought Leroy might be here by now."

"Fuji," Monique said in a low tone, "enough of this shit." She stood and faced him, fists on hips. "Right now, buster. Answers."

"We should move," Fuji said.

"I'm all for that," Monique said. "I'm going to kick a few butts once we get to Leroy's. I'm about ready to now."

"We need to move," he repeated.

"Move where?" Art asked.

"South and east."

"I knew it," Monique interjected. "We're in South or North Dakota, right?"

"No."

"No?"

"We try to find other people," Fuji said.

"What do you mean other people? Where is Leroy?"

"Not here."

"Obviously not right here. Where?"

"I just think that we should explore," Fuji said in his comforting voice.

"Yes," said Art. "The sooner the better."

Monique watched Fuji. *Smooth as silk*, she thought. *He planned to say this at some point and was waiting for the right time.*

"There have to be other people around somewhere," Grace said.

"Of course there are," Monique agreed. "There's probably a road a mile from here."

"Let's find out," Rene said.

"We need footwear if we plan on going far," Monique said. "We've been lucky. But one deep puncture and your foot will be in a world of hurt. And infection."

"Doesn't even have to be deep," John added.

"What do you suggest?" Elaine asked.

Monique coughed. She needed water. "Hides are best."

Elaine rebraided her hair. "What about the bison?"

"Dried out," Monique said. "We might get a pair or two of half-assed foot wraps from it."

"Better than nothing," John said. "I'll see what we can salvage."

Monique, John, and Art made their way to the kill spot. The hide was gone. "Shit," Art said. "The wolves dragged it off."

"Maybe," Monique said before picking her way to the nearby cotton-wood grove.

John surveyed the remains of the animal. Wolves, coyotes, crows, and vultures had taken almost everything. "We should have cut some sinew. Now all the soft tissue's gone."

"We'll get some the next time," Art said.

Monique laughed. "You mean the next time we find a huge, dangerous horned animal with a broken leg?" She said over her shoulder as walked to the trees.

Art shrugged. "Might luck out and find a wounded deer," he said to her back.

"Same difficulties, just smaller scale. Hey, look over here." She stood over a dark shape lying over a fallen log. "Found it."

The three gathered around the ripped hide with hardened edges. "What do you think?" she asked.

"Looks like a huge, hairy potato chip," Art said.

"Could soak it overnight and stretch it," John mused. "We might get scraps that'll work as wraps. Like short ACE bandages. This is not gonna be easy. Bison hide is like cattle leather. If we had sixteen dead rabbits, life would be easier."

Monique made a face. "Ugh. Well, let's get to it." They dragged the hide back to the stream by the camp.

"Let's pull it and set rocks on the corners," John said.

As the hide lay under the gently running water, the other dancers came to look at their potential footwear. Strings of flesh waved in the gentle current.

"No, no, no," Grace moaned. "I'm not putting my feet on that."

"You can line the shoes with grass so your feet won't touch the hide," Art suggested.

"No."

"So then go barefoot," Monique said.

"That is so gross!"

"Grow the hell up," John admonished. "I'm tired of your moaning." Grace stepped back from the rebuke.

"As am I," Monique said. "We are in a situation and you need to deal with it. You have to thank that animal, Grace. Now you have something to cover your feet with, so stop whining." She thought about her son, Robbie. He never complained to this extent and he was eighteen years younger than Grace.

Grace sobbed. Elaine repressed a smirk as she hugged Grace, then pulled her toward the camp. "Let's sit down. I'll fix your hair." Grace followed like a dog on a leash.

"I can make sandals if we find some cattails," John said. Grace stopped and turned around. "Maybe," he added. "I learned to do that a long time ago. But I only used them for about an hour. Can't promise anything."

Grace stared at him a few seconds. "Don't expect Teva sandals," he added.

Elaine tugged at Grace's arm and the group watched them hike up the small rise and stop under a tree.

Monique exhaled and felt a familiar ache in her temples. Rene put a hand on her shoulder. Monique touched it. She turned and, for a second, thought that Rene looked like a picture of Monique's grandmother when she was young. Monique blinked and a breeze pushed a few strands of hair across Rene's face.

Art's laugh caught her attention. He scratched his belly. "That chick isn't going to make it much longer."

"Yes, she will," Fuji said.

"Getting tired of your Gandhi-isms," Monique said as she watched Rene rebraid her hair.

Fuji cocked his head.

John crossed his arms. "I am too, actually."

"Huh?" Larry asked.

"Are we still going someplace?" Art asked.

"Yes," Fuji answered.

"Really?" Monique asked. "Down the hill and to the unseen road where Leroy is waiting so I can kick his backside?"

"Maybe."

"Okay, then," Art interjected. "We need to divide up evenly in case one group has a problem."

Monique laughed. "What?"

"I'm being practical. If something happens to the whole group, then it's the end of the story. If we divide up, then there'll be survivors. You know?"

"Survivors?" Monique asked. "Where do you think we're going? Through the Bitterroot Mountains?"

"Well, no. It's just that, that—"

"We're going about a mile, Art. One of us could scream and Leroy will come running."

"Okay. But . . . say he's farther away."

"We have to deal with Grace," John finished Art's implied statement.

"Yeah. I hate that thought." Art shook his head. "Man, it's like she's got bad PMS all the time."

"Grace is stronger than you think, Art," Fuji said. "You have to be firm with her, but don't argue. Give her choices and she'll come through okay. Leroy wouldn't have allowed her to dance if he didn't think so."

"So you admit it," Monique started. "Leroy knew this would happen and that we'd be stressed."

"Probably."

"Probably, my ass."

"Don't start again, you two," Art said.

"Say that again?" Monique said calmly.

"Look, I'll try to be nice," Art said as he glanced over to where Grace lay under a tree, her arm draped over her eyes as if she were a wilted daffodil.

"Grace has to go along, guys," Fuji repeated. "We all have to go."

"Can we make it?" asked Art.

"Sure. We have to."

"Make it where?" Larry asked.

Monique rolled her eyes and exhaled. "Over the river and through the woods. Wherever the cars are waiting for us to take us home. Right, Fuji?"

"Yes, of course. Cars will take you home."

15

Hoyo
A Quest

Birds hidden in the green leaves chirped and a flock of ducks flapped overhead. A high whistle sounded. The group watched a large bird soaring through the blue sky with a glistening silver object in its talons.

"What's that?" Larry asked. "An eagle?"

"No," John said. "Osprey. It's got a fish." The group watched the ducks descend beyond the trees. "There's a lake over there."

"How did we miss that?" Elaine asked.

"We all went straight north, south, east, and west. This is northwest. C'mon."

They slowly trudged northwest through a stand of pecans, scrutinizing the ground before placing their feet on leaves, twigs, and other detritus. They emerged from the trees to find a small lake surrounded by cattails, reeds, and bushes. Deer, turkey, and raccoon tracks proliferated next to the bank. They heard the ducks quacking and Canadian geese honking. The water sparkled like glitter.

"There's no lake like this around Leroy's place," Monique said.

"Things change," Fuji said.

Monique opened her mouth to reply, then shut it. Thousands of cattails lined the far shore.

John smiled. "Oh yeah."

"Now we have fish," Larry said.

"We also have shoes," John added.

"Huh?"

"Sandals. Out of cattails. I learned from my aunt."

"How long does that take?"

"If you know how to do it, not too long. But we still need the leather."

John and Art used the sharp chert to cut enough cattail fronds to make three pairs of sandals for everyone. Fuji, Rene, and Monique managed to rip the bison hide into strips long enough to wrap around three pairs of feet. John suggested they keep one section to use as a container for food.

John showed them how to use the long cattail leaves as the long warps and the more slender leaves as the horizontal wefts. They had no looms, so John improvised by using a straight, round branch and looping the warps around the stick so the soles were two warps thick. He used the sharp point of his hunk of chert to make small holes for laces in the warps.

"Bone is best for this part," he said. "We could try and splinter that bison's long bones to use as needles. But for the moment, this chert works." He pushed the smaller strips of leaves through to use as ties.

Grace's hands shook as she attempted to weave the leaves. "I can't do this! I can't see without my glasses." She cried and threw down her attempt.

"You can go barefoot if you prefer," Monique said.

Grace put her hands over her face and wailed. "I'll die here!"

"No, you won't," Elaine said quietly. She picked up Grace's fronds and put them in her lap. "We're all learning from John."

The sandal-making lesson proceeded with much cursing, sighing, and throwing. Monique tried on her first pair. "Damn. Too short."

"Wow, dude," Larry said. "You're feet are biggern mine."

"Thanks, Captain Obvious."

"What size are those?" Art asked.

"Big enough to kick your scrawny heinie."

"You definitely need them to cover your toes," John said.

Monique tossed them to Larry. "There you go. You know what they say about men with small feet."

"Small?" Larry looked puzzled. "I'm a size ten."

She raised her feet and wiggled her toes. "Like I said."

Art, John, and Fuji regarded their feet. Elaine and Grace snickered. The dancers spent the remainder of the afternoon weaving.

"On any other day, this would be relaxing," Monique said.

"Oh, it is," Rene said. "It's like beading."

Monique studied Rene's beatific profile. *How can she be so calm?* The more Monique studied Rene, the more familiar she looked. *Her nose looks like Dad's.* Rene looked up and smiled as if she'd read Monique's thoughts. Monique blinked and realized she had been staring. She quickly looked down and busied herself with the reeds.

Art held up three pairs of less-than-museum-quality survival sandals. "Well, I think I got the hang of it."

John alternated weaving his sandals with assisting Grace until she completed her first pair. Her hands stopped shaking and she made another pair.

Elaine mastered the challenge and made an extra pair for Monique. "Thanks," Monique said. "I'll be done in a minute."

"Okay, so it looks like everyone has sandals," John said. "I suggest that those with foot problems start with the hide wraps. The rest of us wear these. I can't say how long they'll last, but if we don't climb over rocks, maybe ten miles or so. We also need to do what Fuji suggested and make walking sticks."

"Why?" Grace asked. "I don't need a stick."

"It will help you keep your balance. And you can test the ground in front of you. If we have to cross a muddy area or a cloudy stream, you can use the stick to see how deep it is."

"Oh."

"And might as well either sharpen it or tie a pointed rock to the tip."

"What for?"

"Wolves and bears," Art said. She gasped.

"You never know," John said.

"Right," Monique said. "Because we can't make it a couple of miles without spears that double as bear slayers."

"Look, I know," John said. "Let's just go with the flow."

Monique sighed. "Good Lord. All right."

Within the hour, each walker possessed a long stick, topped with sharp rocks attached with cattail fronds.

They reconvened for a group meeting, and John outlined his idea. "We have footwear. These sandals will get us down the road a bit. What we need to do now is smoke some fish. It won't be like jerky but it'll last until we find something else."

"If we don't find water, then we'll have to come back," Art said.

"Not if we find something to carry the water." Grace said as she stood.

"Maybe we can peel the reeds and make baskets," Larry said. Art snickered.

"That's right," John said. "We do have to make baskets, but I don't know how."

"For crying out loud," Monique muttered. "We can't make baskets tight enough to carry water."

"Right," John agreed, "but have to carry food. I'll carry it in that extra bit of hide."

"You can't carry much in that," Monique said as she scrutinized the ragged square of hide that John had tucked into his skirt. A long strip to use as a tie would flop on his thigh as he walked. "Maybe four, five fish. We'll have to use our stomachs as canteens. On the other hand, we're not going far." She did not say that she had no intention of eating anything he carried in that smelly bison skin.

"How far?" Grace asked.

"Not far," Monique answered. "This is just an exercise. We'll see Leroy in less than ten miles."

"We should go east," Fuji said.

"Why?" Grace asked.

"Follow the rising sun."

"Why not follow the setting sun?" Grace asked.

"We must go east," Fuji said.

Monique snorted.

The others did not argue. "East it is," John agreed.

"We just bushwhack?" Art asked.

"There are no roads," Rene said.

"None that we can see," Monique interjected. She still was not willing to accept that they were far from Leroy. Surely, he had a van parked a few miles away.

"Okay," John conceded, "maybe we'll run into one."

"No, we won't," Grace sniffed.

John ignored her. "We need to stay together. No wandering off. If we get separated—"

"We're not getting separated," Monique said. "We can't walk that fast. And if anyone wanders off and gets lost, they should just sit down and whistle."

"Right," Grace said as she saluted. "And I'll take the jeep and drive around until I find you."

Only Larry laughed.

Most of the bison meat had gone bad, but they still had two days of dried meat. A few pieces they thought had smoked all the way through were raw in the middle and now stank. "We definitely need fish," Monique said. "I understand that bison has staying power, but my system can't handle that much heavy stuff at one time."

"If we knew how to smoke it right, it would be fine," John said. "We would be able to stretch it out."

Larry tried to fish using a long stick, cattail stalks as line, and a pointed twig tied at the end as a hook. He tossed the line in, waited a minute, and then pulled it out. After three attempts, he got a tug. Larry jerked the line. It flew up and out of the water, minus the twig.

"Just like a kid," Monique said to John. "Eternally hopeful."

"Gotta do it another way," John said as he unwrapped his hide strips and waded into the cold water.

"You're not going to last very long," Monique said.

"A man's gotta do what a man's gotta do."

"If you say so."

John slowly made his way to rocks that stuck up from the calm water. He bent down until just his head showed above the water line. He submerged for a few seconds then stood, sputtering.

"Damn. Cold."

"Hey, man, just wait a sec," Larry said from twenty feet away. "I can catch one."

"That would be helpful," John answered. He walked around the rocks and then submerged again. After ten seconds, Monique stood. She took a step, prepared to jump in, when John suddenly reemerged, took a large breath, and disappeared. A few seconds later, his head appeared and he called for Monique.

"Get over here!" he yelled.

Fearful that he had encountered a snapping turtle, she rushed into the cool water. John thrashed around and as she drew closer, a large gray, writhing shape broke the surface. He had ahold of it.

"Holy shit! You got one!"

"Yeah. Hurry! I can't hold him."

John's hand held the fish's bottom jaw. Wisps of blood streamed from where the catfish raked his hand. Monique took off her shirt and wrapped it around the huge fish. The spines on the tail and head could still poke them, but the cloth top helped hold the slippery bottom-feeder. They carried the fish to the shore and dropped it. Larry rushed over and helped Monique hold it down while John search for a rock. He found a large stick instead and whacked it three times on the head.

"This sucker is at least seven pounds," Monique said.

"There was another down there. I'll try and catch it."

"You're cold. Wait a few minutes to warm up."

John puffed his cheeks and exhaled. "I'm good." Then he walked back into the lake.

"Good thing he knows how to do that," Larry said. "I don't think I could do it."

John submerged three times before he caught another fish, this time a three-pounder. He carried it to the bank and Larry hit it until it quieted.

"Here's your shirt." Larry held it out to Monique. "Smells fishy."

"Not much worse than how it already smelled." She rinsed it in the lake, gave a few squeezes, and shook it out. "Man, I hope this thing doesn't rip." She could just wear her jog bra, but she'd get sunburned.

They carried their catfish to camp. "Damn!" yelled John. "We let the fire go out." He ran to the embers and stirred them lightly while putting dried grass on top of the tiny flame. Relief flooded through him when the flames shot upward.

They cut ragged fillets with the sharpened chert and then used sticks to impale the large strips. Using rocks as props, they leaned the meat over the three small fires and watched the smoke curl around the fillets.

"We should cook the heads too," Elaine said. "Lots of meat on them." She stood and searched for two more sticks. She twisted the catfish heads off and impaled them. "Too bad we don't have a pot to make fish head soup." Grace made a face.

"Normally I would barf at the thought," Monique said, "but right now that sounds pretty good."

Larry returned from the lake carrying another two-foot catfish. He glistened with water drops.

"Hey, look what Aquaman caught." Art laughed. "Way to go, dude. Now you're a noodler."

"No, man. This mud cat took the line and pulled the pole right outta my hand. Had to jump in after it."

That evening the dancers ate dried bison, Larry's fish, mulberries, and clover. The next morning they ate breakfast of another fish John noodled, along with the dependable dandelions. Larry indulged in a few wild onions and sat with his mouth open.

"What's wrong with you?" Monique asked.

"Strong onions."

"You may have gotten ahold of wild garlic. Some of that's like hot pepper. Takes hours to get rid of the burn on your lips."

Larry belched. "Oh man."

"And you smell like a double-garlic pizza."

"I don't like wild onions," John said, scratching his neck.

Art laughed. "Not possible. All Indians like wild onions."

"Not this one. And I don't like corn."

Grace choked on her leaves. "What?"

"I don't like corn either," Art added.

"Just sweet corn for me," Monique said. "Flour corn is too earthy. My *tanfula* and *banaha* need lots of spices and oil."

"Oooh. You're gonna be disenrolled," Elaine teased.

"Chicken is better than turkey," John said.

Grace stopped chewing.

"Buffalo is not my first choice among meats," Art added. "I prefer beef, but I'm on a diet. I mean, *was* on a diet."

"Man, y'all are really colonized," Elaine joked. "It's depressing, you know that?"

"Can't lie," Art conceded.

Elaine slapped him on his back. "I don't like wild onions or duck. And if there's no olive oil on my food, I'm not happy."

"Uh-oh. That's Old World, man."

"You told me you liked duck." Grace sniffled. Everyone turned to look at her. "You ate the roast duck I made for your birthday." Her bottom lip quivered.

"I really liked that muskrat you smoked the other day," Elaine said quickly. She didn't, really. It tasted like chewy swamp meat—but at least she got a smile out of Grace.

Fuji had not said anything. He stood and picked up his staff. "We should go."

"Yes," Monique agreed. "To the other side of the woods, where we'll meet Leroy."

"No. He's not there."

Monique sighed, stood, and hit her stick on the ground as if wielding Moses's staff. "Shit, fuck, damn."

"Is that your mantra?" John asked.

"My mother used to say that when she was pissed."

"You're mad?"

"Tired of all this."

John decided not to argue with her. "Okay, listen up," he said to the group. "We need to get going. We got no canteens. Drink what you can. Then a few more swallows."

Grace sniffed again, still offended.

"You cooked duck the only way I can eat it, Grace," Elaine said. "You can't take offense to someone's taste."

"Let's be on our way," Fuji said.

"We have other things to focus on," Elaine told Grace. "You're a great cook."

Grace said nothing and continued pouting.

"Enough," John interjected. "Everyone drink."

After they swallowed as much cold stream water as was comfortable, the travelers adjusted their boots, wraps, sandals, and clothes and followed Fuji away from their camp.

"These are kind of comfortable," Elaine said about her hide wraps three miles from base camp. "They won't last long, though."

"Not surprised," said John. "I read that Native Canadian women during the fur trade period had to make new moccasins every few days."

"And they had needle and thread, yes?"

"I dunno. Can't have everything."

"And I read," added Elaine, "that those women not only raised the children, cooked, and made other clothes, but they also trapped, skinned, and prepared the pelts for their French husbands to trade. Those men had everything, including credit for doing the work."

"That's not really what I meant," answered John. Elaine knew that. She turned and smiled at him.

They trudged across the tallgrass prairie interspersed by stands of cedars. They stopped several times to adjust the leather wraps. Art had to change a sandal.

After a few miles, Larry yelled, "Hey, I gotta go!"

"Then go," John responded.

Larry scanned their surroundings, but there were no trees in the immediate area. "Just do it, Larry," Monique said. "No one is looking."

And indeed, no one looked. No one cared.

A murder of crows followed them. The eight shiny birds flitted across the treetops like noisy ninjas, cawing and gossiping. Monique loved crows. She ran each morning with peanuts in her pockets, tossing a few to the crows who sat on highlines, fences, and mailboxes. When she first began communicating with them, they scrutinized the offerings from afar. They did not investigate the treats until she jogged away, but it took only a few days for them to recognize her in her orange visor. Soon enough, she got more than she bargained for, because the smart corvids expected their nuts. When they spotted her, they followed and cawed until she gave them what they wanted. It was all worth it when one flew over her head and dropped a shiny gum wrapper as a gift. She cried as the birds cawed from the pecan trees. She started buying peanuts in five-pound bags.

"I wish I had peanuts for them."

"What?" Art asked.

"Nothing."

After six miles, Fuji halted at a thin stream that ran through a small elm grove. "How convenient," Monique muttered.

"Yes!" Art yelped. He prostrated himself at the edge of the water, stared at the clear stream that undulated as if a ribbon tied to a fan. He dunked his head and drank.

The other dancers knelt and splashed water onto their faces. Art waded downstream, took off his skirt, and sat in the cool water.

John plunged his head in and held it under.

Monique walked downstream past Art. She unwrapped her leather straps, then settled her feet into the current. She felt immediate relief. Surreal, she thought. *No noise besides nature and us.*

The group sat in quiet contemplation for fifteen minutes. Fuji stood. "Let's keep going."

No one moved.

"When do we meet Leroy?" Monique asked. Fuji shrugged.

"So that's how it's gonna be? Steve is going ballistic right now."

"You need to trust Leroy. You do, right?"

She lifted her feet from the cool water and wrapped them again. "He better be over the next hill."

The others adjusted their footwear.

John examined a torn toenail. "Yeah, he better be." Fuji smiled and started at a brisk pace.

The dancers did not find Leroy over the next hill. They plodded to another rise a mile away. They did not see him—or anyone else—in any direction from their vantage point.

"Nothing but trees," Elaine said. "No roads. No buildings." She sat on a log and stared at the decaying limbs around it. Her wraps had come untied.

"Leroy," Monique muttered.

"What?" Art asked.

"He has to be around here."

"What if he's not?"

"He damn well better be. I'm sure Steve has declared me missing or dead by now."

Art slapped at a fly buzzing around his head. "If Leroy's not in this area, then he's waiting for us someplace else. Close."

"No mountains," Monique said. "So we're not in Colorado and this doesn't feel like Montana or Wyoming. Too warm. I mean, parts of the Rockies are warm, but there aren't any mountains here."

"We're not in the Rockies," Fuji said.

"Looks a lot like Arkansas," Art said.

"If this was Arkansas, we'd see Tyson plants, rice fields or something," Monique argued.

"We don't see big elms like this much anymore," John said as he touched the bark of a large tree. "Dutch elm disease got a lot of them."

"Now what, Fuji?" Monique asked. "Let's get on with whatever it is we're supposed to do so we can feel better about ourselves."

"I second that," Art said.

"Hell yes," Grace muttered from behind a tree where she squatted. "I've had enough of this."

"Over there," Fuji pointed.

"Over where?" John asked. "I see trees."

"The cottonwoods."

"You mean the tall ones way the hell down there? They're at least a mile away."

"Good place to camp."

"Yeah, well, Leroy better be there," Monique said.

After an hour of trudging over downfalls and rocks they approached a forest of towering cottonwoods. Ferns and old leaves covered the forest floor. Birds and butterflies flitted through the canopy while squirrels chattered at the edge of the trees, closer to the nearby stand of pecans they preferred. The ground felt soft through their leather wraps and reed sandals.

"Good spot to rest," John said. "Anyone see any bear-claw marks on the trunks?"

"No," said Elaine, who had been looking for bears since leaving camp. "But deer have been rubbing."

Monique scrutinized the scuffed tree trunk. "That's old. Deer don't start that until maybe mid-August."

"Yeah, but there's scat everywhere."

"True."

"No bears here," Fuji said with assurance.

"You sure about that?" Grace asked.

"No bears. For sure."

"Look by those trees," pointed Elaine.

"Where? I don't see anything," said John.

She jogged forty feet to some downed branches. "Check this out." She held the five-point antler above her head. "Good weapon," Elaine said, testing the weight.

"There's another over there," said Art, looking around. "And no one's around to collect money for them."

"Hey, and water's over there." Rene pointed to a thin brook almost hidden by grass lining the bank. The narrow stream curved back into the shadows of the cottonwoods.

"This is the place," Fuji said.

"Of course it is," Monique said. She did not see Leroy, nor did she see evidence that anyone had been in this spot.

The group drank the cool water. They waited for their bodies to absorb the moisture, then drank more.

"Gets me off Pepsi," said Elaine.

"Yeah, I think I'm successfully weaned from beer," agreed John. Monique craved a cold beer but didn't say so.

As the dancers ate the smoked catfish that John carried in the hide, a herd of mule deer bounded past, black-tipped tails down. "Damn. Look at that," Art said, his mouth full.

"I've seen more animals in the past few days than I have in the last year," Elaine said.

Blue jays screeched in response.

"We're in a protected area," Monique said. "An animal refuge or something."

"A really big one," Elaine agreed.

"I'll say," John said as he wiped his hands on the grass. "I think we've walked about nine miles."

"Feels like twenty," Elaine said.

Monique looked at Fuji and Rene. Both kept their eyes on their fish remnants.

"My bag stinks," John said. "Fish and bison remnants. Christ."

"We need more food," Grace said. Everyone already knew that.

"This is a burned spot," John said. "Lightning must have hit a tree, then the rains put it out fast because it didn't burn a big area. These pink firewood blossoms come in first after a fire."

Larry had wandered ahead, looking at the ground, bending over occasionally to inspect a plant or the underside of a log. He took a few more steps, then yelled. "Hey, lookee here!" He grinned.

"What?" John asked.

"Dead deer."

Hungry scavengers with sharp teeth and beaks had ravaged the two deer carcasses, a doe and a fawn.

"What killed them?" Art asked.

"Maybe coyotes came after the fawn and got both," John theorized. "Pretty tore up, so it's hard to say. Still meat on the legs."

"Eww—you're not going to eat that?" Grace asked.

"No. We can use the sinew."

"And hide," Art added.

"More shoes," Monique said.

"More shoes," John agreed.

They took the time to soak the hides to clean and soften them. After a few hours, Monique used chert to tear the tough skin into squares big enough for two pairs of small ankle-high moccasins. She molded the damp skins around Grace's and Rene's feet, then tied the hide around their ankles with longer leftovers serving as laces. After an hour, the hide had dried enough so they could take the "boots" off to harden.

John took the two forelegs of the doe and used his chert to detach the tendon behind the dewclaws and behind the knee. He split the tendon and set it on a rock to dry. "There you go."

"Go what?" Grace asked. "What do we do with that?"

"Let it dry and then I'll separate it. We'll have enough strings to wrap five, maybe six, small rocks on the sticks. The reeds we're using are dry and won't last much longer."

"Good," commented Fuji. "Now it's time to rest."

"I'm already itching just thinking about laying in that," Monique said as she watched the others bend and stack bunches of grass.

"Anybody here got allergies?" John asked. "I haven't heard any sneezes."

Rene raised her hand. "Shellfish."

"Pineapple," said Grace.

"How can you be allergic to pineapple?" Larry asked.

"I dunno. My mouth and tongue swell."

"Russian thistle and sugar," Monique said.

"Sugar?" Larry asked.

"Sucrose intolerance. It's not really an allergy, but I have a reaction to sugar. Stomach ache, mainly."

"Damn."

The dancers settled in under the darkening sky.

"As the sun set, the stars awoke," Larry began. "They sparkle like the eyes of happy children."

"Larry?" Monique said quietly.

"Yeah?"

"Shut up."

Elaine arose first the next morning. "Time to get moving," she said in a serene mommy voice. The dancers had covered themselves in grass and looked like burial mounds. Behind the camp, a sleek-furred, long-bodied mink sat on a rock, nervously assessing his surroundings. Grace stood still, watching the weasel.

John yawned. "Another mink," he said quietly.

"Where's the coffee?" Art asked, not expecting a reply.

After relieving themselves and consuming the remainder of the smoked fish that now smelled slightly rancid, the dancers resumed their journey. In late afternoon, they spied a small herd of mule deer does grazing in the shadows, their fawns protected by their mothers' long legs. The does' heads shot up when they sensed the travelers. As one, the animals strode into the forest.

"Whoa," John said. He pointed to the stand of trees across a small meadow.

"Oh my God," Grace gasped. "A bear."

"Yeah. A small one."

"He's okay," Fuji said as he kept walking.

"Hey, wait!" Grace yelped. "You're going straight toward him."

"Not anymore."

A few seconds later, the bear was gone. Fuji shrugged. "We scared it."

They continued for another hour. "Where are we going?" Monique asked.

"This way."

"Don't be a brat."

"A little farther."

"How far?"

"Just . . . through the trees some."

"This damn well better be good," she said before walking to the cottonwood grove to pee.

She returned, then faced him. "What's the point of all this? We could do this at a group therapy session."

"There are other people around," Fuji said.

"What?" Grace cried. "Where?"

"How do you know?" asked Art. "I don't see any signs of people. We've walked at least forty miles. There are no fences, trash, planes, electrical or telephone lines. No smoke rising anyplace."

"A little more north and east."

"Where, exactly, is a little north and east?" Monique asked.

"Skullyville."

"Why in the world Skullyville?" John asked.

"We're taking this route," Fuji answered calmly.

"Oh for—" Monique started, but knew it would do no good to complain. "Jeez. All right. How many of you have been there?"

Everyone raised a hand.

"Okay, then. All of us have seen the cemetery, a few houses, cows . . ."

"Give it up, Fuji," John said. "Why? There's nothing to see in Skullyville that we haven't already seen."

"People we need to see are there."

"Jesus," Art muttered.

"No. Not him."

"Why are the supposed people there and not here?" Monique asked.

Fuji focused on Monique. His pupils seemed to enlarge, as if he had entered a dark room. "There are people you need to see," he repeated. Then he smiled. "Let's get moving." He strode off, Rene behind him.

After another eight miles, they ate young lamb's-quarters and wanted more. John and Monique searched around their rest area but did not find onions or mulberries.

"I'd pull out a fingernail for some turkey eggs," Monique said.

"Me too," John said. "We gotta catch more fish."

"Or another bison. Or a deer. A rabbit. I'd even eat cilantro, and that's worst-case scenario."

John chuckled. "I'd eat beets if I had some. And I hate them."

"Must be a man thing. My husband, son, and father hate them too."

"When are sand plums ready?" he asked.

"At least another month."

"Damn."

"Yeah. I make jam."

"Let's think about finding fish."

"I'm really scared of bears," they heard Elaine say as she splashed her arms in the creek they'd followed.

"There're probably mountain lions around here too," John said. "I'd be more scared of them. You don't know they're around cause they're sneaky. They get behind you, grab your neck, and pull backward. That's how they kill deer."

"Yeah, but bears. I mean, they're wonderful and furry and sacred to many tribes, but so big."

"In the thirty years I've hunted, I've only seen six bears. Four in Colorado and two in Montana. They scare the hell out of me. I'm still afraid bears will tear through my tent, no matter where I hunt. Of course, after I saw *Jaws*, I thought a shark would get me in swimming pools."

"I saw *Night of the Grizzlies* about the maulings at Glacier," Monique said. "I imagine bears on my street in Norman when I run in the dark."

"Why are there so many here?" Elaine asked. "We've seen three."

"Only two reasons. One is that we're not in Oklahoma and we're in bear territory. Like Montana mountains. Or Glacier National Park."

"Or Alaska," Art offered.

"Yeah, but we're not in Alaska or Montana," Monique interjected.

"Don't worry," Fuji said. "They'll stay away."

Monique laughed. "Thanks, Timothy Treadwell."

"They will."

John made a fire that grew quickly thanks to the kindling Elaine and Grace gathered. Larry, Rene, and Monique found a dead, dry oak tree with enough broken limbs to keep a fire raging for days.

The night sky arrived, clear as a planetarium. There were no pollutants or streetlights. The stars shone like crystals an arm's length away. The expanse above the forest grew brighter. Soon the white edge of the moon peeked through the trees. The dancers watched as the round, white moon rose and the stars faded.

The fire crackled. Crickets and cicadas were not yet ready to sing. No one heard distant car engines, rifle blasts from hunters practicing, or cows mooing.

"Besides that fire, it's quiet," Elaine said.

"It is," Monique agreed. *I'm too used to my fan*, she thought.

"Did you see that?" Larry asked everyone. "In the southeast."

"Unless you're blind, you can't miss them," answered Grace. The air caressed the dancers' bare skin. Grace piled more old leaves on her legs.

"Cool. Falling stars," Larry said.

"Meteors," John said. "Stars don't fall."

"When a witch dies, a star falls," Monique said.

"You believe that?"

She knew they were meteors. However, she had seen witches die. "Maybe."

"Hmmmm."

"Every tribal story began with some truth," she said softly.

"Maybe," John countered.

Larry was not through contemplating. "Oh wow. Hey, one's not gonna hit us and wipe us out like the dinosaurs?"

"Doubtful," John said.

Larry gave that some thought. "Hey, John. There aren't any dino—"

"No."

"My God," Grace said quietly to Elaine. "He probably thinks *The Flintstones* is based on a true story."

A high-pitched yip, shrill and exuberant, startled the dancers. Another voice answered, followed by a chorus scattered throughout the forest.

"Wow. Coyotes," Larry said.

"They're not gonna come over here, are they?" Grace asked.

"They come into neighborhoods," Monique said.

Grace sat up. "Should we make a fence or something?"

"With what?" Art asked.

"Coyotes can get through anything we might come up with," Monique said. "Just like snakes can crawl over ropes."

"Ropes?" Grace asked. "What do you mean?"

"Some people think that if you lay down a rope around your sleeping bag snakes won't crawl over it and get into your bag while you sleep."

"Don't worry," Fuji said. "They won't bother you."

"And just how do you know that?" Monique asked.

Fuji shrugged.

"Twinkle, twinkle—hey, how come they twinkle, anyway?" Larry asked.

"They don't," John said. "Light passing through the air bends. You can still make a wish."

"I'm too tired," said Grace.

"Then I'll make one for you," said Elaine.

"How many stars are there, man?" asked Larry.

"Changes every night," answered Art. "Why don't you count them?"

"Good idea. One, two, three . . ."

As Larry lulled the dancers to sleep, the cold moon orbited quietly.

16

APESA
A PLAN

While the others slept, Fuji and Rene left camp and made their way to the creek, where they stopped beside a tall cottonwood. They inspected the deeply furrowed trunk. The stream ran alongside rocks of various sizes and through the edge of the box elder grove. A patch of pink rose mallows thrived in the mud on the opposite bank. They shone white in the moonlight.

Fuji pushed his hair behind his ears. "This old tree has seen a lot," he said. He touched the rough bark gently, as if stroking a baby's cheek. He knelt to drink. Rene dipped her right toes in.

She smiled. "Cold."

"Yup." Fuji dipped his head in, fingertip-scrubbed his scalp, then flipped his hair back over his shoulders, the cold drops flying in an arc above him.

While his hair dried, the six-feet-two Fuji propped his left foot on a log. The five-feet-four Rene wound her long black hair into a tight bun and skewered it with heavy twigs. "I'm alive. Finally." Rene said. "This is how it's supposed to be. I don't think the others understand. It's not what they expected."

"Leroy said it would be hard," Fuji said as he sat down on the log. "He's right. I miss my bread and commodity cheese."

"Smile when you say that," Rene laughed. She flicked her foot at him, water droplets landing on Fuji's legs.

"Arrowheads."

"What?"

"Over there, arrowheads are starting. Gena and I used to pick them in the summer by the creek and cook the tubers like potatoes."

Rene inspected Fuji's face. His eyebrows arched over his nose, a sign of upset. "Your mom, your sister, and the twins love you, Fuji. They'll understand."

"I know," Fuji answered. He stared at the early arrow-shaped leaves. "I hope I do right." Then Rene's smile dropped and she kneeled next to him. She took both his hands in hers.

"Fuji, you remember."

Fuji nodded, "I dream about every part of it. I know what I have to do."

Satisfied with his answer, she nodded. "I was hoping you'd say that." Fuji's eyes focused on the rustling, shiny leaves that reflected the moonlight. "Now what's wrong?"

"Just the same old thing. Memories." He turned to Rene and offered half a smile. "A lot of us died marching. We came from that direction." He nodded to the east. "From Mississippi."

"I dream too, you know. These dreams are supposed to be gifts. I know they scare you." She scanned his face. "Not everyone can recall memories. We're lucky."

"Maybe. But it's also a curse. Every place I look, I see shades of the Old Ones. I feel them being born and I feel them die. I also know the future. You know it too."

"That's why we're here," she said. "Still, lives can be changed just by one small event in the past. That event can alter everything around it. You know the pebble-in-the-water story: toss a pebble into still water and watch how it spreads ripples outward." She tossed a small rock into the water and they watched the silent circles of disturbance expand. "We're not one, but eight pebbles. The water in the creek isn't still; it moves forward. The water seeps into the dirt, nourishes the plants and animals, allows fish to live. Water goes everywhere and does things we can't imagine. No telling what'll happen."

She picked up eight small pebbles and tossed them in. Fuji and Rene considered how the tiny waves rushed outward to overlap and mingle with the others as they simultaneously moved downstream in the flow of time.

17

TIKABI
FATIGUE

Another three days and thirty miles later, the exhausted dancers collapsed onto thick broad-leaved plantain. Monique lay on her side, looking at the leaves. Her eyes widened and she sat up. Her hair had come unbraided and looked wild.

"Ha!" she yelled.

"What?" John sat up. "What's wrong?" The others turned to look at her.

"This. Right here. It's from Europe!"

"What is?" Elaine asked.

"Broad-leaved plantain. I have it in my yard. It's my ground cover."

"Well, that's great," Elaine said. "What's your point?"

"We're still here," Monique said proudly. She noted the blank stares. "This is not from here. Just like dandelions, honeybees, and the sparrows following us. These things came from Europe and Asia. That means—"

"Monique," Fuji interrupted, "many animals and plants arrived here a long time ago. With the colonists. We already talked about dandelions and sparrows. Remember?"

Monique swallowed and touched a thick leaf. She recalled how excited Steve was at learning that plantain didn't grow tall like grass. He wouldn't have to mow the entire yard.

"We're in one of the Dakotas," she said. "Or Arkansas. Maybe East Texas. I visited Stephen F. Austin State University when I was trying to decide if I wanted to major in forestry. There are a lot of trees . . ." She trailed off. East Texas was heavily populated.

Rene walked over to Monique and put her arm around her shoulder. "You're tired. We all are. Go wash up and you'll feel better. We'll fish for breakfast."

Twenty-four hours later, the dancers awoke after a deep sleep.

John felt like he had slumbered eight hours, so he was puzzled as to why it was still dark.

"Hey, man!" Larry called out. "Where's the sun?"

"Too early," Art said, his voice hoarse.

"No way. I always wake up at the same time."

"So do I," said Monique. "The only time I sleep late is when I'm sick."

"It's fog," John said. "Can't see twenty feet." He carefully made his way to where Art sat by the dead firepit with his arms around his knees. John rubbed his fists into his eyes. "Heavy moisture."

"Like a cool greenhouse," Elaine agreed. "I feel it in my lungs."

Grace ran to the group from her sleeping spot. "Oh my God!" she yelled. "Are we in hell now?" Cottonwood leaves that she used as a pillow stuck in her hair. Her clothing had shredded the week before, and Elaine had used cloth remnants to fashion her a diaper-type bottom and a wraparound bra.

"Just like a big cloud," Monique explained. "The sun will come out soon."

"It'll lift." John agreed.

"Are you sure?" Grace panted. "I saw this movie called *The Rapture* where God banished Mimi Rogers to a dark place like this. After the rapture. She stood there in the dark and—"

"This is not hell, Grace," Elaine said. "And it's not purgatory."

The dancers, except for Fuji and Rene, who were at the creek, congregated together, just in case Grace was right. They watched anxiously as the mist dissipated. The blue-and-pink sunrise turned bright.

"Thank you, God." Grace began crying.

The group felt heartened as the sky cleared and birds flew around in search of breakfast. Fuji returned from the creek, his hair and body shining from the water. He had lost fat and was transforming, like a fair-weather gym patron who joined in January and kept his New Year's resolution through summer. He seemed to have collected energy, unlike the others, who felt weak from rapid muscle loss.

Rene came behind him, also wet from her morning bath. "Sheena of the jungle," said Art.

"No, man," disagreed Larry. "She looks like that cartoon Pocahontas." He did not mean it as a criticism.

Monique did not think Rene looked like Pocahontas. With her hair slicked back, Rene looked like the young female version of Monique's father. Now that Fuji had slimmed a bit, Monique felt surprise at the reality that Fuji looked like . . . her. Same posture, same bone structure. "I'm losing my shit," Monique mumbled.

"Great fog, huh?" Rene asked, her voice deep and raspy. "Springtime is wonderful and it's turning to summer. The earth renews herself this time every year. Now we grow stronger, plant seeds, and get ready for cold times."

"Yeah, wow," said Larry.

"Don't forget what the Creator did for us," Rene said gently. "Nanishta created us and gave us life."

"We look to the women in our family to keep us healthy and happy," said Fuji.

John listened, his eyebrows knitted together. Nanishta was an old name; hardly any modern Choctaws used it. He was more familiar with Hashtali, the sun god, although Choctaws did not worship the sun. Most

Choctaws did not believe in those old cosmological stories. He did not know why Fuji threw in that comment about women. John always showed women and the earth respect.

"What's the plan for today?" Monique asked, her eyes averted from Rene and Fuji. Thunder boomed in the distance.

"This way," Fuji said.

The others picked up their walking sticks. Thunder rolled, closer this time.

"You don't have to tell me twice," Art said.

The dancers made their way through an old oak forest. The thick, craggy trunks stood silent and unbending. A recent storm had taken down hundreds of inflexible branches. Sharp twigs and tough bark littered the ground. Monique continued to wonder how Fuji knew to avoid these downed limbs, bramble patches, and poison ivy, while a thorn slid under John's toenail and a greenbrier scratched a bloody line along Elaine's thigh. Monique's plantar fasciitis, however, had abated. She thought that maybe she should try barefoot running when she got home.

"What did tribes used to do during tornado season?" Art asked.

"They knew when a twister was coming," Monique answered.

"But how?"

"They knew the rhythm of the winds. How animals acted when storms were miles away. They knew when something was about to happen. Compared to them, we know nothing."

"I know about mackerel skies," Art said. "Clouds like the sides of a fish. That means storms are on their way."

"We'll keep that in mind," she said.

Larry had squatted to poop in a patch of poison ivy a mile before and could not stop scratching his butt. They stopped at a creek so he could sit in the cool water, but without a corticosteroid cream or an oatmeal bath, he was doomed to misery. *At least he didn't wipe with it*, Monique thought.

After pushing through a stand of cedars, they emerged into a field of fledgling big bluestem grass amid large boulders. What really caught their attention were the enormous cumulonimbus clouds building in the southeast. The largest billowed upward like a white volcanic eruption.

"How in hell did those get here?" Monique asked.

"Oh no," Grace whined.

"We've been walking for three hours in the trees and couldn't see the sky, that's how," John answered.

"Heading into that time of year, I guess" Monique said. "We've been lucky."

"Lucky, my ass," Art said. The day before he had put his foot down between two fallen logs and twisted his ankle. "Damn, this hurts. I feel like the walking wounded."

"I second that remark," Elaine added. "This stone bruise on my heel is killing me."

"We have to find a place to stop, Fuji," Monique said. "We all need to adjust our wraps. Mine are coming off."

Thunder rumbled again.

"Heloba's eggs sound like they're about to roll off the table," Monique warned.

A fat opossum late for his sleep made his way up a tree when the group saw him. He froze as the humans approached.

"Big guy," said John. "What do you think?" He prepared his spear. The bare-tailed opossum turned his head, listening for their decision.

"No," said Fuji. "Leave him."

"Leave him?" asked Elaine. "We need more meat."

"No need. Come on." Fuji stood his ground until John kept walking.

Art hurried to catch up. "What was that about, Fuji? We're hungry." Fuji did not answer. "You have a vision or something?"

"Something." He hurried into the trees. Monique thought again about how easily Fuji was able to negotiate the forests, but she realized this time he followed a game trail.

They moved out of the trees and hiked another twenty minutes through a field of Indian grass interspersed with bois d'arc and pecan trees.

"This way," Fuji said as he set off at a quick pace through the sandstone at the edge of the field. A peal of lightning caused Grace to squeal. The exhausted dancers followed Fuji like hobbits trailing Gandalf on Caradhras peak.

"Why does this look familiar?" Monique asked.

"I give up," John said. "Why?"

She didn't answer until they'd struggled up rock faces laced with pine trees. They banged their toes, slipped, and cursed. All made sure they placed their sore feet securely on the slanted rock, and did not realize Fuji had stopped until he spoke.

"Hurry inside."

Monique knew where she stood. "No way."

"Just get in here."

The group made their way into the dark cave. "Fuji—" Monique began.

"Just a minute, Monique. Everyone get back as far as you can in case the rain blows in. We need to stay dry."

Raindrops hit the rocks outside the entrance.

Monique moved back in the darkness. She stared at the wall across from her and felt her lizard brain awaken. She panted.

"You okay?" Rene asked.

"This is just like Robbers Cave. In the Sans Bois Mountains."

John stood at the entrance. Sprinkles pummeled his bare chest. "She's right. I've been here a dozen times. With my family growing up. With my wife. But the cabins should be over that way."

"They will be," Fuji said. "And there are three lakes."

"Created by damming," Monique finished. "But this can't be Robbers Cave. It just looks like it."

"We haven't seen anyone in ten days," John said.

"That's because Fuji led us away from people," Monique countered. "We saw no planes, heard nothing familiar."

Elaine said, "I've been here too. There are trails and campsites, cabins, a store—"

"Not now," Rene said gently.

"I wrote on the walls," Grace said.

"You what?" John asked.

"I was seven. Came with my parents too. I had a piece of pink chalk in my pocket."

"Same here," said Art. "Camped for a few days."

"Oh my God!" Grace cried. "We're going to be on the next season of *Unsolved Mysteries*."

"This is where Belle Starr, Jesse James, and all them hid," Larry offered. "Is there treasure in here someplace?" He asked hopefully.

Monique sighed. "Sure. Why don't you go look?" She put her hands over her eyes and lay back on the sandy floor. "God, I am sick and tired of forest bathing."

The clouds roiled overhead. A rolling *BOOM* reverberated in the cave. The dense curtain of gray rain obscured the dancers' view of the trees beyond the entrance.

Grace sobbed.

"And so," Monique said, still on her back, "what are we supposed to do?"

"This was convenient," Art said as he unwrapped his feet. "A big storm blows up on us and Fuji just happens to have led us to this cave."

Fuji shrugged. "A coincidence."

"We seem to be having a lot of those."

Monique sat up. "This is not Robbers Cave. It can't be. Where are we?"

"You've known the answer to that all along," Fuji said.

"Don't get mystical with me."

Fuji smiled.

The rain picked up, causing a light spray to hit the group inside the shelters. Thunder boomed again, and a clap of lighting caused the dancers to look outside.

"My family is worried about me," Monique said. "And so are the families of everyone else here. How do you rationalize what we're doing?"

"They know what you're doing. Don't worry," Fuji said.

"Are you serious? Steve has probably gathered his entire extended family by now and they're about to torture Leroy for information."

"What do you mean, 'they know'?" Grace asked.

"Leroy talked to all of your families," Fuji said.

"I'll lose my job, you twerp," Monique said.

"Same here," Grace said between hiccups.

"I'm worried about that myself," Art added. "We're way overdue." Another sharp streak of lightning lit the sky. The dancers jumped.

"Is this what Silan and Mike did?" Monique asked. "They looked just like we do now when I saw them. After the dance. Starving, sunburned, injured."

"Not sure," Fuji answered.

"What do you mean you're not sure? You certainly seem sure about every step we've taken so far. Where did they go?"

"I don't know where they went."

"East James?"

"Dunno," he repeated.

Monique stood and swayed. She felt dizzy and weak. She breathed through her nose like a raging bull. Her heart raced and she knew if the switch flipped, she might slap him.

John stood and put his hands up, palms out. "We're all in this together," John reasoned.

Monique's nostrils flared. "In what together? What is *this*?"

"Leroy has a plan," Fuji answered.

"Those men were hungry and weak," Monique persisted. Fuji shrugged again.

"Now what are we supposed to do?" Grace asked.

"We're still going to Skullyville," Fuji said.

"If this was Robbers Cave," Monique began, "which it is not, then Skullyville is almost fifty miles away. I do fifty miles a week at home when I have the time. And with good shoes. And food. And I can rehydrate. Fifty miles in rotting leather strips and frond flip-flops is a stupid idea. Unless Skullyville is just down the road."

"No, you are correct."

"About what?"

"It's about forty-six miles from here."

Grace gasped. "Are you crazy?"

"And I feel like shit," Art said. "I need a shirt. I'm getting too much sun."

"We can't walk much farther, Fuji," Monique said. She cocked her head. "Oh, I see. You mean we go a little farther, then Leroy will drive us there." Everyone looked at Fuji.

"Maybe," he answered.

"Better be," Monique whispered.

The rain suddenly stopped and the world outside turned bright. Art sighed. "When do we start?"

For the next three days, the dancers followed Fuji through open meadows and dense forests, across streams, and over rock outcroppings. The morning dew highlighted spiders' webs and cooled their legs. It rained on the second afternoon, but they saw the clouds approaching and hurried to a thick grove of post oaks, where they hastily constructed a thatched lean-to made from downed branches, leaves, and clumps of grass they pulled out by the roots. The group sat on decaying logs as they huddled underneath their makeshift roof until the shower passed.

They found water at least once a day, but hunger pangs gnawed. Mulberries, dandelions, and clover were the most reliable plants. Often, what they thought were wild onions turned out to be thick grass. Grace caught a few perch from a small lake. Each night, Monique labored to make the ground conform to her body by removing rocks and digging a small depression for her hips.

Everyone felt the sting of burned skin and chapped lips, and were down to their last pair of cattail sandals. John tripped over ground vines and sprained his wrist in an attempt to keep his face from slamming into the trunk of a downed oak. Monique was determined to keep her running shorts. Every evening, when they camped by a stream, she rinsed them and allowed them to dry during the night. So far, they were hold-ing up.

One night, Monique watched the twinkling stars. *How long have they sparkled?* she wondered. The North Star was in the same place she saw it almost two hundred years later. *Later.* That did not even make sense.

"Hey, man. How long have we been out here?" Larry asked.

"Nine, maybe ten days," Monique answered.

"You sure? I thought it was more like two weeks."

"Nope."

"I thought eleven," John said.

"Twelve," Elaine chimed in.

"Huh," Larry mused. "Feels longer."

"I'll say," Grace added. "Time doesn't fly when you're not having fun."

They ran out of speculations and fell silent. A warm breeze blew some old leaves across Monique's face. *Will that wind keep going? Quiet, then strong, continuous, and never tired, like the oceans' currents? Did I feel this same wind before we came back here?*

Back here. Monique sat up and gasped. "Back here," she said.

"What?" Larry asked. He rolled over to look at her.

"We really are here."

"Yes," Fuji agreed. "We are."

Monique wondered if she would die in this time. What if they all did? Who would bury them? Would their bones scatter? She stared at the stars until her eyes closed and her thoughts faded.

For the next two days, fair weather allowed their kindling to start quickly. The days grew warmer. The dancers ate fish, lamb's-quarters, and dandelion leaves. One evening, Larry returned from a forage with a handful of grass-hoppers. Monique grimaced as he tossed the hapless insects onto the fire, then after a few seconds used sticks to move them to the grass.

"Nice and crunchy," he said. No one else indulged.

Monique found a stand of mulberry bushes and the group ate handfuls of the plump berries, coming away with purple-stained lips and fingers. They drank clear water, although they all knew it contained fish pee and animal excrement, tiny bugs and even smaller microbes. Still, the pure water tasted unlike their tap water back home. No chemicals, no garbage, and no oil sheen. No one became sick, except for one afternoon after Larry had consumed handfuls of unripened mulberries.

"They have to be black, Larry," Monique told him. "Your system isn't going to appreciate those berries right now."

"Hey, man," he responded. "They're just a little harder than the others. Still sweet. Sorta."

Monique knew they were mainly bitter and he would either puke or have diarrhea. As she expected, Larry kept returning to grove of trees downstream from the small creek. The last time, he stayed twenty minutes. John went to check on him.

"Yep. Just like you said," he explained. "He's sitting in the water now."

Despite his ailment, Larry appeared to be the only dancer besides Fuji and Rene who enjoyed their predicament. He constantly commented on flowers, trees, and the clear air. The day before, he'd held his arms out and twirled, like Julie Andrews in *The Sound of Music*.

Elaine now stood straight, but she remained introspective and quiet. Activist Grace had become sullen and thoughtful. Her over-plucked eyebrows and short bangs had grown in some and she appeared more relaxed. She made herself useful as a fisher. Using string braided from the bison's tail, she made hooks with small sticks, one tied to the other with hair to form a pointed J. Then she skewered a grasshopper. She caught several catfish in the creek the first morning after they'd left the cave, and the catch inspired everyone to try.

"What kind is that?" Elaine asked when Grace pulled out a long, pointy-nosed fish.

"That's a pike," said Fuji. "They eat everything."

"Keep him," said John.

They also found camas growing by the creek. "Look! All right," John said excitedly as he ran across the stream to inspect the blue-petaled flower. "These are a lot like onions. We can cook these with the fish."

"What about sunflowers?" Elaine asked.

"Not till later in the summer," John answered. "We can save some seeds and grow our own next year. High protein and easy to store."

"Next year?!" Grace cried out before taking a deep breath and counting to ten. Fishing and quiet time-outs helped preserve Grace's sanity. Elaine, on the other hand, emerged as a leader. She took the initiative in finding food and served as the architect of their lean-tos. She used branches as the frame, then wove in grasses. For roofs, she used the ends of pecan branches, full of plump green leaves that the squirrels chewed off and dropped to the ground. And they worked—when it rained lightly for two days, the group stayed mostly dry.

Larry had not changed much. After he made a crack about needing ketchup for his fish, John took him aside and told him to watch his mouth, and he made an effort not to complain. Larry continued to take delight in catching bugs and roasting them, especially grasshoppers and crickets with huge hind legs, that he called "children of the earth." He talked to himself, but the group figured that was his normal behavior. Fuji and Rene stayed together for the most part. Although they gamely answered frequent questions, everyone sensed they were hiding something.

On the sixteenth day, Grace paced around their campsite. "Can't do this much longer," she said.

"Do what?" Larry asked.

"I just can't."

Art smoothed his mullet. "You have to."

"No, I don't. Are we supposed to stay here until we die? What kind of joke did Leroy play on us?"

"Not a joke," John said. "This is the real thing, unfortunately. We got what we asked for."

Grace coughed. "Then we're stupid."

"Maybe. Life is for learning."

She twirled a hank of hair between her fingers. "Then I guess I'm doing a good job at living."

One afternoon, after a slow and treacherous exploration of a hilltop grove of thorny honey locust trees, Art, John, and Monique stood in a field of green clover. Monique watched as the two men absently stroked their flat bellies. At "arrival," as the dancers called it, they had weighted twenty pounds more. Art felt pleased at reducing to the same size he was when he ran cross-country in high school and his first—and only—year of college.

Monique, however, possessed little excess fat at the start of the dance and now she felt light-headed as her body fed on precious muscle tissue. She could see from the crepey skin on their bellies how quickly they all were losing weight, and they would become sick and weak if they did not find more food. Fish and mulberries were plentiful. Those foods were fine and dandy to use if you were an Indigenous chef and wanted to make a career out of showcasing precontact foods—but that gimmick only worked when you also had plenty of other ingredients. She knew of no Native food activist who only ate precontact foods, and if they said they did, they were full of shit. It simply wasn't possible without community effort. Besides, why would you do that if you had ample supplies of wheat bread, chicken, eggs, cheese, beer, and apple pie? She worried they might starve to death.

Art rubbed his gut and twisted around to look at his rear.

"Skinny butt too," John told him. "You're starting to look like Larry."

"Thanks for the image."

"Just like waking from the starving time." Fuji walked up behind them, grinning as if the carnival had arrived. Monique looked him over. Fuji's face had thinned, his brown skin had tanned even darker, and he seemed older. When he turned his face to the left, he looked a lot like her late brother, Brin.

John rubbed his hand over his taught abdomen. "You act like these were the good old days."

"Depends on how you look at it," Fuji said. "They were good once the people figured out what to eat and how to get it. When everyone worked for the group and not just for themselves."

They watched Grace harvest thistles a short distance away. They took John's suggestion and roasted the roots. He had no idea of their nutritional value, but the thin plant did not taste bad.

"I hope I'm not allergic," Grace said. "They're sticking into my arms and I better not get any little splinters, cause we don't have tweezers."

"Wash in the creek after," John yelled.

"What're these?" she held up green stalks topped with round heads of yellow petals.

"Those are butterballs. We can't eat those."

John turned back to Fuji. "That last part about not being in it for themselves . . . lots of Indians are out for themselves, and power." He rubbed his palm over his short hair. "Ethnocentric too, like their tribe is the best tribe. In 2022, I mean. Some people are tribal and they try to keep the old ways together. You know, to speak the language and all that. But most don't. I think that as man evolves, he gets more selfish."

"You think?" Fuji considered that.

Art had had this discussion with his friends on the Tribal Council numerous times. "Members of our tribe are self-centered. Think about the factions we have. Some full-bloods say the mixed-bloods aren't as Indian as they are. Mixed-bloods say the fulls are backward. Some Christians say that those of us who try to keep tribal traditions are headed for hell. Those who lost the election say the winners don't have the tribe's best interest in mind. Grace says that all the time."

"Maybe man is insecure," Fuji said. "We've got so much technology and things go so fast that it's hard to keep up. Indians especially. We end up competing with each other instead of with the white men."

"You like it here, don't you?" Art asked.

"It's what I wanted. It's what we need."

"Are you sure?"

"Yes."

They stood in silence a moment, watching as Grace struggled to pull thistles from the ground. They heard the slap when she squashed a mosquito on her neck.

"And you think it's possible to return to traditions."

"Yes, I do."

"We may waste away first," Art said.

"Monique still doesn't really believe we're in a different time," John said.

"She believes it. She just hates to admit it," Fuji said.

"I'm still not convinced, but I understand the lesson."

"Do you?"

John sighed. "Actually, no."

18

Nitak hopaki
Long-Ago Days

"Come on," Fuji said.

"A man with a mission," said John. "What's the deal, Fuji?"

"Come on."

"Fuji? Wait!" yelled Elaine.

Fuji appeared not to hear. He walked faster until he reached an oak grove, then he pushed his way through. When he broke free of the branches, he dropped his spear and spread out his arms. Elaine reached him first and would have dropped her stick too if she still had it. A hundred yards away stood two small houses made of logs with mud filler. Both had porches with overhangs and one had a rocking chair next to the wooden door. Streams of gray smoke from their rock chimneys raced toward the sky.

"Oh boy," John said. "Wait a minute. Where are we?" He grabbed Fuji's arm and pulled him back. "Everyone, come on. Get into the trees. We need to talk."

John led them away from the settlement and down an embankment. "Fuji, who are those people?"

"I don't know."

"You don't know?" Monique asked. "You've been telling us that we're headed to Skullyville and will encounter people we're supposed to meet."

"Yeah," Grace chimed in. "Now what? These houses look really poor. What if they're crackheads or moonshiners?"

"They're not," Rene answered.

"How do you know?" Monique asked. "Whoever lives here is barely getting by."

"There's more," Fuji said.

"More what?" Monique questioned.

"Come on."

The group skirted the properties and followed Fuji through the trees. He slowly approached the edge of the forest, and the others gathered around him. "That's the agency building." He pointed to a long, mud-covered log structure with wood shingles and a porch that spanned the length of the building. Three white men dressed similarly in light-colored trousers, off-white button-down shirts, and dark jackets sat on the porch bench. Two held rifles.

"Military," John whispered.

Fuji nodded, then backed up. He led them around the base of the embankment, then found a game trail and quietly walked into the trees, holding the branches so they would not whip the people behind him. He stopped. The others moved as silently as they could through the brush. When they caught up to him, they halted short and gaped.

Under the dark, cool canopy of tall trees, the group saw dozens of graves, some right next to each other. Other graves were situated randomly, like giant mole mounds rising amid new green shoots.

Art said, "Damn. A cemetery."

"There're dozens of graves," Grace said. "My God. There's even more over there to the right. Some look fresh."

"Yes," Fuji agreed. He walked to the edge of the graveyard. The others followed him into the open space. Grasses had been pulled from around the graves in an attempt to neaten the area. Large oaks shaded the graveyard, the branches so dense that the place stayed in perpetual shadow.

Fuji moved to a fresh grave that had a headstone. The others gathered around. "LeFlore," John said. "Not surprising. Lots of Choctaws have that name."

"Yeah, but the headstone says this person died in 1834," Monique said. She stared at the rock, then shifted her gaze to the mound of dirt. "Maybe they recently moved him."

Fuji shook his head. "No. He died within the last year."

Blood pounded in Monique's temples. She felt like she did when she saw her first autopsy. The ground started to spin. John took hold of her arms. "Steady," he said.

"I'm okay."

"Sure?"

"No."

Fuji strode past the cemetery to a road that led through the trees. Rene hurried to walk beside him.

"Hold up," Art said. The pair turned. "What is this? Where is this?"

"Hell," Monique said. "*When* is this?"

"We'll talk in a minute," Fuji said. "Come on."

Fuji meandered through the trees, then slowed his passage down a steep embankment of jutting rocks.

"That cemetery looked familiar," Monique said. "Steve, Robbie, and I did a commemorative march a few years ago. We met at Skullyville."

"Skullyville's not even a town anymore," Elaine said. "It's more of a settlement."

"It's about to be a town," Fuji said. "Iskvlli Kaunti. Also known as Money Town. It was an important town after removal. Trading, annuities are passed out, a way station. In twenty years, the Skullyville Constitution will be written here. This will be part of the Butterfield Overland Mail route. It'll fade after the Civil War."

"I don't recall seeing all those graves," John said.

Monique panted even though she had not exerted herself. She did not remember seeing as many either.

"Maybe some just got covered by dirt, or something grew on top of them," Elaine suggested.

"My God," Grace said. "We really are in a different time." Monique noticed that Grace did not cry.

Fuji stopped in a large clearing. He motioned for the others to sit on an oak log. Monique remained standing.

"This is one of the first settlements for those who were removed."

"Are we going to meet them?" Monique asked.

"No."

"But you said we needed to see them."

"And you did."

She closed her eyes and refrained from blurting out *You little shit*.

Instead, she looked through the trees to the large open area beyond the grove. She took a few steps toward the space. Trees had been removed, and she spotted what appeared to be wooden football goalposts, but closer together. She squinted. Some kind of material waved from the tall posts. She studied the grass. It was worn, churned up in spots. Enormous cloud shadows ran over the ground.

"Is that—?" She pointed.

Rene smiled. "I believe it is."

"What?" Larry asked.

"*Ishtaboli* field," Monique said. "Stickball. Holy shit."

She turned suddenly to Fuji. "George Catlin will draw this."

Fuji nodded. "He already did."

"We're in a Ray Bradbury story, aren't we?" Monique asked quietly.

"Who?" Larry asked.

She ignored him. "Looks like there was a recent game. The field is chewed up. Hundreds of people played and even more watched."

"Catlin must have painted it recently," John said.

"Catlin. Oh yeah," Larry recalled. "And that guy on the cover of a book with two sticks. And a horsetail. Red legs." He scanned the field in hopes of seeing the subject of Catlin's iconic painting, the ballplayer Tullock Chishko.

Monique felt a wave of vertigo. The district leaders Thomas LeFlore, Moshulatubbee, and Nitakechi were still alive. The tribe was just getting their feet back under them. There should be a post office established by now. In about ten years, the Irish would suffer from the potato famine and people of this town would send money.

And her ancestors were alive! Her mother's side of the family settled in Kully Chaha. The other side, led by the Lighthorseman Wood Nall, built their first home in Boggy Depot. Maybe they were there right now. But that was about 120 miles southwest.

She never had relatives in Skullyville. The first time she visited the place, she sensed that the settlement would always be more than cows and a few houses. In many respects, Skullyville the town had died, but its essence remained very much alive. Now, she knew that to be true. She felt the touches of those spirits who endured horrors, lurched to the finish line after the removal march, and then watched their families die. Their spirits flitted through the trees and hung in the air.

"We're going on." Fuji interrupted her musing.

"On?" Grace whined.

"North."

"How far north?" Grace asked skeptically.

"Four miles. Not far."

The group followed Fuji through the dense forest. Greenbriers caught and tore their skirts and left long bloody scratches in their skin.

Once again, Monique wondered how Fuji knew where he was going. He never seemed to use the sun for direction.

"Where we headed?" John asked Fuji.

"Can we get food?" Art asked.

"I wouldn't count on it," Monique answered.

Ten minutes later, the dancers climbed a brushy rise. Fuji stood at the top and looked back at them. Monique was the first to stand next to him.

"Yup. Like I said, John, don't count on it."

The dancers took in the expanse in front of them. "Nothing here, man," Larry said.

"Mounds are here," Grace said.

"You have a grasp of the obvious," Art replied.

"Spiro Mounds," John said.

"Oh," Art said. "Of course."

"We came here when I was a kid," Elaine said. "After we visited Robbers Cave. There were roads, a center, and kiosks. They keep the grass mowed."

"Not now, man," Larry said.

Monique snorted. "Can't have everything."

"What are they?" Larry asked. "Hills?"

"This is part of the Mississippian culture," Monique said. She had also visited the archeological site, but got a refresher about the place from reading Robbie's sixth-grade school paper. "No one has lived here for five, six hundred years. This area was used for ceremonies and burials during the last part of that period."

"So those are burials?"

"Just one is. The Craig Mound. I don't see it from here. The biggest flat-topped one is Brown Mound." She pointed east. "Craig Mound is south of that, I think. Treasure hunters took it apart in the 1930s. All that incredible stuff. Copper, pots, carvings, feathers, leather, things made from plants that would normally fall apart in the air stayed preserved inside. Many things went to Europe. Some collectors sent back the artifacts, but we'll never see most of them. At some point, the looters used dynamite. It was a real disaster."

"Don't you mean it will be?" John reminded her.

"I guess so."

"Can't we do something to prevent the looting?" Grace asked.

"No," Fuji said, "we can't."

"But surely we can find a way to—"

"There's nothing we can do about it, Grace," Rene interjected. "We can't take anything with us, there's no place to hide the contents. It has to happen."

Grace sighed.

"Societies lived here for centuries," Monique said quietly. She had always wondered about the day-to-day life of those long-ago people. Museum dioramas of historic Indians creeped out Steve, but fascinated her. The movie *Apocalypto* had knocked the breath out of her. She knew Mayans were pissed at how Mel Gibson portrayed them as single-minded violent chest rippers. Still, the beauty and the *otherness* of the people mesmerized her.

"Just mounds," Larry said. "We can't look inside them, right?"

"Right," Fuji said. "Walk around if you want."

"Craig Mound," John said and started off. The others followed through the bushes. When they got to the edge, the dancers stood staring, transfixed at the undisturbed thirty-three-foot-high mound covered by a variety of plants.

"So much inside of this," Monique said. "I wish there was a way to protect it."

"No." Fuji turned to the north. "Come on. Camp isn't far."

"Stop. You don't mean Fort Coffee, do you?"

Fuji pointed north. "About two miles."

"We got this far," Grace said. "May as well."

"Why?" Monique asked. "If this is 1835, then white soldiers are still building it right now. They'll be looking for whiskey runners and will stop anyone in the area. That's the main reason the fort is there. Booze is illegal. Why would we go there?"

"Clothes and food," Grace said.

Monique stared at her a few seconds. "Grace, look at us. We would have a lot of explaining to do. We look like we just came over the trail."

"Who said they have to see us?" John asked. Fuji slapped him on the back.

Once again, they set off. Footsore and hungry.

After two slow miles, the group stopped next to a creek. The sun had set, but the stars began illuminating the clear sky.

"Oh man," John said. "My feet have had it."

"Mine too," Elaine said.

"I need more sandals," Art said. "Is there another lake around here?" Monique thought he asked that question as casually as if he needed directions to Dick's Sporting Goods.

Monique leaned against one of the thick cottonwood trees, her knees bent so she could inspect her toenails. Remnants of maroon polish looked like bruises. The others dealt with aches and pains, mainly emanating from their feet. Monique's were calloused, so tenderness wasn't an issue, but two deep cracks in her left heel were. The pain only compounded her worry about Robbie and Steve.

"Make do with the leather wraps until we find more cattails," John said.

"The fort should be through the trees," Fuji said. "I think it's best if just four of us go."

"And do what?" Monique asked.

"There should be a separate structure with supplies. I know there're three main buildings, but I don't know about the smaller ones."

"Wait a minute," Monique said. "If we waltz in there, someone will report it. How do we know this visit won't be recorded—and someday historians won't read about us?"

"They won't."

"Report it or record it?"

"Neither."

"What about shoot us?"

"No."

"All right. I'll go," Monique said.

"Me too," Grace said.

"I'm in," Art added.

"The rest of you stay here," Fuji said. "We'll get clothes if we find them."

"I'd rather have shoes," John said.

"You get what you get," Monique chided.

"We should go now before it's too dark," Fuji said. "The men might be eating now."

"Lead on," she said.

"The rest of you, drink water and eat some of those berries. We may be moving fast."

"Jesus," Elaine said. "Don't get caught."

Fuji turned and pushed through a tangled wall of interlocked branches. Art, Monique, and Grace followed him through the unforgiving trees.

"Damn, this is thick," Art said. "My skirt is totally shot."

"Hell, my skin is shot," Grace huffed. "I look like I'm in a slasher movie."

"Shush," Monique admonished. "Both of you are as loud as squirrels."

"Huh?" Art asked.

"Little squirrels make all kinds of noise in the woods. Try to be a deer."

Fuji stepped out of the scratchy forest, followed by the others. They had emerged to the east of Fort Coffee. The fort complex was composed of three main buildings arranged like a sharp-cornered U atop Swallow Rock that allowed an unobstructed view of the Arkansas River and whiskey-running boats. The river shone in the moonlight. A heron by the shore squawked.

Art started to speak and Fuji put up his hand, then crouched behind a wide bush. Monique, Art, and Grace did the same. "Two men are smoking outside," Fuji said quietly.

"I wonder if that smaller add-on structure to the building on the left is storage." Monique pointed with her chin. "There's a barrel outside."

"Could be."

"And the door's on the outside, facing the woods. We should try that first."

"Good idea," Fuji said. "Let's wait until these guys go inside."

The four dancers watched as the men talked and traded the hand-rolled cigarette back and forth. After the small red glow dissipated, the men walked down the wooden sidewalk and disappeared around the corner.

"Let's go," Monique said. She pushed aside the sharp branches and led the others to the shed. "No lock." She pulled the short rope that served as the handle. The strap hinges squealed as she opened the door. She stopped and then pulled slowly.

Art stepped inside the structure. Moonlight illuminated items inside the door. "Bingo," he said. "A crate of boots and shoes."

Grace followed him. "Stacks of pants on the shelf, I think. Maybe shirts. Here are a couple of knives and a tin cup."

Monique and Fuji crowded in. "How many shoes are in there?" Fuji asked.

"Hang on. Lemme count. At least a dozen individuals. They're just tossed in here."

"If that crate's not heavy, take the whole thing. Grace, grab the pants. Monique, you take the pile of shirts."

"Kind of greedy," Monique said.

"What we don't use we'll leave at the base of the hill. I'll grab that bag of socks."

Art, Grace, and Monique filled their arms and exited. Fuji continued to rummage inside. "Hurry," Grace warned.

Fuji finally emerged, holding a large bundle. Monique closed the door behind them.

"Let's go," Fuji said as he rushed into the thick trees. The thieves carried their booty back to camp and dropped the loot in front of the small fire. "Someone match the pairs of shoes and sort them by size," he said. "Largest to smallest. Lay out the clothes too. We should move quickly."

"No underwear, huh?" Elaine asked.

"There may have been long johns in the back of that room, but we couldn't hang around," Monique said. "Footwear is crucial. What we got, Art?"

"Three pairs of boots and six of shoes. They're pretty much the same size. Like around a men's eight or nine."

"Shit," Monique said.

"Except for this pair. More like a twelve."

"Really?" She eyed the brown boot. "That's gotta be a fourteen and looks like a canoe. That's way too big, even for me."

"What about pants and tops?" Elaine asked.

"Dozen of each," Grace said. "Pants are grayish or brown. One is sorta white. Same with tops. Couple of these are pullovers. All long sleeved. Here are the two largest." She threw one to Fuji and another to John.

"Shoes first," Monique said.

The group tried on hard-soled footwear, trading sizes, complaining at their discomfort. "Man, I can't see getting too far in these," Art said. "These are my size, but they rub."

"Are socks in this bag?" Fuji threw it to Rene.

She held up a thin, gray sock. "Yeah, but really thin."

"Better than nothing," Elaine said.

Monique knew that a thin sock could cause blisters, but she did not want to put that idea into their minds.

"All right. If you can't find any that fit, I got these," Fuji said as he unrolled two soft deer hides.

"Oh yeah," Monique said.

"By the way, where are we going now?" Elaine asked.

"To Kully Chaha."

"How far's that?"

"Maybe fourteen or fifteen miles. As the eagle flies."

"Sugar Loaf Mountain is there," Monique said.

Fuji nodded. "Yes. Nvnih Chufvk. We're not climbing it."

"Why?" Monique asked.

"It's a tough climb."

"No, I mean why are we going there?"

"There's a settlement there. You need to see it."

"You said that about Skullyville."

"And now you know for sure where we are and when."

"So?"

"We'll meet people there."

After deciding on their wardrobe, the dancers started their trek. Monique, Art, and Rene opted for deer-hide anklets they made with the pilfered knives. The others wore boots, but they weren't happy about them. The pants ranged from soft cotton to scratchy wool. Monique wore the top she danced in, along with gray pants that fit like capris. She still had her mesh-lined running shorts underneath. The others chose to wear the shirts with the sleeves rolled up. Larry had to use his skirt as a belt. Everyone carried his or her old clothes.

"Oh man, these shoes hurt," Larry whined. "The socks rub."

"Boots are stiff," Grace winced. "Good thing we kept our sandals."

The dancers walked all day, stopping to adjust clothing and to drink from every stream. They kept looking behind them, expecting to see a posse on horseback.

"No one will follow," Fuji said, not looking back. "They'll think we went downriver."

After a mile, John abandoned his boots and wrapped his feet with hide strips. "Much better," he said.

"We'll camp in that low spot," Fuji said. "See, there's a creek."

The weary dancers spread out in search of food. Grace found a turkey nest with nine eggs that they cooked three at a time in the tin cup. Larry collected dark fruit from a mulberry tree and Monique found a patch of dandelions and chickweed.

An owl's hoot reverberated through their campsite. Monique sat up and reached for her Glock, then remembered it was locked inside her cruiser 187 years in the future. She panted. She looked up and saw the outline of a great horned owl perched on a leafless branch. The large bird raised its wings slightly and puffed up, then settled and hooted once more. The predator's eyes assessed her.

A hand squeezed her shoulder and she gasped. "Monique," Fuji said.

"Shit." Her heart pounded against her ribs. Some Natives believed that owls could be harbingers of bad luck and death. Monique knew firsthand that some owls were shape-shifting witches. Her recent run-in with one such evil family almost killed her, Leroy, and Chris.

"It's just an owl."

"Are you sure?"

"Yes." He squeezed her again. "The witches don't know we're here."

Monique eyed the bird and watched it gracefully launch from the branch and disappear into the sunrise like a World War II Curtiss O-52 Owl aircraft.

19

Nvnih Chufvk
Sugar Loaf Mountain

"And we're off," John said in the morning. "Again." He straightened his back and groaned. Monique knew his sciatic nerve was bothering him, but he wouldn't say so.

"Only a few more miles this time," Grace said. She stood tall, flipped her tangled hair, and pointed to the horizon like Sacagawea.

Grace has come a long way, Monique thought. *In more ways than one. More confident and less whiny.*

The group started slowly, covering two miles in an hour.

"Break time," John said. The group left the thin game trail and entered the shade of blackjack oaks, where they adjusted their footwear. The women rebraided their hair. After twenty minutes, they walked out into bright afternoon. Suddenly, what looked like a cloud passed overhead, obscuring the sun.

"That's not a cloud," Monique said.

"Oh my God," Elaine gasped.

"What are those?" Larry asked.

"Not geese," Monique answered.

John stood. "Holy shit. I think those are pigeons. Passenger pigeons."

The group watched the spectacular flock, their wings making a whistling sound unheard by anyone living after 1870. Humankind had systematically wiped them out.

"We're such assholes," Monique said. "Minks, bears, wolves, bison, pigeons . . ."

"This is the hard part," Fuji said. "We get to see what came before."

"Yeah, before this is all ruined," Larry said.

Monique realized they were no longer on the game trail. "Hey, this is a road. Look. Grass down the middle. Wagons and horses have been on this."

John said, "I agree."

"Where're the people?" Larry asked.

"Can't be far," Monique said. "Those road apples are fresh."

"Maybe we can get horses," Larry mused.

"Hang on," Art said. "The people might see us as enemies."

"They won't," Fuji said.

"Let's go slow," Monique said. "We need to think about this and decide what to say when we run into them."

Too late. They had been spotted. Three men on horses emerged from the oak grove on the opposite side of the road.

"I hope this is the welcome wagon," said John. A branch broke behind the group. They turned to see another man emerge from behind bushes. They were all carrying rifles. Hunters. They were dressed similarly to the dancers, in cloth pants and beige shirts. One donned a worn suit with a thin tie. All wore boots or leather shoes. One had shoulder-length hair; the other three wore theirs short and shaggy. All had dark skin. The riders looked to be from twenty to fifty years in age, although the sun and weather probably contributed to their appearance.

"Are they friendly?" Grace asked.

"It's okay," Fuji said. He put his hand on her shoulder. "We'll be fine." Grace continued to stare at the strangers.

The groups stopped about ten feet from each other, assessing what they'd found. The men behind the dancers walked cautiously around to join the horsemen. The man in front had a pocked face. Another man had a crooked nose.

John thought that even though he, Leroy, Fuji, and Rene were supposedly full-bloods, these men looked more so. He once again considered the signs that somewhere down the ancestral line, more than one *nahullo* had contributed white blood to his family woodpile.

Elaine also gaped. These men were not like movie Indians wearing makeup and reproductions of traditional clothing. These people were simultaneously flawed, dirty, and tidy. She glanced away, then looked back.

A stout man with bushy black eyebrows said, "*Aiokpanchi*," which all eight travelers understood meant *welcome*, but he spoke with an accent a bit different than Leroy and Ninah's.

Fuji repeated it for the group. "He said, 'welcome.'" The men looked quickly at him. Then they spoke among themselves. The equestrians studied his face.

Fuji introduced himself. "*Sa hochifo vt* Fuji." The leader came closer and spoke to Fuji. John thought he caught *apa*, which means eating.

"He said to 'come eat and become presentable again,'" Fuji translated for the dancers.

"We do look odd," said Elaine as she glanced down at her men's clothing.

The lead rider walked with a slight limp. He stood several inches shorter than Fuji, but his demeanor made him taller. "*Halito*, friend. *Chim achuckma? Sa hochifo vt* Geletumma Chinisa." He pointed to the other men. "Simpson Taylor, Isom Folsom, Lemus Battiest." The three men nodded.

"*Am achukma*," Fuji responded.

"*Chi hochifo nanta?*"

Fuji turned to his friends. "Introduce yourselves."

"Uh, John."

"Grace."

The leader asked Fuji another question. "They want your complete names," Fuji told them.

"Oh, right. I guess they do have first and last names," John said.

One man snickered. Then another coughed and grinned. Rene started to speak, haltingly. All the men laughed.

"We understand you," the leader said.

"Oh," Fuji said, mollified. "Well, in that case, everyone, go ahead." And they did.

"Blue Hawk?" one of the men with short hair asked Monique. His wore a homespun shirt with the sleeves rolled up.

"My husband is Pawnee."

"Huh," the man said, as if he was not familiar with the tribe.

When Larry said, "Larry Chipmunk. I mean Larry Chinisa," Gele-tumma Chinisa jerked his head up and looked more closely at Larry. The man next to him made a comment and gestured to the dreadlocked man.

"Are you hungry?" the man asked. Everyone nodded. "This way."

"Now what?" asked Larry quietly as they began walking. "Is that guy related to me?"

"Looks pretty clear, Larry," said John.

"Fuji?"

"What?" He and Rene walked along holding hands, smiles on their faces.

"How's that for an answer?" John asked. For once, Larry stayed quiet.

After a half hour of fast walking, they arrived at a community of a dozen homes spaced fifty feet apart in a clearing and built of wood planks and shingles. Arbors similar to ones the dancers had seen at modern dances sat interspersed between the homes. Chickens scratched in the dirt and a horse whinnied from a small corral. Large pecans, their leaves green and lush, shaded the homes. A few foot-wide trails led from the camp. Children chased one another.

Rangy dogs sniffed the newcomers. The dancers smelled meat cooking. "This looks to be the same time as it was in Skullyville?" John said.

"It is," Fuji answered.

"This world is gone, but it's alive and breathing," Elaine said. "How can this be?"

"It just is," Rene said, her cheeks flushed with excitement. "It's hard to breathe. My mind's going too fast."

The men led them to the center house. Geletumma Chinisa pushed the door open and motioned for them to enter the darkness. There was only one small window and it took a moment for their eyes to adjust to the dim light.

"Sit and rest," he said before leaving.

"Holy shit," Art said.

John licked his lips and scanned the ceiling, the walls, the stone chimney. "Yeah, this is—"

Two young women in calico dresses and stained aprons entered and set wooden bowls full of *tanfula* on the table. One took spoons from her apron pocket. "I'm Viney."

The women did not look down or appear at all subservient. They looked the newcomers directly in the eyes and smiled. The woman with a pronounced cowlick at her hairline said, "My name's Talce. There's more."

"Hey, thanks," Art said with a wave as they left.

"'Hey, thanks'?" John mocked. "What was that?"

"I know, I sound like a redneck Texan trying to speak Spanish from a guidebook."

"Just say it," Fuji said. "*Yakoke.*"

"Hey, this tastes different from how I make it," Grace said. "And it looks different."

"They ground the corn," Fuji said. "They soaked it in lye ash and cooked it all day with hickory oil. Probably squirrel is in there too."

"I do that too. I mean, I thought I was doing it the right way."

John scrutinized his dish. "It's really, uh, thick."

Fuji and Rene beamed.

"We use cornmeal that's already ground," Fuji said. "Not many use hickory oil."

"No squirrels neither," added Larry. "Could use some salt."

"Hush," warned John.

An old woman in a bright calico dress and deer-hide ankle boots entered, followed by two middle-aged women in similar clothes. One of the younger women wore her hair in a bun and the other wore hers neatly combed down her back. The dancers stood. The old woman looked each man up and down, then walked to Elaine, interested in the tattoo peeking through her shirt buttons.

"*Sa hochifo vt* Sara Rose," the elder said as she tilted her head to inspect the colorful tat.

She then scrutinized Fuji, appraising him like a piece of art. "Hmmmm," she murmured. Fuji stood still, holding his bowl. Then she turned to Larry, her eyes narrowing. She reached up to his hair, but did not touch it. She said something to the two other women, who laughed quietly.

She turned her attention to Monique. Her eyebrows rose. She looked back and forth between Fuji and Monique, and then she quickly turned her gaze to Rene. Her mouth opened as if surprised. She looked at Monique one more time before turning to leave. The other women followed.

Monique wished she had a beer.

"What did she say about my hair, man?"

"She wants to brush it out," said Rene.

"Hey, no way. You can't brush it." He touched his locks protectively.

"Let's eat," Monique said. "We need it."

The group spooned the mush into their mouths. It had no spice, salt, or sweetness. "Earthy," Elaine said. No one responded.

The door opened and the elder woman entered, carrying a pie with a lattice crust. She set it on the table, winked, then left.

"Oh my God," Monique said.

Elaine spotted a wooden spoon in the pile of utensils on the small table under the window. She grabbed it, then dug into the pie. She plopped a piece into her bowl on top of the *tanfula*, then doled out pie for everyone else.

"This is really good," Grace said. "Now *this* is sweet."

"Oh yeah," Monique agreed. "Choctaws have been using sugar since before removal. I bet they make biscuits too."

"Hey, I thought sugar made you sick," Larry said.

"I don't care," Monique mumbled through a huge mouthful.

"Maybe they got fry bread." Art sounded hopeful.

"No," Grace said. "We didn't make fry bread. We made biscuits, gravy, cakes, pies." Larry picked up the pie pan and scraped it clean.

Monique stood. "Let's go out."

Here and there, children peeked from behind a house or their mother's dress to look at the newcomers. One man under the shade of a tree watched them from fifty feet away. He had straight black-and-gray-streaked hair parted in the middle that hung to his earlobes. The man quickly moved behind the tree trunk. *That's weird*, she thought. *I hope he's not a creeper.*

"Monique, look," said Elaine. Monique stopped looking for the mystery man and turned her attention to Elaine.

The women had brought cloth dresses over to the dancers. There were also some hard-soled shoes and socks in the pile. "*Falaya.*" Sara Rose pointed to Monique's feet.

"Uh, yeah. Long."

One girl handed Elaine a Bible. "You can have it," she said.

"*Yakoke,*" Elaine answered. The girl shrugged.

"After what they just went through on the trail, I don't think she has much use for that," John observed.

"You can go wash in the *bok,*" another woman said. "The crik. Behind the house."

"Good," John said. "*Yakoke.*"

Monique stood next to a pin oak, watching a man hoe a spot in his garden. He was taller than the other men she had seen so far. His house seemed better built too. Chickens pecked in the dirt and baby pigs—teenage hogs more like it—followed their mama as she dug deeply into the emerging clover.

Her eyes drifted back to the man. He stood and put a hand to his back. She could relate. This was the time of year her back ached and often spasmed from putting in her garden. If she wasn't careful about using her legs to lift, a strain could make it painful to stand.

"You know him," came a voice behind her.

She turned to see Fuji looking over her shoulder at the gardener. "How could I possibly know him?"

Neither spoke for a minute.

The man hoed another row as Monique and Fuji watched. "He does look . . . familiar," she said.

The man took off his hat and wiped his forehead with his sleeve. He spotted the pair, stood, and became still. He leaned on his hoe.

Monique took a step, then stopped. "You should," Fuji said.

"I don't speak Chahta anumpa well enough."

"You don't have to. Come on."

"*Halito!*" Fuji waved.

"*Halito,*" the man said. As they got closer, Monique realized that he was younger than he appeared from a distance. He was dark and sunburned.

"*Sa hochifo vt* Fuji," Fuji said. He nodded at Monique, who said, "*Sa hochifo vt* Monique. Blue Hawk."

The man nodded but did not extend his hand. He looked over and then scrutinized her face. Monique shuffled her feet, unsure of what to say.

"Monique," Fuji said as he continued to look at the man. "This is Thenton Oakes."

"Nice to—" She froze, then knitted her eyebrows and cocked her head. "I . . ."

He watched her under heavily hooded eyelids. Just like hers. And just like her father's and her grandmoth—

Fuji interrupted her confused thoughts. "You know, Thenton Oakes. He signed the treaty."

"You mean—"

"He can talk to you about it," Fuji interrupted. "The treaty. You said you had questions. About the treaty." He arched his right eyebrow.

Thenton Oakes watched her. He was not really leaning on his hoe but acted like it.

No way is this man my ancestor, she thought. *Dear God.*

"What did you plant?" Fuji asked.

"*Tanchi*." He gestured to the knee-high rows of corn. "*Isito. Shukshi. Tobi.*"

Corn, watermelon, squash, and beans. The squash plants were almost as high as the corn plants. The pole beans grew up a lattice attached to the fence. She wasn't surprised. The only tribes that traditionally grew corn, squash, and beans in a symbiotic fashion and called them the Three Sisters lived in the Northeast. The idea that every tribe did that was a myth.

Goosefoot and pigweed grew between the rows. Monique felt a twang of satisfaction that Thenton Oakes did not weed his garden. She recognized all the edible weeds. She looked at his feet to see that he was hoeing up poison ivy.

She smiled but her mouth was dry.

"How long have you been here?" Fuji asked.

Thenton thought a few seconds. "Year."

"How is your family?" Monique asked.

He pointed to the house. "My wife and brother." He spoke slowly, but not because he had a hard time with English. Monique knew that a son, who would be born in twelve years, spoke English and Chahta anumpa with proficiency.

She wanted to blurt out, "Why did you sign it?" But she could not ask the question.

He nodded. "My sister. Friends. Many were sick and died here." Monique waited for more. She had questions, but now that she was in front of the man who could answer them, she couldn't speak.

"*Eho hilha tok*," Fuji said. *We danced. A long time ago.*

Monique thought it curious that Thenton stifled a smile. He said, "There will be more food later."

"*Yakoke*," Fuji said. "We can help you here."

Thenton waved his hand. "Look after your feet."

That evening, a strong breeze ruffled the dancers' hair as they walked through the camp. Clouds gathered. It smelled like rain.

Women cooked the evening meal outside while men worked on their roofs or tended to the horses. Every person the dancers saw nodded or waved, but none invited them to approach. A sense of solidarity existed among these survivors of the Choctaw-removal ordeal; so did an undercurrent of sadness, as if they hoped for a bright future, but were not sure how to obtain it.

A group of men led a horse carrying two gutted deer. After the horse stopped under a tree, women untied the carcasses and dragged them to the shade of another tall pecan. Women and young girls pulled their skirts forward up between their legs and tucked the material into their belts. Men joined in to help. They surrounded the deer and peeled back the hides with shiny knives. The dancers stood wrapped in their blankets to ward off the evening chill while they watched, fascinated at the speed with which they reduced the animals to pieces.

A teenage girl, perhaps seventeen, kept glancing at John from beneath arched black brows. She wore her hair tied back with red cloth. She was dressed in a cotton skirt, a blouse of white-and-red calico, and leather boots.

"A gentle flower," Art commented. John turned to look at Art and rolled his eyes. When he turned back, the girl smiled, revealing a large gap where her a front teeth should have been.

"Good grief," said Art. "In a few hundred years, someone who lost their teeth would have replacements in a few days."

"No choice here, my friend."

Grace and Elaine walked closer to where the community skillfully separated the meat from bones and representatives from the families came and carried off their portions. They hung the hides on a frame, using sinew string to stretch the skin. They completed their task in less than two hours.

"Hardly any blood on them," observed Elaine.

"I can't do it that good even with modern equipment," said John.

"That's because you're not under pressure to do it any better," said Art. "Here they have to dress animals well and they have to do it fast. When we hunt, we're out in the woods by ourselves and nobody looks over our shoulders while we screw up."

Thunder boomed.

The dancers slept in the big house that night, grateful for the shelter from the nighttime drizzle.

"There're about a hundred people here," John said after everyone awoke the next morning and lay atop their beds of straw-filled sacks and thin blankets.

"This is 1835," Fuji said. "Elders and babies died along the way. Like in Skullyville. There are some more settlements not far from here and the rest of the tribe is scattered across the nation. This is where some of the traditionalists are. For now. This group has been here about a year. There will be others."

Grace asked, "And why are we here?"

"Because you asked to be sent back."

"Asked? I didn't ask to come *here*."

"Uh, I think you did," John said. "You're always talking about getting back to the old ways. Now we know what that means."

Elaine sighed. "Looks like we got our wish to be decolonized. Here we are."

"Hey, gang," Monique said, "none of you want *this*. You need to rethink the term you're using. You don't want to dispense with your cars, washers and dryers, coffee makers, and there is no way in hell any of you will give up your iPhones. As Inigo Montoya said in *The Princess Bride*, 'You keep using that word. I do not think it means what you think it means.' Decolonization means to retain traditions, to fight for treaty rights, and to ensure cultural sustainability in modern society."

Monique considered the callouses on the bottom of her right foot, which was crossed over her left knee. She continued. "You don't have to give up what you need while you simultaneously add traditions and try to ensure cultural continuity. Besides, what we see here are not really the old ways."

Grace chewed on her lower lip. She missed ChapStick. "I get it. This is our past, but they're still colonized. They're hurting from removal. Too much death."

Monique sat up. "You would prefer the 1600s?"

"God, no. What I mean is—"

"These people are trying to stay away from whites," Fuji interjected. "This community is only one of many Choctaw settlements. This will be the Moshulatubbee District. You know about that. The tribe is split between the Nationalists, you know, traditionalists, who want to keep the old ways, and the Progressives, who are usually mixed-bloods and want to interact with white Americans. Then there're the others in between. The confused, the depressed, the ones who wished they'd fought harder to keep removal from happening." He glanced at Monique. "And some who are regretful."

Monique considered Fuji's statements. She realized that he never hesitated before he spoke.

"Some things never change," said Elaine.

"This is where my great-great-grandparents will be buried," Monique said, her hands in her lap. "Or, one of them, that is. In that open area. Over there." She pointed out the door to the east. "I know that because of where Sugar Loaf stands. He'll have two headstones. And his son's will be next to it. I don't know where Thenton was buried. Will be buried, I mean."

The room silenced, although they could hear hammering in the distance.

"My great-great-grandfather's not born yet," she continued. "Not for twelve years. Then forty years after that, he'll be shot and his skull bashed in. Pigs will find him on the road over that way." She pointed at the south wall.

"Damn," Elaine said.

Rene squeezed Monique's arm. "It's a gift to know the future. But frustrating not to be able to say anything." Rene did not remove her hand. Monique looked at her. Rene did not blink and did not look away. Unsettled, Monique broke eye contact.

"Well," Monique said as she stood so Rene would let go of her, "he had kids before he was murdered, so . . . here I am." Rene had communicated something to her, but she wasn't sure what.

Fuji leaned forward on his elbows. "We all know a lot."

John took a sip from his cup and set it down hard. "I would say that's an understatement. We don't just 'know a lot' Fuji. We know the future. Monique knows the fate of her family. We know about the Civil War, allotment, statehood, who the chiefs will be. Sanitation, medicine, causes of disease. I mean, we can't invent anything, but we know about inventions. Well, shit. That's just a few of the million things we know and these people do not. Do we have diseases that might kill them? Do we change history? What are we supposed to do now? Tell them? Not tell them?"

"Why are we here?" Elaine repeated Grace's question.

"Yeah, man," Larry chimed in. "Are we like the Terminator?"

"The Terminator was sent back to kill Sarah Connor so she wouldn't have her son," Art explained. "Not the same concept."

"It actually is," John argued. "What if we killed, say, some of the Progressives? The ones who let the whites in. The ones who ride roughshod over the traditionalists?"

A tiny bell dinged in Monique's brain. Once again, she didn't know why and she couldn't grasp the thought.

Fuji brushed corn mush off his shirt and then folded his hands. "We are here to see what life was like. We—"

"Bullshit," Monique interjected. "We could read a book or look at old pictures. We could listen to stories. We're here for a specific reason."

Fuji took in a breath, but not a deep one. "What have you learned?"

Monique looked at him. Her mother often asked her that question, and just as calmly too. When Monique was a child, she frequently became impatient when she couldn't figure something out. Her mother thought it more effective for Monique to solve problems herself than to give her the answer.

Grace attempted to untangle a knot in her hair. She gave up and ripped it out. "What do you mean?" She rolled the knot of hair between her hands.

"We've been here at least four weeks. What I should have asked is *What have you seen?* And don't drop your hair on the floor." Grace froze.

"Take the hair with you and bury it someplace. Or throw it in a fire."

Witches might it get it, Monique thought.

Grace did not argue. Instead, she clenched her fist and answered, "I've seen the inside of a cabin that was made without power tools. The insulation is straw and mud between the logs. That chimney looks like something that I could put together." She tapped the tabletop. "This is a good table, though."

"This is a house that was built for survival," Fuji said. "They had to get something up fast after they got here."

Hammering continued.

"Those buildings they're working on now will be stronger," Rene said.

"What else?" Fuji asked.

Monique snorted. "You mean no pollution? A lot of animals? Clean water?"

Fuji nodded. "That's part of it."

"People," Elaine said. "People trying to start over. Wanting to live."

"Yes," Fuji answered.

"Are we supposed to help them?" Art asked.

"We can help them."

Monique noted how Fuji answered.

"Okay," Art said, "how many times do we ask why we're here?"

"You don't need to ask again."

"What do we do now? Just eat this stuff and wander around?"

Fuji smiled. "You worry too much, Art. But that's okay. You're supposed to. You need to trust Leroy. And you need to trust in yourself."

Dear God, here we go, Monique thought.

Sara Rose and Viney came back in. The latter carried a pie. Larry sat up straight.

"Whoa," he said.

"This is *bihi*," the younger woman said. "Mulberry."

"Did you make it?" Elaine asked to be polite.

"Yes." She took a large spoon from her apron pocket and set it next to the pie. "*Kafi* outside. On the fire." She smiled and then left.

"Coffee?" Art asked. "Did she really say there's coffee?"

"She did," Monique answered.

"This pie looks like my grandmother made it," John said. "Laced over the top."

"Coffee," Monique repeated "From where?"

"A trading post? I don't know. They probably can't get a lot at once," John answered.

Larry picked up the spoon and doled out a section of pie, dropping it into his bowl.

The others watched him take a bite. "Sorta like the other one. Not as sweet, though." Everyone took a turn at spooning a portion.

Monique went to find the coffee. She returned with a full tin cup. "Uh, this is what you call worm dirt. My spoon stands up in it."

"I smell it," Elaine said. "Yikes."

"No filter. Super coarsely ground. Everything is in here." She took a tentative sip. "Oh God."

"So much for coffee," John said.

"Well, we need to repay them for the food," Monique said. "We can help with whatever they're building. Maybe I can help fix garden fences."

"Yes," Fuji said. He stood abruptly. "Let's go."

"What's the hurry?" Grace asked, her mouth full of pie.

"We don't have much time."

"Wait. What do you mean by that? And what did you mean 'trust in yourself'?" Art asked as he shoveled in a huge bite. Mulberry juice stained his lips purple.

Fuji and Rene walked out the door.

"Shit," Art said. "I hate when he gets mysterious."

The dancers spent the afternoon assisting the community. John, Art, and Larry helped shave logs, a difficult chore because the three drawshaves needed constant sharpening, and the handle on one was about to snap. Elaine and Grace helped the women chop wood, an easier task because the wood was dry, and then Grace wandered through the community and stopped at each garden. Monique went back to Thenton Oakes's house, where she tied reinforcing wire from post to post. Her hands ached and bled in a few spots. She kept one eye on Thenton the entire time, fascinated by the heavy eyelids that were a trait on her father's side. She did not see Fuji and Rene.

If Thenton watched her, Monique never saw him do it.

A few hours later, the group sat at the same table in the center house, tired, stinky, and disheveled. "Will we get to see the rest of the tribe?" asked Elaine.

"No," said Fuji.

"How do you know?" asked John. He grew weary of asking Fuji that question. "How did Leroy know who we'd see?"

"We're here because this is where he sent us."

"No, we're here because we walked here," Monique said.

"Hey, dude, wait a sec," said Larry. "Who's the man who looks like me?"

"You'll find out," said Rene. "Leroy wouldn't just let us struggle to find answers." She looked at Monique and smiled, as if she wanted to say something else. Monique noted that she had done that several times in the last few days.

"Oh, no? I thought that's what we were doing," said Grace. "If this isn't struggling, then what is? My God."

The group became silent, then went outside to wash in the creek. After contemplating the stars for a few moments, they came back in and fluffed their thin beds. Soon they confronted their confused dreams.

The next morning, they walked to a wide, shallow stream to bathe. Dragonflies skimmed the surface, hunting insects to satisfy their voracious appetites. Camp crows drank downstream from the dancers. Their intelligent eyes focused on the newcomers.

One of the riders was finishing his bath as the dancers approached. "Good morning," he greeted.

"Morning," the dancers said almost in unison.

They saw that his right arm was twisted, the hand and lower arm facing outward. It looked like the humerus bone had fractured, then got set crookedly. The well-developed bicep muscle bulged out sideways, while his tricep rubbed against his chest. The man's nose appeared as crooked as his arm. He did not seem embarrassed by his injuries. He put his shirt over his head.

He nodded, then disappeared into the bushes.

"Damn," Monique said. "Poor guy. Surgery could correct that."

"This whole thing is bizarre," said Grace.

Art asked, "Really?"

"Think about it. We're from the way-far future and are trying to relate to our . . . what? Second-world ancestors? It's like we came from another dimension. We're of the same tribe, but we're completely different."

John dunked his head in the cold water and scrubbed his scalp. "You sure about that?" The droplets on his skin shone like tiny lights in the bright sun. "We're not that different. Same concerns, same need for community."

"What I mean is that even though I try to learn as much as I can, and I certainly don't look Swedish, these people are the real deal."

234 | DEVON A. MIHESUAH

"Times change," John said before shaking his head and scattering drops of water.

"Intermarriage," Art said. "Missionaries, capitalism, political intrigue. Not everyone would care about what we see here."

"True. Think about our home now," said John. "I mean where we came from. Some Choctaws have no clue as to what it means to be Choctaw. All they know about Indians is what they learned from movies. Chief Hollis Roberts used to wear a headdress to impress dignitaries. We still have Choctaw princesses, and the tribal newspaper has the Chaplain's Corner that only talks about Christianity. Women wear white buckskin and feathers for celebrations and look like they stepped out of an Indian maiden art painting. I'd say a good portion of the tribe are Indians only by virtue of a few drops of blood and a desire to have a connection to the country's past. They don't feel like they're good Indians unless they meet white standards. That's what we are: good little colonized Indians who judge ourselves by what the colonizers think. If the white Choctaws had to actually live among traditionalists, they'd have a nervous breakdown."

The group was quiet. Monique knew that many modern Indians only dwelled on happy history and were pleased to oblige white America's desire to see complacent Indians. So they told tales of fulfilling experiences in boarding schools, military service, relocation, and church. They refused to complain about stereotyping, racism, and sports mascots, and they would not consider the realities of what colonialism had done to their pride and spirits. Few things sadden and sicken culturally aware Indians more than talking about how colonized Natives view the world.

"They don't look like movie Indians," Larry said.

"It looks like everyone here has had a serious injury," observed Art.

"I'm not saying they have to be fashionable," Larry said without irritation. "It's just that the past isn't what I thought it was."

"You can't have it both ways, Larry," said Rene. "They're not completely traditional and they're not just sophisticated and pretty either. They're both."

Larry did not answer. He waded from the water and sat on the bank to dry, his back to his friends who stood in the water. A tree twig with a few leaves still attached to it floated on the calm water. It slowly made its way around a bend and out of sight.

For the next two days, the dancers ate fish, pig, deer, and rabbit, garnished with camas bulbs and dandelion leaves and flowers. Birdsong permeated the camp and dogs barked at forest creatures the humans did not see. Children laughed while adults bustled about on their daily routines. The children were willing to play games, but not to converse. The tribe acted alternately friendly and distant, and their behavior made the dancers feel like intruders. John wiped away tears a few times, and the older people saw him do it but pretended they had not.

On the third day, John and Art followed a hunting party and scouted for deer.

"Damn," Art said for the tenth time in as many minutes. "I can't ride in this hard saddle."

"Sit to the side," John answered with a grimace.

"Right, like a girl."

"No, to the side. Just move your junk around until you find a comfortable position."

"No way is this gonna work—and I probably won't be able to have kids."

Larry followed Geletumma Chinisa for one morning. After Larry tried to speak to him, the man jumped on his horse, ran off, and did not return until dusk.

The next morning, the group sat at the table eating roasted pig and mulberries and watched two young women making brooms from broomweed. "We're part of all this, but we're not supposed to be included in this life," Elaine said.

"I feel like a ghost who wants to hang around her past life but has to go on to the next one," Grace said.

"That's pretty creepy, Grace," said Art.

"And how do you feel?" she asked.

"Like someone in a dream. I got the damn message and now I want to wake up."

"I feel ashamed," said Elaine. "Not just because of our appearance. I mean, no offense, but we are ragged out. We're the inferior Indians here. We know the future and about technology, but I don't think we're the 'new and improved' variety. I feel stupid."

"Don't get too upset," said John. "I feel very stupid."

"I can't walk straight," said Art.

At midday, the group sat at the table, either stirring or picking at bowls of *tanfula*. The ladies had cooked and stirred the corn mush all morning. This batch contained venison and walnuts.

Monique looked out the door. The buildings reminded her of those at the Fort Worth Log Cabin Village, sprinkled with a few structures from the Tsa-La-Gi Ancient Village at the Cherokee Heritage Center.

"I'd pay real money for some salsa and guac," Art said. His hair had grown to cover the tops of his ears. Monique wondered if he planned to keep his mullet.

"Deal with it," John said. "We have to eat everything we're given. That venison in the mush is a bit gamy, but it's good for you, so don't be shy about eating it."

"I liked the pig we had this morning," Grace said. "Good thing they adopted them."

Everyone stopped midbite and stared at her. She ignored them as she scraped her bowl.

"Spanish boars and English pigs make a great combo, huh?" John teased.

"Take the best that you can," Grace said without a hint of annoyance.

Art belched and put his head on the table. Monique reached over and rubbed his back.

On the fifth evening, Fuji came to the center house, where the others lay on their pallets, not yet asleep, and said it was time for them to leave.

"Why?" asked John. "I'm just getting into the rhythm of being an outcast around here."

"Well," Fuji said as squatted down, "you're really not supposed to be here."

"Are you supposed to be here?" asked Art.

Fuji shrugged and evaded the question. "I don't mean you can't be here. I mean you shouldn't stay much longer."

"Fuji dreams of the past," Art said sarcastically. "Don't you, Fuji? Oh, wait, you can't tell us. Right? Forget it." Art put his hand on his battered genitals. "I mean, don't let us know anything important, Fuji."

"Slow down, Art," Grace said. "Go sit in cold water."

"I'm not saying this is scary," said Elaine. "I feel privileged. But my intuition also tells me this isn't right. Like I've seen what I'm supposed to and we need to go. This isn't our time."

Fuji kept eye contact with her for a few seconds. "Yes, Elaine." he said quietly.

"Even if we were born now, it would still be stressful," said Elaine. "Look at how organized these people are. But some limp from rickets and others have bad scars. They spend all their time finding food, training horses, and fixing the houses. It's like our time in a way because we're always busy, always concerned about something. The differences are they don't have medical care or time to mess around. And the things they're concerned about are real life-and-death issues. Not bullshit like a dead iPhone battery."

"Hard life," said John.

"Hard, but pure," Grace said. "Survival is the focus. Not entertainment, not personal achievements. They take care of each other and they do it as a group."

"You just described a tribe, Grace," Elaine said.

"This isn't the whole tribe," Fuji said. *It's just a portion of a group that is disoriented,* he thought. "There are others of the tribe who are different.

The Progressives want to make money, reject their traditional religious beliefs, and leave the old ways behind."

"They've already been doing that," Monique said. "Same with the Cherokees. The Nationalists of both Nations will become angry."

"They're going to have to deal with whites," said Grace. "It's unavoidable."

"Excuse me?" Art interjected. "Did that come from the mouth of Grace the activist traditionalist?"

"Yes, it did," Grace answered.

"They'll learn," said Rene. "They have to. They already got removed from our homelands." She sighed. "Here we see Andrew Jackson's Indian Removal Act at work. They're still mourning." Rene wore her hair in a high bun, secured with sticks. Monique's grandmother had done the same.

"Nothing we can do about the factionalism," Grace said.

"There has to be a way to try and steer the course," Art said.

"I want to make suggestions to them," said Grace, "but I don't think I'm supposed to do that."

"No. You're not supposed to say anything," Rene said, "but it's understandable that you want to."

Another niggle pulled at the edge of Monique's thoughts.

Fuji stood. "Plan on leaving tomorrow. Remember what you've seen. Remember what you've just said." Then he smiled his ultrabright grin that put his friends at ease. Except for Monique. That smile . . . "We're just people," he continued. "There is a higher power." Then he took Rene's hand and they both walked through the door.

Monique stood and watched Fuji and Rene walk to a group of elders. They talked for a few moments and then dispersed. From this distance, Monique could see that the one who stayed behind to talk with Fuji was the mysterious man she had spotted when they arrived. They must have been carrying on an easy conversation because they gestured with their arms and laughed. Then they shook hands like old buddies. Monique thought about why a historic Indian would have the mannerisms of a baby boomer. She nudged John to see if he had been watching. He had not.

"Who was that?" Monique asked Fuji when he and Rene came in for the night. "I know him. I do."

"Just a man, Monique." He lay on his pallet and turned away from the group. "We'll leave early."

Monique lowered her voice. "Fuji, who was he?"

"No one you know." Then Fuji reached out and slapped at her arm. "Don't worry. Go to sleep." Then he fell quiet.

Monique nodded off, trying to remember.

The next morning, the group ate a large breakfast of venison, onions, berries, and roasted corn. "Sorta like cornflakes, but this tastes like the earth," Larry mused.

They quietly washed in the stream, each person attempting to imprint the camp into their minds. A dozen tribespeople met them back at the center house and gave them knives, simple deer-hide foot coverings, and skirts. A few of the women hugged Elaine and Grace and held their hands up in farewell to the men.

"You want another Bible?" asked the girl who gave Elaine a copy when they first arrived.

"This is enough," Elaine answered.

Geletumma Chinisa approached Larry and stood in front of him, staring into his eyes. After a few seconds, he reached up, lightly yanked on a dreadlock, and smiled. "They could be twins," Elaine said quietly to Grace.

"Do right," Geletumma Chinisa said slowly in English. Then he turned and pushed his way through the crowd. Larry raised his hand and opened his mouth to speak, but he could not find his voice. Rene lightly clasped his arm. Larry began to cry. When he lowered his head, tears fell onto her hand.

The dancers gathered their packs full of clothes and utensils. The gift givers said farewell, then melted back into their tribe. The camp then watched and waved from a distance.

"Those Bibles could be worth some bucks," Art said.

"Can't take them," Fuji said. "We'll leave them down the road."

Fuji led the hikers back to their base camp at an invigorated speed. New foot coverings and several days of plentiful food gave them energy to walk faster. As they hiked through the trees, John spotted a black bear meandering through the trunks about two hundred feet from the travelers.

"Look there," he pointed. "He's upwind."

They watched as the bear lumbered around pigeon-toed and nose up, seeking dinner.

Elaine felt simultaneously thrilled and scared. She broke into a trot, followed by the others until they reached the bubbly stream a mile away.

"Wow," Elaine said, breathing hard. She cupped her hands in the water. "He was big."

"Not really," John replied. The run made him weak and giddy. "Still could do some damage, though."

"Thanks for the information." She looked back the way they came, in case the bear had followed them.

"You won't see many bears in the wild," John said. "Remember him."

"You sound like Fuji," said Grace.

"Yeah, well. He's right, you know."

After three hours, they arrived back at the campsite they'd made prior to meeting the residents of Kully Chaha. Fuji and Rene vanished into the box elder forest and had not returned by late afternoon.

"No way they're doing anything but talking," Art said, smiling.

"Gotta get dinner," said Grace. "Time to fish." She returned to the cache of hooks she'd set under a pile of rocks and set out for the lake. Larry and Elaine followed.

John started a fire while Art gathered wood and dandelions. The fishers returned with eight catfish and two large pike. They used their new knives to behead and fillet their catch, then cooked the fish on long wood skewers.

They ate and took out their new clothes. The group tried on the garments and admired their knives.

"Like my birthday, man," said Larry excitedly. "Hey, when is my birthday?"

They were talking about how easy it would be to skin deer when Fuji and Rene came out of the woods.

"I was wondering," said Fuji, his arm around Rene's shoulders, "when do y'all want me to send you home?"

20

CHUKA
HOME

"What do you mean 'send us home'?" asked Art.

"You can do that?" Larry smiled. "Hey, let's go, man."

Art stomped over and put his sunburned nose up to Fuji's. "All this time, you could have sent us home?"

"I couldn't until today." Fuji did not back down from Art's intensity.

John hurried over. He pushed Art back and then leveled his nose with Fuji's. "Until now? Why now?"

"Leroy said not until now."

"So you could send us back, but . . ."

"Not until you had met the Others," Rene interjected softly in the background. All eyes went to her. "You had to meet the Old Ones." She shrugged. "That's what he said."

"He said more than that and we know it," said John. "You and Fuji have been keeping something from us."

"Yes," Rene agreed. "And this was it."

"Who the hell cares what you know? Let's get out of here!" exclaimed Grace. Monique stood still, considering Fuji's offer and how he had made it.

It was not as easy a process as the dancers had hoped. They were so eager to get home that they forgot how hard it was to dance the first time. It proved a feat to keep their minds off the goal of leaving and instead of being grateful that they were still alive. Fuji led the prayers, giving thanks for their food and good fortune.

"I hope he speaks for all of us," said Grace that night after the dancers ate a last meal of fish, dried venison, and duck eggs they found in a nest under some willows. "This has been hell. And we have to say thanks?"

"You're here, aren't you?" asked Rene. She had a bunch of clover in her hands and she crushed it between nervous fingers. "And you're going home. How many people get what they want after praying for it?"

Monique studied Rene, who spoke slowly and with meaning. Something else was going on here, but she had not figured out what.

"She's right," said Elaine. "Now we're asking to go back. Got to be careful what you ask for."

"No shit," Grace said as she walked to the trees to pee.

That evening, Elaine and Grace lay staring at the bright stars while John, Larry, and Art sat on rocks. John rubbed his calves in anticipation of cramps. Monique stretched and wondered how to handle Steve once she showed up looking like she had just hiked the two thousand miles of the Appalachian Trail.

"Do you think people back home have worried about us?" Elaine asked.

"Sure they have," answered John. "I wonder what Leroy has been telling them."

"Maybe we should have a story ready," offered Larry. "Like we decided to go to Canada for a while."

"No, Larry," said Art. "We're not dumb butts who would go on a joy ride."

"People had a problem with Ron Barnes disappearing," said Elaine.

"Yeah, but most of us don't think he died," said Larry. "I mean, the guy was so spiritual. He probably floated up to the sky or something."

"He could have," said Grace. "Now I think anything's possible."

"I keep thinking this has been a blessing," said Larry. "We could keep whining and drinking and blaming white people and not doing nothing to make the tribe better. Not me, man. No more. I'm talking to my brother and Andre again about going in together on a bison ranch. And maybe a tribal horse ranch. A few Chocs have some horses descended from the ones they had in the East and I want to buy some. Maybe talk to Comanches and get some of their mustangs too. The tribe could make money on it."

"How will you describe the people we met?" Grace asked Elaine.

"Old-time faces. Real Indians. But they're like us. Confused and angry."

Elaine rolled onto her side to look at Grace in the starlight. Her cheekbones stood out like pyramids. She reached to stroke Grace's hip and felt bone. Grace had always worried about her weight. Her wish of being thin had been granted.

"I thought all Indians in the past lived for each other," Grace said. "For the good of the group. This is only one group in the tribe and they're human. Like us."

"It's not easy to focus on everyone in your group," said Elaine. "We're used to being selfish."

"I need to change my thinking. The key to being traditional isn't to get rid of white people. We have to focus on values. I think we give up too easily. We have to try." Grace held up her hands and contemplated their outline in the moonlight. "We can do it. The world won't change and the whites aren't going to be gone. No one's going back to Europe or wherever just because tribes want them to go away. We got our asses kicked after Columbus got here. If the world keeps going, then we have to take the best of it. Use what we want and discard the rest."

"Simple, man," Larry said, eavesdropping from ten feet away.

"No, it isn't simple," said Grace. "I thought that the only way we could be a tribe was to have everything traditional. Not traditional from ten or twenty years ago, but I meant old-time traditional. Untouched. Before Europeans came here. Until Leroy did what he did, I hadn't thought about what I was saying. Our tribe can't go back. Not ever. If things were to suddenly change for the whole tribe like they did for us, then most of us would die. Only a few special people like Fuji and Rene could handle it."

Elaine stood while she watched the stars. "You seem different," Grace said.

"Like how?" Normally when Grace posed a comment like this, she was trying to start an argument and Elaine would speak carefully. Now Elaine was not intimidated.

"You go off and get things done. You stand taller."

Elaine did not rush to answer and that made Grace nervous. Grace expected to hear more of Elaine's unsure answers.

"I've always been afraid of losing myself and becoming what others want me to be." Elaine said slowly. "I got caught in the white world because of Mom's family, but then didn't feel right in Dad's Indian world. I was stuck in the middle and I was tired of trying to do both, to please everyone. I'm only going to do what I need to. Fuji tells us to quit complaining."

Grace thought without speaking, which was a new practice for her. Her father was white. Grace's parents loved each other dearly and the family accepted her dad, but not as an Indian. Intermarried whites were not Indians, no matter how much knowledge they acquired. Grace, however, resented the skin color he gave her. The more Grace's father tried to win her love, the more she pushed him away. She saw that clearly now. Her cheeks burned with embarrassment.

"You know, Grace," said Elaine, "there are more mixed-bloods than full-bloods anywhere. Denying that makes it worse. Now I can say I'm mixed-blood and not be ashamed of it. What I mean is, I'm not like Fuji or Rene. But from now on, I'm going to take what I've learned and use it for my tribe. And, Grace?"

"Yes."

"Men aren't the enemy."

Elaine said nothing more and Grace knew that her silence meant if Grace did not agree with her, the relationship would be over. Their history as a couple epitomized a dysfunctional partnership of disappointments, accusations, and verbal abuse. Elaine had found her strength. If Grace would not change, then Elaine was ready to move on.

"I'm sorry, Elaine," said Grace. "I'm a bitch."

"Admitting you have a problem is the first step."

They both laughed. So did the others, who listened to the conversation.

"They saw what they needed to," Rene whispered to Fuji's broad back as they lay under the same starry sky.

"That's true. Although they didn't see everything. There're Indians living all around here, but they don't all get along. It's a splintered tribe now and it'll continue to be."

"That's why we're here."

"Yes. It is."

"I think Monique knows."

"Well, you do look like her father and grandmother. And my eyes are just like my great-great-great-grandson's."

"I hope she gets over Brin someday."

"She won't. But she'll use her anger for the best. Just like we planned. Leroy will see to it that she does."

Fuji woke the dancers at sunrise.

They exited the cool shade and stepped into the still, warm sunlight. A mourning dove cried somewhere in the shade while the eight made a circle in the red clover and swarming bumblebees.

They could not eat or drink once the dance started, and the moist heat further weakened them. The hungry dancers thought it would be impossible to dance with any vigor. None had any excess fat to burn.

There were no drums. They did not need any. Fuji's songs were rhythmical, and he faltered from dry throat only a few times.

John observed Fuji, thin Fuji, dancing for his friends. Rene danced near him, but not at his side. Instead, she danced outside the circle. *She's doing that on purpose,* he thought. But he didn't have the energy to ask why.

He kept watching Fuji dance. The man appeared much lighter on his feet than the last time they did this.

After nine excruciating hours, they finished the first day of dancing. It was a painful night. The dancers were thirsty and their hands trembled from low blood sugar. Monique, John, and Elaine suffered dehydration headaches.

"How come we didn't get stung by the bees?" asked Larry.

"You disappointed?" Art's voice sounded hoarse.

"Bees don't need to sting us," said Fuji. "They just want to get to the flowers."

Around midnight, John cried out from leg cramps. Art and Elaine pulled his toes back to stretch the calf muscles, but as soon as they released them, John's heels contracted again, reaching back for his spine. His friends took turns rubbing his tortured legs and by dawn, the cramps subsided, but not John's fear of their returning.

"I'd give anything for salt and potassium tablets," he said through tough-guy tears.

"What about bananas?" asked Larry.

"Got some?" John asked. Fatigue would not allow him to laugh at Larry. "Need a whole bunch, anyway. Not enough potassium in one fruit to kill this cramp."

"You'll get through it," said Grace. "That's what you Indian marines do, right?"

"Heck yes." John stood for another day of dancing.

A pair of eagles had circled the dancers since sunup the first day, and they became tired after eight hours of watching the peculiar creatures. They rested in the treetops and kept their eyes on the humans. After sundown, they stayed in the tree, curious because one of them cried.

The eagles began circling again on the second morning. They sensed the air changing in the area below them; it became thicker like it did before a storm. Flying became difficult. As the morning wore on, the birds grew agitated and soared higher, where the air thinned. Small swirls of dirt and grass ran around the two-leggeds' feet. As the raptors watched, the wind gathered strength, and soon, the dancers were covered in blowing dirt and leaves. Curious, the birds flew lower and in wider circles to see what might happen next.

Monique shut her eyes and felt giddy, so she concentrated on breathing deep. She opened her eyes again and saw an out-of-focus and dimmer world. Fuji and Rene came close and leaned in so that all three of their noses almost touched. Their faces became clear and detailed.

Rene smiled. "We love you."

Monique opened her mouth to speak but no sound emerged. *What the hell does that mean?* she thought.

"We are who you think we are," Fuji said as he touched her cheek.

"Make sure we persist," he said. Monique blinked and Fuji and Rene had moved forty feet away. She gasped.

Monique held her arms up and the dancers looked distinct. She could clearly see John, Larry, Elaine, Art, and Grace. Fuji and Rene were now gray. At first, Monique thought the tears in her eyes caused her friends to look hazy, but then she realized why they faded.

She remembered Fuji's question: "When do y'all want me to send you home?" Fuji had said nothing about himself.

"Rene!" Monique screamed. The thin young woman with long flowing hair smiled at her descendant. She brought her palm to her mouth, kissed it, then blew the kiss to Monique. She waved goodbye.

Her eyes went to Fuji. "Fuji!" she yelled. Fuji smiled, arms wide.

As before, the wind swirled around her as if it were a Texas blue norther. Before night closed in, Monique had a sudden thought: *How did Fuji have the power to send them home?*

PART III

Time is but the stream I go a-fishing in. I drink at it; but while I drink I see the sandy bottom and detect how shallow it is. Its thin current slides away, but eternity remains.

—HENRY DAVID THOREAU, "WHERE I LIVED, AND WHAT I LIVED FOR"

21

Falamolichi The Returned

Monique stood next to the large tree. Her gaze shifted to the closest rider. His left leg zoomed in and out of focus, as if it were under a magnifying glass. The man's worn cowboy boot with a stovepipe top sat tucked into the stirrup of the walnut-colored saddle that seemed too heavy for the thin horse. She glanced to her right and saw three women. Grainy black and white, like an old photograph. She had seen them previously, but she could not recall where or when. She turned back to the men. She saw one face clearly. It was an ugly one. He smiled, revealing stained and broken teeth, minus the lateral incisor and canine on his left side. Monique raised hard, cold pistols in both her hands. They felt good.

She blinked. When she opened her eyes, the men were gone. Instead, she saw John standing twenty feet away. He, too, was in black and white. Holding a rifle and dressed in clothes her great-grandfather would wear. His long hair touched his shoulders. "John?" she said, but he cocked his head, as if he were puzzled to see her.

Monique then opened her sunburned eyes to the bright sunlight on her face. She looked around. John shielded his eyes with his hand as he studied her, then paused a beat and tilted his head, as he did in her dream.

He looked away and then glanced back at her. He narrowed his eyes and shook his head, as if ridding himself of a vision.

At the sound of a purr, she put her arms out and the dependable Lorraine approached her like a high tide. Monique hugged the furry feline. Lorraine meowed and turned up her motor. "My God, Lorraine." The cat allowed the human to leak tears onto her fur. Monique turned her head and saw the others sleeping like babes—*more like passed out from too much stress*, she thought. Larry and Art lay on their sides, their mouths open as if snoring. John stared up at the sky, fingers laced together over his head. Grace and Elaine held hands.

Fuji and Rene were not among them. *The absence of the presence*, she thought. She felt tears on her face but she did not cry. Lorraine sat on her chest and watched her, unblinking. What did they say to her before they disappeared? That they loved her. And "We are who you think we are." Her head throbbed. She needed to speak to Leroy.

"Like sunbathers at the beach," Monique said loudly to keep from sobbing. "No sunscreen."

John watched the thin trail of a jet slowly cross the blue sky. Then they heard the rev of an engine on the road next to the dance grounds. "That's Leroy's Subaru," he said as he sat up.

"Maybe we do have sunscreen."

Art sat up. "What's going to happen now?"

Monique lay back on the grass, Lorraine on her chest. "I think I'll just shut my eyes and wait to find out."

She heard the truck's engine stop and the doors open and shut. Then she stood up so fast that Lorraine yowled. Monique almost fainted from the sudden movement, then staggered toward her cruiser with the intention of speeding home.

Leroy intercepted her, carrying a jug of orange juice in one hand and a bag of avocados in the other. "It's only Sunday, Monique. Let's all go in and eat." Deb, Mazey, Peta, and Rob assisted the other dancers.

Monique stood, panting. John staggered to her and took her arm. "Monique. John. You're home," Leroy said gently.

Grace tried to stand, but her knees crumpled and she fell. "Damn."

Monique and John made their ways to chairs in front of an open window. Leroy always took advantage of a beautiful day. The temperature was only seventy-five and a gentle breeze cooled them. She assessed her stolen capri pants. They held up well, but her feet were dirty, heavily calloused, and the skin had splits on the heels. Only small sections of maroon polish remained on her long toenails.

"Everyone listen," Leroy said. "You need to drink a glass or two of juice, then go clean up."

The drummers brought out tumblers filled with tart lemonade. The dancers guzzled their drinks, then paused to breathe.

"Oh man, this is good," John said. "Not too sweet."

"There's Gatorade after you finish that," Mazey said.

"Elaine, you and Grace go use the shower in my room. Down that hall. Monique, you go after they're finished. Larry, John, and Art, use the second bathroom, or I have the solar shower bag set up by the shed. All your belongings are in the guest room."

Elaine and Grace made their way down the hall. "I'm going outside, man," Larry said.

"Get a towel and your bag."

John and Art followed the women.

"How're you doing?" Leroy asked Monique.

"You should have said something."

"Like what?"

"I need more juice." She padded into the kitchen. As ice clinked into her tumbler, she scanned the room. The garbage and recycle bins overflowed with the same remains she saw after Mike and Silan had returned. Boxes of crackers, cereal, and instant oatmeal covered the counter. She opened the fridge to see chicken, fruit salad, various casseroles, and the leftovers of their pre-dance dinner. The smells of roasting turkey and vegetables wafted from the oven. Fresh-baked loaves of bread and three pies cooled on top. A large bowl of greens covered in plastic wrap sat on the table, along with dressings and smaller bowls of olives, onions, and other toppings. How did Leroy know they would return today? She would consider this later.

Monique limped to Leroy's bedroom. Grace was out of the shower and slathering herself with Aveeno body lotion. She could see Elaine's silhouette through the shower curtain. Monique then noticed a deer-hide bag atop Grace's clothes on the bed.

"What's that?" The only way Grace could have smuggled that sack was under her baggy shirt.

"Seeds." Grace smiled. "I got four types of corn kernels, green beans, different squashes, cowpeas, watermelon, and okra. Some of those are Old World, right? But these are the real deal. Old seeds and we have them now."

"You have to be careful when growing these. You don't want cross-pollination."

"Oh yeah. I know. Maybe I'll put them in a greenhouse so we can control the pollination. This will be big, Monique!" Grace seemed to have forgotten that she stood there naked. "We're going to start a seed co-op and try to find more heirlooms."

"Sounds awesome," Monique said as she sat on Leroy's bed and rubbed her cracked feet.

"You know," Grace said, sighing, "this was a great trip."

"Glad you liked it."

"You don't think it was worth it?"

Elaine called out, "It's all yours, Monique."

Monique was relieved not to answer Grace's question.

An hour later, the clean dancers sat in Leroy's den, dressed in the clothes they had worn the night before they had left, which, according to Leroy, had only been two nights before. He told them to leave the clothes they arrived back in in a pile, which they could not take home. The exception were the jog bra and running shorts Monique wore as underwear. She wadded those into a ball and pushed them into her bag. She planned to keep them forever.

"We were gone a month," John said. "But to everyone else it was just two days?"

"Maybe thirty hours," Leroy corrected.

"Thirty *hours*?" John repeated.

"This is Sunday afternoon," Leroy answered.

"How do we explain our appearance?" asked Grace. The dancers appraised themselves. Everyone appeared rangy. Their deeply sunburned skin stretched tight across sharp bones. Only Larry had no dark circles under his eyes. Their feet suffered, the soles cracked, hard, and full of small thorns and splinters.

Leroy set out the turkey that Mazey had carved, the wheat rolls piled high in a basket, a bowl of Red Delicious apples, and another of fat blueberries. He quickly sliced the avocados and set them on the counter. The pungent onions called to Monique. She thought of Silan and Mike. Like distance hikers who overexerted themselves on long, dry trails, the dancers craved onions. As did she. The onion smell was more enticing than the turkey. She put three slices on her bread, then layered on turkey, pepper jack cheese, avocado, and a zigzag trail of mustard thicker than cake frosting.

Despite the dancers' hunger, they were unable to eat much. They remained silent and thoughtful as they chewed. Monique picked up a handful of blueberries and ate them one by one. Grace filled a plate with Doritos and licked the salt off them.

Finally, Larry asked, "Where's Fuji and Rene?"

All looked expectantly at Leroy. "Where they want to be," he answered.

Monique noticed that the drummers kept their eyes on their plates. "You mean, they're still back there," Art said.

Leroy sipped his tea.

"When do they come home?" Elaine asked.

"Don't worry about them," Leroy said.

"In a few days, I hope," Grace said.

"Time is relative," Leroy responded.

Monique looked at Leroy. "That's not an answer." She doused a wheat roll with honey.

"They *wanted* to stay?" John asked.

"Fuji had the power to send us home at any time," Monique added.

"Correct," Leroy agreed.

Monique abandoned the roll and made another turkey, sliced apple, and onion sandwich, this time slathered in ranch dressing. She dipped a corner in ketchup and took a large bite.

"I have questions," Monique said, her mouth full.

Leroy nodded. "Eat some more."

Deb brought out a strawberry-rhubarb pie and a gallon of vanilla ice cream. He set both on the table. "Go for it," he said enthusiastically.

Monique thought he sounded like a zookeeper.

"Hey, I will," Larry said as he spooned out a bowlful of both.

Art slowly doled some pie into a bowl next. Strawberry-rhubarb was Monique's favorite, but she didn't have the energy to fix a helping for herself.

Leroy stood. "You all have questions. We'll talk another time. Get more food if you want, then you all go home. If you leave things, don't worry. I'll wash them and you can get them later. Leave the clothes you arrived back in. You can't take them."

No one moved.

"You need to tend to yourselves. Now go." Almost hypnotized by fatigue, they all went.

Monique unlocked the cruiser and threw her bag into the back seat. She turned the key, but sat for a moment before putting the car in gear. She looked in the rearview mirror and laughed. Her sunburned skin accentuated the crow's-feet by her eyes. "Je-sus," she drawled. "How am I gonna explain this to Steve?"

Monique drove home, keeping her speed much slower than usual. She didn't turn on the radio, nor did she call Steve to let him know she was on her way. She needed silence as she tried to remember what had happened the last few weeks. Once home, she backed the car into her garage, turned off the engine, and sat staring at the neighbor across the street as he diligently pulled weeds from his lawn. What a waste of food, she thought. He could eat those dandelions.

They had been gone almost five weeks, yet Steve was supposed to believe that the dance lasted two days. Even if she had fasted for forty-eight hours and sat outside the entire time, there was no way she would look like she had vacationed in Death Valley. She straightened the rearview mirror again. Yep, the deeply tanned skin and wrinkles from dehydration were still there, despite her drinking water and Gatorade until she almost puked. Her eyebrows could use a few plucks and she really needed moisturizer.

She felt like she was on autopilot as she opened the side garage door and walked around the house to the back door. Rover jumped up and down until Monique dropped her bags, knelt, and hugged the excitable dog.

"And so how did you lose so much weight?" Steve asked that evening as he watched his wife down a second plate of spaghetti. Monique didn't bother twirling. She just speared forkfuls and sucked them into her mouth. Steve always ate garlic bread and Monique abstained, but he watched in astonishment as his wife scooped noodles onto a piece of buttery toast, leaned forward, and pushed it into her mouth. She thought she had sated herself at Leroy's but her appetite came roaring back when she smelled the marinara sauce.

"I thought you said you ate at Leroy's. Did he make you lay in the sun all this time? You're not just burned—you look like you got locked in a tanning booth."

"Hey, Mom," Robbie said, delighted to see his mother indulge, "want some more Parmesan?" He held out the container of shredded cheese, then picked up the bottle of Cholula and stretched it to her. She took both, covered her pasta with cheese and hot sauce, took a bite, and then gulped half her beer.

Steve eyed his wife as he ate, and said nothing. Monique could hear the wheels in his head turning.

"I gotta do some homework," Robbie said. "Glad you're back, Mom." He kissed Monique on the cheek and stared at her a few seconds, concerned. He waved to his dad as he started down the hall, turning once to look at his father and then disappearing into his bedroom.

Monique sat back in her recliner, finally satisfied. Lester Holt delivered the nightly news. She held her right foot as she straightened her leg toward the ceiling. The she did the same with her left leg. "Ouch," she yelped.

"What in the hell happened?" Steve asked quietly.

"Splinter. In my heel."

"No. Where did you go?"

"What do you mean? We went to Leroy's."

"At the very least. You look like a different person."

"I am. Got any fruit?"

"I cut up a pineapple. The stem's in some water."

"Yay. Maybe this one will grow."

"You look like you went on a spring-break bender."

"Thanks."

"You didn't go to some weird spa thing, did you?"

She did not respond. Steve stood and took her bowl. Monique grabbed the last bit of bread and popped it in her mouth. She kept her eyes on Lester while Steve watched her down the remainder of her beer.

"You going to work tomorrow?"

"No. Tuesday. We meet at Ninah's tomorrow."

"Want me to drive you?" he asked as he sat back in his recliner.

Monique smiled and got up. She plopped onto Steve's lap. That meant she wanted a back rub. "No, hon. Just a meeting to discuss the trip. I'll be back in the afternoon."

Steve massaged her traps. "Yes," she moaned. "Right here."

"Damn. Feels like cement."

She sighed. "Wanna turn on the Jacuzzi?"

"You know I do."

22

ANOA
INFORMATION

Ninah Strong Bull lived on her family allotment in a small green house with functioning window shutters and a covered, wraparound porch. Deanna Troi, the milch cow, and Cthulhu, the lop-eared gelding, lived in the stone-sided barn, along with chickens, ducks, and the alarmist guinea hens. Ninah liked to tweet and surf the internet. She had a laptop, dual monitors for her desktop, a fax machine, copier, scanner, color printer, and a satellite setup that allowed her access to over a thousand channels. She was partial to Acorn British mysteries and Shudder horror movies.

John and Art pulled onto Ninah's property next to Big Sandy Creek in the heavily wooded area of Citra. The men had hunted for turkeys before they danced and brought a frozen tom as a gift for Ninah. Four other vehicles sat in front, including Grace's red Ford, Larry's bumper-less Chevy S-10 with many dents, and Monique's cruiser that she parked nose out at the end of the drive.

Ninah heard the trucks. She bolted out the front door and down the steps before Art and John turned off their engines. Ninah was ninety, appeared to be sixty, and had no health issues to speak of. She wore her white hair in a single braid to her calves; she tied the sides back with beaded clips made for little girls.

"Been waiting on you," she said mischievously.

"Got ya a turkey," John said as he held up the heavy bag.

"Oh, goody. I'll cook it in my air fryer."

John followed Art through the squeaky screen door. Art took off his jean jacket, nodding to the room. His eyes stopped on a tall, skinny, bald man standing by the rock fireplace with his hands in his jeans pockets. Larry grinned back at him.

"Larry?" asked Art.

"Got tired of the dreads, man."

"I'm impressed."

"So was I," said a deep voice from the kitchen. Out walked Leroy Bear Red Ears, dipping his bag of Earl Grey into a Santa Claus mug.

Grace had claimed the rocker. Elaine sat on the floor in front of her. Both hopped up when the two men came in and gave them hugs. Monique rose from her folding chair to give them cheek pecks. She wore cutoffs and a faded Metallica T-shirt and held a cold bottle of Hite Korean beer that Ninah favored. She wore Teva sandals, her sore feet covered with soft socks.

"Sit, Arthur and John," Ninah ordered.

The two pulled kitchen chairs into the den while Ninah sat in the recliner under a bull-elk tapestry. Ninah had stuck beaded earrings into the elk's ears and a neighbor's son had thumbtacked a stuffed Baby Yoda onto the elk's back.

Leroy sat in the other recliner, legs crossed and sipping his tea, pinky finger sticking out. The returned dancers kept their eyes on him.

Ninah smiled and sipped from a ceramic cup. She smacked her lips. "How is everyone?"

"Great!" Larry said.

"Same here," Grace agreed. "Slept well, although my feet hurt and I need to stop eating." She laughed and nudged Elaine.

"What about you, Arthur?"

"Sat in an ice bath last night. Much better."

"Larry, dear, that look suits you."

Larry blushed and rubbed his bald pate.

John feigned interest in his plate of strawberries and cream cheese dip. "Monique and John, you look good." Ninah did not ask either how they felt.

"Tell us how you managed to send us to another time," Monique said. She looked back and forth between Leroy and Ninah.

"I was about twenty-two around the time of the termination of tribes," Ninah said. "Strong Bull was twenty. Leroy here was seven. I was old enough to understand and see for myself how termination was a disaster. So we decided to prepare for the Renewal Dance. It had never been danced. It was only a legend. Strong Bull and my parents gave us part of the formula, if you want to call it that. But they didn't know the entire ceremony. We talked with other old people before they passed and learned about the dance piece by piece. The first time Strong Bull and I tried it was in 1958. When Leroy turned fifteen, he started going with us."

"Why?" John asked. "Why go back? What is a trip to the past supposed to accomplish?"

"Well, long ago, our tribe was prosperous," Ninah began. "No horses then, but water, trees, deer, fish. Everything the people needed to live. Then strangers came. We became careless and killed deer so we would have hides to trade. We almost destroyed all of them. These strangers brought things to trade that our people had never seen. Like knives, metal needles, plates and utensils. Pots and pans. Horses. Guns. And gunpowder for the muskets. In return, we allowed the strangers to hunt. We didn't want them here, but we wanted what they had. Our lives changed forever."

Monique sighed, bored with the lecture. She knew all this. "A deal with the devil," Larry said. Monique rolled her eyes.

"Yes," Ninah answered. "We got things we that could never let go of. Things they brought made life easier. And the more we used these things, the more we needed them. All of you can imagine that."

"We sure can," said Larry. "Matches, knives, clothes. Our group was a mess without them."

"We wanted the intruders to leave," Leroy said. "They were destroying our world by making us overhunt. Worse, they made us sick. Many children and older people died from diseases. We fought with other tribes, like our brothers and sisters the Chickasaws. So we decided to run the strangers out. They left, but returned. Again and again. The Spanish, French, English. It kept getting harder to turn them away. Our land was too rich." He took a sip of the cooling tea. He wanted to drink it fast because there are few things worse than cold Earl Grey.

"Shortly after you all came home, the white intruders tormented the tribe again," he said. "They kept coming. More white men married Chahta women. They wanted money and used the land to get it."

"Last week?" asked Grace. She screwed up her face in confusion.

"Not really, dear," said Ninah. "To you, it was last week. It actually was a long time ago."

Grace's eyes darted around while she thought. "Well, whites always have tormented us, haven't they?"

"There already were smart Chahtas in the tribe. Fuji is staying around to make suggestions," Ninah assured.

"Fuji said to use what you need from whites," John recalled, "but don't get too close. Keep your identity and culture and accept others for what they are."

"Fuji can't reveal the future to them, you know," said Leroy. "He tells them to continue to take what they need from the whites to make life easier. They will listen to him. He's good at explaining how to survive as Indians in a world that is changing."

"Those ideas will stay with the tribe through time," Ninah said.

"But our ancestors would have had those thoughts anyway," Art argued.

Leroy nodded. "They could have dealt with whites on their own terms. But you see, those from the present who returned to the past had the advantage of knowing what happens through history. Fighting and wishing the enemy will go away aren't always the best solutions."

Leroy laced his fingers together. "This tribe has been split for a long time. Choctaws have different ideas about religion, politics, economics, everything. Some are almost white and don't know anything about our heritage. They think they know all about Indians just because they saw *Dances with Wolves*."

"So we're the only other ones who have been back?" Art asked.

"Others besides us went back long before you," said Leroy.

"You mean Andre Grayson? B. O.?"

"They were among the dancers, yes. Deb Hollow Tree helped write the constitution at Tuskahoma."

"How could he do that?" John asked. "He wasn't a council member."

"No, but he influenced the ones who were."

"You're saying those of us who went back influenced how history was made?" Monique sputtered. "Were our ancestors that helpless? For all you know, anyone from this time who went back completely screwed things up and that's why things are, you know, the way they are."

"She's right," Elaine interjected. "Maybe we made things worse. Hey— can people from other tribes also travel back and forth?"

"I don't know," Leroy said plainly.

"So why don't we go back to those places?" Larry asked. "Wow, man. Think of what we could warn them about."

"That is true," Ninah said. "But we can't."

"Why not?" Grace asked.

"That's not the purpose of the dance."

Monique cocked her head. The little bell dinged again.

"Anyway, others who went back were your other drummers, Mazey Spring and Peta Hayes. They saw our sacred mound, Nanih Waiya."

"I saw that when I was a kid," Grace said.

"Not at the beginning of time. Not when our ancestors emerged from the ground."

Grace's eyes bulged. "What? They watched our people emerge?"

"They did."

Everyone was too shocked to speak.

After a minute, Monique blurted, "What good did that do?" Everyone looked at her. "Seriously. I would do that. But what did it accomplish?"

"What did *you* accomplish?" Leroy asked.

"I met my ancestor who signed the removal treaty." No one said anything. "What did *you* do?" she shot back.

"We advised Moshulatubbee, Chief Greenwood LeFlore, and Nitakechi."

"About what?" Elaine asked.

"The removal treaty?" Monique asked. "You supported the treaty?"

"No," Leroy answered.

"Yes," Ninah countered. "I mean, there was no choice."

"Understand that when we go back," Leroy explained, "we can't change everything we want. Sometimes we can only prevent something worse. We pushed for Article XIV. That allowed those who wanted to stay in Mississippi to do so. We also—"

"Were you there?" Monique asked.

"At Bok Chukfi Ahilha—Dancing Rabbit Creek? Yes, we were."

"Did you see Thenton Oakes? Did you talk to him?"

"Yes. As did you."

Monique lifted her bottle to take a sip but it was empty. She resisted the urge to throw it.

"Why Fuji and Rene?" John asked.

"Fuji had tribal memories. So did Rene. All of you do. You just don't know how to see them. It takes a special person to see the dreams clearly."

Monique sat up straight. She looked at Leroy. Their eyes met and then he averted his gaze.

"I dream a lot," John said.

Monique did a double take. John would not look at her. Leroy said, "When we went back it was January of 1901."

"Oh yes," Ninah agreed. "Very cold. We had to find more clothes." Monique tried to recall what happened in 1901.

"We helped elect Daniel Bell."

That got him blank stares. Leroy chuckled. "Children. Bell. Anyone?"

"There was no Chief Daniel Bell," Monique said. "Right?"

"Chief Bell," Leroy said. "The leader of the Snakes."

"I thought that was Chitto Harjo and he was Muscogee," John said.

"They had Snakes too. Crazy Snakes. Bell was leader of the Nationalists. They were a full-blood Choctaw faction of at least two hundred men who were also known as Crazy Snakes."

"More than that because we count their wives, and other women too," Ninah reminded him.

"Right, right."

"Newspapers and the government didn't count women."

Leroy nodded. "Anyway, they carried on what Silan Lewis tried to start. They disagreed with Progressive chief Gilbert Dukes. After all, he said he believed that the United States had the Choctaws' best interests at heart." Leroy shook his head. "He was amenable to allotment and he knew that meant we would lose our government. Dukes even said the way to survival was 'safe tribal extinction.' He was not a wise man. Bell's faction wrote a resolution to depose Dukes as chief, along with all his appointees. The Snakes appointed their own chief—Bell—and all the other officers."

"Bell wanted the Moshulatubbee District for the full-bloods," Ninah continued. "With their own laws and constitution. He even created his own Lighthorse brigade. They believed in the 1830 treaty that stated the tribe could manage their own affairs. One of their laws was that any Choctaw who leased land to whites would be whipped. If they sold land, the Snakes would kill them. The Progressives were afraid of Bell."

"Those men rode around and told everyone Bell's plans," Leroy continued. "Dukes got afraid and asked Fort Smith to protect him."

"How could Bell do all that?"

"He couldn't. Not really," Leroy said. "The point was to make it clear that they disagreed with how the tribal leadership handled our affairs. He argued that every structure on Choctaw land belonged to the tribe, not to the whites who had moved in. They also petitioned the U.S. government because they wanted to live in the old ways and to follow the treaties."

"I don't recall hearing any of this," Grace said.

"Me neither," Larry said.

"What did they do?" Elaine asked.

"Ultimately, nothing. The Choctaw Snakes had no power. No money. Bell's followers were greatly impoverished. When officers arrived to see what the insurgents were up to, they found old Bell sharpening his saw. He asked them to come in and have a bowl of watery *tanfula*. He didn't have much else."

"So what was the point of supporting him?" Art asked.

Leroy turned his gaze on Art. "Because it was the right thing to do. To tell those in charge they cannot ignore the problems their people face. That they cannot abandon traditions. That those of us who care are still here. *We* are still here."

"Not everything we do results in immediate action," Ninah said. "You'll be ignored most of the time. Sometimes attacked. But at some point, leaders will have to act."

Monique's brow furrowed. "What did you see in Andre and B. O.? They were alcoholics and drug users."

Ninah laughed. "Yes, yes they were," she explained. "But while some people stay the same all their lives, others just need some nudging to change. They had problems, but Leroy, Strong Bull, and I agreed they had much under the skin that would be useful to the tribe. We were right."

"We are still here," Grace repeated.

"Then and now."

"Hey," said Larry, "who was the guy that looked like me?"

"Who do you think he was?" asked Ninah.

"An ancestor? He had my name."

"You have his name," corrected Leroy. "How many Chipmunks are there in this tribe?"

"Not many. Just my immediate family—my cousins have another name."

"There's your answer," Leroy said. "The older Chipmunk I met when I traveled back was a war leader. He had your nose if I recall correctly. Or should I say, you have his nose?"

Larry swayed on his skinny legs while he thought about his relative who died a long time ago, but whom he'd just met.

"It's not only whites we have to worry about," Leroy said. "It's us not knowing who we are. All of you had doubts about yourselves and about what you're supposed to do as Indians. Now you're different people."

"You're right about that," said Grace.

Monique realized that neither Ninah nor Leroy looked her way.

"All of you were determined to get rid of whites and to be traditional. Life can't be like that," said Ninah. "We have to work with whites, but we keep our identity and are proud of it. We don't have to be who they want us to be. Each of you now has plans to make the tribe stronger. More solid. You are the future of our people. It's the combination of several things. You needed to see what it was like in the old days. From seeing the past, you can create the future. That's the purpose of the dance."

Leroy nodded. "It's in the blood of some of us to want the past. The way it really was hundreds of years ago, not to say you want 'decolonization' just to make a political statement." He glanced at Grace.

"Point taken," she said. "I've aged several hundred years recently."

"We know, Grace," said Ninah.

"Some need the old ways," continued Leroy. "Some aren't interested in the white world and what it offers. Others like some of it, while many like most of it. Like me and Ninah."

"Can't do without my television and computer. Or my oven," Ninah laughed. "I'm not going to be ashamed of what I like. I couldn't stay with the Old Ones. Neither could Strong Bull or Leroy. That's the way it is."

"We all got what we wanted," Grace said. She smiled at Elaine. "I got seeds and we're starting a seed collective. Larry's starting a bison ranch. Art's running for council. Monique's not angry anymore."

Monique thought that was a presumptuous assessment of her mental state. And she noted that Grace did not mention John.

"Here we are. A strong people. Surrounded by whites." Grace laughed. "But like a mountain, they can't tear us down. We can only do that to ourselves."

"Now you know how to be strong," Ninah said.

"I *feel* strong," Grace said with all the fervor of the recently converted. "I feel *blessed*."

Monique did not feel anything except skepticism. "When are Fuji and Rene coming back?" she asked.

"We'll see," Leroy said as he stood.

"This is tough," said Larry. "I don't get it."

"I don't think you have to," said Elaine. "Things are the way they are. Now we deal with it."

"Wait a minute. This means I'm not the leader of the rival faction anymore," Grace said in mock distress.

Ninah stood and walked over to the young woman. She took her head in her two soft, wrinkled hands and pulled it down so she could kiss her cheek. The other unique individuals with strengths, weaknesses, and plans for the future rushed to join them.

Monique hung back. She noticed that John stood a few paces from the others as well. So far, all she had heard were maudlin reasons for dancing and enduring what came after. No way did her group go on such an arduous journey just to become inspired. Or to bring back seeds. Now that she'd gone through the ordeal, she wanted more of a payoff. A deep undercurrent of murky thoughts pulled her off-balance. She could tell that John felt it too.

Leroy looked at Monique and then winked. She knew that Leroy and Ninah had lied.

PART IV

The future is history.

23

AIA^{N}LI
TRUTH

Monique smiled, hugged everyone one more time, and then excused herself. She told the group that she had to get back for a friend's birthday celebration. Except that friend had already had her party two months prior.

As soon as she hit I-75, she sped up and held up her iPhone. She found the number she wanted and pressed the blue call icon.

"It's me," said a gravelly voice.

"East?"

"Yes, ma'am."

"Where are you?"

"Where do you want me to be?"

"I'm on my way to your house. I'll be there in fifty. You better be too." Monique hung up and flipped on the light and siren. She sweated as she flew through Ada, thankful that she had missed the lunchtime traffic.

Forty-eight minutes later, she turned onto Raptor Lane and saw from four houses away that East's blue truck sat under the carport. She pulled into the drive. The detective saw the illuminated lamp next to the sofa through the large front window. Lulu came to the glass and waved, smiling. Silwee peeked over the sill and held up a yellow plastic dump truck.

"You better be in there," Monique said aloud.

Lulu opened the storm door before Monique reached the first step. "Hi," she said. "Come on in."

Monique entered and removed her sunglasses. Sidewinder the wiener dog and the mutt Cottonmouth raced to her, nails clicking on the wood floor. Both jumped up and down, raking her bare shins.

"Enough, you two." Lulu grabbed them, holding one dog under each arm. "I'll be back," she said as she hauled the squirming dogs down the hall and into a bedroom.

Monique stepped in and saw a man on the sofa. He sat wrapped in a Pendleton blanket and seemed to be melting into the sagging cushions. Shaggy hair hung on either sides of his face.

"East James?" Monique asked.

"That's me," he said. He got to his feet. Monique was shocked at his appearance. He held out a hand from underneath the blanket wrapped around him. Monique took it. His grip was strong, but his fingers felt bony.

Lulu brought in a tray filled with sandwiches, chips, and cookies. Silwee followed with two cans of Pepsi. He set them on the side table next to the sofa. "You want a drink?" Lulu asked Monique.

"Maybe later."

"What ya want, Daddy?" Silwee asked.

"Sandwich."

Silwee picked up a thick half of a sub. Lettuce fell out. The boy looked over his shoulder and grinned at Monique.

"Let me help," Lulu said. She placed a napkin under the shower of tomatoes, lettuce, and pickle slices. She restacked the ingredients.

East took the offering and bit into it. Eloise ran to her father with a paper towel. She put it in his lap.

Monique watched East chew. No one in her group looked as exhausted as this man. He appeared smaller than his smiling photograph with the catfish, as if he had been ill and recently recovered. Eloise stood with her hands on her father's leg, scrutinizing his face. Monique realized the girl was worried.

"When did you get here?" Monique asked.

East closed his eyes, chewing. "Coupla hours ago."

"Where have you been since calling me from Leroy's Tuesday morning at two thirty?"

"Leroy's."

"This is Monday. You weren't there when I was at Leroy's on Thursday for our dance and you weren't there yesterday when we finished."

"True."

"You just told me that you were at Leroy's."

"I meant that I've been in the country." He took another bite. He motioned to a Pepsi can.

Lulu opened one and handed it to him. He drank deeply. "Were you with Silan Bohanan and Mike LeFlore?"

"No. Haven't seen them since the dance."

"You've been by yourself since the dance was over?"

East took another bite. "Sometimes," he mumbled.

Monique watched him eat. He was tired, hungry, thirsty, and his face peeled from sunburn. He kept the blanket wrapped around him. Maybe he had a cold.

Eloise brought him a Pedialyte Freezer Pop, a flavored icicle that replenished electrolytes. Monique ate those in summer after long morning runs. She also knew people used them to relieve hangovers.

Lulu picked up toys. "Come on, kids. Let's clean your room." They disappeared down the hall.

Monique sat and crossed her right leg over her left as she stared at East. "You look like shit."

"You're not looking so hot yourself."

She also smelled his intense body odor, but didn't mention that. "So my husband tells me." Elle the cat jumped in her lap, startling her. "Damn, cat." Elle purred and stretched out on Monique's right thigh.

274 | DEVON A. MIHESUAH

East sat still, unblinking, then asked, "Where did you go?"

"Leroy's."

"We all *start* at Leroy's."

Monique looked down the hall to where Lulu and the kids laughed in a bedroom. "It's okay," East said. "She knows."

She nodded. "Skullyville and Kully Chaha."

"When?"

"1835."

He took a third bite of his sandwich, then scrutinized the remainder of his meal. "Beats a squirrel sandwich, right?"

She didn't know if he meant the sub or the trip. "Why didn't you come back with Silan and Mike?" she asked.

East held up a hand and examined his thin fingers. "Because I danced after they did."

"After? What do you mean?"

"After they danced and they went to wherever they went, it was my turn. By myself." Monique licked her dry lips. She could not fathom why Leroy would allow anyone to go alone.

"Did you know what was going to happen?"

"Yes and no."

"But why did Mike and Silan say they that saw you when the dance was over?"

"Did they? They didn't see me."

Monique thought back to their conversations. *Did East go home?* she had asked Silan. *Dunno*, Silan had answered. *I left first.*

I pulled out after him, Mike had said, pointing to Silan.

No, she realized, they had not seen East and were tricky in how they said this. Elle kneaded her thigh. "Ouch. Stop that." She turned to East. "Where did you go?"

East sighed and put down his sandwich. "Wilburton."

"When?"

"I went back to 1892."

She stared. Her group left Fuji and Rene in Kully Chaha almost sixty years before that. "Who knew how to send you back here? And then back to the present?"

"Ron Barnes."

She thought a moment. "He's the one who danced with Leroy years ago and never came back, right?"

"Oh, he came back."

"Ron returned? Where is he?"

"He left again."

"Wait a minute. He just comes and goes?"

"Yes."

"Do you know where he is now?"

"Last I saw him was a few hours ago in 1894."

"But you said you went to 1892."

"Correct."

"That's a two-year jump."

"Look at me."

She did. She inspected his worn face, sun- and wind-weathered skin. It was now almost eighty-six degrees outside and he wore socks. Two thawed ice packs that had covered his knees now lay on the floor. He took another bite of his sandwich, chewed slowly, and closed his eyes.

"You stayed *two years?*"

"I needed to be there for him."

"For who?"

"Silan."

"You mean when Silan and Mike were there?"

"No. I told you—I don't know where they went."

"So what are you talking about? *Who* are you talking about?"

"I don't mean Silan Bohanan."

Monique's heart pounded so hard her fingertips jumped. "Silan *who?*" she hissed.

East took another bite.

"Silan *Lewis?*" she whispered. He focused on the wall behind Monique. "East?"

"I rode with him that night."

Monique gasped. *That night.* By the end of *that* evening, the full-blood Nationalists Silan Lewis and Simeon Wade had led almost sixty men on a revenge killing spree. The newly elected chief, the Progressive Wilson N. Jones, had removed Silan Lewis from his position as sheriff of Gaines County. Silan did not support Jones or his Progressive political agenda. Simeon Wade had run unsuccessfully for Gaines County ranger and blamed his loss on the Progressives. Nationalist grievances against the Progressives were so extensive that the Last League of the Choctaws, as they called themselves, planned to assassinate prominent and wealthy mixed-bloods and white men.

"What do you mean you 'rode with him'?"

"Just like I said. I rode with Silan."

Monique tried to envision the extraordinary experience of riding with traditionalist Choctaws, each one pissed and armed with intent to kill.

"To Hukolutubbee's," East continued.

"Gaines County sheriff Joe Hukolutubbee," Monique recited from the history she knew well. "A full-blood who supported Jones, and the Nationalists thought him a sellout. Hukolutubbee was sleeping on his porch. He got up when he heard a noise. Then was shot by sixteen men."

"Seventeen."

Monique's eyes widened. "*You* were one of the shooters?"

East picked up his sandwich and took another bite. He did not appear to be thinking as much as enjoying the turkey sub. "Yes," he said casually. No one was going to punish him. Not now.

Monique's eyes burned with tears, but she felt a growing excitement. "How did you get a gun? How did you get into that group?"

"I speak Chahta anumpa. Said I had just arrived from Mississippi. Getting a rifle was easy."

"Did Leroy send you back to do that? Kill Hukolutubbee?"

"No."

"You just decided to join the killing party?"

"The opportunity was there. You wouldn't have passed that up."

Monique huffed. "I would never . . . I mean, if I had only three months to live, I might consider doing something like that to a person who deserved it. But—"

"Bullshit. If you could have, you would have."

Monique blinked. A split second later, she knew that she couldn't deny what he said. "Answer the question. Why did Leroy sent you back?"

"Leroy sent me back to kill Chief Wilson Jones."

Monique stood so fast her chair fell backward. Elle did a flip and landed on her feet. "*What?*"

East crunched a blue corn chip.

Monique took a step forward. "East? Leroy told you to kill Jones?"

East was unfazed. "Jones was the Progressive chief and unsupportive of the traditionalists. He rigged the election."

"Answer me."

"Yes. I just told you."

She swallowed. "My God."

"You know what Jones and those Progressives did."

Monique did know. "Well, clearly you didn't kill him."

"I did."

"You're delusional. Jones was not assassinated."

East took several pulls from his can of Pepsi. "It took too long to deal with Hukolutubbee. Then we rode to McAlester and by that time there were about, um, maybe sixty of us."

"And you went after Jones?"

"That was the idea. We rode thirty miles that night. I got saddle sore." Monique thought of Art and snorted.

"We knew it was another sixty miles to the chief's house in Caddo. I knew from history that within hours, everyone there would know what had happened to Hukolutubbee. Jones barricaded himself inside his home. I thought about taking the MKT train, but there was no way I could get there before Jones found out about the other killings."

"Did you kill anyone else? The Nationalists killed more people."

"No. I wasn't a part of those other killings. Anyway, even if I had taken the train, people might wonder about me. I'd be arrested. So I decided to wait."

Monique picked up her chair and sat back down. She started to drag her fingers through her hair, then remembered it was in a bun. Elle leaped back into her lap. Monique put her hands on the cat as if it were a lifeline. "Back up. What in hell was Leroy thinking? You can't just kill the chief."

"Why not?" East crumpled his sandwich paper. "Jones manipulated the election results. There was a recount and Jones won by only eight votes over the Nationalist Jacob Jackson. Some poll books from Nationalist districts were missing and that would have made all the difference. As you also know from history, Jones proceeded to support only his Progressive base. He went after everyone who he perceived as against him. Over half the voters supported Jackson. And Jones refused to serve the interests of everyone. Including traditionalists."

"I understand all that," Monique snapped.

East took a chip from the bag and put it in his mouth. "Do you? It's not just history." He leaned forward. "Some things never change. It's also the reality for many skins. Right now."

Her nostrils flared. "Actually, I understand perfectly."

East seemed pleased. "Good. Then, as you know, Jones already took all the Nationalists out of their positions. Including Silan Lewis. Jones put in his white cronies."

"They weren't white."

East waved his hand as if shooing a fly. "They sure acted like it. Racist, self-serving, ignored the fulls and the poor. His National Council even passed a bill to support martial law. That man was the wealthiest in all of Indian Territory and he did nothing for the traditionalists." Monique thought he overstated a bit. Still, she agreed with most of what he said.

"And you killed him."

"I was at his inauguration speech. Dude was coming out of the out-house. I was ten feet from him. I worked my way closer and was within arm's length. Shot him in the left kidney."

"No, you didn't."

"He was deader'n a dog's bone within minutes."

"Jesus, East. If you had killed Jones, all hell would have broken lose. The United States couldn't try a Choctaw unless he killed a white man. Choctaw tribal courts heard all the Nationalist cases. The juries were already stacked with Progressives and one of the judges was on the Nationalists' hit list. Silan Lewis was the only person executed. If Chief Jones had been killed, all those other Nationalists would have been shot."

East shrugged. "Correct."

"And," she continued, "the tribes were already on alert because allot-ment was coming. Killing Jones would have hurried that up. The U.S. government was looking for examples as to how we couldn't manage our-selves. By that time, Nationalists were outnumbered. Whites were all over the place. And there already was talk of statehood."

"True again. Everything you just said. It happened. All the Nation-alists with Silan were shot. The U.S. government came in. Not only did it shut down our tribe, it also shut down the Cherokees, Chickasaws, Muscogees, and Seminoles. We lost everything. It was a disaster. We really got it wrong."

"Fever dream."

"Not a dream."

She straightened her legs. Elle rolled with the movement like a Coman-che on horseback. "All right. I'll go along with that for the moment. How did you get away after you killed Jones?"

"It was total chaos. People running everywhere. Ron was waiting with horses behind a hotel. We made it a few miles down some roads, then game trails though the forest—and no one followed. It rained. Got off the horse. Fell off, actually. Within an hour, we danced and got back to

Leroy's house. Lulu called you at two a.m. or something like that. It took a few minutes for Leroy and Ninah to realize it was a mistake to kill Jones."

"*Ninah* was in on this?"

"Well, yes. I rewrote history and not in a good way. Ninah made me return almost as soon as I got back to Leroy's house. Lulu and the kids were waiting for me at Leroy's. That's why we were all together. I made that call to you to keep you from making a bigger deal out of me being gone."

Monique thought about the brief conversation she had with East in the middle of the night while she sat on her kitchen floor. "*Kil-ia*," Silwee had yelled to his father. Then "*Miti*."

"Then you went back. Silwee knew what was about to happen. He was telling you *Let's go! Come on!*"

East smiled and pointed at her. "Good catch. Anyway, when I went back the second time, I didn't kill Jones."

"There was no other way to change history?"

"It was my doing that changed it. So when I got close to Jones the second time, I just let him go. I watched that son of a bitch give his speech, then let him walk away."

Monique's left temple pounded. It was not the little bell. The migraine gremlin was awake and pounding the drum. She wondered if she had any Tylenol 3s left in her cruiser. Simultaneously, she considered this messed-up story. If Lulu was waiting for East, then Leroy told her when East would return and that East had to go back to rectify the problem. That also meant Leroy knew when Monique's group would return. No wonder the drummers were at Leroy's on Sunday afternoon. As was a kitchen full of food.

"I had enough time to cram down a roast chicken and a pecan pie," East continued. "Leroy had a lot of other things to eat, but we had to hurry. I swallowed vitamins as I started the dance. You know, three months before we all danced—the week before last—Leroy told us to go to the Indian Health Service and get our vaccinations up to date. We all got flu shots and I got a tetanus booster. Silan also needed a hepatitis booster. And the dentist replaced our old fillings."

Silwee and Eloise laughed. Their joy could be heard the length of the house.

Monique sat with her mouth open. "Hang on. There is nothing in historical documents or oral testimonies that mentions Jones being killed."

"You wouldn't have seen any. We changed events within two hours. I was on the fast track back."

"That's a fast dance."

"There are several versions of the Renewal Dance. You went through one of them."

"And Ron came back with you?"

"Yes. He always does when we make big plays. To assess."

Monique dropped her jaw again. She knew she looked like a shocked opossum. *Big plays. We had to hurry.*

"East, we can't just walk through the door of the WABAC Machine and go to whenever we want."

"The what?"

She realized he was too young for the Rocky and Bullwinkle reference. She shook her head. "The DeLorean?" He blinked. "And you probably haven't seen *Edge of Tomorrow*. No?" She tried again. "*The Terminator?*"

"Oh yeah," East said. "Well, we did go where we wanted. Events were changed back to the way they were supposed to be."

"How can Leroy pinpoint exactly where you need to go?"

"Detective, you don't question what medicine people know and how they got that knowledge. They're special and it's not for me or you to play anthropologist."

"How astute of you."

East nodded.

Monique's left foot tapped as if she were at a sewing machine. The cat purred, its tail as rhythmic as a pendulum. "What did you do for two years?"

"Talked to Silan. Rode around with Ron. I watched Silan's execution by those Progressives."

"His execution?"

282 | DEVON A. MIHESUAH

"November 5, 1894. Today."

"Today??"

"Just watched the circus a few hours ago. All these self-righteous Pro-gressives thinking they were big men." He shook his head. "Silan. He was murdered. He was supposed to be shot through the heart but he caught a lung shot instead."

Monique already knew this story but was mesmerized by East telling it. He had been there.

"That man lay on the ground suffering." East dropped his head and sniffed. After a few moments, he gathered himself. "The sheriff smothered him with his handkerchief. Silan came back for his own execution. He didn't deserve that." He pulled a tissue from the box on the table and blew his nose. "Ron sent me home after Silan died. About three hours ago. I wish I could go back and kill Jones again."

He sniffed again and looked at Monique. His eyes were red and his cheeks wet. "I woke up in Leroy's yard. His cat was purring in my ear. Again. Acts like that one." He motioned to Elle, who meowed in agree-ment. "Mazey and Deb were there and they fed me more, but I wanted to get home. And here I am. They said y'all were at Ninah's. Haven't even showered. I smell like where I was."

He stood and dropped his blanket. He was dressed in a dirty beige high-stand collar, button-down shirt tucked into faded black button-fly trousers. A small-collared jacket with only the top button fastened revealed the thin leather belt.

"Good Lord. You look like you stepped out of *Tombstone*." Headache drumbeats echoed in her skull.

"Yeah. Without a mustache."

You witnessed the execution of Silan Lewis, Monique thought. The real-ity that East spoke with Silan Lewis and then witnessed his death was shocking enough, but her immediate thought was what she expressed: "And my uncle wanted you to kill Chief Wilson Jones."

East nodded, sniffed, and sat back down. "He and Ninah wanted to see if that might make things better for us today. Actually, Ninah's the one who comes up with these ideas. Leroy gets us to act on them."

"All of us who just danced were at her house. Why didn't they tell us?"

"Not everyone is down for this stuff, Detective. Most dance and become 'renewed,' as promised."

She thought about Grace, Elaine, Art, Larry, and John. "Actually, I think John might be down for it."

East nodded.

"So, these schemes are experiments."

"Yes."

"Dear God. Where did Mike and Silan go?"

East took several gulps from his tumbler of soda. "Mississippi."

"When I saw them on Monday, they looked more rugged than you."

"Why might that be?" East asked.

"If it's anything like what we went through, I'd say hunger, not enough clothes, aches and pains—"

"Mississippi," he repeated. Elle yawned.

Monique's brow furrowed. Then she understood. The pain in her right temple migrated to the left part of her brain like water pouring from a Japanese rocking water fountain.

"They went over the trail?"

"Yes."

Weather-beaten skin. Red and sunken eyes. Sore feet. Ravenous. *The trail*, she thought.

"I called them while driving home," East said. "Don't know details yet. They're on their way here. Won't be long."

"What were they supposed to do?" Monique asked. "Learn from the experience?"

"No. Keep a group from drowning while crossing a bad part of the Mississippi."

"Did they succeed?"

"Apparently."

On cue, she heard a diesel truck. She saw through the window a dually truck pull into the yard. Silan Bohanan jumped out, followed by Jodi, then Mike and Saralese LeFlore.

Lulu hurried from the back room and opened the door. The LeFlores and Bohanans filed in. "Just sit anywhere," Lulu said. They all nodded to Monique, but rushed to East.

They hugged and backslapped. Monique assessed the three men. Silan and Mike appeared healthier and more rested than they had a few days prior, but still rough. Everyone smiled.

"I got lotsa bean dip and cookies," Lulu said as she hustled to kitchen, followed by Saralese.

Monique listened to them chatter and clink ice cubes into glasses. The women distributed drinks, bags of cookies and chips, and cans of bean dip. Saralese gave Monique a bowl of ice cream. The two women then settled next to their husbands on the sofas. Elle purred, happy to see them, but the cat did not move from her vantage point on Monique's lap.

Elle meowed. "Are you related to Lorraine?" Monique asked.

"Animals know," Mike said, before cramming two cookies into his mouth.

Monique stroked the cat's head. "Know what?"

He shrugged. "They're perceptive," he mumbled. Monique put her hand on the cat's back.

"You look like you went on an adventure," Saralese said.

"Ya think?" Monique's feet ached and she longed for a bucket of ice water to soak them. "There's more to this dance than just going back and having an epiphany about how to behave in the present. East told me he's a hit man and killed Wilson Jones."

The only sound for a few seconds was Elle's purr.

Mike nodded as he chewed. "There's that," he mumbled.

"Yes, there *is* more," Jodi said. Monique recalled the first time she had seen Silan's wife. She'd worn tight jeans and a gray T-shirt and had seemed casual about her husband's exhausted state. Today she wore the same jeans and a red T-shirt with *No More MMIW* in white letters stenciled across the chest. Missing and Murdered Indigenous Women. Thousands of women, girls, and boys in the United States and Canada were just that. And the problem was prevalent in Oklahoma. Jodi appeared as relaxed as she did the first time Monique met her. Her eyes were sharp and friendly.

"There's something else I'm not being told," Monique said. She breathed hard through her nostrils.

"What did you do?" Saralese asked.

"I went back and met my ancestor."

"That's not all you did," Saralese said.

"Right. You mean besides hike for weeks half-naked, wearing reed sandals, eating berries and weeds, and shitting in the woods?"

Saralese looked to East, who nodded. She continued. "Now you know what it's like." Monique spread out her hands in a *so what?* gesture.

"For the next time."

"What next time? I'm not going back."

"We all go back," Saralese answered.

"You have?"

"Yes."

"Fuji and Rene didn't go back again. They traveled with us and will stay for a while." She still was not sure how to interpret her last encounter with them. *That had to be a dream*, she reasoned.

East leaned forward and clasped his hands together. "Both of them have done this before."

"They *have*?" Elle was unfazed by Monique's outburst. The cat turned onto her side and watched her human cushion. "When did they go back the first time?"

"They didn't go back. Fuji and Rene came forward."

Monique sat up straighter. "What does that mean?"

"Fuji was born in 1813. Rene almost two years after that."

Monique ground her teeth. Elle purred loudly and tapped Monique's forearm with her paw. A feline attempt at comfort.

She snorted. "How can that be? Are you saying Fuji's mother, Christine, was born in the 1700s?"

"No," East said calmly. "Fuji and Rene were sent forward in 1819 when he was six and she was four. Christine and Inge adopted Fuji. Rene went to Rosa and Arlan."

"I don't—"

"They were sent ahead to the future before their group started on the removal trail."

"Who sent them?"

"Ron."

"Why?"

"Because they died going over the removal trail in 1833."

"Died?"

"Yes."

She had so many questions that she didn't know what to ask first. "They're the ancestors of Leroy. And Strong Bull."

Monique sat still. Her skin tingled. "Leroy is my uncle," she said.

"Yeah," Silan said.

"Fuji and Rene are my ancestors."

"They are," East agreed.

"And you already knew all this." Everyone nodded.

"So did you," Lulu said. "You aren't sure, though."

Monique felt dizzy. Lulu stood and took Monique's bowl and cup to the kitchen.

Lulu smiled when she returned. Monique took the full cup, sipped, and coughed. Heavy on the vodka, but balanced with lemon juice. She took another healthy swallow.

"Wait a minute," Monique said, dehydrated enough to already feel slightly lit. "If Fuji and Rene died, then Leroy and Strong Bull wouldn't exist. Neither would I." Monique sat back. "How would they have known that Fuji and Rene wouldn't make it?"

"Threads of time," East said. "Different possibilities. Fuji's parents knew these things."

"Christine and Inge."

"No," East corrected. "His real parents. His father's best friend was a *hopaii*. A prophet. You met him."

"Who?" she shrilled.

"Thenton. Fuji and Rene's daughter married Thenton's son."

Monique choked and vodka shot from her nostrils. Lulu handed her a paper towel. Monique forced herself to take a breath. "Oh geez. My ancestor. A prophet. Signed the removal treaty?"

"He knew he had no choice."

Monique sighed and took another gulp. "But how could Leroy send them back with us if Leroy hadn't been born yet? Hell, how is Leroy here at all? How am I here?"

"Leroy was born right on time," East said. "Just like his ancestors were. Fuji and Rene went back to 1835. With you."

"How many people knew about the adoptions?"

"A few. They wouldn't have thought too much about it. Two Choctaw kids from Mississippi needed families. They just didn't know from *when* they came."

"There is no historical record of Fuji or Rene."

"This is true. Fuji and Rene are referred to by different names in the historical record. Tandy and Ellin. You will see that they are your great-great-great-grandparents."

"Oh God," Monique croaked. "I know those names. They're on the 1860 county census. And now they're dead."

Lulu gave her a wan smile. "Well, yes, Monique, both of them would be dead by now."

"Their families will be devastated," she said, sobbing. Monique knew that if something happened to Robbie, she would not survive the loss.

"Maybe," East said. "Probably. But I'm pretty sure that Christine and Inge and Rosa and Arlan have been given hints. The elders will explain it to them. And Gena is an interesting personality. She might dance someday."

Monique sniffed. "But I don't understand how Leroy and I could have been around Fuji all these years if he and Rene were *here* and not in the past."

East drank from his glass, then coughed. "Ron Barnes went back many times," he said, seemingly changing the subject.

"How many? I only know about two."

"Oh no," Mike laughed. "More like a dozen. He's like, uh, a fixer. If one thing didn't turn out right, he goes back to put it the way it was. In the case of Fuji and Rene, on one of his trips, Ron purposely wanted to see Fuji and Rene as children. In their original homes. The ancestors of all these medicine people, right?"

"I . . . I guess. How did he know they were our ancestors? Never mind. Go on."

"Well, Ron met Thenton, who knew from Strong Bull who Ron was and why he was there. Thenton told Ron that Fuji and Rene needed to leave, that they would die soon. Ron then went to Skullyville *after* the removal to make certain they were dead. Like Thenton predicted, Rene and Fuji weren't there. They had died. So Ron hurried back *here* to discuss their deaths with Leroy and Ninah."

Monique blinked.

"Time usually works fast, but sometimes it slows," Silan explained.

"My God. Ron flits back and forth?"

"Pretty much. Yeah."

"Ron went back again," Mike continued "Before the removal. The parents agreed to let Fuji and Rene go forward to our time. Then they danced with your group and went back to where they should be. Had your great-great-grandmother. Right on time."

"That makes no sense. If Ron hadn't gone back to talk to Thenton, Fuji would have made it to Indian Territory. We know that. Leroy is here. I'm here." She took a big swig.

"No, Monique. I just told you. Ron went back because Fuji would *not* have made it."

Monique felt nauseated.

"Well, we can't really explain all this," Saralese said. "But we've seen enough to know that time moves in different directions. Threads are all around us. Time is not linear and it's not circular."

Monique rubbed her eyes. "Okay," she sighed. "What's the point of all this?"

"You know the answer to that, Detective," Silan said. "The Renewal Dance is a way to change things for the better."

"You can't just change God's plan," Monique argued.

"We can if we're allowed to," countered Saralese. She smiled and pointed upward.

Monique followed her finger, then realized she was pointing at something much higher than the ceiling.

"We see what sticks," East said. "Sometimes, like with Wilson Jones, it's a mistake to change the order of things."

"And sometimes it's just a dance," Jodi said. "Dancers take a trip and become rejuvenated. More committed to culture. They become activists or something. Like the people in your group. But other times there is more, uh, specific purpose behind what we do."

"Have you been back?"

"Yes. I was supposed to assist in the difficult birth of a child. And I did. That child ended up murdering Pushmataha when he was a teenager. *That* changed things for the worse. So I went back again and saw to it that the child died."

Monique drained the vodka. "You killed a baby?"

Jodi nodded. "Sort of. I just didn't help with the birth."

"How did you even know about the difficult pregnancy to begin with? And who was the mother?"

"Wife of a prominent headman. That story is known well enough. Lost their infant son in childbirth. So we thought it a good gamble to fix it. Didn't stick. So I fixed it again. And I brought back that cat."

Monique looked down at Elle. The cat that was technically almost two centuries old blinked its one eyelid.

"Something had gotten ahold of her," Jodi explained. "Probably a coyote. Her eye was a mess. I knew she wouldn't make it. I brought her back and took her to the vet. Full of worms too."

Monique wondered if Leroy had also rescued Lorraine from the past.

Mike cleared his throat. "Silan and I went over the trail. We were to make sure our group took an alternate course. Otherwise, everyone would have died crossing the Mississippi River at a bad spot."

"How did you manage that?" Monique asked. "You were escorted by troops. White men. What happened to them?"

"They, uh, went into the river," Silan said without smiling.

"Seriously?"

"As serious as colonization."

"What about their families?"

Silan shrugged.

Death and dying. One life for another. "How did you know what would happen if you changed events?"

"Multiple trips back showed how scenarios would play out," Silan said. "Same answer as before. Leroy and the others could change the situation once they realized how things ended up in the present."

"So why don't you go back and kill Hitler? Andrew Jackson? Columbus?"

They all shook their heads no. "This dance is only for us," Mike answered.

Monique tried to envision time-traveling Indians whooshing through the cosmos like event-changing fairies. If every tribe could change the past, things would be completely different now. No poverty, diabetes, reservations—and the Native population would be substantially higher. Word about the invaders would have reached the East and West Coasts and Alaska ahead of the Spanish, Russian, Dutch, and English killers. No fur trade with the French. San Salvador Natives would know about the opportunist Columbus before he washed up on their shore. Or would they? She considered what East had said about the failed strategy to kill a chief. Monique realized that perhaps she was being overly optimistic.

A thought hit her like a brick through a window. "My brother!"

"Uh, you have to talk to Leroy about that," East said.

"I could go back," she cried, panting. "Prevent him from being killed." Elle meowed.

Saralese held up her hand. "If all of us could bring back our loved ones by changing an event, we would do it as fast as we could put on our skirts," she said. "Don't get your hopes up. This dance is about the good of the entire group. Community. Not individual wishes. I already asked."

Monique planned to ask Leroy anyway. "I can't take all this in right now," she said.

Silwee and Eloise ran down the hall laughing. They jumped on their parents' laps and turned to face Monique. Both smiled. She wondered if these children were adopted or maybe from the future. They seemed to know what she was thinking.

"You shouldn't stress about it," Lulu said.

"Oh, no?"

"Kids, go outside for minute." Lulu waited until she saw them on the porch with their colored chalk before she spoke again. "You are who you are, Monique. And now you have jobs to do."

"I don't know what the hell you mean by that, but I'm not going back. Wait. Jobs?"

"But you have already," Mike said. Before she could protest, he held up a hand. "You saw something. In black and white. Parts of that vision were clear. You felt that you had an immediate purpose, but you didn't know why."

"How did you—"

"And the first time you experienced that was between the time of the dance at Leroy's and when you arrived in the past."

"Yes."

"What did you see?"

"That first time, two blurry men on horseback. Then after the dance— before we arrived in 1835—I saw three women. The men were up to something. I had things in my hand, but I don't know what. If I'm passing myself, then why don't I see myself?"

"Because," Silan said, "in a thread, you become yourself for a few seconds, then you move on. That dream wasn't a dream. It was your reality. Or, one of them. You encountered it as you passed yourself going further back in time with your group last week. It actually was a future event."

"No. The men were dressed like Confederate raiders."

"What I mean is, it was an event that happened *after* you arrived in the past."

"I don't get it. I didn't encounter those men last week. And I didn't do anything," Monique argued.

"Not yet," East said. "Not in the way we understand things."

Monique wondered if she'd had a stroke at the dance a week ago, was in a coma, and imagining everything since she woke up facedown in a field of clover. Everyone sounded insane.

"And I saw John," she remembered.

"Oh yeah?" Mike asked. "Doing what?"

"He was indistinct. Dressed like East is right now. And he was holding a rifle. An 1878 Browning single shot." *How did she know that?* She wondered. She did not recall learning about such a weapon.

Monique watched as the others smiled. They were pleased. "What?"

"He has a task," East answered. "Just like you."

"Killing someone?"

"Not necessarily. Maybe his job is to convince someone."

"Convince someone? Of what?"

"Dunno."

"I did not sign up for this," Monique said.

"You didn't really think that meeting your ancestor was all you would do?"

"I didn't know what to expect."

"How do you feel about it?" Lulu asked.

"How am I supposed to feel?"

No one answered.

"All right," Monique acquiesced. "I'm angry that we walked a hundred miles. That our ancestors walked much farther in winter. That they died."

"Were the others in your group angry?" East asked.

"Well, at times, yes."

"But not like you."

"John is."

East nodded.

You could use some anger management, Leroy had told her. "That's why Leroy got me and John to dance," she said quietly.

"It seems you do understand, Detective."

Elle's purr intensified.

Monique considered the relaxed cat on her lap. The plants in the window looked the same as when she was here last. Silwee and Eloise laughed on the porch. She stroked Elle. She picked up the cat and put her on the floor, then she stood and walked to the window. A woman across the street pushed a lawn mower. Sparrows twittered in the grass. A red Smart Fortwo motored past. *Dang, that car is small,* she thought. *How safe can that be?* All this took less than a minute. *Time moves on,* she thought.

Monique turned to face the group. "This is it for now. But I'll be back."

"Yeah," East said, "we know."

"Wait a sec," Lulu said. "I have something for you." She stood and hurried to a back room. She reappeared a few seconds later and handed Monique a package wrapped in white paper.

Surprised, Monique took the bundle. She was unused to receiving gifts. She untied the bow and pulled back the white wrap. It was the blue ribbon dress she'd admired in the den the previous week. The ribbons were her favorite colors.

"It's beautiful. Why?"

Lulu winked. "You earned it."

"Thank you," Monique said as she hugged the smaller woman.

East stood. "Detective." Monique faced him. "You're disappointed."

Monique ran a hand over the material of the skirt. "I can't believe Leroy told you to kill someone."

"Why not?"

"He's my uncle."

"So?"

"This is fucked up."

"Some might say that."

"How many dancers go back and kill people? How many times has this happened?" *Hundreds?* she wondered. *Thousands?*

He shrugged. "You didn't know about Jones because we corrected the mistake." Silwee rushed in from the front yard, his face flushed. He held up a rock and laughed.

Eloise came next, her hands and face dirty. She stopped and hugged Monique's right leg and then ran down the hall.

Monique smiled. "Where is Ron Barnes now?"

"Someplace," East answered. "Preparing for the next event and the next mistake."

AFTER

Maybe I was a mercenary, but you'd never know it to look at me. I was clean-cut, nice car, nice house, even a housekeeper who came in once a week.

—MAX BROOKS, *WORLD WAR Z: AN ORAL HISTORY OF THE ZOMBIE WAR*

24

Abi
Killer

Monique drove down Raptor Lane, feeling numb, but not disoriented enough to pull over.

She took several long pulls from her water bottle, then settled into a cruising speed ten miles above the speed limit.

She absently ate popcorn from the bag in her lap, spilling pieces onto the seat and floor. She popped a Diet Rite and drank half the can, then felt behind her on the back floorboard for her box of Clif Bars. She ripped open a wrapper and ate the White Chocolate Macadamia Nut bar in two bites.

She pulled into Leroy's driveway and looked around. His Subaru was not here, but Lorraine stood next to the woodpile waiting for her to exit her cruiser. Monique figured Leroy had gone to the store. She grabbed her flask and walked directly to the dance arena. Lorraine followed her. Monique lay down on the grass with her sunglasses on, giving brief thought to the chiggers. Lorraine politely observed the human from a few feet away. Monique registered that the cat did not try to lie on her. She closed her eyes.

The sun started to fall behind the tall cottonwoods. Monique felt comfortably warm in her shorts and T-shirt. She took deep breaths and imagined fluttering leaves in front of a blue sky. She heard the distant cawing of the crows that she loved and the closer chirps of soaring purple martins. A gentle breeze blew over her, but it was not chilly. Silence came with the calm. Her blue sky and green leaves dulled to gray.

She was back by the tall tree.

Monique checked her weapons. Each hand held a Colt Single Action Army revolver with a seven-and-a-half-inch barrel. They felt comfortable in her grips. She could not recall how she got the weapons, nor did she know why she was standing in the woods. Two malevolent men with bad intent watched three women garden a field. Monique and her fellow dancers had not encountered these people on their journey. Where did these weapons come from? Who were these men and women? One thing she did know: the weapons would fire, and in her competent hands, she could hit most targets with accuracy.

She focused on the nearest man and could not see his face, but his form was visible. She took aim and her right index finger pulled the trigger. She watched black blood blossom from his left breast. He dropped from his saddle. The other reached for his rifle in his saddle sheath. Her left index finger sent a bullet into his neck. Blood exploded in a black burst. He fell backward onto the horse's rump and tumbled to the ground. The two horses trotted twenty feet away, then stopped and looked back. *Used to gunfire*, she thought. Time skidded forward like frames in a film reel.

Smoke drifted up from the two pistols. On the ground in front of her were two dead men, their shirts soaked with blood. She regarded the women. All three had emerged from behind the trees where they had taken cover.

The women looked at Monique, eyes wide. One smiled. Monique smiled back. She felt calm. Peaceful. A job well done.

Monique stepped into the open and yelled "*Halito!*" but she heard no sound. "I killed them."

The women smiled and waved. Perhaps they'd heard her. Monique started toward them, but a strong hand grabbed her shoulder. She turned to see dark eyes in a thin, worn face. Salt-and-pepper-colored hair hung to his earlobes, like Captain Jack of the Modocs before the U.S. Army hanged and decapitated him.

"I'm Ron," the man said. She could not hear him, but he was clear nevertheless. "Time to go."

She understood but did not want to obey. Monique turned back to the women and tried to pull away from Ron. His grip intensified. The scene turned foggy.

"Nice afternoon," said a familiar voice. She opened her eyes. Leroy stood over her, looking toward his garden. The fading blue sky highlighted the yellow banana in his right hand.

Lorraine moved closer to Monique and sat, unblinking, her tail raking the grass.

"You asshole."

Leroy did not respond.

"Fuji and Rene."

"What about them?"

"You could have said something. Hell, *they* could have told me. I had to figure it out."

"They knew you would."

"How long have you known?"

"Since before they arrived here as children."

"And when did they know?"

"Same."

"And y'all managed to keep the secret."

Leroy took a bite of the banana. "This is a special place," he said, changing the subject. "Don't know exactly why. Maybe someone from the past came here and made it so. Regardless, we make our journeys from this point. We see many things."

"A mystic. Just like Fuji and Rene."

"Correct."

"A hundred-mile journey. My skin is shot to shit and my feet look like roadkill. Yeah. I saw many things on my journey, Leroy. Why the secrecy?"

He did not respond. She realized he meant something else. Monique did not sit up. She lay still, looking up at him. "What the hell did I dream?"

"It wasn't a dream."

She recalled what East told her a few hours prior. *Threads of time.* "Why didn't you tell me?"

"You're the type who needs proof."

"I killed two men. I felt good about it. I knew how to use those old guns. And I knew where the men would be and why."

"Monique, those women were friends and we know those men assaulted them. Those Southern boys raped and killed two of them. Choctaw women. Strong women. The third escaped. A descendant of the woman who got away was a Code Talker in World War I. Another, a young man, is now an attorney specializing in environmental law. And another is a primary activist in the Missing and Murdered Indigenous Women movement. If the other two ladies had lived, well, who knows what their descendants would have accomplished? You'll make sure we find out what the other women do. If it turns out that their descendants didn't do anything of importance, well, you'll go back and fix it. Just let them die. But we think they did something of significance. Ten years ago, Ron saw a woman in a thread who looked like one of the killed women. She was in Congress. In D.C., I mean. With the same last name on her nameplate in front of her. Maybe a descendant, maybe not." He paused a few seconds. "But why else would Ron see her?"

Monique's eyebrows drew together so furiously they almost morphed into a unibrow. "I'm not a hit woman."

"All of us are multifaceted."

"If you start with the 'We all have two wolves inside of us' story, I'm going to slap the crap out of you *and* your two beasts."

Leroy chuckled.

"You're suggesting that I'm a killer?"

"You just said you felt good about shooting those men."

"It was a *dream*, Leroy."

Lorraine walked closer to Monique. She sat next to her head and purred. The cat waited for Monique's attention. Monique turned her head and looked into the green eyes.

"You've got a steady hand. And good instincts."

"You're assembling a team of assassins. Jesus. Leroy, you're vile."

Leroy ate the last of his banana, then folded the peel like origami. "You're trying to wound me and it's not working."

"We can't just fly through time and kill people who we *think* will cause screwups in the future."

"We could settle for current realities—or attempt future possibilities."

"So you're saying that I'm over a barrel."

"Not at all. I knew you were supposed to do this. Thirty years ago. In a thread."

"Leroy, I'm forty-five."

"Your current age doesn't matter. It was in the 1930s when I saw you."

"That was ninety years ago."

"Time is relative. Winter. You were bundled in a fur coat. Waiting in the dark for a justice to come out of the Oklahoma capitol building."

"And I had a gun, right?"

"I don't know yet. Could have been a knife. That was my second dance."

Monique sat up.

Leroy continued. "During my first dance, when I was sixteen, I saw John in a thread. That thread was around 1920. He killed two men plotting to bilk allotments from fifty families. I saw John again in a thread when I was thirty. That one took place at an earlier time. Later I realized he was there to talk to Solomon Hotema."

"The Choctaw witch killer?"

"The same. In 1899, Hotema was about to kill three innocent people he believed were witches. John was to intervene. I wanted John to steer Hotema toward the right people."

"Real witches."

"Yes."

"But Solomon killed those innocent people. He went to jail."

"John hasn't spoken to Hotema yet. He can prevent their deaths."

"That can't be." However, as she said it, she realized that he told the truth. "Does John know?"

"He knows because he has passed himself in time. Just like you when you saw yourself. But he hasn't accepted his new reality. He'll probably be over here tonight or tomorrow."

"How do you know Art and the others won't tell people about what happened to us? If they do, this could turn into a real shitstorm."

"They won't tell. Neither will anyone else who went back."

"How do you know that?"

"Because I told them that if they talk, they'll be sent to some random point in time with no way to get home."

Monique gasped. "Are you shitting me?"

Leroy did not nod or shake his head. He simply stared at the hawks circling the fields.

"You really are a dick."

He did not respond.

"How many people are in your, uh, squad?"

Leroy shrugged and did not answer her question. Instead, he said, "We need to tend to those Confederates. You'll arrive with enough time to find your weapons. Then Ron will return you right after. The task will take about an hour. Our time."

"And how long in way-back time?"

"Dunno. But you know how to deal with it."

She snorted. "And how am I supposed to get pistols?"

"You already know they were in your hands. You found a way."

"What about Steve?"

"What about him? I can deal with him. I always do."

Monique knew that to be true.

"And when you're finished with those Confederates, there's something else. A pipeline is about to go in. Right across the Kiamichi River and not far from where aggressive fracking is causing too many quakes. That pipeline can't happen. You will need to erase the roots of that project. They go back to Oklahoma statehood."

"By 'roots,' you mean one of the Sooners."

Leroy nodded. "Boomer Sooners. Gotta appreciate the mileage the university gets out of that."

"I don't."

"When will you be ready to go?"

She picked up Lorraine and set the cat on her lap. She petted the mottled fur as she watched a hawk land on a power-line pole. Another flew above it, shrieking its invitation to soar. Her headache had disappeared.

"So, this is how I channel my anger." She was not asking.

"It is." Leroy watched the hawks.

"What if I die back there?" She took a sip from her flask.

"You won't. Your dad didn't. But he got sick on the removal trail and died after he returned."

"What?" She inhaled water and coughed until her face turned red. "My father?"

"Of course."

"Dad died when I was twenty. He got sick, lost weight, and just . . . died."

Leroy shrugged. "Many people died after the removal," he reminded her.

She thought back to the days prior to her father's death. His appearance had distressed her. Drawn face, chapped lips, thin and bent physique. He coughed relentlessly. She had always thought that he had simply deteriorated from undiagnosed cancer. Now she knew otherwise. Maybe pneumonia. And now she realized that her father had not gone on a hunting trip with Leroy the week before he died. He had danced.

"It's your destiny, kiddo."

Monique snorted at the name.

Despite her discomfort and anger at Leroy, Monique considered the satisfaction she felt from shooting the Confederate men. Maybe she would encounter her father and brother in a thread. She felt a sudden thrill of anticipation.

Leroy and Lorraine waited for her to speak.

Monique coughed and tracked the hawks that streaked overhead. She smiled.

"Got any beer?"

Afterword

I spent the summer of 1991 at the National Museum of Natural History and the National Museum of American History, courtesy of the Smithsonian Institution American Indian Community Scholar Internship. On the first day, I stopped in the American History bookstore and found Otto L. Bettmann's *The Good Old Days—They Were Terrible!* (New York: Random House, 1974). Even though the book had been published many years prior, to my chagrin, I had not seen it. It is a fascinating, albeit occasionally stomach churning, chronicle of life in the second half of the nineteenth century. *The Good Old Days* prompted me to consider how many times I had heard someone say that they wished they could visit another point in time. Wild West enthusiasts, Civil War aficionados, and historical-romance fans are just some people who might imagine themselves living in the past. For sure, many people have fantasized about going back in time to kill Hitler. No doubt, many Natives desire to time-travel and dispatch Columbus, Hernán Cortés de Monroy y Pizarro Altamirano, overzealous missionaries, Russian fur traders, and Andrew Jackson, to name just a few colonizers. I certainly have, but I also have wondered what our present life would be like if this actually could happen. Would things be better? Would the hundreds of North, Central, and South American tribes have true sovereignty, with thriving cultures, clean environments, healthy minds and bodies, and control over their resources? Or would more nefarious individuals take the place of these well-known historical figures who caused so much misery to Natives, and make things even worse? I started jotting notes for this novel shortly after that summer. Because my job is to write nonfiction, however, I pushed this project to the back burner. The story herein is much different from what I originally outlined over thirty years ago.

The characters in this book are aware of the extreme violence within the nineteenth-century Indian Territory, as well as the factionalism between the Choctaw Nationalists and Progressives. Many of the people described are real. I patterned Thenton Oakes after my ancestor Lewis Wilson, who signed the removal treaty in 1830. I am not as agitated about my ancestor's action as Monique is about hers, but I have wondered why Lewis signed and if he regretted joining in. Lewis and his family did not benefit in any way that I have found. His son, Charles Wilson, was a staunch Nationalist and became a Lighthorseman, sheriff, court clerk, and treasurer of Sugar Loaf County in the Moshulatubbee District of the Choctaw Nation. Members of the rival Progressive party murdered him in 1884, and he is buried in the Vaughn Memorial Cemetery in the area once known as Kully Chaha, at the base of Nvnih Chufvk (Sugar Loaf Mountain), where Monique and the other dancers visited. Ten years later, Silan Lewis and other Nationalists, angered over the actions of Chief Wilson Jones, did embark upon a killing spree of Progressives; Silan Lewis was the only Nationalist punished for it. And the man did indeed return for his own execution. I chronicle this dramatic and violent history in *Choctaw Crime and Punishment: 1884–1907* (University of Oklahoma Press, 2009). My first attempt at dramatizing Charles Wilson's death is in the story "The Death of Matthias Lamb," in *The Roads of My Relations* (University of Arizona Press, 2000).

There is no Renewal Dance (at least, not that I know of), so readers interested in time travel will need to investigate another portal to the past.

As in my other works of fiction and nonfiction, I do not reveal ceremonial aspects of my or any tribe. Cosmological entities among the Choctaws are well documented and easily accessible.

Thank you to Marie Landau for her impeccable copyediting, to Leigh McDonald for another beautiful cover, and to the KU Hall Center for the Humanities for the generous Vice Chancellor for Research Book Publication Award. And to Josh, Tosh, and Ari for their continued support. A special thanks to Tiffany Midge, who listens.